BULLET HOLE DRIVE

A Pedal To The Metal Citywide Demolition Mystery

the

Karl J. Niemiec

BULLET HOLE DRIVE

ISBN 978-0-9833663-6-2

Portland's Blood Red

Karl restored and drove B.R. for 27 years in LA

Dedication

This action pact love story is for every man, woman, and child that ever fell in love with a Corvair. And for my mother, Alice Stafford, who gave me my first Corvair joyride.

I guess I fell in love with the Corvair when Mom showed up with one in Jupiter, Florida in the summer of 1961, having driven it down from Farmington, Michigan. We, the kids, took the bus down there ahead of her, and she surprised us two weeks later with her blue 61 four door. My grandpa just loved that car. He would smoke his cigars, flick ashes, and come in the back window to hit us kids. I still remember sleeping on the back floor as my mother drove at night.

I also remember it coming to a slow-motion crashing-end one winter night rounding a bend in the road with us sliding and hitting a road barrier rock broadside. Mom went to a bigger car, an Impala after that. I found out later in life that my pop worked to help build the Corvair at Fisher Body.

Years later, then just a bigger kid living in LA, looking for a car for my novel/film-detectives to drive, I found my first Corvair and pulled it out from under a tree. Thus commenced a 30 year love story, spanning two movies and four novels that included my 66 Blood Red and black convertible Corvair.

My Blood Red is also featured in the *Jozeph Picasso Alien Trilogy Filmmaking Adventures*, **Alien Made, Alien Biz, Alien Mobster**, on the front and back cover of this book, and in the current film **Law of Average – The Endless City**, driven by me, Detective Joe Average, my latest film trilogy – out 2018.

Wishing you many Corvair joyrides.

Karl J. Niemiec

Table of Contents

OTHER BOOKS BY KARL J. NIEMIEC

At
http://amzn.to/karlniemiec

POLO (Script, Novel, and Audiobook)
The Game of Halloween (Script, Novel, and Audiobook)
The Polish Gang
Alien Made
Alien Biz
Alien Mobster
P.D. (Puppy Dog) Brown
Prolific Screenwriter (Course Book IUPUI)
JungleBall 3D (Game)
Three Position Footballs (Game)
Three Neo-Noir Stage Plays
Potential Killers (Stage Play)
The Original Bikini Car Wash –
Murder Mystery Picture Book
One Lucky Pony (Screenplay Format)
Young Authors Club (Children's Course Book)
Audition Monologues That Work
Audition Scenes That Work (Books I&II)
Saving Paradise (Screenplay Format)
Write to be Published (Course Book IUPUI)

1 BLOOD RED CORSA

Portland Cooper gripped his cordless phone in a meaty, grease-stained hand. He shouted into it as he turned his muscular back on his Corsa shop's work yard and stuck a greasy finger from his other hand into his left ear. He was in the middle of one of those days where he would gladly hurt an ex-friend.

A steady pounding came from Jorge, a young Mexican, who used a shrinking hammer on a rear corner panel of a 1960 700 blue four door Corvair. Hissing and snapping sounds came from a cutting torch underneath it, as a blue flickering light and shooting sparks rained down on the oil stained concrete.

"What do you mean? There wasn't a scratch on those heads," Cooper yelled. "Don't feed me that BS, Marty!"

Cooper's voice was deep, dark and calculatingly mean. He was a man who knew what he wanted and wasn't afraid to seize it by the throat and drag it home. His broad shoulders were thick from work, his hands wide, his arms strong, and his legs long and lean from hours of toil. His dangerous smile wasn't handsome in any way, yet his harsh dark eyes had a certain twinkle in them that made him approachable, trustable and yes, even loveable.

Gwen Hawkins, Cooper's girlfriend, pulled through the open electric gate and into the work yard from the dead-end alley. Mick Jaggar's pucker-lipped voice came whining over the car's Blaupunkt about the lack of satisfaction. She parked her father's hand-me-down black 1963 split window Sting Ray in one of the parking spots that ran along a cinder block wall leading from Cooper's two story home to the remote controlled wrought iron gate. The house was a custom designed one bedroom with a den upstairs and a Corvair parts store for a first floor.

Gwen got out of her car. She waved to Finn, a gruff sailor, using the cutting torch under the 700. When she caught Finn and Jorge checking out her long shapely legs she pulled down her black leather skirt and gave them both an astute smile. Finn winked and Jorge gave her the big toothy. Class hung all over her. It shown in all the ways she carried herself; the casual dark hair that splashed on her purple silk blouse, the classic way she wore just enough pearls, her real nails perfectly manicured, the alluring sent of island breeze, with just a hint of Malaysian blood in her eyes, and not an ounce of flesh wasted. Why a true work of nature hung around with a punch in the face like of Portland Cooper and his cronies was beyond her mother's imagination. But thirteen-years of pure physical bliss couldn't be all wrong.

Cooper stood with his back toward Gwen. He rhythmically punished his head against the closed paint booth door. It was situated between a pair of double door work stalls filled with Corvairs under restoration. From the sound of it, Mick wasn't the only one not getting much satisfaction.

"Look, Marty, get out of that stinking girly shop and get my heads over here," Cooper said. "Ten minutes, or I call Delma to tell her where you're hiding out."

He stepped into the number two booth and picked up the shop's wall phone. "I'm dialing. It's ringing. Hello, Delma, this is Portland Cooper. How are you? Yes, I know, the same to you. Hang on a minute. You still there, Marty? Hello, Delma? Never mind."Marty had gotten the message. Cooper hung up twice in disgust. He turned to see Gwen tapping her hi-heel in the shade of the work stalls with her arms crossed in front of her. He hooked the cordless to the belt of his work pants and eyed her suspiciously. Gwen had that look on her face, again.

"Whatever it is, I'm busy," he said. His voice deliberately hard. "But go ahead, what is it?"

"We can start with a cordial hello, how was your flight."

"Sorry, we don't work on those Frenchy jobs." Cooper headed over to a 1966 red and black convertible blood red Corsa parked in the number one work stall. "Where's Roger Kelemen?"

"Why yes, New York was lovely this time of year."

"That wasn't you last night?"

Gwen slugged Cooper. It hurt. She checked to make sure she didn't crack a nail on his rock hard arm.

"I have something legal to talk about."

"Yeah? Go hire a lawyer." Cooper reached inside the blood red Corsa and turned on its ignition. The Corsa leaped to life. He glanced at Gwen's expression. He knew better.

He went around to the rear and opened the engine hood. The specially designed 190 hp engine purred under his touch. It should, Cooper made his modest living building them.

"Portland, I think Roger is missing."

"Missing where?"

"Missing everywhere. No one's heard from him."

"You know Rog, he's impulsive. He'll call."

"Roger stood Mother up for dinner last night. He was never that impulsive."

Cooper straightened up. He really didn't like where this conversation was headed. He could feel it in his balls. He could sense it in every past stitch and bullet hole in his body. When Gwen's voice got that "I need something looked into" quality his arthritic knee twinged in panic. It was a survival alarm for the other knee to start running. He asked anyway. "Roger stood Irene up?"

"Yes, Mother's little birthday dinner for Jack. It was her first no-show in years. Mother was furious."

"Your mother deserves to be."

"Please, I'm worried. Something's happened, I know...."

"Don't start with the queer feelings again, Gwen." He went back to adjusting one of the four turn cut-out carburetors. "Last time I had my head broken in three magical places."

"Please, Portland, just this one last time?"

"No! Just forget it. You've had me up to here with alligators, dumped in the Mojave Desert, and once, while covered with dirty motor oil, one of your so-called buddies lit me on fire and pushed me out of an airplane -- without a parachute. So I'm not in the mood right now to help more of your dizzy showbiz friends. Got that?"

Gwen stuck her tongue out at Portland's back.

He began to replace the four chrome air cleaners.

"But this is Roger. You know, our close childhood friend, the kid you argued and fought with all the time."

"Your close friend. To me he's just another lousy actor who owes me money." He thumbed the engine's belt retainer before going to a deep grease-stained sink to clean his hands.

"You crud, you don't mean that."

Cooper turned to look at the shining Corsa. It was beautiful, better, a masterpiece. His art, his original interior design. Right down to how the black leather flowed from the dash and glove box panels, down through the center of the bucket seats, over the headrests, and across the backseat. Like two black racing stripes flashing over the interior. All the standard metal and plastic were covered with red leather and the door panels were in seamless black with a strip of black carpet at the bottom. Even the visors were black and trimmed in red leather. Right out of his day-dreams, thirteen years ago. And here it stood again, a nightmare on four wheels. Just looking at the gorgeous thing was worth seriously hurting someone. All it was missing was a set of Kelsey-Hayes.

He didn't want to say it but he had to. "When Rog picks up his Corsa and flashes three G's in my face, I'll kiss him." He wiped his hands on a clean garage rag. Gwen looked puzzled.

"What...?"

"Right, you didn't know." He tossed the rag hard into the beautiful red and black backseat of the Corvair.

"I didn't." She glanced down at the unfamiliar license plate and the cheap spoke hubcaps. It didn't fit any rational conclusion. Not yet. It was identical, almost, maybe six people could tell the difference at a glance. One of them was Roger Kelemen.

"Why would Roger want a Corsa just like yours?"

"I don't know. Why don't you…? Cooper stopped himself. She would if she could. "I only built the engine. Roger said it was for a good friend's Corsa. Instead of picking up the engine they dumped the Corsa off here. So I installed it."

"I'm still drawing blanks on why?"

"I'm drawing them on how. It's nearly identical to mine."

"Who's it registered to?"

"R.J. Kelemen. A custom shop treated it like a hot potato this morning. Didn't even have me sign anything. Just left it in the alley and took off running. Go ahead, look closer. They even duplicated my leather interior package."

Gwen checked the stitch count on the driver's red and black bucket seats. It was a perfect replica of his interior design, even completed with red end-pads on both headrests. "This isn't leather."

Cooper growled. "I want my money, so where is he?"

Gwen ran her hand over the custom wood steering wheel. "That's why I'm here!" She checked the instrument panel. The gauges were all there, oil temperature, oil pressure, cylinder head temperature, exhaust temperature, volts and amps. All perfectly aligned in the black dash control and glove box panels. They were accented by a red leather center console with the FM/AM stereo radio, ashtray, cigarette lighter and red leather dash pad. Cooper always prided himself that no one else had a leather Corsa package like his. It won him many trophies over the years. But now this fake love letter. This would not end well, she thought. So she tried her best to change the subject with something even more repulsive to Portland. "Speaking of money." Gwen looked over her shoulder at Portland."Mother said if you cleaned your nails, you could come to dinner tomorrow night."

She stood up, turned to face Portland and smiled nicely at him. After all, this was a substantial breakthrough in her mother's and Portland's combative black sheep relationship. It wasn't as if they disliked each other. They merely stayed out of each other's hair. In other words, Portland could visit anytime he wanted to, only he never wanted to when Gwen's mother and stepfather were home.

Cooper glanced at the grease still under his nails. "I'd rather repack a rear axle bearing."

Gwen started one of her classic pouts as Cooper's engine whisperer-ears perked up at the whirl of a familiar Corvair engine hustling down the alley. Marty's using cheap gas again, he thought.

Portland took his wireless phone out of his belt and slowly pressed Delma's numbers again. He stopped a number short as a beat up 1962 white Corvan pulled sharply out of the alley and skidded to a stop in the middle of the work yard. "THE ELECTRIC CHAIR" in big blue and black letters was stenciled across the double side doors advertising Marty Owen's electrical gadget company. Marty rolled out from behind the wheel dressed like a beach ball. Some people called Marty an electrical wizard. His wife just called him a cheating fat pig that needed to be electrocuted. He hiked up the back of his sagging pants to cover his ass crack, allowing his fat belly to remain hanging over his abused brown leather belt. He stopped when he saw the look on Cooper's chiseled face and the phone in his hand.

"What took you so long?"

"What are you talkin' about? I'm three minutes and thirty seconds early," Marty defended himself.

"You were supposed to be here at 8 a.m."

"I'm tellin' you they had scratches. Hiya, Gwen...what's with the face?"

"Never mind, let me see the heads."

"I ain't got 'em."

Cooper pressed the last number."Hello, Delma? Yes, this is...same to you...I've got Marty here."

"All right, all right...I hocked 'em last night in a crap game at Malcolm's."

"What'd you get for them?"Cooper put the phone down on the Corsa fender. Delma could still be heard cursing into the blood red paint. Cooper began to unsnap the boot covering the folded down convertible top.

"Hundred-fifty."

"A hundred-fifty? "This was medieval torture."Malcolm knows they're worth twice that much...a piece!"

"I know, Coop... I couldn't help myself. I was drivin' by and I just stopped...you know, and they were in the van, and I was feelin' lucky or horny or something, I don't know...maybe I should've settled for a Snickers. Hey look, here's fifty bucks, I didn't lose everything."

Cooper didn't take the money. He folded up the boot looking at Marty, mustering as much disgust in his expression as he could. "Forget it, Marty, just forget it."He picked up the phone.

"Hello, Delma? Never mind."He clicked her off the line.

"What can I do to make this up to you?"

"Short of having a fatal heart attack?"

"Preferably."

"Nothing. Just tell Holland to call me...tonight."

Cooper got into Roger's convertible Corsa. He reached over and hit a toggle switch on the center console just below the bottom row of gauges. A hydraulic motor began to hum as its cable pulled a black canvas top out from the well and down over the car's interior. He pushed it again and it went back up and folded down into the well. He hit a different console toggle. A window went up then back down. He hit another toggle and the door locks went up and down. Cooper shifted his eyes toward Gwen "Shit. Roger must've gotten a hold of my blue prints."

"I thought you kept them locked up," Gwen said.

"So did I." Cooper put the Corsa in reverse.

"Wait a minute, where are you going?"

"Out of my mind. You comin' or stayin'?"

Gwen opened the passenger's door and slid her title little bottom in beside Portland. Her grace made everything, even a hardnosed angry grease monkey like Cooper, look sociably acceptable.

"Buckle up, we're going for a test drive."

Gwen found the seat belt and strapped it around her tiny waist. "Hey, at least he didn't copy your seat belts," Gwen said.

Cooper growled!

"What does the suspension look like?" Marty asked.

"Mickey Mouse," Cooper answered.

"Figures. Hey, I heard Roger's got his 911 back on the road."

"Big deal." Cooper looked at Gwen.

Gwen's eyes brightened with surprise.

Cooper shouted over his shoulder at the two men working as he backed the Corsa out of the number one work stall. "Jorge... lock her up. Thanks, Finn."

The two men remained unaware under the noise. Cooper just shook his head and tossed the cordless to Marty.

"Never mind, I'll sign them out." Marty backed out of the Corsa's way.

"You're putting cheap gas in your van again."

"No I'm...." He looked at Gwen."Okay, I hear ya."

Gwen smiled knowingly at Marty. "There's no arguing with the Engine Whisperer."

Portland pulled Roger's Corsa into the dead-end alley and out to Laurel Canyon Boulevard. He raced the car through its gears knowing damn well the car ran perfectly. And when he gets his hands on Roger, he'd bury him in it.

2 THE WALL OF BLAME

Cooper drove Roger's Corsa fast along Mulholland Drive. He turned right on Beverly Glen and headed back into the Valley and made a right on Dickens in Sherman Oaks. He pulled the Corsa to a stop at the curb and got out.

"Stay put."

"But...."

Cooper gave her a look that Gwen knew all too well.

"Oh, all right. Leave the keys. Portland?"

He leaned back into the Corsa.

Gwen hated it when he got into one of his moods. "The spare key is under the larger flower pot."

Cooper's dark eyes narrowed as he turned the ignition on but took the Corsa's key with him and walked towards the Condos. So Gwen tuned in the Angel's game.

Cooper walked through the open courtyard and pounded on Roger's door not expecting an answer and didn't get one. He looked for the hidden key and let himself in.

It didn't take a genius to see the place was a shambles. Whoever did it wasn't there to steal anything. About five grand of stereo equipment lay scattered on the floor, their insides exposed. Eight top of the line Cerwin Vega speakers were sliced up. Roger's pride and joy collection of hundreds of collectable records, eight tracks, and cassette tape jackets were torn open.

The furniture was ripped inside out. Every book was off its shelf and picture frames smashed. The carpet was pulled up and away from the walls. Only the drapery and windows were still intact. The job was sloppy but thorough.

The kitchen and dining room were more of the same and worse. Every piece of china and electrical appliance had been crushed or split open. Drawers were spilled out onto the floor. Someone had taken a fire axe to the master bedroom.

Cooper entered the spare bedroom and stopped in his tracks. "What the hell?" Two walls were completely covered by pictorial murals. They were blowups from sixteen millimeter black and white movie stock, and depicted Cooper's Corsa and Roger's Porsche 911 on Ascot Speedway's dirt race track when they were teenagers.

The other two walls holding the window and door were stripped of their drywall. But the undamaged shots showed continuous action. Cooper ahead, Roger on the outside, the two of them neck and neck. The Corsa and Porsche bumping as they made a turn. Finally, the Porsche crashing into a four foot steel crash wall, and detonating into a ball of flames.

It really wasn't Roger's fault. The 911, cool as it looked and drove, had known carburetor problems. It was first designed with too narrow of rims and tires. It was sensitive to side winds which caused over and under steering. Twenty-four pounds of lead behind the corner of the front bumpers helped, but unfortunately not enough in this race.

Cooper always felt Roger deliberately under steered the 911 into his Corsa, but never got Roger to admit it. He couldn't figure out why Roger would risk such a move. But shit happens on the track at that speed. There had to be more to it than what he knew. There was a lot of insurance money changing hands after that wreck. A lot more would have changed hands if Roger had died. Gwen wouldn't hear of it. But Cooper had snuck a look at the 911 once anyway. He found nothing to explain what he felt had happened. Roger losing control. That meant nothing. Did someone try to kill Roger? Leaving Cooper to blame? Did Roger find out? Did he always know? Is that what it's all about after all this time? Or is Roger making an innocent foolish move on the outside again.

The last picture was obviously taken by a less grainy thirty-five millimeter still camera. It showed a much closer shot of Roger on a stretcher being put into an ambulance moments after Cooper had pulled him from the burning wreckage. Gwen, in her teens, looked on, her hands to her face, tears in her eyes. Cooper's face was covered with dirt, smoke, and anger. In the background were the victorious Corsa, the smashed, smoldering Porsche, and shocked, much thinner, Marty Owens.

So, Cooper thought, thirteen years later, Roger had put the 911 back on the road. Hair stood up on the back of Portland's neck. What was the actor up to now? Where was he? Who A-bombed his condo? Why were the other walls torn up but not this one? Were they looking for something or just trashing the place? Was there something in the mural that tipped them off? Did they find what they came for? Why in hell would Roger duplicate Cooper's custom Corsa down to the stitch?

Cooper studied the murals. He had never laid eyes on them before. In fact, he never knew they existed. If Roger had won, the film probably would've made it to all the networks. He thought back to the last time he'd been to Roger's condo, maybe three months or more. This room had been closed. The damage to the door indicated the door had been locked. So someone had their fatal race on sixteen millimeter and thirty-five millimeter. Cooper tried to envision how Ascot Park looked like back then. The camera person must have been positioned at the top of the grandstands and had come down afterwards to get snapshots of Roger. Or was there a second person, a photographer taking stills. Did Roger have it arranged? If he didn't, how much did it cost him to get the film? Why hadn't he shown it? Did Gwen know?

Cooper studied the mural closer from the beginning again. There it was in black and white. Roger had forced a move to the inside and caused the Corsa to nip the Porsche's rear-end, shooting the silver bullet into the steel wall and crunching it like a Coors Light can. Roger had broken both his legs, fractured his collarbone and punctured a lung. There were rumors of facial bone fractures but that was kept from the prying media for reasons Cooper was sure those handling Roger's career knew best. Regardless, he was never the same dickhead preppy Roger Kelemen after that crash.

They had raced many times before that. Often while being chased by a thick-necked cop named Brubaker. By the time these photos were taken, neither one of them had a driver's license and Brubaker had crashed one too many black and whites, the last a Mustang, and got his butt put behind a desk. Full out through the canyons and back they'd compete against each other. On Laurel, Coldwater, Beverly Glen, Benedict, all across Mulholland from Bel Air to Beverly Hills to West Hollywood and onto all the freeways, crisscrossing Los Angeles and into the San Fernando Valley. The Corsa/Porsche duels, to see who the better, smarter driver was.

This was the only officially staged race on a race track because both were banned from the streets. The first and the last official race. Roger was in the middle of filming a movie at the time and Paramount had lost nearly ten million because he couldn't complete the film. Or Lloyd's of London did.

Things were never the same between them. Roger's career was never as strong. Sure, he'd done a lot of television since then. But the big studios wouldn't touch him. His body was racked with pain. They put him on pain pills. That eventually led to illegal drugs and affected his short time memory. It didn't stop Roger, Jack and his agents, Jerry and Ruth, from blaming Portland for all of Roger's professional short comings. Even though Portland saved Roger's life by pulling him out of that wreck before it flamed up. Roger never blamed Cooper to his face. He didn't have to. The spin in the media took care of that.

It didn't help that from that race track Portland's dad had introduced him to Don Yenko and he ended up driving one of

Don's best Corsa Stingers in SCCA D Production national championships. At times he had the Stinger running 140 mph. No one believed a Corsa could win the Daytona International Speedway championship. But with Yenko's limited-production close-ratio transmission and a fearless kid like Portland Cooper behind the wheel, there wasn't anything the Stinger couldn't do that the Porsche could do. That little six-banger was amazing. It just needed to breathe.

Then in the spring of 1967 Uncle Sam called and Cooper spent the next four years rebuilding helicopter engines in Corpus Christi, Texas, and learning how to test fly them. By the time his extended tour of duty had finished, so was the Corsa. General Motors dropped the car in 1969, therefore so did the serious race tracks. Porsche offered him a job designing engines, so did Ford. GM never came calling. He turned the others down. After drifting for a year, he settled back in North Hollywood because he grew up there and it was close to all the auto junkyards and recycle heaps where he knew the Corvair would end up. And of course, still close enough to Gwen.

He opened Cooper's Corsa Shop to keep as many of them alive as possible. To hell with Nader and his book "Unsafe at Any Speed". He loved his Blood Red, it was fun to drive at any speed. Through it all, Gwen Hawkins was always beside him. But lurking in the background, ready to take Cooper's place at anytime, was Roger Kelemen. Cooper reached back behind his left temple and without realizing it, began to scratch at a four inch scar he received about three weeks after these race photos were taken. All Cooper could really remember about receiving the scar was that three large men threaten to harm Gwen after they jumped him outside a malt shop on Melrose. The message was to stop poking around a wreck yard where Roger's 911 was stored. They beat him silly and left him bleeding in an alley to make sure he got it. He had. Loud and bloody clear.

He and Gwen had just finished a tiff inside the malt shop about Portland going on the race circuit without her. Cooper insisted she stay in school. She wanted to come with him. It almost seemed like the end for them, Gwen attending UCLA with her preppy friends and Portland hitting the road with new race track groupies in every town. It seemed so minor now but then it was big enough to end things between them. In more ways than one. The beating somehow changed that.

Ten minutes after leaving the shop, when Cooper had not returned to pick her up out front as promised, Gwen headed toward where they had parked and found Portland stuffed in the malt shop's dumpster. There was no proof of where the beating had come from. Maybe Roger sent the message, maybe Jack, Gwen's stepfather, maybe Paramount. It didn't have to make sense. Cooper got the sticky picture. So he dropped it.

But he and Gwen had made one thing perfectly clear to each other from that night forward. Gwen was his girl, and he was her man, no matter where he went or how long he was away, or how many books she had to read to finish school. Anyone that had a problem with them loving each other best bite the bullet. As long as Portland was alive, Gwen would be his to love and to cherish. As long as Gwen wanted him on whatever terms they chose, they'd be together as one.

It was emotional blackmail to be sure. Gwen for keeping his mouth shut. A deal was a deal, whether said, written, beaten or otherwise. Otherwise suited Cooper just fine. That was over a decade ago. Had it been that long?

Cooper picked up a picture of Roger, Gwen, and himself. He remembered the shot. It was taken on his mother's camera. Gwen and Portland had just graduated high school together. They were happy and laughing. At least Gwen and Roger were. Cooper's face had been scribbled over in ink and a pen stuck through his heart. He let the picture drift to the floor.

Cooper examined what was left of the other walls. He looked down into the stripped studs and found only crumbled plaster. In the far corner Roger's desk drawers and files were spread about. A Phillips screwdriver was stuck into a wall stud below the window near a tool box dumped out on the floor.

Cooper pulled the screwdriver out, looked at it and tossed it aside. He went to the desk and examined the scattered papers and noticed that someone had failed to pry open Roger's old transistor radio after having stripped the last two screws in their haste to look inside. It sat there crushed. Cooper recognized the Regency TR-1 as the transistor radio Roger kept in his 911 and carried to the beach in his pocket. He always had an earphone stuck in his ear so no one else could hear. There was something about it. What were they looking for?

He bent down and selected a larger Phillips screwdriver. With great care and with subtle touch of an artist, his skilled fingers worked the last two screws out and took the radio apart. At first he didn't notice anything unusual. But a closer examination revealed a standard twenty pound typing paper folded and taped neatly to the inside cover. It was stuck in place by file folder labels. Cooper easily pulled it free. This hadn't been here long. He looked around the floor. Nothing hadn't been broken or torn up. He unfolded it and took a moment to take it in. It was a list of addresses and names of Irene's dinner guest. Properties that they owned and worked at but didn't live in, office buildings, beach houses, and ranches. It was handwritten by Roger and signed with his autograph. Why it was stuck in there, Cooper wasn't sure. It had to mean something. Even if only to coked out Roger. Copper folded it up and put it in his pocket. He left Roger's ground zeroed condo, keeping the door key just in case.

Outside, Cooper walked across the small, shrub filled courtyard and knocked on another condo's door. What a waste of a day, he thought. The door swung open from his knock. A strong familiar smell hit him as he pushed the door open.

"If you ain't got a gun, you're dead," came a man's gravel loaded voice from within.

"Nick, it's me."

"Cooper, baby... come in. Who the hell left the door open?" Cooper heard a slap of flesh.

"Ouch, I didn't know," said a young girl. "I had to pee."

"You didn't know. You'll get us blown away, goddamn it! Then you'll know! Come on in, Coop. I've got a surprise for ya."

Cooper entered, pulling the door shut behind him. He locked it. He had enough surprises for the day. In the living room, unshaven and smelly, Nick sat on a dilapidated green floral print couch. He held a loaded, fully automatic water pipe on his potbelly with one hand and a loaded fully automatic twelve gauge sawed-off shotgun in the other. The two scantily clad women, Dorothy and Bonnie were waiting legs crossed on the floor, antsy for their turn at the pipe. Nick sat in only his white army issued cotton boxers. The air wasn't on. The windows were covered so that no outside light came through. The place was hot, sweaty and had that dirty bathroom stink. They must've been trying to keep the air in the room to recycle the fumes. The girls sat in their panties and men's a-shirts. Nick had buried his right leg in Korea from the upper thigh down. He didn't try to hide it. The girls only had minor shaving scars and hot ash burns. Nick put the shotgun down and soaked a cotton ball stuck on the end of a wire in 151 rum. Dorothy held up a lit candle.

"Have a seat, my friend. Get your shit off the chair and let the man sit down."

The rum burst into flames. Nick held the fire over the glass water pipe's bowl and lit the white rock. He inhaled and handed the pipe to Bonnie. Dorothy, the older unnatural redhead got up and moved her things quickly and got back in line.

Cooper didn't sit.

"Sit down, you're givin' me a stiff neck," Nick said.

"A least something's stiff," Dorothy murmured.

"As long as I can piss out of it, it works. Here, fill your face?" He finally exhaled, pulled the pipe from Bonnie, took another hit, and held the pipe up to Cooper.

"Hey!" Bonnie, the younger of the two women said.

Cooper held up his hand. "Pass."

Nick shrugged and Bonnie grabbed the pipe back and gave Cooper a set of greedy thankful eyes. What a shame, Cooper thought, the kid was barely old enough to bleed, and here she was pumpin' flesh for a face full of death.

"How about something else? Grass, coffee, booze? How about these tits?"He held Dorothy's breasts."You want some?"

"Maybe later."Cooper sat down.

Nick took the pipe and put in another small rock and handed the pipe to Dorothy. She was just slightly old enough to be Bonnie's mother and knowing Nick, was. Jesus, what people will do for this crap. White death. A zenith flash.

"No problem, I'll put them on hold. Here, look at these pics. Not bad for a gimp that can't get it up, huh, Coop?"

The two women sighed and eyed Cooper wantonly.

"It's my birthday, I'm celebratin'. You want some shit?"

"No, thanks. Nice pics, though. That you?"

"You like that, huh?" Bonnie asked. "Go ahead feel, their genuine authentic."

"You want some, Coop? Give him some. I got matching sets?"

"Real nice, but I'm interested in Roger in the background."

"You into guys, big fella," Dorothy asked, running a long painted fingernail up Cooper's leg, hooking it into the flap of his fly and resting her palm on the bulge in his pants. "Someone must be a happy camper."

Cooper removed her hand, gently patting it before letting it drop. "My friend's into guys...he stood her up."

Nick seemed to be wigging out. Dorothy stroked Nick's chest with her other hand. She toyed with the thick graying hair.

"You still with me, Nick?"

"Yeah, yeah, just buzzing on c-train, Coop buddy...you're lookin' for Roger."

"That big ratfink movie star?"Bonnie asked.

"If you're looking for the dickless wonder, he ain't been around in three or four days," Dorothy said.

"That right, Nick?"

"All I know is he came over, wouldn't drop his pants for the girls, snorted two Gs of my stash, and mumbled something about becoming a multi-millionaire, then split."

"Did you happen to notice anyone at Roger's place?"

"Two nights ago...late...two guys," Nick answered.

"A big guy and the other was the kung fu type you see in those beat 'em up foreign movies," Bonnie said.

"The big one was blond, kind of dumb looking in a cute sort of way. You know what I mean? They used a key to get in. Nick wouldn't let us talk to them."Dorothy pulled on Nick's chest hairs and he bolted upright.

"Aaahhhh! You stupid bitch. Give me that pipe!" He took it from Bonnie and repacked it and gave it to Dorothy."Here, stick this in your face and shut the hell up."

"How long were they there, Nick?"

"Maybe half an hour. Made noise. Roger wasn't with them."

"You didn't happen to report this?"

"Oh sure, I call the cops all the time."

Cooper got up to leave.

"Let's take some more pics," Dorothy said.

"There ain't film."Nick opened his eyes and reached for the Polaroid behind his head.

"Who needs film to pose like a rose?" Bonnie said, sitting up happily. "Hey, mister, you want to take some pics?"

The Corvair car horn honked two short one long. Cooper didn't look away. He just backed his way to the door and opened it. "Next time. Happy birthday, Nick."

Cooper shut the door as Nick started clicking the camera at Dorothy and Bonnie who crumbled to the floor in a tangled flurry of suggestive poses.

Gwen sat in the car listening intently to the Angels game. She had her head back against the headrest, pretending to have her eyes closed.

Cooper came up slowly taking in a 'kinda' dumb looking, in a cute sort of way,' heavyset blond gorilla sitting in a black 67 BMW 2000CS. It was parked in the wrong direction eight cars down and across the street.

"What's the score?"

"Two to one, Angels in the third. What took you so long? Cooper got in the Corsa.

"I checked with Nick. Roger hasn't been around in three or four days."

"See, what did I tell you?"

"I know, you and your queer feelings. How long has blondie been watching us?"

Gwen straightened her neck. "In the Beamer? He just pulled up about a minute ago. There's another car up about half a block. A blue Datsun Roadster. He got out and came to talk to this one and went around back. So I honked. He hasn't come back out this way."

"Thanks." Cooper put the key back in the ignition, starting the Corsa. He put it in gear and drove off, pretending not to take interest in the Beamer or the gorilla behind the wheel.

The meat in the 2000CS waited a moment then followed. Cooper was nice about it and let him keep up. It didn't figure that the gorilla knew where Roger was, if Roger was alive. But Cooper had a few questions he wanted to ask him anyway. Like who he was, who he worked for, and what he wanted?

Cooper dropped Gwen off out back of his Corsa shop. He got out of the Corsa, leaving the engine purring, and opened the walk gate. Gwen went in and opened the electric gate with her genie and pulled her black Vette out. Cooper waited outside the gate until it closed behind her car. He stuck his head into the Sting Ray's open window.

"How about dinner?" Gwen asked

"How about it?"

"Will you show up or what?"

"I'm not hungry."

"This is your first serious invite in years. You better be there with bells on your toes."

"I'll think about it. Call me later."

Gwen made one of her faces and Cooper kissed it. Her plush lips engulfed his thin flesh as his hand slipped down over her ripe upturned breast and taunted a nipple with his heavy thumb. He pulled his face back and their eyes locked not knowing what would happen next. It was always like this, as though danger drew them together. The excitement opened up a fire in their hearts. An obsession that would not end. A fear of never touching each other lovingly again.

"You'd better go."

"Tease. Tell me dirty stories then send me home."

"I've got work to do. Thanks to you."

Gwen's expression changed to concern.

"Don't worry. Drive fast. Don't stop and get me a status on those addresses."

Gwen blew him a kiss and sped out of the alley.

Cooper watched her go as a baby blue 67 Datsun Roadster pulled into the alley. It rolled up along Cooper's property and stopped just short of blocking the gate. A young Asian greaser, dressed in black with gray lizard cowboy boots stepped out and leaned on his car trying his best to look intimidating.

Cooper tried not to snicker.

The blond gorilla climbed over a neighbor's rickety fence across the alley and leaned against its dry-cedar. He crossed his thick harry arms over his chest. Just passing the time of day, and innocently covered up a gun under his left arm.

Cooper stood his ground between them, keeping the two hoods in his peripheral view. He kept his eyes more or less focused down at the opening of the alley. It made his two new friends nervous because they had to keep jerking their heads around trying to see what the hell Cooper was looking at.

"You Portland Cooper?"the gorilla asked with a squeaky German accent. Like maybe he'd been kicked in the fatherland once too often.

"Maybe...who wants to know?"

"You're better off not knowin'. Is this Mr. Kelemen's car?"

"Maybe...who wants to know?"

"Told you we should've thumped him first." The slant eye hiked up the sleeves to his black cotton turtleneck. It was hard to tell, but he was most likely Japanese. His face had several scars, just as likely from kick boxing as from kissing moving rickshaws.

"I don't take to thumping, if you know what I mean," Cooper said, balancing his weight on the balls of his work boots. "Maybe you girls should spell it out."

"We want the car."

"Come and get it."

The heavy set one stepped within arm's length."Nothing personal." He unfolded his hand away from his gun and tried to grab the front of Cooper's work shirt. Instead, he got an up-close and personal face to cinder block interview with Cooper's wall. It took off a layer or two of skin above his bushy blond right eyebrow.

The short one came with a kick at Cooper's chest. Cooper grabbed it by the boot heel and flipped him on his back. He added a swift steel-toed kick of his own to the hood's left ribs.

The slant-eye let out with a string of oaths about Cooper's ancestors while Portland wheeled around and jumped back into the Corsa.

The heavy set reached for his gun this time. So Cooper slammed the Corsa into gear, running over the German's toes. This action raised the gorilla's pitch another octave as he dropped the gun to reach for his shoe.

Cooper was headed into the dead end alley in first. He hit the brakes then jammed on the gas as he cut the wheels heavily to his left and stepped off the pedal. The rear end did exactly what Nader said it would do. It spun around on the loose gravel until Cooper had the Corsa facing out of the alley.

The judo-junky leaped into the backseat as Cooper zoomed past. Portland put his boot to the brakes again sending the greaser over the windshield and sprawling onto the hood. He raked his teeth across six coats of blood red paint.

With the tires still rolling forward, Cooper crammed it into reverse, with a clunking grind. He hit the accelerator while cutting the wheel to the right. Spinning the frontend of the car around this time. It flung the screaming greaser off the hood, reptile-uppers first into his hopping mad pal. Pinning the hairy German's back against Cooper's work yard wall.

Cooper sped off in reverse then spun the car around again as the two thugs struggled to get off each other. Before they could limp to the Datsun Roadster, Cooper and the blood red Corsa were nothing but hurt feelings.

Gwen hadn't bothered to go around back to park in the lot behind her Beverly Hills, PR office. She left her black Corvette on Canon and went into the front, turning off the alarm but not turning on the overhead lights. She was at her secretary's desk, as she hung up the phone. Gwen was clearly puzzled about what she had learned, but not impressed. She held out the neatly folded piece of paper Portland had given her. Why would Roger hide this list in his favorite radio? Was it a message? If it was, whom did he expect to find it? Cooper? Her? The police? Someone tore up Roger's place. What were they looking for? Surely not this list. If something bad were to happen to Roger, is this list a clue as to who did it? Looking at the familiar list of names again, she hoped not. She wasn't looking forward to Portland's take on it. Even though she had no choice.

About an hour later, Cooper pulled up to the gate where Gwen lived in the guest house. Her stepfather owned the massive home years before Gwen's mother married him. The three of them had lived there comfortably ever since with two maids and a cat. Gwen did own a beach house in Malibu off Broad Beach Road. She spent most of her weeknights in the guest rooms at her mother's because it was much closer to her PR business. It made spending time at the beach seem more like getting away from it all. Plus she was closer to Portland.

Cooper used the street access buzzer. The gates rolled back. He drove the Corsa up the steep cobblestone drive to the two story home overlooking West Los Angeles and pulled in behind Gwen's 64 Vette, and a new XJ Series II-white Jaguar, the XJ12. There was also a 76 white Cadillac Eldorado convertible, driven by Gwen's mother under a carport incased by bougainvillea of bract colors not normally encountered in nature. As Portland once discovered the hard way by attempting to climb up to Gwen's room, they had nasty thorns.

Cooper sat watching. It looked like no one else was there but them. He didn't think he was followed. But one never knew. Lights from a fountain glistened on the cars and water spewed from a large fish held by cherubs. An eight foot white painted cement wall encased the elegant romantically lit, manicured grounds. Almost all the lights were off in the massive home. Cooper waited in the car until Gwen surprised him by coming out in a cream silk evening gown. Cooper couldn't help but smile at the pink bunny slippers. He had bought them for her nearly twelve years ago and she still wore them despite having nearly fallen apart.

"Portland, do you want to come in?"

"This will just take a minute. Wow." He let out a low whistle as her statuesque form walked in front of the light from the gardens. She wore nothing underneath. It clearly showed.

"Wolf." She saw the scratches on the hood. "This isn't?"

"Relax, it's Roger's. Our blond friend and his grease-job pal tried to take it from me. What'd you find?"

She saw the scrape on his hand and frowned, "Like you said, just a list of names and addresses. I made a few calls and they are still in the names on that list. There are recent appraisals on all these properties in the past six months. But nothing has changed as far as the deeds go yet. I don't quite understand what it means. What's going on, Portland?"

"I'm no Einstein either?"Gwen gave Portland a copy. He looked at it while drawing his nails across the back of his head, subconsciously feeling the scar again. "What do you make of it?"

"Well, of course, we know them all. Jack's name is fourth on the list. Roger's in some sort of trouble, isn't he?"

"Notice there's no mention of you, me Roger or Irene?"

"No. But look, that's our Calabasas ranch address and we had a current appraisal done for insurance purposes about six months ago. It's in Jack's name only. It was about the same time all these other properties had one done."

"I'm not invited? What a heartbreaker. So someone needed to know what all this was worth. Could be Roger. But why?"

"This is a list of mother's standard dinner guests."

Cooper nodded his head. Yes, he remembered them. Once in awhile he even watched them come and go and listened from the veranda where he'd meet with Gwen for a secret kiss and a beer she'd sneak from the barman. They weren't part of his life and he most certainly was not part of theirs. He was referred to as being Gwen's neighbor friend. With a few other creative adjectives thrown in at times due to the race accident.

Dear old Roger always filled in for Portland during family events, like dinner, Bar Mitzvah, movie premieres and holiday parties. Not that Portland wanted to attend any of those events. If Gwen's mother, Irene and Irene's second husband, Jack, were to attend, it was just simply assumed that the little boy who had lived next door was simply otherwise occupied. Gwen often invited him and just as often didn't. He always turned her down anyway. Cooper let the thought fade and tried to put two and two together but kept coming up with odd numbers. Something was missing from why this was all happening.

"What does Roger want with a Corsa just like yours? After all the fights you two had over it and all those races."

"I don't know. But those pictures…someone has our last race on film. Why didn't he ever tell us? Or better yet, show us? It would've been worth a few laughs."

"Not to Roger."

"Or to Jack's production company if they mean anything."

"Don't start up with that again. It's old hat."

"So are the fifteen stitches I received a few days later for sniffing around his 911."

"Are you looking for an argument?"

"What we're looking for is Roger. I'm just wondering if the two incidents have anything in common. We do know a lot of money changed hands because of that race."

"You just don't like Jack."

"True. I also don't like getting the hell kicked out of me. I would've fried his ass long ago if he wasn't your stepfather. He's a crook and bilked millions of insurance money."

"The money went to Paramount, not to Jack."

"He got his share. Check his contract."

"What do you know about his contract?"

"A few things are standard. Others weren't."

"Are you saying that wasn't an accident?"

"I'm saying Roger forced it, causing himself to lose control. But I don't know why he would lean into me. Unless he didn't."

"That again."

"Just because I found nothing, doesn't mean there wasn't something there. It could've been removed."

"Jack did not try to kill Roger."

"I didn't say he did. There are other people involved here."

"Jerry and Ruth? They are his agents."

"They are on that list."

25

"This is ridicules and has nothing to do with that race."

"At least we agree on that it's ridicules."

"See, you came here just to piss me off?!"

"No. I came here hoping to get some answers. But all we seem to know for sure is that Roger is missing. His place is trashed. My car is duplicated and wanted by someone bad enough to get tough about it. That and our last race was secretly filmed. And now a list of prime real estate is hidden in Roger's favorite transistor radio that reads just like your mother's dinner list. Oh, yeah, and Roger has his Porsche back on the road, or one just like it, and...."Cooper stopped.

"What else?"

"He also has a drug problem again according to Nick."

"Goddamn him!"

"You care to guess at the board?"

"Roger plans to race the cars again?"

"Only if there is money to be made, would be my guess."

"Wait, maybe Roger's been working on his script again."

"I thought it was about racing boats and set in Florida."

"Yes, it is or was, as far as I know."

"So he could've rewritten it to add our cars."

"Maybe. These people will be at dinner, ask them about it."

"Do I have to?"

"These people are all family to Roger. Practically raised him. Took him off the streets of Hollywood. If Roger has a script that involves racing cars, they would know. All things considered, I'm sure no one is happy about it."

"Wait a minute. How much money has Roger hit you up for?"

"Not that much. And not for a few months."

"How much?"

"Twenty-three grand...on a signed IOU."

Cooper shook his head as he got back into Roger's Corsa. "And now he's building cars and talking about being a multi-millionaire? Look, keep it clamped about this, even to Irene. By the way, will I eat with you or in the kitchen with the help?"

"Portland, don't be rude. Mother would be furious."

"I'll call you about it. Call me if you hear from Roger."

Gwen kissed him gently. "Promise me you'll be nice."

"You want nice? Gee, am I stuck in Bel Air again? Everything is so nice, I'm getting goose bumps." He drove off.

Gwen turned toward the house and caught a glimpse of Jack, her stepfather, turning away from an upstairs window. Years ago Jack had barred Portland from coming into the house.One stupid grease footprint on a new white carpet was all it took. But it was more than that. They all blamed him for Roger crashing his 911. It's true, Jack never cared for Portland. It's true Portland was a smartass and never took to Jack. But it wasn't fair that Roger was invited to dinner and holiday events all these years and not Portland. Even if Portland preferred it that way. Even if Portland was in Jack's eyes a troublemaker, a wiseass, a non-conformist, and thought he had something on Jack, like insurance fraud. It still wasn't fair to exclude him.

She smiled to herself when she remembered Portland's first day in school. He stuck out like a pickle in a lollipop jar. His light green cotton, short sleeved shirt, rolled up with cigs. His hair slicked back. His pointed black dago boots. That cocky smile. He was everything her mother feared. But she felt her father would've taken to him, maybe. Her grandfather sure did. What a dream boat he was though, and living right next-door. Stay away from that boy, she told herself. But she couldn't. He was the outsider, the rebel with an attitude. Stay away from that boy, her girlfriends told her, but she couldn't. He was manly and trustworthy. Stay away from that boy, her mother told her. He wouldn't and she couldn't. Even after all they'd gone through. No ring, no promises, just a special something. So her classmates shunned her. Even the boys. Even to this day. All except Roger. The boy movie star. The family business friend. Always there in a pinch when she needed him.

When Portland's family moved away, Roger was there to hold her hand. When Portland went to war, or on the race circuit, he was there to hug her. Always the friend, the third wheel. Lunch, dinner, parties, an escort whenever Portland couldn't make it, or wouldn't. From the start, she never had to say anything to Roger, he already knew. He loved her, she knew it. But it wasn't like the excitement she had with Portland. They were best of friends. There was always that feeling, that understanding. A connection. All the fun they had with their cars that year. Porsche - Corsa and her dad's black, hand-me-down Sting Ray. Only to have it all end with a tragic crash into a wall. It wasn't Portland's fault. Even if he goaded Roger and was blamed for it. Things were never the same between Roger and Portland after that. That was also when Gwen knew she had made the right decision. It had to be Portland, because it was Portland Cooper she loved. Not because he won the race or saved Roger from burning up in his 911.But because of whom Portland was inside. What she saw in him on the islands when his family came to visit. It was him she needed by her side. Forever. She could see in her grandparents' eyes that they had approved. Portland was the one. From the start, he was a man with heart who could fully understand who she was, and love her the way she dreamed to be loved. From that day, Roger would remain her best friend, her client, and Portland her lover. Had it been thirteen years?

The last few years Roger drew away. Pleasant on the surface but life was troubling. Now he was in real trouble with drugs again. She knew it, she had that feeling. She saw it coming without really seeing it there. But she had failed him. He came for money, and she should've given him time, love, friendship. She should've listened when no words were being spoken. She should've known and done for him what he had done for her. Been there for him. But no, she had failed him.

Poor Roger. Wrapped up in drugs again. How far had he gone this time? How many times can he throw it away trying to hide the pain? He'll call, she knew he'd call. Call me, Roger. Call me. I'm thinking of you, dear friend. I'm here, call me.

3 BOTTOM OF SANTA MONICA PIER

Cooper pulled up to his shop gate, got out and let himself into the work yard by punching a code. He got back in and drove Roger's Corsa into the paint booth and locked it and the door to the stall. His stomach did a Tarzan yell reminding him that it hadn't been fed since seven that morning. To make sure its master wouldn't forget, it immediately began to gnaw on Portland's backbone.

He entered the house through the parts shop and climbed the back stairs to the kitchen making sure he was still alone. He got halfway up the stairs when the phone rang. He raced up the remaining steps two at a time. His machine picked up. Cooper reached it as it beeped. He turned up the volume to monitor the call.

"Coop, it's Holland. Call me."

Portland pressed the intercom button as he bent to pull off his socks. "Hold on, I'm here."

Any car part ever made, Holland could get it over night. Legal or otherwise... and usually both. She'd fly it in herself if the price was right.

"I've got your heads."

"Who fronted Marty for them?"

"I did."

"All right, drop them by, I'll cover it."

"Forget it, Coop. I won it back. Hear you're trackin' Roger."

"Seen him lately?"

"Yeah, I saw him. He's been feelin' pretty good. Dropped an IOU on my blouse at ten percent weekly."

"When?"

"Four nights ago."

"How much?

"It's confidential...you know what I mean?"

"It's important. Two semi-toughs tried to take his Corsa."

"Two g's."

"That's all?"

"That's my limit for guys like him. What's the problem?"

"I don't know. I think Roger tried to do something stupid to get a hold of a large sum of money and now he's disappeared."

"Gwen asked ya?"

"Who else?"

"You ought to marry that broad, my friend. Or I'm gonna hook her up with my brother."

"Yeah, I'll ask her tonight."

"Marty said that maybe Roger nabbed your blue prints."

"Any truth to that?"

"I don't know, could've been from photos, but I heard he had the work done someplace up in Bakersfield. Pretty dame close I hear. Pissed, huh?"

"You bet I am. Except for the suspension and fake leather, it's identical."

"When did it arrive?

"Early this morning. I never should've put the engine in it.

"Have you checked your blues?"

"I'm about to."

Cooper went to a small safe he kept in his closet. He twisted the combo and opened it and pulled out a leather satchel to check to see if the blue prints to his Corsa were still there. They were. Maybe Roger did use photos. There's been plenty taken over the years. "Everything looks in order."

"I can think of several hows, but I can't think of any whys."

"Gwen thinks maybe he's got a script or something."

"Makes some sense if he did. But why bother with your car?"

"I should've been suspicious when he said the engine was a gift for a friend. He even had me sign it paid upon installation."

"That sounds like Roger. But the question is still why? We all know how he feels about you and your Corsa. By the way, last time I saw him he had his Porsche back on the road. It looked pretty good. Sounded even better."

"So I heard. Was it the original body?"

"Claims it was. I'll believe it when I see the weld Finn did and VIN number."

"Roger's got a reason. It may be distorted, but Roger's got a reason. Stay in touch with Marty, will ya?"

"You want the heads tonight? I'll bring beers."

"Tomorrow's good."

"Be that way. See you then."

Cooper hung up and went into the bathroom and turned on the shower. He had his T-shirt up over his head when the phone rang again. He pulled it off and tossed it toward the hamper and hit the intercom again. "Coop here."

"Roger called!" Gwen's voice was stressed.

"Yeah?"

"He wants to see you!"

"Will you calm down? I'm tired. Give it to me nice and slow now. Where?"

"Midnight, on the Santa Monica Pier."

Cooper checked the clock on his dresser. It was ten-thirty already. "I've got to wash up and eat something."

"I'm worried. He wouldn't tell me anything."

"Gwen, I'm starving. I'll call you from Santa Monica. Bye."

"I love you."

"I know...get some rest." Cooper hung up and continued to undress. He stopped and pulled his trousers back on when a silent alarm began to flash above his bedroom door frame. The dull clatter from a master lock falling on concrete came from down in the work yard. Someone had cut the padlock on the number three work stall. Cooper had dropped the lock enough times putting his car away to know what the sound meant.

He rushed to the window and carefully parted the curtains to look out over his Corsa shop. Shit. He was right. The big blond gorilla and his judo junky friend were back and had scaled the fence. The big guy had a pair of lock cutters and was pulling Portland's Corsa out of the third work stall by its bumper, while the Jap tried, in vain, to jimmy the box on the electric gate. Marty had rigged it. Only God could've jimmied it without the code. The slant-eye pried at the box with a screwdriver and got immediately knocked on his ass by a vicious bolt of electricity. He sat there a moment with his black eyes dilated until some sense of where the hell he was came back into his slicked-back head. He got up to examine the gate with a much more respectful attitude. He kicked it.

So whoever these two were, they didn't know about the identical blood reds, Cooper thought, as he fetched his new Colt Python Mk V out of a dresser and went back to the window and silently slid it all the way open. Gwen had given him the gun for Christmas. Interesting girl. He checked the 357 to make sure the safety was on and stuck the revolver's throat in his pants. He had a mind to just shoot the two clowns right there from the window, not kill them, maybe just blow a finger off or two. But he figured he'd better have a word with them first. Besides a bullet could ricochet off a bone and chip the paint on his Corsa. Then he'd have to kill the bastards.

Was Roger having the car stolen because he couldn't pay off the work, or didn't want to? If they weren't working for Roger, then why does someone else want it? Was it for money he owed? Could it be that simple? Money? Cooper climbed barefoot and shirtless out the window. He moved across the slope of the roof, to the roof of the work stalls and eased himself down a homemade rope and peg fire ladder to the ground.

He came up behind the blond gorilla and fought back the urge to plug him right there for putting his finger prints on the

Corsa's paint. He thumped him instead. Cooper took out his hanky and wiped the finger prints off the engine hood. Afterwards he searched the limp body and pulled out a Czech CZ 75, its clear plastic handle revealed three shells. Cooper slid past the slumped over body, got in his Corsa, pulled out a hidden key and started it. He stopped at the gate as the slumping body rolled over into a full unconscious sprawl.

Mr. Judo, unable to pick the gate lock, stuck his pug face into the open Corsa window and got a quarter inch of cold steel stuck up his flat nose. "How'd you...what the...?" He crossed his dark slanted eyes to see how much trouble he was in. Lots. Three of his past lives flashed before him and all of them ended with Cooper's grinning face.

"Evening...what's your name?"

"Teatro."

"Teatro, didn't you catch my drift earlier?"

"We got a job to do."

"And now you've got two seconds to tell me what you're looking for or I split your eyebrows. One, two." He clicked back the Python's hammer. The metal click echoed off Teatro's teeth. "Nice knowing you." Cooper tensed his trigger finger.

"We don't know! We're just supposed to get it and deliver it!"

Cooper stuck the five inch barrel all the way into Teatro's mouth. "Where?"

"We're to wait for a call."

The big one rolled over on the oil stained concrete below them, groaning. His blond hair fast become matted in blood at the base of his skull.

"What's your buddy's name?"

"Dexter."

"Dexter. Dexter, get your fat ass up off the ground. You're beginning to embarrass Teatro here. Isn't he?"

Teatro nodded his head politely.

Dexter rolled over again. He sat up still in a daze and groaned louder. His thick brain pounded like World War III.

He spat up on himself before remembering where and who he was, and wasn't happy about either.

Cooper put the car in gear. He pushed a hidden toggle switch under the dash and the gate opened.

"Tell him to follow us."Cooper let out the clutch.

Teatro's command came out as an unintelligible plea. Dexter crawled along trying his best to stand up. He finally made it with a wobble and followed them out of the work yard into the dark alley.

"You've got a way with words. Reminds me of someone I met in the service."

Teatro didn't seem to care if he was kidding or not.

Cooper dropped the thought as Dexter caught up with them and the two thugs walked beside Cooper's Corsa with the barrel's sight still scratching Teatro's tonsils. Cooper took them out to the dead-end alley and over to Dexter's BMW.

"By the way. Nice car."

"Thanks," Dexter answered warily.

"You got a spare?"

"Yeah, so?"

"You got a knife?"

"No."

"I got one," Teatro said, willing to admit anything to get rid of the hard-on stuck down his throat.

"Shut up, you idiot!"

"Give it to him," Cooper demanded.

Teatro reached down to his gray lizard skin boot and pulled out a ten inch switch blade and handed it back to Dexter.

Dexter reluctantly took it.

"Now slash a tire. Slash it! Or I spread his tonsils all over your chubby face."

"Slash it, for Christ's sake!"

"Getting religious on me, huh?"

34

Dexter bent down and with great reluctance, slashed a tire. It hissed out in twelve seconds flat. Doing so was almost as painful to him as taking it on the back of the head.

Cooper respected his feelings but told him to slash another radial anyway. Dexter closed the knife. Teatro screeched something about the mentality of Dexter's posterior.

"All right, play it tough. Drop the knife.

Dexter dropped the blade.

"You, back off." Cooper pushed on the gun.

Teatro gladly backed off in a fit of gag reflexes.

"You, over here."Cooper was beginning to enjoy himself. Shooting these two punks would've been too easy. Besides, he had to get out to Santa Monica soon, and the police would have probably frowned on him for leaving two unattended dead bodies lying about his property. At least until they ran their ticker on these two and discovered that Cooper had done the world a great favor in eliminating two of the biggest dumbshits ever to stain a police blotter.

Dexter came over and stood next to the Corsa.

"Closer."

Dexter inched closer.

"Turn around and drop your pants. Drop them!"

Dexter turned and methodically drop his pants.

"Let's go," Cooper ordered, "this isn't Vegas."

"You're sick, man. Are you gonna give me a great big kiss?"

"Exactly. Now grip your knees, Dexter. Stick your face to the sky and pucker.

"Guy's a pervert." Dexter bent over and turned his face up at the starless night.

Cooper stuck the cold 357's barrel up under Dexter's balls.

"Tell him to slash the tire." He stuck the gun further up making sure it was uncomfortable.

"Tell him!"

Dexter began to smart off, thought better of it, and told Teatro to slash the tire.

"Good choice."

Teatro slashed a front tire. They watched the tire's life hiss out. Teatro was good at it. Probably practiced.

"Now let this put a print in your memory." Cooper pulled the trigger before Dexter had time to react. The bullet ricocheted off the cement and punched a hole in the side of the BMW.

Dexter stiffened up and passed out cold into Teatro's arms.

"Now isn't that romantic."

"You've got poor taste, pal."

Cooper recocked the gun and pointed it at the Teatro's head. "I never miss twice."

Teatro backed off, dropping the stunned gorilla face first to the loose gravel.

Cooper drove off as the gate closed.

"We'll pack heavier next time, smartass!"Teatro yelled.

"Good. I hate shooting unarmed girls."

Cooper made a right on Laurel Canyon. He headed to the 101 north, then took the 405 south to the Santa Monica where he headed west, making damned sure he wasn't followed.

Cooper pulled into a small parking lot just south of the Santa Monica Pier. He parked his Corsa in front of a sand filled volley ball court. Far enough away from the pier to give him time to look things over. Sea scented moisture hung in the air thick as saddle blankets. He got out of his Corsa and pulled an old gray sweatshirt out from under the driver's seat and slipped it over his head. After pretending to study the rhythm of the pounding waves he strolled under the pier where two blue gazebos stood guarding the darkened Hippodrome building and carousel.

Even though the Santa Monica Pier survived lack of use and public neglect over the years, the whole area was poorly kept. The pier and the businesses around the pier had taken on a dilapidated look and there was no one else stupid enough to be slinking around in the poor lit night on a Sunday evening.

Several studies had been done for the redevelopment of the pier, of which Gwen and her mother took part in, but they were never acted upon. Cooper couldn't help thinking that maybe someone would finally do something honest about the desolate conditions of the Santa Monica Pier when they found him missing and his blood staining the old rotten planks.

Cooper stayed in the shadows until he reached the stairs near the black top bike path and a junk food stand. He took his time climbing the mildew covered wood planked stairs. He cautiously searched through the darkness. Portland had no idea what Roger had in mind, whether he'd be alone when he found him, or dead, or more likely, both.

Cooper didn't like that the pier was closed. If security were supposed to be around, they weren't in sight. The parking lot behind the row of pier shops and restaurants was empty. A dumpster was overflowing with vegetable boxes, food scraps and rats. This had to be a bad setup. It was there in his head... a distant Taps...a solitary trumpet blowing sadly...da da da....

Then why didn't he just turn around? He looked out over the parking lot. His Corsa was still there. Go home, Cooper. This is stupid. Stop, turn back. What are you looking for? Roger? Death? Let him come to you if he needs help. Let Death do its own leg work. Don't take the punch, fool. Run, go home...go home now. The thoughts rang true in his head but his feet kept him moving forward, drumming to the danger of a heartbeat. The excitement, the challenge, that at any moment, any turn, any blink of the eye, any press of the pedal, it could end, top speed into a ball of nothing, he could die...go home, you fool.

Someone stepped out of the shadows of the farthest gazebo, silhouetted in the dim parking lot lights against the gray mist in the starless night sky. He, whoever it was, seemed alone.

Cooper silently crept barefoot along the wood planks in the shadows of the carousel until he was an easy gunshot away from the figure. Cooper couldn't see the person's face but no one else he knew had such a full head of blond hair but Roger. He wore the back down to his shoulders and the front blow-dried and moussed back, only something was wrong. His hair seemed unkempt, very un-Roger. He looked edgy, rubbing his hands together. His nose was running and he kept sniffing and wiping it with the back of his white sport coat sleeve. Roger always was a little snot-nosed preppy brat. He had it bad this time. Cooper had seen Roger strung-out on coke before, but he never looked like this. He'd always been able to keep it together. There had to be something else going down with him. Now in theater three, Roger Kelemen as the cokey... again. When Roger finally turned toward the light trying to pinpoint where Cooper had gone, Cooper could see Roger's ashen face was unshaven, his cheeks deathly hollow, his eyes sunken and dark from lack of sleep. His trademark white cotton suit looked more lived in than normal, like he was the band on the run, the vulpes in the fox hunt, and the rodent in a field of prey.

Had a job, ain't got no clothes. Spent my money all up my nose. Had a wife, let her slide. Cut two lines, she'd take one side. Saw a doctor, he said to quit. Looked at him and said eat my shit. Tossed the bills when things got heavy. Still paying on the fifty Chevy... cocaine. The silly little rhyme ran through Cooper's head. Roger had written it on a Christmas card to Gwen five years ago from where he was drying out. His second time around. He had taught himself to play guitar. Better think up some new verses Rog, Cooper thought. Because Santa's here and there's been a lot of new snow this year.

Cooper tossed a dried lollipop stick out of the eclipse from the carousel. Roger turned toward the sound. "Cooper?" He had fear in his voice. He looked over his shoulder. Both shoulders at the same time if he could.

"It's me."

"You alone?" Roger sniffed back snot, wiping his face again.

"Don't think so little of yourself, Rog." Cooper came out of the darkness and moved to the railing next to Roger.

"Bite me. Is that my car?" Having someone by him, even if it was Cooper, gave him courage. He wasn't alone in the dark now. Everything would be all right. The first step was over. Cooper was here with the Corsa. Just make it through this one night. Just this one last deal and he'd be set for this one life.

"You bring my cash?" Cooper asked.

"Yes."

"In that case, you're looking at it. I hear you also rebuilt your Porsche."

"You've got good ears. You packing?"

"Do I look lopsided to you?"

Roger pulled out a Chinese silenced pistol, a type 67 from what Cooper could see. An old gun, hadn't been made since 1968 though some of those captured in Vietnam were still around. And not likely traceable.

"Just mentally. Put them up."

Cooper did. He wasn't surprised, even expected it from his old pal. What the hell was Roger up to, though? Why is he including him in his drugged out bullshit after all these years.

"What do you want, Rog?"

Roger fumbled around Cooper's waistband. "Nothing, just turn around." He took Dexter's Czech out of the back of Cooper's pants. His hands shook as he fumbled with it to put it in his jacket pocket. They'd be here soon. The second part would be over. They'd get what they were looking for and Cooper would be out of his way forever. Too bad he couldn't stick around for the grand finale but the jerk had to get too cute for his own good taste. Should've just let them take the car. Now he had to go. So where were they?

Cooper got one close look at Roger's face in the light. From the looks of it someone had danced on it, maybe kicked some sense into him or maybe he had taken a bad fall during a coked out coma. Cooper bet on the boogaloo. Either way Roger looked like he had spent a lot of time speaking to ralph on the big white phone.

"In my back pocket you'll find a list of names."

Roger took the paper out and unfolded it and held it to the light. It was the list of names and address.

"Big deal, you found my Christmas list."

"Hidden inside your old transistor radio?"

"So I'm eccentric. How's the engine run?"

"Better than new. Why'd you copy my Corsa?"

"You're the smart one, figure it out. Did the custom shop put the radio back? I had a hell of a time finding a working AM-FM Stereo."

"Should've called me, I've got three in my workshop. By the way, a couple of your good buddies stopped by to listen to it. Know them?"

"Not personally. They...." Before Roger could finish his reply his back stiffened. Someone else had a gun to his back.

Cooper turned to see what was up and caught a glimpse of a butt from a Browning before it crashed down on the side of his thick skull. His mind turned to oatmeal and raisins, two scoops and boiled oats. He wasn't out but his legs and arms felt numb. Someone had stuck him with something strong, quick and effective. A sharp piercing jab into his thigh. The gray clouds from above came storming down on him and wrapped themselves around his head. The blurry six heads surrounding him seemed like twenty. He tried to move his right arm and sensed his left earlobe wiggle. It felt as though he took a fast cold bullet to the spine. Making him wet his pants as he lost all motor control. An engine gone dry, but denying him that certain satisfaction of being a new man.

His hands were tied. A cement block was strapped to his waist. A rope was looped from his hands to his feet. Muffled voices, scuffling feet, joined a thousand shades of wet gray. He slid over the planks. Then up, up, up and down, down, down, down, where a cool thud engulfed him as his body slapped on the water's surface. Only to sink below its wetness near the end of the pier. It immediately became dark, lonely and deathly cold. As the lights faded from above, his ears popped, his eyes stung, his lungs ached. Portland Cooper fought to clear his senses as his body crashed against old rotting pylons at the bottom of the sea.

So this is what he'd come for. Barnacles ripping at his flesh. The tide rolled over and over Cooper as the sheer shock of being twenty feet below and not being able to see, breathe or willfully move brought his own frantic survival instincts back. The frigid water sent a left jab to his face with the full meaning of if you don't move sucker, you're gonna die!

Move, move, move! What little strength he had he used to rub the cement block against the sharp crustacean with his thick rippled stomach muscles. Faster, faster, faster, sit-ups, sit-ups, feel the burn, move past the wall. Was it working? Time ticked by, one, two, three, three and a half...to the beat of the blood pressure building up behind his eyes. No man would live beyond four minutes. He had to move faster.

Up above, only silent, unnoticeable air bubbles escaped to the surface. They burst into the night as speechless as a breath in the wind, a will to the living, a last rite for the dying. No shooting star. Nothing.

Gwen pulled her Sting Ray to a stop not far from where Cooper had parked his Corsa. Only it was gone. She got out despite it being so dark and quiet. She looked up to see two security officers headed out on the pier, drinking coffee. She couldn't sleep so she drove over to Portland's place and found his shower running. She knew something had gone wrong, she could feel it.

Waves rolled heavily in from the sea, crashing amongst the giant pylons. Something bobbed in between the white caps. Something white or gray. Gwen sprinted down to the water edge, kicking off her shoes when she reached the sand.

The light barely made it out thirty yards. But it didn't matter. She knew it was Portland, half dog paddling, half bobbing. Gwen waded out, put her arms around Portland's

41

thick chest and guided him toward the sea soaked sand. Waves pounded them sending them sprawling into the knee deep water. They half crawled, half hopped, up to the wet sand.

Cooper choked up water. His hands were still tied, so were his feet. Seaweed was wrapped around Portland's chest and waist. A torn mildewed Winchell's coffee cup, assorted toilet papers and sea foam were stuck to his neck and face. Christ, the Santa Monica Bay wasn't even fit for drowning. Gwen pulled at the seaweed to get at his abdomen to push. Cooper pulled her away as he rolled onto his side and threw up.

Cooper plopped back, helpless on the beach, a flounder out of water. The block was gone. Water kept pulling at his ankles so he pushed himself up on his hands and knees and flopped forward onto dryer beach, getting a face full of prime coastal real estate. It felt better than feeling dead. He choked up more of the Pacific, putting forth upon this Earth what she had so graciously given him. Salt water and sand.

Gwen pulled the remaining seaweed off him. She waited for Cooper to regain his breath as she ran her finger along the scrapes on his back.

Cooper stiffened.

"Lie still, let me untie you."She picked at the wet knots.

"Your friends are always so interesting." His chest heaved up and down. He coughed again and burped loud and proud.

"Rude."

"Thank you. Felt even better."

"What happened?"

"Use your wild imagination."

"I had all these bad vibes."

"I'm having a few myself."

"Where's Roger?"

"Hurry up so I can strangle you, will ya?"

"Did you see him, is he all right?"

"My head hurts like hell, thank you."

"Portland, please. What happened?"

"I'll explain on the way home."Cooper pushed himself onto his bare feet and managed to stand up. Blood rushed to his brain. He tried to focus on the parking lot.

"Where's my...?"Had he survived the grasp of the ocean depth, or was hell really the polluted Santa Monica Beach? "Where is my Corsa?"His head swam. He could still feel the insistent tugging of the ocean. The waves that splashed against the pylons called out his name. Portland, Portland, as if they wanted him back. Where was his cherished blood red? He tried to remember where he parked it. No. It's gone. How? He took a step forward, recocked, teetered, his eyes rolled back and his knees gave way as he swooned into Gwen's outstretched arms. His 210 pounds of packed muscle hit her like a giant wet medicine ball. She stumbled back, digging her dainty feet into the sand, struggling, losing beach, trying to set Cooper down gently on the sand.

"Portland, Portland... damn you. What was I supposed to do? Roger's not as strong as you. Or as heavy."

Gwen fell backwards with Portland flat on her.

Portland, Portland, Portland. Come feed the ocean crabs!

4 DEATH OF THE BLOOD RED

Cooper lay face down in bed. His T-shirt read 'Corvairs Eat Porsches!" He began to come to. Marty waited beside the bed with Gwen. The look on their faces said it all. Portland opened his eyes suddenly and tried to sit up but Marty held him down.

"Stay down, Coop. Everything is okay."

"What day is it?"

"July 21st, 1979."

"It's still Saturday night, Portland. You've only been out for a couple of hours.

"Doesn't feel like it. What happened?"

"You went down for a ten count."

"What? Let me at 'im."

"Portland, you're in your bed. I called Marty. He helped me get you here. Doc will be here shortly."

Cooper rolled over letting out a mild groan. His body ached, twinged, stung, and just plain hurt all over. He looked around him trying to focus is eyes. It didn't help much.

"You took a nasty bash on the side of the head."

"Someone drugged you. I found this stuck in your thigh." Gwen showed Portland a broken needle.

"And you've got scratches on your back and arms," Marty said."You kept mumbling something about an AM-FM stereo radio and the Corsa locked in the paint booth, so I called Jorge to keep an eye on it. The radio seemed so important to you we took it out. Here's some aspirins."

Cooper waved them off. He didn't recall saying a thing. He thought a moment. Radio... radio... Roger... the pier, Roger was concerned about the radio. "It's Roger's. They took my Corsa at the beach. Let me see the radio."He rubbed his face. Gwen handed him a glass of water. He drank it down. He needed a beer. His jaw hurt.

"Tomorrow," Gwen said trying to mother him."Doc said..."

"Now!"

"Doc wanted us to call him when you woke up. He wants to talk with you," Marty said.

"Just give me the radio, Marty. And bring me a beer."

Marty sulked away. "I'm just tryin' to be a pal."

"You big brat." Gwen said.

"What? I'm sittin' here with a golf ball on the back of my head. All on account of your stupid client."

"Oh shut up! He's our friend."

"Guess who was standing on that pier with a gun to my ribs when this golf ball arrived?"

"Roger?"

"Bingo!"Portland sulked.

"This is getting serious."

"One scratch on my car and I'll show you serious."

"Who'd Roger have with him?"

"I don't think they were with him. More than likely they followed him. Or they made him set me up. Somebody wants me out of their way. Those other two thugs showed up here again after I talked to you. I left them in the alley with two flats. So I'm pretty sure it wasn't them."

"Maybe they had another car nearby."

"Maybe, but they weren't friends of Rogers."

"No?"

"They don't even know him."

"How do you know that?"

"They didn't know about the identical Corsas. That takes both Roger and Jack off the hook on hiring them. For now."

"Don't start."

"You want me to go to the cops?"

Gwen looked down to her hands. Did Jack have anything to do with all this? "Maybe Roger just wanted to switch cars on you. Maybe not pay you?"

"Nice try. I don't think it's the car any longer. I think it's something in it."

"Are we still talking about the insurance thing?"

"You mean fraud?"

"Well...?"

"I think this goes deeper than that. Much deeper. He's got something we don't know about on them, I'm guessing."

"What makes you...?"

"They would've bounced me a long time ago if they were worried about me."

Marty and Jorge showed up with the radio.

"You gonna live, boss?" Jorge handed over the radio.

"Don't worry about mister wonderful. A thump on the head won't make him a better person. By the way, I've moved in," Marty said.

"No way."

"Thanks to you, Delma dragged Sheila off the stage and nearly beat her to death in the middle of Victory Boulevard. Sheila had nothing on but a G-string. One thousand a piece for bail. Gwen covered it."

Cooper shot Gwen a glance. "I always miss all the fun. Hand me a screwdriver out of that drawer."

Jorge opened the drawer and took out a Philips and handed it over. "Roger's in trouble, huh?"

"Big trouble when I get my hands on him." Cooper started to take the radio casing off. "If the people he's hitting on don't kill him first."

"I don't understand. What could Roger have on anyone...and don't start up about that mailing list. Those are all my mother's longtime friends."

"Marty, how many people in LA keep a paper hidden inside their transistor radios with a mailing list of Gwen's mother's dinner guests?"

Marty gave it a quick calculation on his fingers. "Let's see... I don't know, maybe one...two at the very most."

"He owes nearly all of us money," Cooper said.

"Don't look at me," Marty said.

"It's hard not to."

"Already he sounds like Delma."

Cooper took the last screw out of the radio's casing. "Drum roll, Jorge, please."

Jorge beat on a dresser top with an ink pen and tire pressure gauge form his shirt pocket.

Cooper opened the casing. Inside wrapped in paper toweling was what appeared to be a postbox key. "Oh lovely, just what I've always wanted."

"A key?"

"Not just a key... maybe a postbox key." Cooper opened the toweling and read aloud what was written on it.

"This is the key to your death. If you have legs, run. If you can't run, swim. If you can't swim, fly. If you can't fly, goodbye." Cooper handed the key and paper to Gwen. "It's for you."

Marty took a look at the note. "I don't get it." He got up and went across the hall to the den.

"You're not supposed to. But one thing is for sure, this key is worth a lot more than just a bunch of addresses."

"Elliott's office building, Jack's ranch, Frank's beach house, and Jerry's Big Bear cabin. Property they could live without."

"Or Roger would love to live with."

"But why did he hide the list in his radio like that? It's just a list of property," Gwen asked.

"You mean other than coked out paranoia?"

"Yes."

"I'm thinking he left it as a clue, in case something was to happen to him. Maybe he thought a list of who's involved would keep him alive if people knew he had one. We're talking a coked out Roger here."

"Please stop saying it that way."

"If you wanted it sugarcoated you should've taken your troubles to a Baskin Robins."

"Ha, good one, Coop."

"Don't be jerks. Roger's our friend. And he needs our help."

The doorbell rang from out front of the parts store on the first floor of Cooper's home. No one, but the postman ever used that door. Not even UPS or Girl Scouts. Cooper motioned for Jorge to go down and see. "There's a gun in the drawer."

"Never touch the stuff. Parole." Jorge sprang up and went down stairs to see who it was.

Marty came back from the den with a bottled Miller for everyone. He popped the tops off and passed them out.

"Ahhhh." Marty sat down, relieved.

Gwen and Cooper sipped their beers.

"Oh shit. Hey, boss. You better come look."Jorge yelled from downstairs front door."And bring my beer, Marty."

"Now what?" Portland asked.

Marty helped Cooper out of bed.

"Oh my god, it's Roger."Gwen ran for the stairs.

"Hey, don't worry about me. I'm fine."

"Keep him up there, Marty."

"Help me. If it is Roger I want to punch him in the face."

"I heard that."

Marty helped Cooper to the stairs and down them. What the hell did they shoot him up with?

Downstairs, Gwen and Jorge stood staring out the front door at something in the yard. Their faces were drawn. Their eyes seeing but not believing.

Things were starting to look bad again. Cooper didn't like it. If it was Roger, they'd be out there. Maybe a spaceship had landed, or a belly dancer was selling girl scout cookies in her underwear. Or an elephant was humping a Volkswagen full of

Beverly Hills naked cheerleaders. Let it be anything but what he feared most, no, what he knew it was. Please, not his Corsa.

Marty helped Cooper to the door. The others wouldn't look at him. He felt like a Christian about to pick door number one.

Marty looked out the door before Cooper dared to look. He was speechless. That ruled out belly dancer and elephant.

"What?"

The others continued to stare in disbelief.

Cooper couldn't take it any longer. He looked, and wished he hadn't. It wasn't true as long as he didn't see. But now that he had, Cooper half floated, half stumbled out into the front yard. He was a zombie, a jelly fish, a limp rag, the pain no longer mattered. His heart hit bottom. He tripped and stepped on it. He went involuntary to his knees. Tears came to his eyes.

His friends could only look on with pity, sorrow and agony for him. They wisely stayed away.

Cooper edged across the grass on his hands and knees to what was once his hot little blood red Corsa. His baby, his dream, his creation. It lay there quietly, a heap of blood red and chrome scrap metal. Its guts spilled out across the sidewalk. Its engine hammered to a pulp by something big and mean. The red and black leather interior and top knifed and bent to useless nothing. The wheels were off. The tires slashed. His prized Kelsey-Hayes were nowhere in sight. Whoever did this probably didn't even know what value they had. In the center of the heap the antennae stuck up bent where it had been stabbed into a bucket seat. An unpaid grease stained parking ticket from the smashed glove box waved in the damp breeze. Cooper took the paper and read what someone had scrawled on it with his own black magic marker he kept in the crushed ashtray.

"What does it say?"

"I've got powder burns on my balls."

"What?"

Cooper went back into the house. "It's a thank you note."

"Huh?"

They followed Cooper into the parts level of the house and slowly closed the door behind them. The light shut off and the gleam from the chrome died. Cooper went directly up to his bed and laid back down.

The others stood at the bedroom door. There was nothing they could do or say and it was painful knowing it. They would've given anything to get Cooper's Corsa back for him. They watched him. They knew that no matter how close they had come to Portland Cooper, this man's true best friend, silly as it may have been, wasn't necessarily a dog, it was his childhood vision, his blood red Corsa. Gwen came to the bed and sat down beside her lover. She understood. Their love was real, an adult thing between them. But his Corsa was from his childhood dreams and his tie-in to those days of living with his father. A reminder of how that life was suddenly taken from him by people who did not understand how much the Corvair had meant to its drivers. To his father, to kids like Portland.

Ford was still building its Mustang. Vettes were still being built. Camaros were, too. But the Corsa's extended design life had been cut short at ten years of production. Even before it was fully perfected. It was only now being kept alive by day dreamers. Hundreds of thousands of them, just like Portland Cooper. Cooper helped keep those dreams alive for many of them. His Corsa was a living breathing thing. It meant more than what met the eye. It gripped the hearts of rebel Corsa lovers across the nation. This feeling in Cooper was so strong nothing could interfere. Something wonderful and personal, like an invisible friend. A comforting blanket. Gwen understood that in him. She loved that kid in him. It wasn't just a car. It lived for him, it breathed, it ate, and it had never let him down. Never. He never owned another car to drive, and never wanted another car...just his beloved blood red.

Now it was gone. Because of Roger.

She looked back toward Marty and Jorge, at the pain in their eyes. She wanted to cry for them, she wanted to cry for

Portland. Because she knew they wouldn't cry for themselves. But the tears wouldn't come. She was so shocked she couldn't even cry for herself. A knot gripped her stomach and the sorrow in her heart was devastatingly real. The tears just wouldn't come and it filled her full of unbearable frustration.

Gwen motioned for Jorge and Marty to go. They went into the den. She stroked Portland's head, pulling the dark straight hairs from his forehead and rubbed his thick furrowed brow. An era in their lives together had come to a violently sad end. It was piled in the front yard of Portland's home. She picked up the thank you note and read it to herself.

"What does this mean?"

Cooper reached for the nearby lamp he made in shop from a Corsa piston. It went out and the room became illuminated from the work yard below. He lay looking at the light seeping through the curtains for awhile, thinking, not sure what it meant. Then it came to him. Simple, clear, and smooth like the purr of his Corsa's engine.

"Take better aim."

5 BLUNT FORCE TRAUMA

At seven the next night, Gwen stood at her parent's front door greeting the guests as they arrived by couples in expensive foreign cars for an hour of cocktails before dinner. They were mostly well-established, stodgy men and women with drawn-back smiles and stained dentures. These well-to-do, movie people had adorned Irene's dinner list even before Gwen and her mother actually moved into the house. They were more than guests, they were practically family. Gwen gave each one a hug and a kiss as they entered while at the same time keeping an eye on the drive. Where was Portland? He had called from a phone booth just outside of Kansas City to let her know that he might be a few minutes late. He found some interesting background on their buddy, Roger Kelemen.

After circling the Van Nuys Airport waiting for clearance to land, Copper finally arrived a half hour after everyone else in Roger's Corsa. Holland had flown Portland in her Cessna at night to Kansas City and they headed back that afternoon. KRLA played on the Corsa's radio. The top was down. He parked behind a blue four door 73 Mercedes Benz 280 sedan. And walked to the front door where Gwen met him with a big relieved smile. She noted his smugness. They were let in by a pretty doorman. Despite all the frowns and grumbles, Portland looked rather James Bond-ish in the new dark blue suit and gold tie Gwen had bought him. She loved to buy him clothes, he hated wearing them. But under all the grease and finger scabs, Gwen suspected that Portland was really a closet gentleman.

It had been a few months since Portland had actually come inside. It was still the same large overly spacious rooms with a panoramic view of Westwood and UCLA's red brick buildings through the bay windows that extended out from the broad, white-carpeted living room. A bar was tucked into a box-like room dividing the living room from the dark wood, book-shelved study. The tactfully elaborate furniture hadn't changed in a decade or more. Maybe some added over priced art, but there was still the one-of-a-kind, hand carved grand piano off in a corner, ceramic elk, and glass sculptures, even one from Art Linkletter's son in front of the bar. Everything shimmered with money, class, and style. Right down to the white marble hall with Portland's favorite ornate gold and silver Chinese trunk by the front door his mother had given them. A true tribute to Irene's astonishing taste and her ability to keep every elegant object from clashing with the next. Sort of a lime sorbet in between courses. Not a speck of dust, a smudge, a finger print, or his greasy footprint among them.

Some of the things that Gwen's mother, Irene, already owned were from her first marriage to Gwen's father. He was from Kuala Rue, a small Malaysian island in the South Pacific. Every once in a while Cooper would look at Gwen and he could see the island bloodline in Gwen's smile or twinkle in her eye. It was definitely in her long dark thick hair. And she had the cutest feet. He smiled thinking of how he would hold them.

Her grandfather was a very interesting character from a long mixed bloodline, some originating from those islands. He wrote a children's book series based on myths and legends of the islands of an ancient cave civilization that span from the origins of man, featuring The Little Island Princess. Portland's mother had bought the Chinese trunk the first time Portland and his parents had visited the islands for Gwen's coming of age ceremonies, back when they were both just sixteen. The year they had moved in next door. Looking at Gwen now, dressed in her slim hip hugging silk floral dress, Cooper had to smile again thinking of the two summers they had spent on the islands. Exploring the waterfalls and jungle looking for away into the caves below the island described in her grandfather's books. Until disaster struck them when her cousin drowned in a jungle whirlpool beneath the falls. The old man had taken to seclusion since the death of this grandson, having already lost Gwen's father to murder.

Portland actually cut a secret deal with Gwen's grandfather and now owned a small, barely accessible by land, cove on the far end of her family's jungle. He had started to build a boat engine repair shop before running into some trouble on the islands. He was due back there to finish a rebuild of a PT boat engine as soon as Holland could fly in the parts. He'd finish the construction while he was there. Thinking of the trouble he was about to experience, he wished he could gather the guys and leave now.

"What?"

"Nothing. You look very beautiful tonight."

"So do you, James. Martini?"

Cooper's eyes narrowed. James was also her father's name.

The same bartender mixed drinks at the bar. The same waiter went around taking orders as another familiar face served hors d'oeuvres. Jack Rotenberg, a heavy-set drinking man, mingled with the guests in a short walk-through between the bar and a set of remote control glass patio doors. His graying black hair widow peaked at the center of his low brow, sort of like Eddie Munster, just above his bushy eyebrows. His skin was blotchy from long years of good whiskey and his face was bloated from living too well. His stocky frame stuffed his brown suit to the gills and his stubby arms never seemed to bend at the elbows as he hoisted his V.0 on the rocks up to his broad lips. His dark puffy eyes shifted toward his second wife, Irene, who was still pretending not to have been waiting at the door worrying whether she was about to receive her second no show. Her drawn-back smile hid nicely her second facelift. Her pinkish red hair was done up on the top of her head and complemented her flawless pale skin like a flamingo on a bed of lilies. She wore a black silk dress that not surprisingly hung rather elegant on her with one simple strand of pearls.

"Portland, my dear boy, how are you?" Irene asked.

"Sober." Irene took his hand, looked it over quickly and gave it a satisfied squeeze.

"You naughty boy, go have Jack fetch you a drink."

Gwen went with him.

Irene smiled with approval at Gwen and tried to get a glimpse of Cooper's shoes as he went into the living room. They were new of course. Cooper had promised to dress in an airport hotel Gwen had rented for him.

"How was your flight? What did you find?"

"Down, Miss Moneypenny, I'll tell you later."

Gwen pulled him close."You promised to be nice."

"Did you see? She checked my nails. And right now I bet she's checking my shoes. I'm marked for life."

"She is not." Gwen looked back catching Irene looking away, pretending to fuss over the presentation of hors d'oeuvres. They crossed the carpet to the bar. "It's just your imagination."

"I bet."Cooper couldn't help but glance back to see if he left a trail. So far so good.

"Still have your shoes on, I see."

"Had them sandblasted on the way over."He shook Jack's out stretched hand.

"Gentlemen, you remember Portland Cooper. His family lived next door in the sixties. The auto people."

"Advertisement, Jack," Gwen corrected him.

"Of course, car adds."

Jack put his hand on the shoulder of the man speaking in a high voice with thinning reddish hair. "This is Frank Laska."

Cooper remembered Frank. Over the years he hadn't gotten any manlier. Though age had rather an elegant effect on the director and he had lost some weight.

"Of course, it's been a long time."Frank held out a limp hand. Cooper was forced to take it.

"You remember Jerry Goodricke, don't you, Portland?"

Goodricke was in his late fifties and completely bald with very thick, large, dark-rimmed glasses. He wore a dark blue suit with a white shirt and red striped tie. The agent armor.

Cooper glanced at his reflection on the top of Jerry's head and adjusted his tie. Gwen caught the gesture and pinched his buttock. Cooper remembered Jerry as being a taller man but with power comes less of a need to impress and old habits like shoe lifts were forgotten. Jerry and his wife were Roger's first and only agents. Cooper had visited their offices often years ago with Roger to pick up sides during times when Roger had no driver's license from racing in the streets. Jerry even stuck a few pages in Portland's hands once and asked him to read something with Roger. When Portland was finished, pleased with himself that he could actually read at all, Jerry told him outside the door, "Don't call us, we'll call you."

When Roger got Portland outside in the street, he told him that Jerry had him read on purpose to make Roger look good in front of the other two men who were casting a big picture at Universal. Portland just hiked up his jeans with pride, combed his DA in the window of a Rodeo dress shop, and replied, "Yeah? Let's see those clowns rebuild a transmission." So much for an acting career.

Jerry looked up at Portland. His thick glasses magnifying his cloudy blue eyes like a gold fish in a glass toilet bowl. "You're not, that damn kid, from next door, are you?"

Cooper looked at Jack.

Jack smiled mischievously.

"Mr. Hot Rod, sure I remember you. Elliott Pascal." Elliott towered over the others. He was a good inch taller than even Portland but his shoulders and upper back where curved from sitting over a typewriter most of his life. His hair was shockingly white in patches above his ears and at the very base

57

of his chin like a two tone black and white 57 Delta 88. Someone had done a dental job on him that probably cost a down payment on a good house in Watts. He gave Cooper his best distinguished smile, adjusting his paisley ascot as he extended his long fingered hand.

Cooper took the writer's hand and received a massive shake. "Nice to find you've thought so much of little ole me, Jack. Or is it still, 'Old Man Rotten Berger?'"

"Very funny, Mr. Cooper. Let me buy you a drink."

"Miller in a bottle, if you have it, please."

Gwen shot Portland a nasty look. Portland faked a yawn. Gwen made another one of her faces and Portland turned his back on it.

Elliott's wife, Sophie entered. She swung her form freely from side to side. At forty-eight she had kept every inch of the figure she'd had at thirty, thanks to a rigorous work out, diet pills, and Dr. Fromstein. Her mass of natural blond hair rained down on her bare shoulders. Her red knit dress was cut low in the front and showed enough cleavage to drown in. She had a set of legs that started just below her naval. The last time Portland saw her she was getting out of the Blue Mercedes in a pair of black leather pants that looked better on her than any stud bull could've imagined. A waft of high octane perfume engulfed the bar area as Sophie nudged alongside her husband. Her mixed green catlike eyes locked on Portland. Immediately Cooper's troubled knee started to ache. Gwen pinched him hard again. Old green-eyes was definitely not getting enough.

Cooper remembered seeing Sophie in several of Roger's beach blanket movies, and a disco cop spinoff series on CBS that tanked after six shows. But nothing in the last few years.

Hollywood rumors had it that none other than Howard Hughes had brought her to town as a little over developed teeny-bopper and kept her under tutelage until he discovered her in bed with one of the bell hops, a waiter and the night barman. Jerry and Ruth represented her as far as Cooper knew. She had one of those tans a woman could only get from working endlessly at it. Her perfectly upturned nose divided her set of startling eyes in a way only nature could achieve. Gwen had said the Hughes stuff was just bullshit, but Cooper couldn't have cared less about where she was from anyway. The bartender gave Cooper his beer. Cooper waved off the glass and napkin and held the bottle up to his lips and tried to keep his eyes where they belonged.

"Thank you."

"You're welcome, sir."

"This lovely thing is Elliott's wife, Sophie. Sophie, Portland."

Sophie held out her manicured hand and Cooper took it. Nice, red nails, and real. She gave his hand a seductive squeeze as she spoke, her voice deliberately husky."Gwen darling, where have you been hiding this one?" If she purred any harder someone would end up changing the litter box.

"Watch her, she's a sap for a pretty face," Elliott said.

"It wasn't his face I...wait a minute. Aren't you that cocky hoodlum with the funny red car?"She stepped back and gave Portland a lascivious onceover."My, how you've grown. Oh, anyone ever tell you that you look like Sean Connery? With more hair, of course. You should cut it, maybe try washing it. You could double for him."

Portland shot Gwen the evil eye. It was amazing how fast people of showbiz stature could turn ugly. Gwen fought back a smirk. But failed miserably.

"All right here, let's get down and do some serious drinking," Jack said. "Gwen, what can I get you, honey?

"Champagne, please."

A waiter came in and offered baked mushrooms stuffed with seasoned spinach and pine nuts. Sophie took two and a napkin. Cooper passed. The bartender poured Gwen's champagne. When Gwen wasn't looking Cooper leaned into Sophie and said, "They grow those in bullshit, you know."

Sophie stopped chewing and spit it out into the napkin.

Gwen caught a glance of their interaction while taking a sip and pulled Portland out of the room. "What did you say to her?"

"You know, normal Hollywood party bullshit," Portland said.

Irene came in with Jerry's wife, Ruth, a rough looking chain smoker with nicotine stained dentures and gray hair on her head and chin. She wore a dark green one piece dress with white buttons down the front and a white and pink flowered silk blazer, sort of like bathroom wall paper on the run. But sheik. Standing next to her husband she could have spit on the top of his head. She had so many wrinkles on her face and neck that if a surgeon were to perform a face lift on her he would probably have to start the tuck somewhere around her arm pits and chance giving her a permanent wedge. She wore bright red lipstick that did nothing to hide how big her mouth was and held an ashtray with a smoldering cigarette in one hand and bourbon on the rocks in the other. Her voice was at best described as sultry, now gone ugly from smoke, booze, and just plain overuse.

Following them was Frank's date, Tracey Abbott. She carried a ding-a-ling smile that seemed endlessly trapped on a face that had victim written all over it. Her dark brown eyes were warm and trusting. She had high round cheek bones with a tad too much blush and her clothing said working girl all over them. Her brown hair was long in the back with short moussed-up curls on top that peeked out from a flat black hat with a little strap that came under her pudgy chin. She had a slight hook to her nose and had a body and mind born for dinner, a movie, and the famous one night stand. At her price, when she wasn't posing as Frank's date, or having her heart broken by some bar-hopping-stud, she was the best secretary Jerry and Ruth ever had.

"I knew I'd find you all pestering the bartender. Let's take it into the living room. Jack?"

"Right behind you, dear."

Irene led them across the white carpet past the piano.
Tracey took Frank's arm as they went. Frank gave her a peck
on the cheek and glanced back to see Jack stopping Jerry and
Ruth. Jack turned his back on Frank and pretended to merely
linger behind with the two agents, the Goodrickes, instead of
actually trapping them behind the piano.

"Listen you two, don't deal with this problem on your own,"
Jack said, making sure the bartender wasn't listening."Sam
doesn't like outside help. Is that clear?"

Jerry kept a smile on his face as he glanced around the room
catching Elliott's eyes before they darted away.

"There's no way we're giving in to Roger this time. I don't
care what Sam says. This was supposed to end years ago and
we were supposed to get our payback from it. Now here we go
again. He's a mess. We don't care how it ends. Just end it."

"Talk some sense into him, Ruth."

"I'm sorry, Jack. We understand that Elliott and Frank have
agreed to go along. But we just refuse. We'll rot in hell first."

Jack downed his drink and slammed it on the piano. "You
just might." He walked off in a huff.

Gwen followed Cooper into the kitchen. Two male chefs, a
tall handsome blond and a short older Puerto Rican, prepared
dinner with two young Mexican assistants.

"Portland, Mother will scream if she finds us in here."

"What, and crack her face?"

Portland continued out the back door past a white catering
Ford van with "Along Came Mary" painted on its side and made
a left and headed around to the front of the house to where the
cars were parked. He took a slim jim, his preferred lockout tool,
from the Corsa backseat and used it to open the door to Gwen's
stepfather's white Jaguar. He sat on the passenger's front seat,
took out a small black prototype transmitters from his pocket,
reached up under the dash, and pulled down a hot wire. He
pulled out a pair of wire cutters and spliced the wire from the

black box into it. He put a ground wire under a screw from the dash frame.

"What are you doing?"

"Trying to stay alive."

"You just bugged Jack's car?"

"So, have it sprayed."

"Okay, I'm sorry, they were rude."

"Forget that. This is one of Marty's little inventions. He calls them audiosurveillance kits or something like that. Basically that black box is a transistor amplifier that transmits sounds caught by this miniature microphone. Some snoop magazine is paying him to develop it. There's another devise for listening in. I'm not sure how it works but it will turn Jack's car phone into a one-way party line." He pulled out a black miniature battery powered drill and dug a small hole into the receiver of the cellular phone. "He's trying to get a patent on it. He actually could make a bundle from these. Car phones are tough nuts to crack." Cooper stopped and looked at Gwen. "Don't say anything to Delma about the patents."

"Why would I?"

"Just don't."

"Does this snappy attitude have something to do with what you found out about Roger in Kansas City?"

"Okay, here it is in a nutshell." He slipped the small black bug, the miniature microphone, no bigger than a fly, into the hole he drilled into the phone. He then took out a tube of black calking from his pocket and patched the hole, using a square piece of plastic and pressing it against the calking to give the patch texture. After he pulled it away, the little hole had virtually disappeared. He put the car phone back in place. He looked at Gwen. She waited with a scowl on her face. She hated it when Portland made her wait for information. "We all know Roger ran away from his foster family in Kansas City and made it big somehow ten years later in Hollywood. Right? Isn't that the garbage you've fed the press all these years?"

"Yes, so?"

"Yeah so, what we didn't know, because Roger wasn't about to tell us, was that six months prior to running away, he was involved in an identity thief case where he was the key witness in putting a man and a woman away for ten years."Cooper grinned up at Gwen as he got out of the Jag and relocked its doors. "He really ought to get an alarm."

"What? Are you sure about this?"

"Positive. I looked up Thomas Walker. I know him from a local Corvair Club in Belton just outside of Kansas City, The Heart of America Corvair Owners Association. I met him for the first time at a swap meet out that way in 73. You remember Marty and I drove out there?"

Gwen nodded indicated she remembered.

"Well Thomas sold me heads and still calls me once in awhile to sell me parts. He told me when we were loading my shipment into Marty's truck that he knew Roger way back when. Heard about our race on the news. At the time I didn't care as much as I cared about the tornado coming in. So I didn't ask how he knew Roger. But now that I do, I looked him up while out there this morning. By the way, Thomas thought Roger was a pompous dick, even way back when, while staring in local theater together."

"Not fair."

"Hey, just the facts, lady." Portland crossed over to the blue four door Mercedes."This belongs to the tall writer guy with caps, doesn't it?"

"If you're referring to Elliott, yes."

"Shit, the alarms on. I hate untrusting dinner guest."

"They wouldn't have to if you'd stay out of them."

"I'm not admitting to anything that happened while known as the hoodlum living next door."

"Just don't leave cigarettes and their radios on."

"Don't know what you're talking about."

Cooper took off his coat and pulled a tarp out of the Corsa. He unrolled it beneath the Mercedes grill, scooting under on his back. He used a long modified screw driver with a bent tip to grab the hood release cable. "Press down on the hood...gently."

Gwen leaned her bottom on it. The latch popped.

"Get ready to run."

"Portland!"

"Nothing's fool proof." He stood up and slowly lifted the hood just enough to get his hand inside. "Don't breath."Cooper held his own breath."Now hold the hood."

"I will kill you if we get caught."She took the hood with both hands and held her breath.

"Sshhh... motion detector."He reached in further with a socket wrench and with absolute concentration loosened the battery positive cable and slipped it off. A smile crossed his face. "The guy spends these kinds of dollars on a car and for two hundred more, I couldn't have done this."

Gwen dropped the hood on his arm.

"Thanks."He lifted the hood.

"You're welcome. Why are you doing this?"

"Mainly because I have the opportunity. Okay?"

Gwen wasn't buying it.

"Honest, Gwen, I don't know yet." Cooper popped the lock on the driver's door. "But it might work to our advantage to hear what they have to say when no one's supposed to be listening."

"So what else did you find out? And make it fast, Mother will be looking for us soon. If she isn't already."

"Well, Thomas now edits a small throwaway rag in Kansas City he inherited form his uncle."

"So?"

"So, he did some research for me in the archives."Cooper got in and began the same procedure for bugging Elliott's car.

"This is beginning to stink."

"It gets thicker. Thomas located a picture of two of the three defendants."Cooper took an old news clipping out of his shirt pocket and held it up for Gwen to read. "Here, take a look at this. Add hair and lifts to the person on the right and who do you have?"

"Jerry Goodricke."

The shot was of Roger when he was in fifth grade, holding a fish that was the length of his arm. The man next to him with wire rimmed glasses, a full head of hair, goatee and a broad smile on his face was definitely Jerry.

"Alias, Henry Duncan. But get this. He was one of Roger Kelemen's first foster parents."

"What?"

"Yeah, I thought you'd like that bit. Take a look at this." This time Portland handed her a snapshot.

"Oh my, that's Ruth."

"Also known as Bertrand Duncan. Homeroom mother of the year. Both fulfilled eight years of a ten-year stretch for stealing the identity of the Jacksons. A young married couple on their way to Kansas City to teach at a private elementary school."

"Wait a minute. Back up. Jerry and Ruth were Roger's first foster parents?"

"Neat, huh?"

"No it's not. So Jerry and Ruth were pretending to be the Jacksons. Teachers at a Kansas City private school."

"Yes, an elementary. It's closed now. Apparently the real two Jacksons never made it. The case was only brought to life during an unusual long drought that revealed the original Martha and Davis Jacksons' car in a pond. A third defendant out on bail was supposedly burned in a car crash with his brother three weeks before the trial. There are no known photos or family. His name was Eddie Waller and his brother's Tim. Eddie posed as Fred Mall, the elementary school principal who created the private school and lived in a condo above Tim's photo lab on the street level. Seems that angry parents, after finding out that their kids' education were being stolen by frauds, might have burned the lab in retaliation. But no one was alive to pressed charges. The original Fred Mall who had no living relatives was never found. You see where this lovely story is going?"

"Yes, and I don't like it. What about mug shots?"

"There were no charges against the one brother who owned the photo shop. The fire was left open as an unsolved arson that destroyed all content of the photo shop. But no one seemed to remember what happened to the mug shots of Eddie."

"This is horrible."

"Depends on how you look at it. Someone paid good money to make photos and the past of Tim and Eddie Waller go away. Thomas found those of the Duncans in a theater scrapbook sponsored by his uncle's throwaway. All the microfilm of the case in the library is gone. There is no record available from the closed school that has pictures of Tim or Eddie. The court house was of no help either. I even spoke to the prosecuting attorney's wife who said her husband never discussed his business with her. He's now dead. The law firm that represented Eddie and the Duncans is no longer in business. Eddie was never pictured in the yearbook himself. He used pictures of Fred Mall. It was Tim who printed the yearbooks and class photos. Apparently Fred and Eddie looked enough alike to make it work until the real Jacksons showed up dead."

Portland got out of Elliott's Mercedes and relocked the doors. He pulled the hood down again and had Gwen hold it. He reached in and reattached the battery cable. He held the hood and motioned for Gwen to move away. He eased the hood down and pressed it back in the locked position and reached under to remove the modified screwdriver.

"Where'd you learn that, prison?"

"It's one of Holland's tricks." Cooper moved over to the Corsa and put the slim jim, the pocket tools, and the tarp away.

"Your friends will get you into trouble one of these days."

"Why not? Yours do."

"Touché, jerkoff."

66

"Thanks, you've finally noticed it. Jerry and Ruth ran a children's agency about the time Roger became their client."

"Elliott Pascal wrote and Frank Laska directed most of Roger's movies."

"And Jack produced. But that doesn't necessarily mean that Elliott, Frank, or your stepfather have anything to do with this. Even if the car the two brothers died in was a white 56 Jag." Portland turned and sniffed the air. "You smell something bad about to happen?" He headed back to the kitchen door.

Gwen followed. "But all of their names are on that list.

"True."

"What are you planning to do about it?"

"One, I'll get even with those two knuckleheads for my Corsa. Two, I'll find out who put the four iron to my skull. And three, I'll help Roger, if he's still alive. If he's dead, he's in hell, and there's nothing much I can do about that."

"You think he's dead?"

"Maybe...let's eat. All this Bond crap is making me hungry." Portland opened the back door to find Irene glaring at him.

"Come inside, you two. Dinner is about to be served." Irene flounced back through the kitchen. She didn't bother to hide her anger as she informed the head chef on the way by that they were finally ready.

The circular dining room table was set for ten people with irreplaceable one-of-of-a-kind china and flatware. The guests milled around looking for their place cards as if Irene ever changed their places at the table. Irene did her best to mask how upset she was with Cooper and Gwen. Gwen dug her nails into Portland's arm. Portland just smiled and dug the new grease from his nails and wiped it on his napkin in protest. Gwen grabbed his hand.

The two would-be actors who had served during cocktails came in and assisted the ladies with their chairs and napkins. They poured a Wine Olympics award winning '76 Trefethen

Vineyards Chardonnay from the Napa Valley. Gwen cringed when she saw the look on Portland's face. Portland, who sat between Sophie and Irene declined the wine. Instead he leaned in and whispered his desire for a cold Miller. The waiter nodded politely and went out toward the bar at the end of the marble hall. Gwen shot Portland another look. Portland smiled again.

"Well, have you all met Portland?"Irene asked.

"You've met everyone, haven't you, Portland?"

Frank's date, Tracey, cut in."I haven't met him, yet."Her voice was so innocently stupid it was almost charming.

"Sure you have," Jerry said, while ordering a scotch on the rocks. He removed his glasses to wipe a smudge and placed them up on his bald head.He closed his eyes and squeezed the base of his nose, trying to breathe.

"No I haven't. Who is he?"

"Portland Cooper. Tracey Price," Jack said.

"Pleasure," Portland said, taking the beer from the waiter and holding it up as if to toast.

"I'm sure," Tracey answered.

"Here's hair on your lip." Cooper drank deeply from his beer.

Irene looked over at her daughter. Gwen flushed.

Ruth rubbed her chin.

"Portland used to be a neighbor," Jack said, his voice dark from having his mind on other things.

"Now I'm just a stand-in for my buddy, Roger Kelemen."

"You're a friend of Rog?"

"Sure, we're all Rog's friends, aren't we?"

Tracey picked up her wine."I just love Roger, he's such a party animal."

"Speaking of Roger, has anyone seen him lately?"

Ruth looked over at her husband."He's in Florida."Jerry nodded in agreement as the waiter returned with his scotch.

"Working at the new Burt Reynolds Dinner Theatre maybe? Or is it preproduction on his new action movie?"Portland asked.

"Just on a vacation," Jerry answered.

"Is he? For how long?"

Jerry sipped on his scotch. "Until he wants to come home."

"All of him, or part of him?"Portland asked.

"Excuse me?"Jerry asked. He shifted his eyes over to Jack. Jack looked over at Gwen.

"Portland," Gwen said, a little bit embarrassed.

"Just kidding. Say, how is his drug problem, anyway?"

"Who said Roger had a drug problem?"Jack demanded.

"Mutual friends. People he's been buying it from."

Tracey finished her wine, immediately it was refilled.

"Sure, I've partied with Roger lots of times. We got so high one time he couldn't...."

Frank gave Tracey a stern look."Tracey."

"What's wrong with a little partying?"

"Is Roger in a rehab, maybe?"

"I said he's on a little vacation," Jerry said with more than anger in his voice aimed at Tracey."End of discussion."

"Seems that Florida isn't a place for a guy on the loose with a coke problem."

"Portland," Gwen said, trying to slow him down a little bit. Maybe bringing Portland into this mess wasn't such a good idea. She looked over at her mother.

Irene was thoroughly interested."Does Roger have a drug problem again?"

"Not that I'm aware of, honey," Jack said.

"He was supposed to attend Jack's birthday dinner. Why didn't anyone tell me he was vacationing in Florida? In fact, when I spoke to him on the phone the day before, he gave me no indication he wasn't right here in LA," Irene said.

"You'd think if the guy needed rest, his good friends would send him home to Kansas City where he grew up. Maybe to his foster parents. Am I wrong? Jerry, Ruth?" Portland picked up his beer and watched as the urgent looks ping-ponged around the room again. The two waiters came in and cleared away the appetizer course.

Elliott, breaking the silence, cleared his crusty voice. "We are aware that Roger has a rewrite on a script he wants to direct. We've all read it. He's been after us for years. There are no plans of making his film at this time. Is there, Jack?"

"No, there's not," Jack said.

"So now Roger is writing and wants to direct his own scripts. Don't you usually write Roger's films, Elliott? And you direct them, Frank? I mean, the nerve of Roger wanting to cut you two out of his new project after all you've done for his career."

"Is that true, Jack?" Irene asked.

"Yes, Irene. This is nothing new. We're not making Rogers film. Let's get dinner served. Portland, Roger has wanted to direct for years. He bugs us on every project to direct. And he has, on some of the TV episodes. This is a script he's done many drafts on. He has always brought his projects to us first. We always look at them. Right, Jerry?"

"Of course. This is a rewrite of an old boat race script. No one wanted to put money into it. Water shoots are expensive. He destroyed several boats in it."

"Plus, no one will touch his projects in his condition. Right?"

"He does not have a condition," Jerry said.

"You guys wouldn't be planning to finance Roger's film with your own money, would you? Maybe sell off some investment properties? Even a grease pit like me knows that's not a good idea."

Oh crap, now he's done it, Gwen thought. She looked away when everyone looked at her. "May I have more wine, please?"

"Mr. Cooper, it's no business of yours whether we decide to be involved or not." Elliott sounded much like Gregory Peck with a southern drawl in *To Kill a Mockingbird*.

Cooper smiled nicely at Elliott. "No problem, how about this? Last night, someone chopped up my Corsa and dumped it on my front lawn in thousands of unusable pieces."

Jack looked at Jerry. Jerry shook his head.

Cooper dropped the smile. "Minus my Kelsey-Hayes."

Sophie, Elliott's wife, leaned close. "Why would anyone want to do that to your funny little red car?"

"Because they thought it was Roger's funny little red car. Roger had someone make it look just like mine. Anyone have a guess as to why? Maybe it had something to do with his script rewrites from boats to cars. Not to mention they were looking for this."

Oh god, here comes the rest of it, Gwen thought. She hid behind her wine glass avoiding even her mother's eyes.

Cooper took out the key that he had found in the Corsa radio and held it up in front of him. Glances ping-ponged around the room again. Cooper watched their faces flinch. The key meant something to everyone except Irene and Tracey.

"It's a key," the brilliant Tracey said.

"Are you saying whoever cut up your car is looking for that key?" Ruth asked.

"You want me to say it louder? You can also lay odds that the same people tried to drown me in the bay last night. While, by the way, Jerry, I was being frisked by you know who."

A puzzled look covered Tracey's face. "Who, Jerry?"

"I don't know what he's talking about," Jerry said.

"Portland, you'd better go. Gwen, show Mr. Cooper out."

"Did I miss something, Jack? Does Roger have a new script? Is he on drugs or not?" Irene asked.

"Never mind, Irene," Portland stood. "The grease ball from next door has once again made himself unwelcomed. Good night, and thank you all for a lovely and enlightened evening."

"Goodnight, Mr. Cooper."

Cooper drained his beer and smile politely at Tracey.

Everyone turned to watch as Gwen led Portland down the marble hall to the door and outside.

"Gee, what an intense guy," Tracey stopped when she saw the looks she got from the others. "Of course, what do I know?"

"Nothing. Now shut up and eat!" Jerry told her.

Outside, Portland moved toward the Corsa.

"You son-of-a-bitch."

Portland turned and leaned on the car, facing Gwen. "Feel better? Irene doesn't know a thing. Neither does Tracey. But everyone else is in on it. This little key had them all sweating. You can bet it has something to do with Roger, those properties, and his script rewrites."

He got into the Corsa behind the wheel. Gwen got in on the other side. "Where do you think you're going?"

"I need some cheering up."

"No. Every time you get depressed I get in trouble."

"Oh, come on. Remember our prom night?"

"Who could forget? I spent the night in jail. I could've been flying helicopters in Nam instead of fixing them in Texas."

"Then I probably saved your life. Didn't I? So you owe me."

"Get out."

"Remember, you parked under that valley oak overlooking all those lights and popped that bottle of champagne."

"It went all over my dash. With those damn two inch acorns dropping down on us. No thanks."

"That tree is still there. I actually had lunch under it."

"You did not."

"Want to bet?"

"What will I win?"

"A ride back in time, I guess."

Cooper headed the blood red Corsa down the driveway.

"You sure know how to make a crappy time exciting."

"Yeah, that's me, Mr. Excitement.

"Let's stop for Champagne."

"Somehow, I'll regret this."

6 RIDE BACK IN TIME

With the lights from the Valley shining behind them, Cooper and Gwen glided through the night in Roger's Corsa.

The radio played "Run Through the Jungle." Gwen put her head back against the headrest and closed her eyes. Memories of their romantic high school days filled her loins.

Portland couldn't help but smile seeing the peaceful look on her face considering he just two fingered her life in the eyes. She hadn't changed much. Any man would kill to have her. In fact, Portland wasn't sure if a few of her friends hadn't tried, Roger included. He questioned many times over why she stayed with him all these years. She was a worldly woman, near royalty where her father was from, who could've married long ago, but with all the high priced friends she's had, none had ever come between them. Over thirteen years of Gwen getting him into trouble. And he loved almost every minute of it. He pulled off Mulholland down a small dirt service road just off Pacoima Road. Los Angeles winked then faded behind them.

Thanks to being lost in thoughts, Cooper didn't notice Dexter and Teatro passing them and continuing east on Mulholland in Teatro's 1967 baby blue Datsun Roadster.

Portland pulled the Corsa to a stop under a massive bending valley oak that was slowly being pushed off the cliff by the march of time. The view of Los Angeles had completely disappeared around the last bend and a broad view of the San Fernando Valley's night life had taken its place. Its lights spread openly north to Los Angeles National Forest. Fog was rolling in from the south-west, but on the north side of the Hollywood Hills the air was still warm, humid and clear.

"Do I have to say it?"

"You will anyway."

"I'll settle for you popping the cork."

"Seems every time we come here, I'm popping something."

"You big stud."

Cooper took the foil and wire cage off the bottle and popped the champagne. It spurted straight up. Gwen went down on it and sucked up the French bubbly before a drop could get on the red and black leather seats.

"You've been practicing."

"Rich girls drink a lot of champagne."

"I don't want to know."

"We forgot glasses again."

"No we didn't. Let's have your shoes."

Gwen took them off and Portland smelled one.

"You rat, they're new."

"I know."

Cooper poured two shoes of champagne and they toasted.

"Have I told you lately how much you mean to me?"

"You have your ways. Seems like just yesterday and it's been over eleven years since that cop interrupted us."

"Brubaker. Boy did he get an eyeful."

"He wouldn't have if you hadn't gotten your knee caught in the horn?"

"That was your foot."

"You big greaser...kiss me."

Portland pulled Gwen to him and they kissed. In zero to sixty flat they were in the backseat with their clothing off like two teenagers seeking thrills on Blueberry Hill. Their bodies hot. Their hearts racing. The impending danger of making love out in the open heightening the need to experience the true essence of lust. His body, her body, mingling on the Corsa faux

leather like two panthers in heat, clawing and biting, and....
"Ahhhh," Gwen yelled.

Up on Mulholland Drive the Datsun Roadster pulled to a stop. Teatro and Dexter got out and snuck down the dirt path toward the sound of the Corsa's radio. They were still bruised from their last encounter with Cooper so they were being careful not to let Cooper get the upper hand on them again. They held their guns at their sides and clung to the edge of the service road, getting brush in their faces. Dexter had trouble with the rocks under his sore foot.

Down at the end of the road the Corsa rocked back and forth at a quickening, frenzied pace. A front spring squeaked.

"Feels like she needs a lube."

"Am I hurting you?"

"The car, Gwen, the car."

The two thugs neared the end of the path as Portland and Gwen climaxed together with loud satisfying groans, cries, murmurs of love, and sighs that faded into heavy breathing purrs as they bathed in each other's sweat.

"What the hell was that?" Teatro asked.

"Shhh, they're gettin' it on."

"Yeah? I'd like a little of that myself. You see that ass?"

"Shut up."

An acorn let go of its branch and dived-boomed onto the hood of the Corsa, bouncing up and striking the windshield before it rolled away. Cooper sat up trying to regain his breath, watching it. He looked up at the tree. It was talking to them. He turned back to look up the path, listening for footsteps.

Gwen pulled him back down on top of her.

"More."

"Wait? Someone's coming down the path."

Gwen moaned aloud."It's just mother nature joining in."

Cooper reached under the seat and pulled out an old Smith and Wesson revolver.

About six years back, Gwen had paid for Portland's concealed weapon permit so that her PR Company could hire him as a personal bodyguard for a cousin of Mayor Tom Bradley who was traveling in a celebrity golf tour. So began a string of celebrity related security jobs Gwen hired Cooper for. Not all of them were as dangerous and costly as finding Roger.

Cooper sat back up, glancing at the path to make sure it wasn't the Police surprising them again. It was dark, but it didn't take much light to recognize the spike hairdo on Dexter's head and his heavy torso. Cooper squeezed off two rounds at their feet before the two thugs realized they had been spotted.

Dexter and Teatro dove for cover into the brush and slammed head first into a hidden sandstone cliff behind the thick ivy. Lights ran roughshod through their brains like a rock concert as they bounced away from the concealed stone.

Cooper jumped in the front seat and started the Corsa. Gwen rolled off the backseat and onto the floor, deliberately keeping her head down.

Still nude, Cooper had the tires spinning in the dirt. He swung the Corsa around, having no choice but to head back up the path towards the two thugs. He held his gun across his body on the door ledge to steady it as he passed the two staggering men in second gear already. He fired at their feet as they climbed back onto the road. The two shells ricocheted up into the rocks behind them and they could only hit the dirt as the Corsa zoomed by them in the dark. Dexter got off a couple of wild shots but Cooper already shifted to third as he disappeared into a flood of dust beyond the ivy covered cliff.

Cooper headed east on Mulholland Drive nearing Laurel Canyon. He and Gwen were both still naked. Gwen crawled into the front as Cooper handled the curves in the road at near sixty. She found the late July wind blowing past her naked skin exhilarating. Boy, if Jack hated Portland now. What would he say if he saw this? Back when they were sixteen and Brubaker caught them bare assed, Jack nearly had a fit and had it out with Portland's dad. Mr. Cooper asked his son to wear protection and told Jack to back off. He knew they were in love.

Gwen let out a yell up to the sky as she extended her body, standing up in the front seat, holding onto the windshield. Her long dark hair jetted back behind her like a race horse. Portland nearly killed them taking a good look. Following her legs up from dainty feet past cute little ankles to cutout calves and slender thighs that ran up to her tightly wound buttocks. He caught just a glimpse of hair blowing over her shoulders in the wind. Jesus! What a body, what a woman, what a nut!

"Watch the road!"

"Sit down, you're embarrassing me."

"Why? No one can see me."

"How about the grandma getting her mail at the last turn."

"You liar."

"Cross my heart."

Gwen sat back down. She wiped herself on Portland's shirt. "Thanks."

"I wouldn't want to stain your seats."

"They're not mine, they're Roger's."

"Sorry, I forgot." Her nylons went flying one-by-one out of the car as she scrambled for them. Cooper whacked her on the bare butt leaving behind a huge pink hand print.

"Ouch! You shithead!

Cooper's shirt went out the back after the nylons.

"Sit down!"

"We're losing our clothes!" Gwen looked back at a set of head lights gaining on them. "Oh, oh, here they come." She nabbed her skirt and blouse as they swirled in the back.

"You ripped the buttons off my blouse."

"You wiped yourself all over my shirt."

Cooper looked into the rearview mirror and caught sight of the headlights swerving on a curve behind them. No one would take the turns like that unless they had a good reason. Cooper down shifted and passed a slow moving Buick just missing an on-coming Fiat. Horns blared and the yellow Buick pulled over, making it easier for the Datsun to pass.

Gwen pulled on her blouse. "Red light!"

Cooper slammed on his brakes at Laurel Canyon, then pushed the pedal to the metal, cutting through the intersection as the crossing traffic hesitated.

"Jerk off," a guy in a baseball cap yelled from a swerving black 1973 Pontiac Trans Am. He revved his 455 Super Duty in protest.

Portland and Gwen looked at each other. "Don't look at me, you're driving."

At the south-west corner of the intersection, off on a dirt patch, where people often left their cars for sale, sat a Mustang patrol car. Inside it were two cops, Brubaker and George eating hot dogs and drinking coffee.

"Twenty years ago you could see...."Brubaker froze. "What the...?"Brubaker looked at his rookie partner.

The kid kept chewing. If he noticed, he wasn't interested.

Brubaker let out a long gross burp that made George check his own shirt.

"No shit."

"Did we just see what we thought we just saw?"

"Yeah, nice tits, too."George took in half his dog.

The baby blue Datsun zoomed by just making the yellow. George tried his best not to notice. He checked his new watch, sipped his coffee, and thumbed through a new issue of Guns Are Us magazine. He had twenty minutes left to his dinner break and wasn't about to waste it on a tits-and-ass chase game without a proper invitation.

"I mean the car. That was a red Corsa." Brubaker rolled his stocky frame over the seat and pulled the shotgun off its mounts. He turned his eyes on George still eating and reading behind the wheel.

George bit into his hot dog again. "So what? Just dumb kids racing. Hand me a napkin. Wait ten minutes there will be two more, just as stupid."

"Kids, my ass. That's Cooper and his Corsa. Never mind, just drive.   I've waited ten years for this."

"Listen, I didn't let you drag my ass all the way up here to spend my dinner break chasing some dumbshit that's not on my turf, so call it in. I haven't eaten in eight hours."

"Start this car. Or I'll throw your ass out!"

George looked at the seriousness of the older white cop beside him. He didn't know who this Cooper was, and didn't much care. He wiped the sweat from his dark face with a mustard stained napkin. And made sure what little he did eat wasn't still in the corners of his mouth. He flicked a flake of relish from his deep lined forehead. Goddamn crazy son-of-a-bitch. He patted down his hair in the rearview.

Brubaker cocked the shotgun, its sharp click dangerously filling the car. He was careful not to look in George's direction, so no one could prove it was a personal threat.

George's back stiffened and he quickly took his eyes from the mirror. He didn't need any proof. He threw his hot dog out the window, started the Mustang, turned on his flashing headlamps and went after the two cars.

Cooper made his way to the Hollywood Freeway, nearly ending it all when a Toyota four-by-four pulled out in front of them at Floye Drive. Oh what a feeling!

The Datsun Roadster managed to follow thanks to the Mickey Mouse suspension Roger had left on the Corsa. Even so, Teatro wasn't able to handle the unfamiliar course as well as Cooper. Twice he nearly sent them on a short cut, scenic route tour of the Valley, via some unsuspecting person's backyard.

After getting a late start, the Mustang was just back far enough so that Brubaker and George were unable to get a read on the Datsun's plate. But it wasn't the blue Datsun Brubaker wanted. No, he wanted only one car and only one driver - the shithead, loud-mouthed, Portland Cooper. Images of the past ran through his mind. Life was fair. Because he had escaped from the desk job Cooper helped give him. Now after spending only three months of dinners staking out his old beat, he came into contact with the one person he most wanted to see mess up. Cooper. Portland friggin' Cooper and his blood red Corsa. Even if Brubaker wasn't behind the wheel. Even if it was part of his deal, no driving on duty, except for emergencies.

"All right, Brubaker," he could hear the Captain yell, "why in God's name did you blow that rookie's head away and take over the car? How many times do I have to tell you? No more driving! Unless it's an emergency."

"But, Captain, it was an emergency." Brubaker laughed out loud. The point was he was out from behind the desk and on the Corsa hunt again. The scent was strong. He could smell the duel tetraethyl lead exhaust. He could taste premium fumes trapped in his teeth. Better yet, he could see the one person he hated most in the entire world, Portland Cooper. It was like time hadn't passed him by. He was on Cooper's tailpipe again. Only now he had a new trick pony car. A muscled up Mustang. A very effective high-speed pursuit vehicle that could handle these roads much better than what he drove before. There was no way Cooper could out run him now. No more of those boats they used to stick him with. He had an eight cylinder primed to run and a package wrapped around it built for speed. And no one, not Cooper, not Roger Kelemen, no one would make him eat their dirt, or crow or any other stink again.

"You're driving like an old woman! Let this thing breathe."

"Eat it, Brubaker! I ain't ending up behind a desk because of your bullshit."

At the freeway, Cooper headed north on Cahuenga West and entered the Hollywood Freeway at Barham and mingled with the traffic heading into the Valley.

The Datsun decided to get out of the chase. It slowed to blend with traffic heading south on Cahuenga West into

Hollywood to see if they could shake the Mustang in the low lying mist as it crept up the pass.

But the Mustang crossed the Hollywood freeway and headed north on Cahuenga East, catching up with Cooper and Gwen at the Barham traffic, and followed them down the ramp heading toward the101 Ventura Freeway West into the Valley.

Cooper did his best to blend in with the north-bounders but Brubaker and George pulled up alongside of him anyway and waved him over with his shotgun. Cooper had no choice other than to cut to the slow lane and stop just short of Lankershim below Universal Studios. Traffic continued to zoom by as they didn't bother to change lanes to make room for the two cars on the shoulder. The two cops got out of the Mustang with their guns unlatched and approached Roger's Corsa. Gwen managed to have herself covered but Cooper was still completely naked.

"What now?"

"I'm open."

"You sure are."She looked down at his lap. "Exciting, huh?"

"You don't look bored."

"It's the wind."

"Yeah, I bet."Cooper looked in his rearview mirror at the two approaching officers."Whatever happened to the good old days when you could race around town and only be bothered by incompetent asses like...."His eyes blinked twice from the glare. That couldn't be. He blinked twice again, hoping beyond hope that his eyes would clear. That what he saw was just a fathead mirage. They wouldn't."Oh, great."Cars whizzed by even faster now as the traffic thinned out. The wind began to blow north through the pass, a bad omen as to what was about to happen.

"What?"Gwen turned around and a white chalk veil dropped over her face. It couldn't be. "Brubaker."

Brubaker headed toward Cooper's side of the Corsa. A fat phantom of the past. The overhead light cast a smug villainous mask over his hooded eyes. The north bound lights that rose out of the mist rolled over the Cahuenga pass, throwing his expanding heavy shadow over and over again at the Corsa as he approached. There was no mistaking that big dick walk. It was him, a rebirth of an angry past.

Brubaker drew his gun in case Cooper tried to make a run for it. He stopped just behind Portland's left ear, ready to kick the door if it opened in the wrong manner. "All right, Cooper, hold it right there."

Portland looked over at Gwen's ashen face. "You heard the officer. What are you waiting for?"

George came up sniffing around behind Gwen. He checked her out hoping for another peep show and looked disappointed when he found Gwen almost completely covered.

Gwen held Portland's sport jacket tight around her neck trying to disappear under it. Creep.

Brubaker reached into the backseat to pick up Cooper's pants and found the gun and the half empty champagne bottle.

"What's wrong with you, boy? Every time I bust your ass, you've got your pants down. Now get these on and get your naked butt out of this piece of shit.

"You too, ma'am," George said. "And to the back."

Cooper pulled his pants away from Brubaker and struggled to put them on while still seated. Not easy to do when under pressure. "I thought they had you behind a desk."

"I have one year before retirement. They gave me a choice. So I'm back and I'm here to make life miserable for you.

Cooper finished pulling his pants back on. He stepped out of the car and stood next to Gwen at the rear of the Corsa. Cooper in suit pants and socks. They looked at each other. It was their prom night all over again.

Someone yelled from a passing truck. "Cool Corvair, man."

Cooper wasn't sure if he wanted to laugh, strangle Gwen, or just punch Brubaker out for old times' sake, and run for it.

George kept his gun on them while Brubaker reached in to the car and pulled out Cooper's gun. He smelled it.

"Cuff him, George. If he gives you lip, jack him on the hood."
Life was beyond fair, it was just...Cooper with a fired gun.

George played it up. It wasn't often he had such a gorgeous audience. He holstered his gun and reached back for his cuffs.

"Wait a minute, I've got a permit."

"Let's see it."

"In my sport coat. My wallet."

Gwen opened the sport coat to reveal the inside pocket.

George reached inside the sport coat pocket, clearly against procedure. He made sure he brushed up against Gwen's erect braless nipple under her blouse in the process. He looked her straight in the eye as he withdrew the wallet.

"Excuse me."

Gwen just gave him a cold stare. She had him setup for a clear knee to the balls. She glanced at Cooper who was shaking his head. Gwen let the opportunity pass.

George took the wallet and handed it over to Brubaker. The old cop opened Cooper's wallet, again against procedures and took out Portland's permit and driver's license. He didn't bother with the registration to the car. A big broad satisfying smile spread on his thick face."Still not smart enough to keep your driver's license renewed on time though, huh?"

"Ah, I'm sure it'll be in the mail any day now."

George opened his handcuffs.

"Lean over the back of the car and spread your legs, please."

"What? In this neighborhood?"

George jacked Cooper up over the hood and slammed his head down in the paint.

"What should I do, Portland?"

"I haven't forgotten you either, young lady. Rest assured I want nothing to do with your mother and stepfather again. So I suggest you get this bucket of red shit out of my sight before I have it impounded for littering the highway." Brubaker headed back toward the Mustang.

"Take the car back to my shop and have Jorge lock it up. Wait there for my call and have Holland arrange for my bail."

George pulled Cooper off the engine hood by the back of his hair and the handcuffs. He jerked him toward the Mustang.

"Just how fast will this thing go?"

"Ask, your fat friend. I believe he wrecked fifteen cars trying to find out."

"So that's why the captain said...."

"You looking for trouble, George? And screw you, Cooper. It was less than seven cars, and I haven't gained a pound since back then."

"Yeah, well, you were fat back then, too."

George jerked on Cooper's bare muscular arms. Noting the red inked CORSA on his right shoulder. Gwen got into Roger's car and started it. She looked back at Portland as they tried to stuff him into the back of the Mustang. Cooper watched her as they jammed his head into the car. He wanted her to beat it. She knew that. Who knows what kind of hairless angry cat they would've let out of the bag if Brubaker got a whiff of what was really going down. She pulled into traffic as George began to read Portland his rights.

Brubaker had Cooper and no one would wipe the smirk from his face that night. Portland Cooper behind bars. In just three months he'd caught Cooper up to his old shit. Naked with a fired gun. Life was good. Maybe a miracle would happen and that big-shot super star Kelemen would run a stop sign in front of him or better yet, litter. He'd love to fine that big mouth arrogant punk in his souped-up 911. Life was sweet. Life was great. Life was getting even. Life would even be better if he had Kelemen behind bars, too.

Marty pulled up in his white Corvan and bounced out. Cooper and Gwen got out of the passenger's side. Gwen stifled a smile trying her best to look innocent. Cooper didn't say a word. He just looked about his work yard at all the familiar faces.

The dead-end ally and open work yard were packed tight with all kinds of Corvairs. A 1962 Greenbrier had its rear doors open and a keg of Miller sat in a zinc tub full of ice. Cooper looked around at the others. Twin purple 63 Monza four door sedans had all their doors opened and two teenage girls with tattoos and body piercing sat in front of a blaring stereo. Elvis sang 'Jail House Rock.' A nice touch.

Cooper nodded to Mr. and Mrs. Thompson, the black couple in swimwear. They were an elderly retired lawyer and teacher that still lived up the block. She was his junior high math teacher. He had gotten Cooper out of trouble a couple of times. So Portland kept an eye on them when they weren't traveling all of North American in their white with red stripe 68 Corvair Ultra Van. Somehow they had squeezed its smiling face up into the yard and against the east cinderblock wall. Their gas grill was out, ready for ribs and chicken that sat in a cooler waiting.

Another kid in his early twenties, who was well over six foot eight, sat in a Corvair dune buggy that Cooper hand built for him. A group of teenagers sat around a white Monza with a blue stripe that jetted across the engine hood and pointed down across the doors toward the back of the front tires. Another one of Cooper's creations. A young couple smiled from inside their artesian turquoise 140 Corsa coupe with their factory installed A/C running, while their two children slept in the back.

All the other cars belonged to older Corsa Club Members who sat in their all original show Corvairs. All the men had their shirts off, suggesting that they were naked in their cars. Real hilarious, but Cooper didn't let on. They applauded Cooper as he walked among them. Cooper looked at their smiling faces, from teenagers to parents to grandparents. What a sack full of misfitted nuts. He had personally worked on every car in the yard. Some he had completely rebuilt from the ground up as long as ten years ago. Some of the others he had bought and sold as is. He walked into his work yard and the smiling faces parted to let him pass. They turned to watch him go. There it was. His beloved Corsa. His funny little red car. Piled in a final resting heap in the center of his work yard. Not a single part not cut or smashed. An American flag hung at half-mast from a pole sticking out of the heart of the metal. Sixty-six votive candles burned at the base of the scrap pile. Sad was all it was.

Cooper wasn't sure what to say. He felt a hand tugging at the back of his tongue pulling all his thoughts down into the pit of his stomach. What could he say to these friends? "All right, you clowns. You've got a big mouth, Gwen."

"It was Holland's idea."

Holland, about twice Cooper's age with long graying hair pulled back in a tail, and a smartly chiseled face, looked on with her pilot's steely blue eyes, still sharp as razors. She smiled from her pristine baby blue '61 Lakewood station wagon, its white top reflecting the overhead work lights. One of six Corvairs she owned. Cooper was the favorite son she never had. Her late husband adored him, too. He spent many of his last hours here chewing the fat with Portland, keeping himself busy, while she flew cargo planes across the US. "Some of us Clubbies thought we'd welcome you home."

"They come to pay their bills, too?"

"We're family, not stupid," Marty said.

Snickers broke out among the crowd. It was a good thing Gwen was decent enough to bring him a change of clothes.

"Go ahead, have a little snicker and go on home, it's late."

"I, ah, invited the NoHos over to party," Marty said. "Some are still on the way. Kind of, you know, a wake for your Corsa."

Finn, got out of his 1964 black convertible Spider. He spoke with a voice of a man who had lived on and off the sea his whole life and who had been drinking on and off the whole evening. He looked like a castaway from an old Captain Blood movie. "Aye," he said. "We aim to catch who done it, and jump start their scrotums." A cheer spread through the crowd.

Marty handed Gwen and Cooper a beer.

"I'd like to make a toast," Holland said. "To Cooper's Corsa, the first and the best car out of our pack. May it rest in peace."

No one made a move. "P. E. A. C. E.," she added.

Everyone chugged their beer except Cooper."Wait a minute," he said and moved over and poured another beer. As he and others downed their beers he poured the other over the pile of steel and leather. One by one the others came over to pour what was left of their beers onto the pile, making sure not to put out the candles. The beer oozed out the bottom at their feet.

"What do you say, Coop? We got a party?"

Cooper looked over at Gwen. She had tears in her eyes. They all had remembered the man she loved. Corny, but touching. He pulled her close. "Yeah, Marty, we've got a party."

Another cheer let out from the crowd as the girls with the spiked hair turned back up their stereos. Jorge and his wife opened up the trunk of his white 1965 Corsa and pulled out snacks as the others crowded around the beer keg as the Thompsons plopped slab of ribs and chicken on the hot grill. Filling Cooper's Corvair yard with the sweet smell of barbeque.

Gwen leaned her head on Portland's shoulder. It was just amazing, she thought. All these people had come on a moment's notice. All for the same love of a car. The blood red Corsa. This wonderful mistreated, misunderstood band of Corvair lovers. She wrapped her arm around Portland's waist. She loved this man. Underneath the hard exterior of a ruthless person, beat the heart of a real caring, sensitive man who was capable of love, understanding and devotion...for his car. She laughed.

Cooper kissed the side of her face. "I love you, too."

"I know."

Early the next morning, a few hours before sunrise, Cooper sat at his desk in the upstairs den. He leaned back in his chair with his hands folded behind his head. His feet were propped up on the desk. His thighs held the dregs of a warm beer. His half awake eyes studied the photos on the wall of Corvair Club rallies and races.

A poster of Portland next to his Corsa was behind him. A shelf was full of racing and show trophies with a few pictures of Cooper, Gwen, Roger, and Marty with their cars. Three framed car magazine covers had Portland and his Corsa featured on them. One read, "A BOY AND HIS DREAM CORVAIR."

Portland picked up a framed picture off the desk. It was a shot of him and his dad in front of a Chevy dealer. His dad had his arm around him, giving him a set of keys. Portland was happy but embarrassed. His hair was slicked back in a Ducktail, the D.A. they called it back then. He was definitely way too cool. A big printed sign overhead read: "HAPPY 16TH BIRTHDAY, PORTLAND COOPER." The showroom window in the background was full of red and black balloons. Behind the window, all by itself, for the world to see, was the exact Corsa Portland had designed in his high school auto shop class. Down to the very stitch count in the leather headrest.

Portland sipped his beer, grimaced at its temperature and swallowed. A teardrop fought up into his eye but he managed to fight it back. What a great man his father is. He had met with the heads General Motors Design personally and submitted Cooper's blue prints. He was finally on top of the advertisement world. The hot new company. The new Corvair ad account had finally brought his advertisement company out of the red and into the black. He could finally give Portland's mother the life they had dreamed of all those years. A home in Bel Air. No more North Hollywood. They'd be able to put Portland in the best of schools. This was the big time now. General Motors was knocking. And the great American sports car dream show was answering. People were buying. Loving the Corvair. So in '64 they packed up and moved in next door to Gwen's family.

Cooper hated the move away from his cool pals to snobby Bel Air. He put up quite a fuss. Even took off for a couple of days and slept in the sand at the beach. But when he finally showed up to find Gwen and her mother Irene standing at his new front door, he was smitten from moment one. Gwen had turned to see him pull up in his Corsa, the sun hitting her face perfectly, and smiled. His hood heart melted and he was in love. He never told her that. Played it cool all these years. But it was from moment one that he knew she was the girl for him. His mom saw the look on his face, and she knew in her heart that the Coopers were home.

But even bad dreams had an awakening. Nader, the expert, who never drove a Corvair, or owned a car, had put an end to the dream in 65 just as the new modal hit the showrooms. GM pulled their money from Portland's dad's firm so fast that his dad nearly lost everything by 67. He had to sell the house. Portland was in Corpus Christi defending those dreams by then. But nothing could protect his dad from corporate raiders and his old man was forced to sell out the business and take his remaining loyal clients to a firm in New York City.

Patrick Cooper was never the same. He was never his own man after that. It nearly broke his mother's heart to have to leave California, Bel Air and their independent dreams behind.

Soon, Portland would have to call his dad who was now retired down in Miami, and tell him what had come of his prized Corsa. The man had called in so many favors to have it built for Portland...the kid with grease in his blood, under his nails and on his shoes. Soon, he'd have to give him the dirty details. Soon, but not until he found more answers...not until he knew exactly why...and got to kick some serious ass for it.

He set the picture of his dad down on his desk and reached over and fingered his black and red racing jumpsuit. Sleep was racing up behind him and his toes couldn't reach the brakes. His matching helmet and black driving gloves hung with the suit. A poster of him in the outfit drinking from a victory cup while Gwen planted a big one on his dirty cheek hung behind the suit. A red and black hard top Corsa with the number sixty-six on the doors and two black stripes over the hood and deck was in the poster's background.

Maybe he should've taken those offers from Ford and Porsche. Maybe he should've come back and driven those other cars instead of staying loyal all these years to the Corvair. The Corsa. An outdated dream. Maybe. The world was full of too many maybes. Maybe the world was flat and life was just one big long drag race on its way to drop off the face of the Earth.

He let go of the jumpsuit and looked over at Marty crashed out in Cooper's black leather La-Z-Boy, with a beer on his protruding stomach. Sounds that came from his closed throat weren't quite as polite as barnyard ambiance.

"Am I wasting my time, Marty?"

"With what?"

"Playing with these funny little cars."

"Did you see those people out there?"

"Yeah. A bunch of crazies hanging onto outdated dreams."

"They need you, Coop. They look up to you. You keep those outdated dreams alive. I know how you feel. The Corsa was meant to live. Let to evolve into what it could've been. But it didn't. Without guys like you, it hasn't got a chance in hell. Who knows, maybe GM will revive the Corvair someday if enough of us keep believing. It ain't a half bad living. Shit, all of us would kill to have a woman like Gwen in our front seats. So shuddup."

Cooper sat in silence a moment. "Marty?"

"Yeah, Coop?"

"Thanks for the party."

"Anytime." Marty closed his eyes and started snoring again.

Gwen came in wearing a soft yellow nighty and carrying a blanket. She took Marty's beer and covered him up. She came over and held her hand out to Portland. He took it and she pulled him up onto his feet. "Come on, slugger, let's go to bed."

Cooper picked up the picture of his dad and put it under his arm and swung his other arm around Gwen's shoulder and headed for bed. "Good night, Tinker Bell."

Marty snorted and rolled over, pulling the blanket up around both his chins. "Good night, Delma."

Jerry and Ruth Goodricke's office was in an older brick two-story Beverly Hills building. It was about a block off the Wilshire Boulevard, on South Beverly Drive, where some kind of media event was taking place. Inside, ditzy Tracey sat behind the reception desk gabbing on the phone about personal shit. Cooper entered, and didn't bother to stop at her desk as he headed toward the inner offices. He'd been there before. Tracey looked up surprised to see someone dressed in gray sweat shirt, jeans, and work boots zoom by her desk. "I'll call you back." She hung up, realizing who it was. "Mr. Cooper? Jerry still doesn't want to see you."

"That's all right, I still don't want to see him. But I have to. In here?" Cooper headed for a door leading down a hall towards Jerry's office.

Tracey tried to stop him. "Mr. Cooper, don't, stop!"

"I love it when you talk dirty." Cooper made it to the inner office door first and went in.

Tracey stopped to think over what he meant by that, as Cooper let the door shut between them and went down the hall.

Tracey rushed back to the phone to buzz Jerry. The intercom picked up on the other end and immediately a silenced gunshot pushed through the receiver. The squeaking of a chair and heavy eye glasses tumbling down to the floor mat came next. Quickly followed by the deadened, hollow thud of a skull smacking a stack of papers on a heavy wood desk.

Cooper ducked inside an office which appeared to be Ruth's. She wasn't in. Cooper drew his gun and re-entered the hall and quietly made his way past a mailroom with a copy machine in it to Jerry's office. He looked in. A window was open leading to a fire escape. Curtains blew in the subtle soot-filled breeze. Not much of a view unless crowed alleys, electrical transformers, dumpsters, and power wires did it for you. The people attending the event taking place down the alley had taken every available legal parking space in the area. Cooper turned back to scan the room. Nothing but a dead agent was out of the ordinary.

Tracey's voice still came over the intercom. "Jerry, Jerry, Jerry." The intercom clicked off.

Jerry lay lonesome on his desk. He wasn't about to answer anyone but his maker. His non-seeing eyes stared toward the open window. The side of his face pressed flat against a coverless screenplay. Seemed Allen Smithee, the unaccredited writer, had torn it off before pulling the trigger and making the story come true. A dark ugly hole split the difference of Jerry's bushy salt and pepper eyebrows. The starkness of his pale head made the hole and the deep red blood seeping from it onto the white page of the script all the more graphic. It must've been a small caliber because it didn't blow the back of his head out.

Cooper leaned in to see what Jerry had been reading. The title was printed there at the top center of the page, just above Fade In. From the looks of things, Beverly Hills Drive had just apply Dissolved To: Bullet Hole Drive. Apparently, the screenplay was already written, cast and had a killer ending. Guess someone didn't want to own up to writing or directing this death scene. Unless they could negotiate a final cut.

Cooper went to the window and looked out again. So much for pumping Jerry for info. Or baiting him into explaining what the hell was going on. Whoever dropped by to kill Jerry most likely came and went through the window. Despite his name being on the top of the list, Cooper also had the feeling that Jerry was the weakest link to Roger's faked Florida vacation. Someone else had the same idea. Jerry had a lot at stake if something were to happen to Roger. If Roger were having some kind of problem, it was most likely Jerry and Ruth he would come to first with his complaints. After all, what were agents, foster parents, and former fellow identity thieves for? Cooper turned back to look at Jerry again. He really couldn't see Roger having the balls to kill his own agent. Nor his foster parent. He didn't see any of Irene's guests as a cold blooded killer who would kill a longtime friend and business associate. Not even Jack. So who did? There was a piece missing.

Was all this about making a movie? Did Roger kill Jerry over this? Why else would he blackmail them besides money? Or was he? Did it have something to do with the photos on Roger's wall. Or more than likely the identity thief trial thirty years ago? Who were Eddie and Tim Waller? If they really had perished in a burning car crash, why have all their pictures along with all other fiscal evidence of their existence disappeared so completely? Were Eddie and Tim Waller real?

Cooper looked out the window again. The fire escape ladder was down. Maybe he should use it. Someone stuck him with a body. Did someone dangerous know he was coming? Is this a warning for him, the others on the list, or for all of the above? He didn't feel like fielding murder questions, especially since he didn't have the answers. Somehow this all seemed much deeper than an insurance scam. Whatever this was about happened way before Roger became Super Star Roger Kelemen. Wherever Roger was, Cooper hoped he held all the blood stained cards. Otherwise, he was as dead as Jerry. Cooper looked back at Jerry. One thing was for sure, dead agents don't read scripts.

Tracey came into Jerry's office not understanding what she had just heard. She only saw dead Jerry then Cooper with his gun drawn and screamed something along the lines of bloody murder. After the reality of the moment hit her she started thinking straight. "Holy-shit, I'm unemployed!"

Only in LA? Probably not. A job is a job, and when the boss gets it in the head, business can tend to die along with him.

Two of the building's security officers rushed the room. If Cooper had been the killer, these two clods would've easily been his next two victims. Instead Cooper didn't move. Making sure he didn't get plugged by a couple of scared rabbits.

"All right, drop it right where you stand."

Cooper shed his gun onto the desk. Someone had watched too much television growing up.

"He barged right in and shot Jerry."Tracey started crying hysterically."I just bought an Alfa Romeo. Now what will I do?"

"Check my gun, it hasn't been fired. I have a permit."

"Move away from the window, hands up."Cooper did.

The dumpy security officer checked Cooper's gun. It smelled clean. Cooper showed his permit. So he handed it back to him.

Cooper put his gun back in its holster. Keeping it visible. "Someone went out the window as I came into the room."

"You get a look at him?"

"Yeah, Allen Smithee."

Two plain clothes cops showed up, one black one white. The other security officer took sentimental Tracey out to the hall.

"Someone went out the window as he came in. I checked his gun. It's clean. He says he saw an Allen Smithee."

The brighter looking uniformed officer gave Cooper a look. He knew his Hollywood lore.

"I have a permit."Cooper flashed it. "Can I run along?"

The black cop gave it a once over and checked Cooper's gun for himself.

"You know him?"

"Jerry Goodricke. His name is on the office door."

"Don't be a smartass."

"I just stopped by to say hello. I've known him for years."

"Well, cancel any lunch reservations, Mr. Cooper. We'll need you for awhile. Have a seat out in the reception area, and send Officer Harris in for me. He's at the door with a note pad."

"Sure thing, Officer." Cooper exited Jerry's office.

"Get a complete rundown on this guy," the black officer said to his partner."If you have to, bring Mr. Cooper in and hold him overnight."

Cooper reentered the lobby to find Tracey still crying.

The place was full of young cops holding back crusty reporters and a handful of shifty paparazzi who had escaped the political bullshit down the street to cover something important...like a BH murder. Tracey had the morbid media eating from the palms of her hands. She even managed to unbutton her blouse a little and had hiked up her skirt to show a tad more thigh. A field reporter from KTLA Prime News held a microphone in her face and Channel Five's camera lights filled the room. Andy Warhol strikes again. Her fifteen minutes were on the clock. The paparazzi tried to rush the room when they saw Cooper. A couple even managed to pop off a few shots before they were pushed back out the door.

Cooper stopped just in time, keeping his back to the clicking cameras. He turned to one of the young cops and lowered his tone to a deliberate room clearing sotto voice, "Hey, you hear, they found another body out in the ally?"

"Figures. Who?" Harris answered.

"They don't know yet. Pretty gruesome. I hear there's a trail of body parts across Beverly Hills," Cooper said raising his voice. "Arms, legs... all over the place."

"Christ what a mess," Harris said.

Immediately the jammed room emptied of reporters and photographers as they rushed down the hall leaving Tracey in Hollywood misery. She shot Cooper a nasty look and buttoned up her blouse. How dare he waste a second of her limelight.

Cooper winked at Tracey as she left and turned to Harris taking notes at the hall door. "Excuse me."

"Just a sec?"

"Look, I didn't get his name, but he wants you inside."

Harris looked up from his pad. "Me? You sure?"

"I think so, you're Harris?"

"Correct."

"He said now."

"Thanks." Harris left.

Cooper turned to the other young cops, "Excuse me. Could you cover this door for Harris, please?"

"Yes, sir."

Cooper stepped out the door into the now empty hall and turned back to the officers. "And make sure no one comes in or out. Especially, her. Got that? No more reporters in here."

Cooper headed down the hall and exited the building.

One block over, the Corsa sat in the slim shade of a date palm with its top down. Gwen waited with her head back, catching a few winks. She wore large purple sunglasses. Finally the sun had burned through the morning overcast skies. A perfect reason to fill the backseat full of shoeboxes.

Cooper approached the Corsa making sure he wasn't being followed. He saw the shoeboxes and gave Gwen a look.

"I got bored."

"Anybody we know come by," he asked, getting in quickly and driving off?.

"Like whom?"

"Like Roger, maybe."

"You said he was dead."

"I said maybe. His script was on Jerry's desk."

"So?"

"Must've been a killer script, I guess."

Cop cars were all over the place and the whining howl of an ambulance filled the air. Gwen looked around until she noticed that Cooper was doing his best to be inconspicuous.

"What did you do?"

"Nothing. Someone ventilated Jerry's head and left it on top of Roger's script. Ruth wasn't in at the time. I snuck out. They'll be looking for me."

"What?!"

"Relax, he didn't feel a thing."

"Oh, my god. You don't think Roger did this?"

"I'm trying not to. So, who's next on that list after the Goodrickes?

Cooper drove on as Gwen took out the list.

Minutes later, Portland stopped out front of Elliott and Sophie Pascal's two story white pillared home off Sunset and Alpine in the two million dollar district of Beverly Hills. There wasn't a gate, so Cooper pulled into the horseshoe drive and parked at the front door. He got out of the Corsa, making sure they were still alone. He knocked on the door as Gwen tried to dry her eyes and fix her make-up in the rearview mirror. A heavy set, Mexican maid answered the door in all white.

"Hello?" she said in perfect English.

"Is Sophie Pascal in, please?"

"Is she expecting you, sir?"

"Eventually."

"Sorry?"

"Just tell her that Portland Cooper is here to see her."

The maid stepped back and closed the door in Cooper's face.

Gwen wiped her eyes and blew her nose in Cooper's hanky. "What are you up to, Portland?"

"I'm hoping some of these pigeons are just rats with wings."

The maid reopened the door."I'm sorry, sir, but Mrs. Pascal wishes not to be disturbed. She's meditating by the pool."

"Well, all right, I'll call later."

"The maid closed the door in Cooper's face again. He walked to the right of the house to a gate under the arch of a carport that led around back. It wasn't locked.

"Portland, she doesn't want to see you."

"Then why did she let me know she's out by the pool? I hear a rat-wing fluttering."

"Aren't we the poet today. Mention the disappearance of her little girl just before she married Elliott, if you're not getting anywhere with her. It's a card she never plays."

"Another rock turns over. Stay by the car and honk twice if anyone shows up, including Elliott. Pigeons are harmless – but they carry germs and will shit on you if you let them."

Cooper went through the gate and Gwen got out of the Corsa to try on some of her new shoes.

Sophie lay on her stomach completely naked beside the dark blue tiled, tightly landscaped pool. A token waterfall tinkled down from what looked like real rocks, but weren't, and pitter-pattered into a two person Jacuzzi that overflowed into the jagged kidney shaped pool. Three or four different kinds of squat palms sprang up from a fake rock-like oasis. The assorted wild flowers crept out from under the rock formations, creating a manicured but free styled wilderness that was supposed to give the bather a sense of hiding amongst an ever so gentle nature, and not stuck in the overcrowded inner trappings of Beverly Hills. The line of English beech tree hedges that encircled the grounds was nearly thirty feet high and almost impossible to see through without great effort. Which, Cooper was sure, Sophie anticipated as she lay au natural on her stomach in all her cleanly shaved golden glory.

Cooper came up from behind and deliberately blocked the sun. Sophie didn't bother to look up.

"Mucho funny, you want to cover me with a towel?"

"Not very."

"Then get out of my sun."

"I'm insulted you knew it was me?"

"Who else would be so rude?"

"Maybe the person who just ventilated Jerry's forehead."

"What? Jerry who?"

"You know, Jerry, as in agent, as in get me a job, Jerry."

Sophie sat up, turning her back to Cooper, but not before he was able to memorize that she hadn't a strand of body hair, anywhere. How interesting. God had smiled on this woman. So had money. She probably spent every waking hour fighting Mother Nature. From what Cooper could see, aided by a tuck here and a nip there, she was way ahead of the game. Cooper handed her a towel and poured her a double vodka martini from a freshly iced shaker on a glass pushcart. For safety's sake he never turned his back on her.

She downed the drink with experience.

Cooper shuddered and looked at the phone, noticing the recent oil stains. "Don't con me, you already knew Jerry took it close range to the head."

"How graphic, Mr. Cooper. That was Irene, they also found Ruth's body in her Koi pond."

"She must've gone home for lunch."

"You don't think I had anything...."

"Don't get your dimples in an uproar. What do you know about a movie script, Bullet Hole Drive?"

"You won't start with this Roger crap again, will you?"

"Appallingly so. When was the last time you saw Roger?"

"You know, you are such a bore. Why don't you undress and get interesting?"

"I like my tan lines. They fit my personality."

"From your grease stained t-shirts, no doubt."

"Correct. Now, when was the last time you saw Roger?"

"Weeks."

"Why was he blackmailing you and Elliott? Was it over this script, Bullet Hole Drive?"

"Don't be silly. He has no reason to blackmail any of us. And surely couldn't get much if he tried."

"Look, all I want to do is find Roger."

Cooper handed Sophie the computer read out.

She looked it over. Her face showed nothing. Actresses. "Isn't he in Florida? This is obviously his postcard list."

"Roger's got a problem, Sophie. You know, a bad habit, and he needs money. No one will insure his movie in that condition. You all know it. Which is why I think he's blackmailing everyone on that list. To get his movie made."

"That's ridiculous." She leaned over and poured herself another drink.

"I don't know if Roger killed Jerry and Ruth, but if he did, then everything he does makes sense to him. You are next on that list. So help me find him before he cast you in the part of your lifetime."

Sophie handed Portland back the list. "I don't know what you're talking about. I've known Roger since he was a little kid. He hasn't the guts to kill a bug. I assure you, I was not asked to be in a film written by Roger Kelemen. If you haven't noticed, I'm a TV actress. I haven't read for a film in years."

"But you've read it."

"Everyone who needs to know in this biz knows that Roger wants to do this car script. Elliot has drafts of it in stacks on his shelves. And you are right, no one will insure it if Roger has a known drug problem. So if Roger has this problem, I'm sure Jerry was taking care of it. But they'd only attach names to his project, if someone with money were interested."

"Evidently Jerry didn't take care of it quick enough."

"Are you saying he killed them?"

"I got my bets on other people."

"Then go pester them. I'm losing my sun...do you mind?"

"It's your skin. Is Elliott at this address?"

"That's none of your business."

"I hear your little girl disappear before you married Elliott."

"Have you found her?"

"I'm not looking."

"Then that's none of your business either. Is it?"

"I'm not a cop. I'm just trying to help Roger."

"Then help him and leave us the hell alone. Is that clear?"

"Clear as a bullet to the skull."

Sophie revealed a Colt from under one of her pool pillows. "Sidewalk punks don't scare me."

"Wow, I guess you are a TV actress."

"I also know how to send intruders limping out of my yard."

"All I know is that my funny little car was chopped up, that Roger's missing, and now Jerry and Ruth are dead. All because of a little key hidden in a radio and the meaning it has to your shrinking rat pack of friends."

"Good day, Mr. Cooper."

"Don't bet on it." He turned and left the way he'd entered.

Sophie watched him until he was out of sight and reached for the phone. Maybe now she'll get real work in this town.

Cooper rounded the corner of the house and found Gwen with her mouth held shut by Dexter. Teatro held a gun his way. The situation looked bad with the shoes piled on the driveway.

"Gwen, you're such a flirt."

"Gordamerithhhh."

"Let's have it," Teatro said. Cooper handed over his gun. "Now the key."

"Search me."

"Would you like me to put a hole in her head?" Dexter asked.

"Just like Jerry and Ruth? Jack would love that."

Gwen pulled Dexter's hand away."Ruth, too!"She bit it.

"Aaahhhhhh..."Dexter slapped her.

"Careful, she likes that."

"We didn't ice 'em, pal."

"Why would we?"

"Jerry just hired us to pick up this car. Someone else offered us a better prize to deliver it elsewhere."

"That wouldn't have been a Roger Kelemen, would it?"

"Maybe."

"I hope you enjoyed the chop job we did on your Corsa?"

"About as much as you enjoyed your powder burns."

"Get in, the new boss wants to talk." Cooper got in behind the wheel and Teatro got in with him.

Gwen pulled away as Dexter went to pick her up. She grabbed for her shoes and began to throw them at Dexter.

A come-hither pump missed its mark, striking Cooper on the back of the head. Dexter fought off a pair of gray sandals, grabbed Gwen by the waist and threw her over his shoulder. When he realized he had a wildcat by the tail he clumped her. Gwen decided wherever they were about to be taken would hardly be worth having her head broken over, so she shut up. Dexter took her over and stuffed her into the front seat of the BMW. He got in behind the wheel and followed after Teatro and Cooper.

The Mexican maid came out into the drive. Her face lit up like a pirate discovering the secret of Treasure Island. She wandered out amongst the fortune in shoes.

"America...this is such a great country."

8 HUNG WEST OF CATALINA

Fifteen years ago, one of twenty-nine ships classed as Project B30, and built between 1949 and 1954 in Gdansk Shipyard – Poland, was reported sunk at sea off the coast of South Africa during a disastrous storm after being ransacked by pirates. Yet at sunset, the now painted pink and blue 285 ft refitted coal and ore freighter ship, was anchored just west of Catalina, California. Dinner was taking place on the bow. Loud music played and men and women danced to a rumba beat between piled movie props, sets and durable equipment. All secured and covered in black tarps. Glistening in tow were two matching thirteen-metre Riva speedboats. Both luxury icons, with twenty coats of varnish mahogany, were made in Italy in 1955 and reported missing from the canals of Venice late last week. They were flown in the day before strapped to the belly of the gutted out shell of a 68 Bell 204 Huey. The UH1B, was fastened to a landing pad on the upper deck. Another group of men were gathered at the stern of the ship shooting caged birds with shotguns.

Down a ramp built into the cargo hull of the ship, once filled with Russian ore, crates and grip equipment now filled most of the open spaces. On one bulkhead behind a drawn curtain was a torture chamber movie set. Gwen Hawkins laid there, sedated and shackled by fake chain to a wooden rack prop. But otherwise she was physically if not emotionally unharmed.

Hanging outside the curtain from the same bulkhead on a false dungeon wall from matching designer chains with his toes barely able to touch on a set of wooden pegs was Portland Cooper. His jeans and gray sweatshirt were torn nearly beyond recognition and had bypassed infectiously filthy, as though he was dragged across Los Angles to the helicopter that brought him there. Someone had given him a thorough beating to go along with it. He looked every bit the part of a political prisoner from the thirteenth century. Type casting at its best. Only his black steel toed work boots gave him away.

Roger entered to the beat of the music, looking sick, as though he'd accepted an invitation from Satan to rot in his own personal hell. He wore the same white slept-in linen clothing from the other night on the pier. He suffered from Saturday Night Fever and had thrown up all over himself. He was still unshaven, with even darker luggage under his eyes from dancing all-nighters with the silvery spoon. His fingers tapped on a Miller can as he came down the ramp and stood before Portland thinking of how wrong this all was. He wished it could just go away. He didn't want this to happen.

"You awake, Coop?"

Cooper opened his eyes. "I don't know. Am I, Rog?"

"How's it hanging?"

"Yuckity, yuck."

"Too bad about your Corsa."

Cooper refused to give him the satisfaction of a reply.

"It's your own damn fault. Besides, they will kill you in the end anyway. So what does it matter?"

"Yeah well, before they do, you mind telling me what I got my foreskin stuck in this time?"

Roger stopped, looked around the hull at the empty crates to make sure they were really alone. He went back to secure the door and dogged it down, pushing a crate in front of it, just to make sure. He took out a nasal spray bottle full of vodka and coke and took a blast up the left nostril. He checked behind the drawn curtain for Gwen's slumbering form before taking a blast up his right. The shoes didn't match her jeans and blouse, he thought. How un-Gwen.

"The movies."

"Tough union."

"Yeah, time to pay your dues."

"Snuff films. My lucky break."

"Killed in your own car. Sick, huh? It's not how I originally wrote it. But hey, you know, once you cash the check, you can't complain about the rewrites. Know what I mean?"

"Of course I'd be a bit biased. Where's Gwen?"

"She'll be fine as long as you hit your marks and die on cue."

"So what the hell are we doing out here in this dingy?"

"We still have to shoot the boats and helicopter stunts first and we need you alive for that. There are jetpacks and all kinds of crazy stuff. We're waiting for the sun. Actually, it's just a one shot deal. The speedboats are awesome wood Rivas, fast as all hell. Right off the canals of Venice. We need to blow up a few things out here. In a couple of days we go ashore to shoot the stunt car race scenes around LA. They've already taken killer footage of you hanging and getting your ass kicked. The dailies were very lifelike. You finally found the roll that's perfect. A punching bag with very little dialogue. Full of grunts and groans. I'm talking Oscar nomination here."

"I don't remember seeing a camera."

Roger pulled back a curtain. "They had it set up and rolling the whole time. I saw the footage. You took it good."

"So you duplicated my Corsa and rebuilt your Porsche so you could race them all over again on film?"

"Yes, the permits are all in place. I take it you saw the cars at the marina?"

"Bullet Hole Drive, I also saw the script in Jerry's office."

"Like the new title? Catchy, huh?"

"More than I'll like the ending I bet."

"Well, you see, Coop, the bad guy driving your Corsa crashes and loses this time. The good guy in my Porsche gets the girl and wins. The way it should've been all along."

"Come on. You're still holding childhood grudges about me and Gwen?"

Roger took another blast of vodka and coke up his left nostril with such violent force that it nearly put him on his ass. "I never knew what she saw in you. I still don't. If you hadn't moved in next door to Gwen she'd be mine. We'd have kids and a grand house, and life would be different for everyone. But no, you and your greaseball Corvair had to move in and ruin everything. I'm just getting even anyway. You tried to kill me. So screw you, I'm just killing you back."

"You didn't actually die, Roger. Remember?"

"My life died as I knew it when I hit that wall. My career went to shit because the big studios won't touch me. My face doesn't shoot the same. My bones are out of whack. And this nerve damage in my neck is driving me mad."

"Yeah, kissing a wall at ninety will do that to a pretty face."

"You think any of this is funny to me? Do you honestly think I'd do this many drugs if I weren't in so much goddamn pain"

"I'm sorry you feel wronged. But you did it to yourself."

"Bullshit! You goaded me onto that track."

"You should've said no."

"How could I? Daring me in front of Gwen and the other kids. You asshole, how could I have said no and saved face? I was in the middle of my first A-list film. I was somebody. Two more weeks and I would've been making the big money on my nest five films. You took that from me. You should've left my stupid ass in that car to burn. You made me a laughing stock in the papers. I still get hate mail from people who call me a loser for being a bad role model by screwing up my life."

"I saw those race pictures on your wall, Rog. You were losing and you tried to force your way past me against the wall."

"Bullshit! I had your ass. You pushed me into that wall."

"You really believe that, don't you. Look, I didn't understand what happened. I still don't. Suddenly you were up against me. I went to the yard to check your car. Someone beat the shit out of me for it. They left me bleeding in a dumpster on Melrose. Threatened to kill Gwen if I snooped around again."

"I heard you were trying to pin insurance fraud on Jack."

"I was just trying to figure out why you made such a stupid move when I out drove you and had you beat fair and square."

Roger's eyes filled with hate. He believed Cooper tried to kill him. He had to believe it. It was the only way to get right with everything in his head. "Admit it, Coop, you'd love to get me out in that street again. You and that stinking Corsa. Well, it was me that put that grease print on Irene's white carpet. I took your old boot and I set you up bad. Now I'll finally beat your Corsa – even if it's only in the movies. Wrote that part in myself. It was meant to be a big surprise."

"Nothing surprises me when it comes to you, Rog. Better get your laughs now. I'm not the only one who knows about your little problem."

"I'm not the one with the problem, Coop, you are."

"Gwen knows, Holland knows, Nick knows, Marty knows, you planning stunt movies for them, too?"

Roger paced the floor in front of Cooper. His mind raced trying to scan the possibilities. So what if they knew? What could they do? What could they prove? "They won't prove a thing. Your death will be on film. You think you're so clever messing with me? You don't know shit. What you do know is just enough to get you killed!"

Roger stopped to take another blast up his nose. His nose instantly gushed with blood. It had bled before so the amount of blood he was letting didn't seem to faze him. He just took out a stained hanky from his pocket and tilted his head back. It was part of his life. It was part of being a cokey. It was part of having no membrane left inside his nose. It was just his blood!

"Why don't you just stick a bazooka up there, Rog?"

Roger lowered his head and his eyes narrowed. He kept the hanky to his nose and talked through it. "Look, you stupid grease monkey, I'm still a name, so don't talk down to me."

Cooper thought a moment. Hanging way up there where he was it was hard not to talk down to Roger. Maybe if he waited long enough, Roger would bleed to death right there in front of him. It would save him the hassle of having to kick the living tar out of him when he found a way to get down from the wall.

"Excuse me, Mr. Superstar, I don't want to interrupt your menstrual cramp, but how long do you think they will let you live? No one's going to bank your film with you looking like Dr. Jekyll. They'll just take you out. Get you out of the way. You know it and I know it, so you got to know they are thinking it."

"They won't lay a hand on me, they're my friends."

"Two of your friends just signed with the big showbiz agency in the sky. Who's next."

"It's a long story."

"Bore me. It'll take my mind off how bad you look. Maybe."

"I'm not good at telling it."

"Then answer this. Who are Eddie and Tim Waller?"

This stopped Roger in the middle of a blast up his nose.

"Oh, didn't Gwen tell you? I took a little plane trip to your hometown. Someone burned up all of Eddie's and Tim's pictures but I got one of your foster parents, Ruth and Jerry. Supposedly Eddie and his big brother Tim burned in a white Jag. Stop me if the bells hurt your ears. By the way, which one of our friends has a fetish for white Jags?"

"You're turning into a real cankerous butt sore."

"Jack Rotenberg is Tim Waller, isn't he?"

Roger checked behind the curtain, giving him time to think.

Cooper pretended not to notice. He didn't want to be right about this. It would only hurt Gwen and change Irene's life beyond repair, which wouldn't be such a bad idea. But as much as he disliked Jack, as much as he thought Irene was a pain in the rump, he didn't want to hurt either of them. Nor change

Gwen's life forever because of Roger and his coke problem. Right now, all he wanted to do was get Gwen and himself the hell out of there, alive, and maybe kick some sense back into Roger in the process.

"None of this will do you any good." Roger stopped for just a moment. Telling Cooper everything wouldn't help. It couldn't hurt at this point. But there were a lot of things he couldn't tell Cooper. Bad things he couldn't tell anyone, not even Gwen. He looked inside the curtain again. Gwen's face was peaceful. It was amazing what a little chloroform could do to smooth a women's disposition. Killing Cooper was one thing, but dealing with Gwen and Irene because of it would be a horrible drawn out mess. True he was in love with her back then. And if it hadn't been for Cooper...but things were different now. They were good friends, buddies sure, but now...shit he messed things up. There was no real chance of her loving him back. He wasn't so far gone to believe that. He just needed money, wanted his life back. Why did she have to stick her nose into this mess? Why couldn't she just leave things the way they were, sense that he was pulling away because he wanted to? He had the matter all under control. He didn't need her goddamn help, and he sure didn't need Cooper sticking a wrench into his affairs. Shit, the cars would've been wrecked, all evidence destroyed. All that property and money would be his. Cooper wouldn't have known a thing until the night of the screening if those clowns had just picked up the engine. Goddamn Jerry and Ruth anyway for not going along. Then hiring those two incompetent idiots to grab up the Corsa. How could Jerry underestimate what someone mean and nasty like Cooper would do to them?

He looked back at Cooper. What a shame it all had to end like this."Two shitfaced fools stole Jack's Jag and drove it off a cliff during the trial. Or someone grabbed them both up and put them in it. I don't know for sure. There wasn't' enough of them left to tell anyone about it."

"How convenient. Good old Jerry and Ruth took the identity theft rap for pretending to be teachers. But they couldn't pin the couple's bodies in the pond on them."

"Because it was an accident."

"Yeah, but now, Jack and his brother paid them back with The Old Hollywood Memo to their foreheads. Or did you?"

"Talk all you want. It doesn't make a bit of difference right now. They're dead, you soon will be, and I'm rich again with a film in preproduction. Isn't life just wonderful?" Roger laughed, choked and snorted more coke simultaneously. His nose bled.

"That's pretty cool, Rog. You learn that in improv class?"

"Shut up. I scraped the streets of this town like a cockroach while Jerry and Ruth were in jail. How do you think I felt? I was just a dumb kid and they were the only family I knew. I didn't understand any of the reasons or the seriousness of what was happening to me. All I knew is that my good life, my great private education, had ended with them. They took it all away. Everything I had. My bike, my clothes, my toys. The next foster home they put me in didn't' work out as well. So I took off and came here and lived off the streets and what little money I had saved in roles of nickels."

"Yeah, I'm gettin' the sniffles just listening to you. So what did you do, work the streets? "

Roger punched Cooper in the stomach and backed off seething. Cooper let out a grown. That wasn't quite the reaction he had anticipated from Roger but at least they were getting somewhere. Apparently those days on the streets weren't as innocent as they might have seemed. At least not to Roger.

"You calling me a queer?"

"That's between you and your analyst."

"It's not what you think. You prick."

"I could care less, but I doubt it."

"You don't fool me, Cooper. Playing Mr. Hard Guy, like you grew up in the alleys of North Hollywood. Shit, you graduated from Bel Air with honors and could've gone to engineering school if you wanted. The big joke, you didn't even buy that stupid car yourself. Your rich daddy gave it to you for your sweet sixteenth birthday. I bought mine, you punk. You're nothing but a rich daddy's boy pretending to be cool shit. Well, you're not. You may fool Gwen with your tight jeans, dirty t-shirts and all that gunk in your hair. But I know who you really are. You're a poseur. You're really just a lucky upper middle class hood wannabe. Slumming with grease monkeys because they make you feel superior. You don't know what it's like to be on the streets. And you never will. Well I do. I lived it. I'm from those streets. I survived them. I dragged myself out of the gutters of this town and made something of myself. Something that you'll never be. I'm somebody. You hear me, I'm somebody. I'm Roger Kelemen. And I'm tired of you thinking you're better than me because you've got Gwen."

Roger paced again, trying to calm down. It was useless anger. He knew Cooper didn't give a crap. Hanging there all beat up because of him. He checked behind the curtain. He reached over and ran his hand along Gwen's leg. She was so beautiful lying there. He looked back at Cooper. The boys had really done a number on him. Well, good. "Shit. You thirsty or hungry or anything?"

"I'll take a swig of your beer."

"Sure, man, here finish it. I'm sorry."

Roger held the Miller up to Cooper's mouth. Cooper took a good strong pull before bringing his legs up and scissor locking them around Roger's throat and extended arm. The half filled beer can dropped down on Roger's head, then fell with a clatter to the fake stone floor. Roger choked and more blood gushed from his nose.

"What the hell are you doing, man?"

"What does it feel like?"

"You're choking me."

"That's right, Rog. Unless you do exactly as I tell you, I'll squirt your eyes across the hull of this ship."

"Let go of me by the count of three, or I swear I'll bite you." Cooper didn't let up. What's a little bite amongst friends. The two men stared into each other's eyes. Cooper's blackened and bleeding, Roger's bloodshot and bulging.

"One." Cooper increases the pressure on Roger's throat. "Two." Again Cooper increases the pressure. This time Roger could barely make a sound. "Tthhrree." Cooper slightly tightened his grip on Roger, knowing that with all the blood blocking his breathing passages as it was, he could cancel Roger's subscription to Life Magazine accidently.

Roger's eyes bulged out further and he slowly began to lose consciousness. Funny, Roger had that same look on his face at the ball field when Cooper cold-cocked him for shooting his mouth off about Gwen in front of a bunch of guys. Roger and Gwen had attended a showbiz event together just days before Portland moved in next door. Roger wanted the guys to think that Gwen still belonged to the Hollywood hotshot and not to a North Hollywood greaser. So he alluded to the general public that he'd had his way with Gwen. Just blatant enough for the passing greaser to overhear the snickers. Frats being frats, and greasers being what they were at the time, Cooper felt impelled to make Roger take it back. Roger stood firm on his story, so Cooper clobbered him. Funny as it seemed, Roger just stood there like he was standing now, with his eyes rolled back and bulging and his nose bleeding all over the place. It just went to show that smart mouth punks never grow up. They just got older. Cooper eased off. Roger sluggishly tumbled back to earth.

"Say Uncle."

"Uncle, my ass, you son-of-a...."

Cooper increased the pressure, choking off Roger's words.

"Say, Roger has a drug problem."

Roger wouldn't say anything if his life depended on it. Of course it did. It had nothing to do with admitting he had a drug problem. Roger had no problem with admitting that. It was just that Cooper was trying to make him say it. "Eat me."

Cooper increased the pressure. "Say it."

Roger choked again.

"Say it!"

Stars twinkled before Roger's eyes. They shot around in the impending blackness like miniature fireflies as the blood vessels inside his eyes swelled to block his vision. Cooper would kill him this time. This wasn't a schoolyard, teenage, bullshit brawl - this was life and death. Cooper's or Roger's, and this jerk wasn't about to ease up on him. Shit. "Rooggeerr haassa druuuga proobleem." The words squeezed out like Heinz Ketchup.

"Say it again and mean it. Say it!" Cooper eased off a little.

"Roger has a drug problem."

"Okay, now I'll rest on your shoulders and take the weight off my arms. What I want from you is some answers." He put pressure on Roger again. "Is that clear?"

"Yeah, yeah, yeah, for Christ's sake, get the hell off me."

Cooper left his legs on Roger's shoulders."Whose ship?"

"Jack's brother owns it. He calls himself Sam De'Ogo."

"Now we're getting somewhere. So Jack's brother Tim now calls himself Sam De'Ogo?"

"Don't mess with him, he's a killer."

"Aren't we all. So he's into the movie biz now?"

"Real estate, antique cars, boats...any kind of biz that makes him happy, and lots of money."

"And you blackmailed them all. That's stickin' it in pretty deep, Rog. Why hasn't he killed you?"

"As long as Roger's happy, Roger's tape stays hidden."

"So this key is hiding a tape. How tactful of you. Only you don't have the key, I do."

"The key won't do you any good."

"So far it's kept me alive."

"Look, Coop, without that key it's impossible to get to the tape and it'll only stay where it's at. You're dead meat anyway. Why not hand it over so Gwen doesn't have to die first?"

"You wouldn't kill, Gwen."

"Of course not. Unfortunately, Sam would."

"Now, how did you maggot your way back into all this?"

"Okay, I ran across Jerry in a crowded elevator."

"And Daffy is hung like a buffalo."

"Honest, I was delivering sandwiches to offices out of a cooler. But after I realized who it was, I couldn't let him see me that way. I didn't expect him to be out of prison. He never sent me a post card, letter, or anything. As far as he knew I was living with another family. So, I followed Jerry around town for over a week. Learned that he was an agent and what his new name was. That's when I realized I had to make a move if I wanted to be an actor. He pushed me into plays when I was a kid. So it made sense. Then one afternoon, I followed both he and Ruth up to Jack's place. Wasn't easy, I didn't even have my driver's permit. I was just thirteen in a stolen car. Remember I thought Eddie and Tim were dead. But both Jack and Sam were there. About an hour later Elliott and Frank pulled up in a van full of movie equipment. Then Sophie showed. You should've seen her back then. She had her little girl with her. Five or six."

"So you just hung around."

"Listen, I couldn't very well waltz up and say hiya, guys, remember me? The kid who helped ruin our lives? The kid who knows who you really are. I had to have something on them. It wasn't enough just knowing who they really were. Even if Elliott, Sophie, and Frank didn't. I thought Sam would just kill me. He would have. So, I read up on bugging devices, stole everything I needed, and snuck up to the house and wired it. I made four different crude audio tapes of them shooting Sophie's little girl. Nothing funny like I thought it would be. They were legit, just working with her trying to get her to remember some stupid sitcom lines. You've seen Sophie, well, you should've seen her daughter. An angel, but she was a little touched."

"How so?"

"I don't know...just touched. Sophie and her husband back then were having a bad go of it. He wanted to go back home and took off. I guess Sophie needed help raising the kid by herself so she got her into acting through Jerry and Ruth. They set her up to read for a pilot that Jack was pushing. They had her doing simple stuff. Walking, sitting...but no one laid a finger on the kid. I swear. She could've been a big hit. Lit up the room when she smiled."

"Jerry and Ruth found the kids through their agency?"

"Yes, it was an easy transition with both their teaching backgrounds. Sam bought the agency. Jack executive produced, Elliott wrote, Frank directed and shot. Sam is the silent money guy. He keeps a very low profile. It was harmless easy money stuff. It didn't matter if the series took off or not. They made money. If it did, they made more. But don't kid yourself, it's Sam's productions. He's got a lot of people I don't know working for him now."

"I don't understand why Frank and Elliott are involved in all this charades. Why would they?"

"You don't walk out on Sam. They don't know that Jerry and Ruth did time. No one knows about Jack or Sam's disappearing act. They've made a lot of money working with Sam."

"So where's the girl?"

"She's living with her father. He came back and took off with her when he found out she wasn't happy."

"That's it?"

Roger nodded yes.

Cooper increased the pressure. Maybe Roger was telling the truth, but most likely he wasn't. Maybe Sophie never tried to find the child because she sucked as a mother and was afraid of the father. For the kid's sake, he hoped it was true. But he had a feeling it wasn't. He gave Roger a good strangling jolt.

"I will personally cut your balls off, you prick."

"Maybe I'll end that lame threat now." He squeezed again.

"All right, all right. It's all true. Sophie never reported her girl missing. She never heard from the kid again. Elliott eventually married her. The next day I approached Jerry. He was glad to see me at first. Until I told him about the tapes. He beat the shit out of me right there in his office. Jack came over and he beat me some more. Sam came and made them stop. When he heard all I wanted was to act... to be their star... make them money, he made them see it my way. They were making it happen for other kids, why not me? Sam made them say yes. Jerry and Ruth signed me. You know the rest. We made a lot of money together shooting cheesy stuff. If I hadn't of done that stupid race. None of this would be happening."

"But you never destroyed the tapes?"

"Sure I did. Years later after I dubbed one cassette copy."

"Together they made you a star thinking they got off easy. Frank and Elliot just kept working."

"But even stars run out of money."

"Had a job ain't got no clothes...spend my money all up my nose. Isn't that how it went, Rog?"

"Shit, Portland, it wasn't just drugs. You know me, I pissed it all away. But this time, I'm getting clean. I'm walking out with everything. Thirty million dollars of their real estate, two million cash and a chance to direct and star in my own script."

"All that for a little tape of who they really are?"

"And you."

"Me?"

"Killing you is the sobering part of the deal. Payback to shut me up. Make sure I don't come back looking for more."

"And a deal's a deal."

"Right. That's why it's got to be in that car. So it's a car stunt accident caught on film."

"So, who tossed me off the pier?"

"That was two of De'Ogo's men. They brought me here. Hell, Jerry would've had me killed if Sam hadn't stepped in. But who do you think came up with the snuff stunt car idea?"

"My good buddy, Roger Kelemen."

"It made them say yes to me directing."

"I or Gwen show up dead, you'll go down, Roger."

"No I won't. They won't be able to pin it on me. Stuntmen die in the movies all the time. And for the record, I had nothing to do with them torching your Corsa. I want you to know that. No matter how much of a dick I think you are. Or a prick you think I am. I wouldn't do that to you or your car. Honest. You pissed those two clowns off all by yourself, not me. It wasn't supposed to be like this. Building your Corsa for my movie was only supposed to be a joke. That's why I didn't tell anyone, not even Gwen. If I had planned any of this, I would've just used your car. I was gonna cast someone to play you. I just wanted to see your face at the premier. Honest, Coop, a joke. They wouldn't touch the script as a boat race, so I got the idea to change it to cars. I put a lot of my own money into getting those stunt cars ready to do a trailer to raise funds. I tried to do it on my own. But I couldn't get further funding. Not even overseas in upfront distribution. Nobody would touch me. I bet Sam and Jack made sure of that. When people in the industry heard I wanted to destroy cars in my film, they laughed at me. Laughed in my face, because of what crashing my 911 did to my career. Not even Jack and the others would help me direct my film. After all the money I've made those bastards, they wouldn't take me serious as a director of my passion project. You know how much that hurt inside? How much that disappointed me that after all this time and money none of them believed in me enough to help with my dream? They are my extended family. But they don't really know me, or even love me. So yes, I'm blackmailing them all again. If for nothing else, to teach them to respect and fear me. Respect what I've done for them. Fear that they bought those properties doing Roger Kelemen projects, and that I can take them away. So screw them all."

"You cut them out by writing and directing. There is no deal to take a piece of if you are also the production company."

"So what? It's just one film."

"So you're stuck killing me, and probably Gwen to get it made. Congratulations, you've finally made it in Hollywood. You're officially a backstabbing dickwad like them."

"Ah shit, I can't go through with this. Let me get the key to those chains. But you're on your own in getting off this ship."

Cooper let up on his grip. Roger slid his arm free. He quickly pulled Cooper's Colt Python Mk V out of his coat and stuck it in Cooper's backside.

What comes around goes around, Cooper thought.

"Now drop the legs and start talking."

Cooper lowered his legs and put his feet back on the pegs.

"You're a real demented person, Rog. You know, despite our many differences of opinions on cars, you hating me, and me stealing your girl, we're supposed to be friends."

"You're just like them. You never really liked me."

"Gwen did, that was good enough. Come on, let me down."

"I can't... you never should've stuck your nose into this one. I've got to deliver or they'll kill me. Now where's the key?"

"Like I told you. It's still in the car."

Roger pulled open the canvas wall revealing the other parts of the castle's torture chamber set. He picked up a cattle prod and stepped over to where Gwen was strapped to the rack. He yanked on the crank and Gwen's eyes popped open and she let out a scream into her gag. Roger stepped back toward Cooper menacing the cattle prod.

"Looks like fun, huh, Coop? We searched the car. You want to sing now...or do I need to pluck a few more nerves?

Cooper swung out with his right work boot as Roger turned back toward him and caught Roger square on the jaw with the steel toe. Cooper could hear Roger's vertebras adjust from the neck cracking blow as Roger's head pivoted on his shoulders. Blood splattered on the false set walls from his nose and mouth. Roger flopped over Gwen's belly like a dried sack of cumquats.

The gun hit the false deck with a clatter. He was still breathing but not moving.

Gwen rubbed her face on Roger to get the gag off. She strained to see Roger's face. She couldn't. She couldn't see Portland either, and her head felt like it was stuffed full of cotton candy.

"Roger? Oh no, he's passed out. Rog? What happened?"

"I just kicked him in the head."

"What for?"

"Because I couldn't reach you."

"This isn't my fault."

"No? Guess what, I'm hanging in the hull of a ship. While you slept, three gentlemen took turns beating the crap out of me on film. I'm sure I look pretty because I'm feeling awful special. But don't worry, all this pain won't last long because our pal Roger has plans to kill me in a demolition snuff film."

"Oh, I suppose you think a rack is fun."

Cooper changed his tactics. "Oh, Gwen, darling."

"Yes, dear."

"I know who tore up my Corsa, who four-ironed my skull and recovered your man-child superstar. Can I go home now?"

Gwen ignored him. She worked her hand loose from the fake shackles. The effort badly scraping the skin off the back of her thumb in the process. "Ouch! I'm bleeding...and...." She picked up a rag and smelled it. "Chloroform. I've been put to sleep!" She slapped Roger on the back of the head. "Get off me, Roger."

"You through?"

"Yes!"

"Why so angry?"

"Shut up!" She began to go through Roger's crumpled coat looking for the keys. "Boy, he smells."

"Next time I'm leaving you at home."

"Please do, nothing, damn."

"The keys are to your left on the floor."

Gwen twisted her body to see. There was no way she could reach them with her right hand shackled. "Oh, shit." She bit her lip as she pulled her other hand free. It too, bled. And hurt. She hit Roger again and pushed him off her to the floor.

"They just don't make racks like they used to."

"Keep it up and I'll leave you up there. How long have they had me breathing this crap?"

"They came in every so often. So hurry up, they're due back."

"Jesus, I've got a headache."

"Yeah, I'm not in the mood either."

"Will you shut up."She brought her hand up to check her throat."Someone took my pearls."

"Get me down from here, and I'll buy you new ones."

Still shackled by the feet, Gwen leaned her slender body off the rack and managed to scoop up the keys and free her feet. She moved over and slid a chair under Cooper. "Those were from my grandmother."Gwen undid Portland's hands. He crumpled to the floor as she sat in the chair and cried into her hands. Cooper fought back up to his knees and held Gwen. He looked at her wrist. They were both bloody. He kissed them. Someone would pay for this. That someone was a man called Sam De'Ogo.

"It hurts, huh?"

Gwen looked up from her hands. "What?"

"Your wrists?"

"The hell with my wrists. I want my pearls."

"Did Roger ever mention a secret between him and Finn?"

Gwen thought it over."Not that I recall."

"Well, Finn did to me once, in a drunken stupor. Something he welded for Rog. Said it was deviously clever."

If Finn held the answer to the tape Roger was hiding, then Finn was in danger. He leaned over and checked Roger's watch. Finn was on his boat at the Marina. Roger's Corsa was not far away. Somehow he'd have to pay Finn a visit. But first things first. He and Gwen had to get off Sam De'Ogo's ship.

9 DYING STUNTS YOUR GROWTH

Cooper discreetly undogged and opened the door to find himself in a small enclosed passageway. Only it wasn't as empty as he would've liked. Three young punks were supposedly guarding the hatch and his only way out. He recognized them immediately as the three studs that eagerly took turns pounding him in his hidden screen-test. The two black ones, Ben and Taylor, stood with their backs to Cooper. They both tapped their toes, craning their necks to check out the scantily clad babes that pranced about the bow in drunken stupors. Ben was stocky, built like a linebacker who didn't make the cut. He kept grabbing at himself and muttering something about white chicks to Taylor under the volume of the music. Taylor had his stiff hair cut in a high flat top with over two inches shaved completely off above the ears. He just shook his head and laughed at his rude friend. His skin was dark as ink and seemed unreal against the setting sun. A black hole against the sky. Cooper could still see his big open hands eclipse the light as he backhanded his face. He stood about six-two and weighed all of one hundred and seventy pounds. From his accent and jungle camouflage Cooper placed Taylor from one of the Caribbean Islands.

The smallest of the three was a bright white, sandy haired kid, barely out of puberty, named Cherry. Sweet Cherry, as his two pals referred to him, fancied himself as a real mean killer. He took extra long turns at punching Cooper's ribs and face with black leather fingerless gloves. They had extra thick and coarse canvass sawn over the knuckles. So that when they struck Cooper's skin, each blow felt like sand paper. He sat just inside the darkened passageway on an apple box behind his two dancing pals. He stuffed grub into a greasy face that was painfully covered with inflamed acne. His gun was stuck down in the back of his faded 501s. His sleeveless blue jean jacket had a big Harley patch stitched on the back. Underneath he wore only a black T-shirt. Goosebumps lined the skin under his white arm hairs from the advancing cool night air.

Cooper eased out the door shielded by the beat of the music. Every muscle in his body was screaming prison-rape. He'd had blood in his urine when he relieved himself in the corner of the ship. He didn't mention it to Gwen. He had shredded a costume jacket to make bandages for Gwen's wrist and found a tube of Super Glue and a roll of Scotch Tape on and art director's cart. He used them to hold together the gaping cuts above his left eye, cheek and lip. He had used the silk lining of the same costume sleeve to stop the bleeding that came from the missing three tooth bridge. He swallowed it after Taylor had knocked it loose. No sense losing it.

He hadn't felt this bad since being the only one of three men to survive a crash in a helicopter on a test run off the coast of Corpus Christi. The turbine engine seized and it dropped out of the sky like a dead bird. They found him floating with the other two men tied to seat cushions. He'd gotten a medal and an early ticket back home for diving down to the wreckage to retrieve his two friends. He recalled those eight hours floating as he slid his hand around Cherry's face. He timed the grab so that the punk had his mouth full. As painfully as possible he dragged him inside, walking backwards, and using Cherry's own gun as incentive. Cooper pined Cherry in a corner out of sight. He held his hand over his mouth and Cherry's gun to his head. He made sure Cherry remembered who he was before he put his lights out with the same rag they held over Gwen's mouth. He added a punch to Cherry's face just to relieve tension. The fast motion shot pain through his ribs but it was worth it. Gwen helped him drag Cherry over to the rack where they had Roger gagged and stretched out. Gwen went through Cherry's pockets and found her pearl necklace. Cooper let Cherry drop hard to the false deck and kicked him. Roger screamed into his gag. So Gwen held the rag over his face and he was out before she counted to ten backwards.

Cooper went back out to the archway and snuck up behind the two brothers and stuck a gun in both of their backs. Ben and Taylor stopped scratching and stiffened.

"Walk backwards."

They stepped backwards into the hull of the boat. Cooper made them throw their guns over to the bulkhead of the passageway before he stepped through the door leading down into the hull. Gwen came over with the rag freshly dampened and held it to Ben's mouth while Cooper held guns to both their heads. Ben dropped to the floor, doing a nice free style flop. Gwen stepped over him to Taylor and held the rag over his mouth and Cooper added a smack of the gun handle to the side of his head as he dropped. Gwen poured the remainder of the intoxicating fluid over the two bodies and followed Cooper up and out of the hull. They secured and dogged the door behind them. Cooper picked up the two guns left by Ben and Taylor and gave one to Gwen. She looked at it and decided she wanted the other because it matched her shoes.

Cooper tucked two guns into his pants leaving his Colt Python in his right hand. He led Gwen out the hatch onto the portside deck. He made sure no one had taken notice of the missing three men and snuck aft along portside away from the movie crew and dancers milling around the bow.

The spit and polished ship barely resembled the old Polish steamer that had been refitted. Instead of its original gray, black, and white, the coal and ore freighter shown with a light blue and was faintly trimmed in Pepto-Bismol pink, with black accents. As crazy as the color combo sounded, with the portholes cut into large bay windows, it was quite pleasing to the eye. Especially since the ship's natural lines themselves were very stark and boxy, like a floating Miami apartment building.

Nearing the stern, Portland stopped at the sound of a twelve gauge shotgun blast. He couldn't help looking down at his body to make sure he wasn't the target.

He snuck over to a stack of ark lights. Looking through the pile to see an eccentric, bearded, troll-like man wielding the twelve gauge pump. While two Mexicans released live doves from a cage. Each dove fled for its life out over the water before getting blasted to tiny bits, having their remains fall onto the twenty coats of varnished mahogany Riva speedboats. It was then, Cooper realized that they weren't moving.

"Pull!" De'Ogo demanded, letting out a wild, drunken laugh before he steadied the gun.

A tall young man handed an older man a dove and the balding Mexican let it go as he crossed himself. The two men closed their eyes. The dove exploded at the sound of the shotgun.

"Damn birds," he swigged from a half-filled Jack Daniels bottle."They keep flying over the boats. I need a real living fight back challenge."De'Ogo looked at the two Mexicans."How about, it, Paco, you want to play?"

Paco shook his balding head and backed away.

"Zev? I'll mail your yaya a million pesos."

The younger Mexican shook his head.

"Cobardes hediondos. You'd sell your sister for a ten spot. But won't put your ass on the line for some real money. You're lucky you two can drive a car in this film. Or I'd shoot you both right now for the sake of smelling your blood. Pull. I said, pull."

Zev and Paco let loose another dove.

Cooper came back to Gwen. She was listening at the cabin hatch to voices inside. He peered into a hatch porthole.

A robust, elderly man, the director of cinematography, with pepper graying hair used a storyboard to explain a stunt shot to two stunt coordinators. Slim shot a lot of De'Ogo's action films and knew Sam moved on without shooting the same stunt twice. He preferred to shoot a bunch of different versions and used the one that worked best. With dubbing them in so many languages, it really didn't matter if the action made perfect sense as long as there were enough explosions and dead bodies to market the film overseas to distributors who kept pouring money into this shit. They were up to eight of these a year now. This one was different though. It actually made some sense. There were some cool cars, boats, and helicopter stunts. He didn't like the idea that a coked out actor was supposedly directing and starring in this one. But he'd worked with Kelemen a few times. He'd seen him work high before. The guy always seemed to pull it together. Had his lines down. Knew how to hit his marks. Moved on action and said his lines when cued. He was great at one takes. Plus his script was good. The pay was great. Living at sea, he could hide most of it. De'Ogo was just crazy enough to throw anyone overboard if they put up a fuss. It wouldn't be the first time a death or two were really dead obscure stuntmen that no one would miss. Yes, De'Ogo was a twisted bastard and the work often got dangerous. Just the way Slim liked it.

The bigger of the two coordinators was as big as Cooper and wearing a white jumpsuit with a gold star on its back. He held a helmet with a tinted shade and plucked at the chinstrap as he listened to the Slim explain what he wanted. A jetpack sat on a desk.

"Remember, I need you to come out of the sun. It should be perfect in about twenty-five minutes." Slim looked up to find the stunt man picking his nose.

"You listening to me, Harry."

"Yeah, just tell me how you want the approach?"

Cooper eased back the hatch dog.

"Come down across the stern. Blast the three men guarding the hatch. Go in, kill the man attacking the girl. Take her up to the top deck where you encounter three other men, who you waste. Remember, you're doubling for Kelemen. We can't see your face through the shade but there's reflection. Don't look directly at the camera. Just move deliberately and keep yourself three-quarters toward the camera as much as you can. Pause on your mark, give me ten seconds while we hit you with a second camera zoom. Then move on. Hear that music, that's what will be playing over this scene. Move to it. Don't rush. We'll get one shot at these boats. Our permit covers just the stunt and three explosions. I don't want to have to cut the shit out of this footage and won't get to bring in a second copter or re-permit. Something's going down with that guy in the hull. So De'Ogo's got us on a tight schedule. By now, you're here. The girl then hangs onto your waist and you go back toward the sun. Listen closely to me, both of you. Drop down into the portside speedboat."

"That's the boat on the left?" Harry asked.

He nodded. "They are both wired in sequence to blow. You don't want to be in the first boat to blow."

"Those are expensive boats. How'd we get them?"

"We got them. And we're blowing the shit out of them is all you need to know."

"Seems simple enough, Slim. Help me with this, Bill."

"Wait a minute. Go over this second part again," Bill said.

"Harry jets to the Huey as the second boat charges. Sweet Cherry is in it. You take it out over the dumping area, point it at the sun and you both bail," Slim said.

"Where's the other speed boat?"

"It crosses the other boat in flames as it blows over here. Remember, we need you to swim under water for over thirty seconds, while Harry swims to Cherry there won't be divers. Harry, don't forget to pull the float on the pack. We well have divers in the water to pick you up only after we blow the second boat. Don't worry, guys, we'll match everything. I'll blue screen anything that doesn't work."

"What about Cherry?"

"What about him?"

"Why isn't he in here?"

"Leave that up to Sam."

"Yeah?"Harry looked over his shoulder at Bill. They both knew if Cherry was meant to get out of that second speedboat alive he'd be there talking to them about it right now."

"We detonate everything in that order so land in the correct boat. You piss Sam off who knows what he'll do. "

"We'll be awful close. Why doesn't he just do this one in the studio?" Bill asked.

"You know Sam likes reality. And we like a job."

"Guys a reality whack job if you ask me."

"No one's asking you, Bill. So keep your mouth shut. His money's good. Always has been," Slim said.

"You have to be a little nuts to be in this business," Harry said, as he went for the jetpack.

Cooper entered with his gun drawn. Gwen was behind him, her gun pointing at Slim.

"Do you mind, young man?"Slim examined the demeanor of the ragged intruder and the stunning woman behind him."We are about to shoot?"

"So are we."

"Shit man, who did your makeup? That's awesome."

"Shut up, Bill," Harry said, realizing Cooper wasn't acting.

Bill took a good look at Cooper's gun as the reality of it sank in. "Holy shit, you're that...."

"Step away from the pack, both of you."

"Wait a minute, pal, that's expensive equipment," Slim said.

"If you're nice, you'll get it back."Cooper looked the room over."Step into the head. Let's go, all three of you."

The three men backed into the small cubicle.

"Take off the suit."

Harry hesitated, looking at Gwen trying to find a connection of help. She gave him nothing. Cooper pulled back the Python's hammer. Harry unzipped the suit and stepped out of it, standing there butt naked. Cooper tied the door shut with a bungee cord. He dropped what was left of his own tattered clothing and put on the jump suit. Gwen helped him on with the jetpack. He put on the helmet and lowered the tinted shade.

"Like it?"

"It's you. But where's the leaf blower hose?"

Cooper stuffed the pair of guns into the suit belt. "You've had too much chloroform." Portland pulled down a long heavy hemp rope and stepped out of the cabin with it. He tied one end of the rope to the railing and tossed the rest over the side. He turned to Gwen. "Meet me at the bottom."

Gwen looked over the railing seeing the rope trailing away into the sea. "What? I haven't had that much chloroform."

Cooper turned away with a grin. "Be there."

He headed back toward the stern of the ship as he started the jetpack. His feet left the deck. He had to get one of these. What a way to beat LA rush hour traffic. Not that he ever came across much on his way down stairs to his Corsa work shop.

10 Kamikaze Jetpacker

De'Ogo turned his head toward the sound of the jetpack. He handed the empty shotgun to Zev. "See what's going on."

Zev and Paco came round the corner and got Cooper's boots square in their faces knocking them both on their butts. Cooper swung out over the water into the setting sun. The kamikaze jetpacker. The two men hit the deck overplaying the moment and got up laughing it off.

"You monkey's ass, Harry!" Zev yelled.

Sam squinted into the sun. What was Harry...? "What the hell! That's not Harry. Shoot him down!"

"What?" Zev asked. "Sure it's Harry."

Just then Harry, Bill, and Slim exited the cabin at a run. They didn't see the knot on the rail straining from Gwen's swinging weight.

"Give me the gun," Sam said. Finally, he'd get his live hunt.

"Don't shoot him down in the water. We'll lose the jetpack," Slim yelled racing along portside.

Cooper opened fire on the ship giving himself cover as he headed out over the water toward the speedboats.

The men on the deck scattered. De'Ogo weaved through the bullets and picked up his twelve gauge pump, tossing it aside when he realized it was empty.

Cooper swung over the portside Riva speedboat. Paco and Zev opened fire at him from where they hid.

De'Ogo crawled along the deck to a gun rack and took out his beloved fully automatic M3 carbine and a full 30 round 30

Carbine cartridge magazine. He loved his M3 because it was just like his M2 but with an active infrared scope system. One of about 3,000 produced. He traded his M2 for the M3 with a dead man who wouldn't sell it to him while researching the inhabitants of a small group of remote Islands in Malaysia. He later ate the crocodile that ate the dead man's body. He used the horrid footage in his first well crafted film, of two men from opposing armies lost on a remote island during World War II. The first of many unknown men to have died in his action films.

He got a kick of showing his little brother the film after Jack had married into the family that owned most of the island. The father of Irene's late husband had proven to be very allusive. Of course he denied having anything to do with the death of Irene's late husband who was shot in the back on a Miami, Florida beach during a press junket of one of The Little Island Princess Books. One of those unsolved mysteries he would answer Jack. The fact that he had arranged for Jack and Irene to meet shortly afterwards was purely coincidental. Almost as much as that Sam now planned to kill Portland Cooper, Irene's daughter's boyfriend, with the same scoped rifle. Sam chuckled at the irony of his secret as he got back onto his knees. Jack didn't need to know everything. Even if Jack suspected what Sam had done to create a life for him once again.

Cooper blasted the towrope, ripping it apart, as he shut off the backpack and dropped with a jarring thud into the left speedboat. The speedboat drifted free from the ship. He reached under the control panel for the ignition wire and almost got the ignition key in the eye. How considerate of De'Ogo to leave the key. The inboard engine roared to life. Cooper jammed the speedboat into action as a .30 caliber bullet ripped through the glass windshield. He headed directly for the shadows of the ship out of sight of the men above.

As Cooper sped toward Gwen, she kept her mind focused on how Portland taught her to swing from massive mangroves trees into the East Malaysian River to chase after small crocodiles while they visited her grandfather. Well, Portland had chased them. Gwen got the hell out of the water as soon as possible. But this was different. A hell of a lot different. Was Portland completely crazy? Swinging out and hitting a moving speedboat while being fired upon by angry men with fully automatic rifles? The man was a screaming lunatic.

"Aaaaaahhhhhhh!" is all she could think of yelling as she pushed away from the hull of the ship. She swung out over the water. Her heart was in her throat. On the way back toward the ship, she dropped with her eyes closed right onto the Riva's mahogany deck. She tumbled crotch first, over the shattered windshield and into Cooper's head. Knocking them both for a loop to the floor boards as he caught her. At the bow of the ship, Cooper reached up with one hand and managed to turn the speedboat east toward Catalina Island.

As the speedboat got back in range Zev and the others wasted their small caliber shots. De'Ogo stopped his men from firing hand guns. They couldn't hit their own mothers from inside her womb with them. He rested his arm on the ship's railing and took aim at the fleeing speedboat, using the M3's infrared scope system in the fading light. He did his best to steady the gun under the rush of the hunt. His heart pounded. Human prey once again. Ah, buck fever. Perhaps if he didn't kill him right away he could prolong the enjoyment of the hunt by wounding him once or twice first. Or perhaps he'd aim at the explosives. Just shooting Mr. Cooper, even wounding him badly on purpose, seemed too easy from this distance. Even if he probably killed Roger to get out of that hull. The thought of Roger Kelemen actually dead saddened him. Stopped him for a moment. Little Nickel-Boy Roger dead after all they'd been through. All the pain, the sorrow, and the finding each other again. All the films and TV they'd done together. Roger dead? It actually angered him to think it might be so. Roger, despite his drug habit and shortcomings as blackmailing troublemaker was family. He had hoped to look after him now that Jerry and Ruth where no longer able to be his parents. Was he dead? There was no reason to shoot this film if he was.

"Someone see if Roger is dead down below."

Gwen crawled along the Riva's deck trying to reach the bow when De'Ogo's second round pierced the side of the boat inches from her face. Gwen looked toward the hole in the boat and could see the pink and blue ship through it. She screamed at the top of her lungs when she saw what was bolted just below the hole. Cooper turned to see Gwen backing off while pointing to enough plastic explosives, bolted tightly, to turn the boat into tooth picks and them into miscellaneous body parts. Another bullet pierced the side of the speedboat just two inches south of the explosives. At least De'Ogo was a sport. Cooper reeled the boat around and reached down to pull the detonator wires.

Gwen tried to remove the explosives but they wouldn't budge. The speedboat now headed back out to sea about two hundred yards from the ship. Cooper kept zigzagging the speedboat, trying not to give De'Ogo a clean shot as he headed directly into the setting sun. But every time he tried to cut toward the Island, De'Ogo sent a round ripping through the side of the boat.

Again De'Ogo didn't aim to hit Gwen or Cooper. He was having way too much fun. Live prey at last. Not just dumb birds, but humans in a boat full of high explosives. So one was his step niece. Who could blame him for having a little fun with his prey? Even a cat would play with the mouse before he killed it, ate it and spit out its bones. So he played. He sent bullet after bullet screaming through the hull of the Riva, boxing Cooper away from the Island.

By this time, they had revived Roger strapped to the rack and he had come up on deck with Cherry, Ben, and Taylor. His coat's right sleeve was covered with blood. They helped Paco and Zev pull the other speedboat in. Roger, Paco, and Zev armed themselves with high-powered rifles and climbed down into the speedboat, ready to set out after Cooper.

De'Ogo had smiled at Roger, despite being angry with him for letting Mr. Cooper loose from the hull. This changed things though, knowing Roger was alive and the movie was still a go.

Mr. Cooper wasn't just prey any longer, he was once again his way of keeping Roger under his thumb. Force Roger to become a killer just like himself. To prove on film that he was if need be. Mr. Cooper's death was De'Ogo's and Jack's way out from under Roger's tape and the past they shared. "I want him alive!" Sam yelled to them. "He dies as planned in the car on film. Do you understand me, Roger? Don't screw up this film. Or it will be the last one you'll ever direct."

Roger looked back at Sam. Blood was crusted on the side of his face. He moved his sore jaw back and forth. He had no plans of leaving Cooper alive to get back to the mainland and that key. He'd, kill him for sure. He no longer gave a shit about directing his stupid film. Accidents do happened!

"I mean it, Roger."

"So do I."

Cooper tried again to head toward Catalina Island but each time De'Ogo's bullets ripped dangerously through the speedboat. So Cooper was forced to head back out to sea.

Roger swung around toward the island, cutting Cooper off. The rest of the movie crew crowded portside, watching and cheering. They were a mix-matched collection of drifters and grifters that De'Ogo had pieced together from around the world.

Unless they were stupid like, Bill, they weren't about to question anything Sam did. The few who had, naturally were no longer with them. Somehow they always tended to stray away from the production into the night. Sometimes sudden departures were accompanied by unexplainable screams of terror. It was true what countless dead people had said about Sam De'Ogo. He was a demented killer whom no one double crossed. He had a sick liking for twisted people. Especially one, that was very twisted these days...the American actor, the one with the coke problem, the boy he created, Roger Kelemen.

The Huey took off from the ship's launching pad with Bill as its pilot. Ben, the stocky linebacker who kept grabbin himself and Sweet Cherry hung on for dear life as they lifted over the ship and headed after Portland and Gwen.

Within seconds it caught up with the speedboats, hovering overhead. To the north, Roger tried to box them in while shots from both Paco's and Zev's rifles skipped off the deck, blasting through the windshield and whizzed over Cooper's head.

Ben scattered wasted shots from a 45 automatic while Sweet Cherry leaned out the UH1B's cargo door taking lazy potshots with a scoped semiautomatic deer rifle. It poked holes between Gwen's feet. Gwen tried to fill the holes with her fingers as they sprang up. She stopped trying when she realized how futile her attempts were and how bad the splintered wood was on her cuticles. She used the gun Portland gave her to fire back at the helicopter, scattering Ben and Cherry back inside.

Meanwhile De'Ogo had turned to his cinematographer. "Roll the camera, Slim. I want everything. Bring both detonators."

Sam had to say no more. Slim turned to Harry and Taylor. "Have them set the camera right here. Bring the 4C35, zoom and filters with two 370 m mags. I want all of this. Taylor, the detonators are in my office. Get them now?"

The two men went on their missions. Harry ran to a group of watching grips and gaffers and barked out Slim's orders in Portuguese. They scattered. But Slim was rolling by the time De'Ogo had his two detonators.

The camera zoomed in on the helicopter as it caught an eddy making Bill involuntarily bank the controls drastically left. This sudden change of direction threw Sweet Cherry off his grip and out of the copter's cargo door. He ungracefully landed in Cooper's speedboat. His weapon hit with a thud, striking Gwen on the arm. She picked it up despite the pain and stuck it unladylike into Cherry's face as he crawled toward her.

"Meet your new dental plan." Gwen gave him a deadly look. Cherry backed off.

Cooper had no choice other than to leave the Riva's controls to dispose of Cherry from behind. The boat cut so heavily into a massive swell that it nearly sent everyone out for a swim. Leaving the semiautomatic behind, Gwen managed with great difficulty to crawl through both of the men's legs. Cherry got more kicks in than necessary so Gwen was forced to claw one of his legs. She got kicked in the nose in the process. Finally she reached the controls as Cooper heaved the biker over the starboard side.

Standing up in an out of control speedboat at sunset in deadly sea, while wrestling a squirming, terrified, screaming teenager over the side, to most likely his death, wasn't as easy as it looked. Particularly when his body felt like it had died already and gone straight to a scrap yard. He wavered in the funny jumpsuit, still with the heavy jetpack strapped to his rear-end. He turned around to look at Gwen with a satisfied look on his face only to find Roger's speedboat charging them portside. His only chance was to sit down on the deck.

Gwen timed it perfectly and cut hard right behind another passing swell. Roger's boat caught the wave at its peak, causing it to glance off the other boat's bow at an upward and mobile angle. Sending his boat airborne. The sudden unexpected airlift knocked Roger, Paco, and Zev on their butts. Cooper picked up Cherry's semiautomatic and squeezed off three quick shells at Roger's out of control speedboat. The bullets caught the boat on its underbelly as it flew overhead. Only to sputter to a stop at the bottom of the next swell. Roger and his two south of the boarder friends climbed back into view. Cherry tried his best to swim toward them.

"Holy Fellini, that was great!" Slim yelled, swinging the camera up smoothly and zooming in to catch the look on Roger's frightened face.

"Whose side are you on?"De'Ogo answered. His step-niece was good and Mr. Cooper was a very lucky man, he thought.

Cooper took back control of their boat and handed Gwen Cherry's rifle. He headed the boat directly toward Roger's and pulled Gwen down below the deck. He strapped a bungee cord from a Styrofoam lifesaver to the steering wheel and stretched it out to the captain's seat to hold the speedboat on course. The helicopter tried to divert Cooper by hovering overhead but the boat was on automatic now.

Roger's and Zev's manic fusillade ripped through the hull and aft deck of Cooper's charging speedboat. Roger, Paco, and Zev were sitting ducks in the water and knew it as they all finally ran out of ammo without stopping Cooper.

"Get in closer. I've got one shot," Ben yelled from the cargo door at Bill who was white knocked on the Bell 204's controls.

"Any stinking closer and he'd smell your breath."

"He's gonna ram the other boat. He's on fire! Pull back, pull back," Ben yelled as he tried to get one more shot at the engine.

"Do I have to frame him? Shoot!"

But Ben just turned from the helicopter's cargo door. His gun dropped. Blood seeped from his mouth. He fell out the door.

Down below, Gwen and Cooper looked at each other as they smelled it."Gas!"Flames leapt up from a punctured spare gas can under the bow. The flames flashed out above them, ripping apart the front of the deck. It threw debris over top of their diving bodies.

As soon as the disintegrating wreckage had cleared over—head, Ben's body dropped down out of the sky like a large gift from a giant seagull. His cadaver tumbled off the seat cushion onto Gwen holding Cherry's still smoking rifle.

Gwen looked sickly at the man she had just killed."Will you stop catching them!"

Cooper looked up through the flames and squeezed off two shots with his Python, striking Paco in the shoulder, and sending the Dramamine starved Mexican backwards and off the starboard side of Roger's speedboat.

Gwen leaned over the side of the speedboat in a fit of dry heaves after having just fed the perch.

The Huey tried to divert Cooper again but Cooper kept sending bullets up at it so Bill was forced to keep the helicopter weaving and bobbing behind the speedboat.

Cooper stood up to restart the jetpack. They were just ten yards away from Roger's boat going wide open. Things were happening so fast there was no time for second guessing. Gwen turned away from the sea, staying on her knees, and wrapped her arms around the front of Cooper's legs. Cooper allowed the helicopter to maneuver overhead then jetted them out of the racing Riva. Gwen screamed and hung on for dear life doing her best not to burn her hands on the jetpack's flames by holding his pockets. Cooper caught the Huey just as Bill decided to bailout and pulled up on the Huey's controls. Cooper reached out for its fleeing landing gear. The combined push of the jetpack and the pull of the ascending aircraft were like a hand reaching down their throats to short sheet their stomachs.

Cooper overshot the landing gear with a numbing crash to his shoulder as he hit a cross bar, pinning himself against the underbelly of the UH1B. Gwen climbed up his body. Nearly pulling his legs out of their hip joints. She latched onto the landing gear as Portland managed to turn off the jetpack and let it slip from his body and fall to the sea.

Roger and Zev leaped out of their speedboat as Cooper's flaming torch crested a wave and surf-boarded right over the top of them. It hit the next wave headed full speed towards the ship with its flames creeping toward the explosives.

"Holy shit, did you see that?" Slim yelled.

"Just make sure you get it all. Zoom in on Roger and the other shitheads in the water. Pan over and follow the other two. Keep it smooth in case we can't cut."

Meanwhile, both Cooper and Gwen had climbed into the helicopter's fuselage through the cargo door. First Cooper made it in, followed by Gwen straining to make it on her own. She knew there was no time for Portland to help her, but that didn't stop her from wanting to punch him in the face for not offering.

Bill turned and nearly dirtied his pants when he saw them. He fought to get a knife out of his boot before Cooper cold get to him and won. He threw it badly at Cooper and it went harmlessly out the cargo door under Gwen's left armpit. Her eyes widened. Hanging out with Portland was so much fun.

Bill did the only sensible thing he could do, he pulled back on the controls sending Gwen to the back of the helicopter on her already tender ass. But Cooper leaped forward and snared a grip of Bill's seat with one hand. He pulled himself up behind Bill with pure instinct to live. He held onto the seat with his legs. This move freed both hands so that he could pound Bill's forehead against the cockpit's side panel until Bill let go of the controls. Cooper reached around and freed the safety harness, yanking back on Bill's collar and pulled him out of the pilot's seat. He threw him back toward the cargo deck.

"It's gonna crash, follow it down, as I light it," Sam said.

"Bill is still in there."

"There's no way he'll right her in time. When the tail hits the sun, we go."

So much for the easy part, thought Cooper. The helicopter was spiraling upward out of command by the time Cooper grabbed the controls. Screw the pain. He pulled himself into the pilot's seat with his left hand while his right hand leveled out the Huey. Thank you, United States Air Force!

"He did it."

"That wasn't Bill. It's him. Cooper."

Bill looked down to find Gwen with a gun covering his frontal lobe. He adjusted his Yankee cap. Gwen's cool eyes cut like daggers threw it, dissecting his life. She meant business. He could see it in her slightly island eyes. In the grip of her fleshy lips. In the cut of her square jaw. But most of all, he could see it in her manicured finger tips. They gently squeezed on the cold metal, with a vacant quiver. Just a touch of sudden death. He could see it alright. The little lady wanted to live. She was first class from a long line of survivors and there wasn't a thing he could do to dissuade her. Life could be so simple. Bill politely tipped his cap and leaped out the cargo door as Cooper banked the helicopter. Bill hit the cold churning sea below just in time to see that son-of-a-bitch-Cooper swing the lady and helicopter toward the island.

"I'll be damned."Slim still had the camera rolling getting everything. Men and women scattered away from the stern. "That son-of-a-bitch can fly, too?"Slim yelled.

"On the boat, on the boat," De'Ogo screamed.

Taylor and Harry stayed as long as they could stand it. They hopped from one foot to the other, like kids wanting to break for the nearest bush and relieve themselves. Finally, as the racing thirteen-metre Riva got within thirty-yards, Slim yelled for them to scatter. He didn't have to say it twice. They sprang across the deck to safety.

But Slim held his ground...and racked his own focus on the charging speedboat. This was his kind of moment. A one chance shot. Get it or die trying. He loved that he had to rack the focus himself. The shot was all him. He stood on his tip toes, practically leaning over the railing. Goddamn coward, his subconscious screamed! Have faith, as he fought to steady his knees. As insane as De'Ogo was, he was as much a master of timing! Have faith. The Riva skittered across the third to last crest before the ship, aiming straight at the camera. It couldn't have been a better shot."Get it. Get it! Get it!" Time stood still as the Riva shot up and off the last swell like a missile launching. Gravity grabbed it bringing the engine and stern underneath as the flaming bow flipped up and back. De'Ogo's shot was impossible. The explosives were hidden from view and moving, with only a split second to react. One shot.

"Get it!"

De'Ogo pulled the trigger. The hum of the camera filled the air. The gun had clicked empty. But the speedboat wrenched up into the air anyway, exploding, throwing water, debris, and bits and pieces of fiberglass, wood and metal at the ship.

The flames had reached the explosives. Riva wreckage blew past them as the camera continued to roll, headed toward the last four sprocket holes per frame. Slim pulled back through it all, taking the blows as they came, to find the fleeing helicopter. "You crazy son-of-a-bitch!"

"Keep rolling! Zoom out. Here it comes."

The helicopter made its way toward the island while Roger swam to his floundering speedboat and was met there by Sweet Cherry, Paco, Zev, and Bill.

No wonder the pilot couldn't maneuver the aircraft, Cooper thought. The thing was nothing but a stripped coffin robbed from a graveyard. The rattle of the turbine engine jittered his aching ribs and the controls were stiff and rusty. If he didn't know better this thing was meant to die out here.

"Meant to die! Oh shit," Cooper said.

De'Ogo reached for the red detonator. "You still got him?"

"Full frame... crawling in."

"Get as tight as you can, then zoom out and follow it down. On three. One...."

The sun continued its fiery magic hour glow. The tick before it sunk below the horizon. This was Slim's favorite shooting period. The light was gorgeous as it sank into the sea, throwing vivid hues of nightfall against the approaching clouds.

Cooper turned back to Gwen. Her eyes were locked on the fuselage across from the cargo door and a familiar block of gray.

"Two...." De'Ogo's continued.

There wasn't time to think. They met at full tilt going out the cargo door.

"Three...."

Their bodies collided in midair. Death was in their eyes.

"Three and a half...."

Through the camera, the last scintilla from the dazzling sun disappeared perfectly behind the tail section of the helicopter. Its explosion burst out from where the celestial ball had just vanished. The Bell 204 split in two and spun out of control. Seconds later it crashed into the glowing water two hundred feet above a designated Naval explosive dumping ground. Just like Roger wrote it in the script. De'Ogo had timed it perfectly. And thank you, Mister Cooper, Slim thought. If you're still in one piece, take a bow.

De'Ogo chuckled to himself. Roger was a dangerous drugged out dumbass but his script was a brilliant way to solve all of Sam's problems.

"Got it. Jesus."

"Let it roll and print it all."

Ten minutes later the ship pulled up alongside Roger and the stranded men. They tied up the crippled boat and came on board. De'Ogo looked at Roger. Roger shied away.

"Mr. Kelemen... be at my table in ten minutes. Replace Ben, Slim. I want to see dailies in an hour. Send for my helicopter. Make sure there are no bodies floating around."

"It'll be jumpy."

"Edit, Mr. Director of Cinematography, edit."

De'Ogo walked off, his clothing smoldering.

Roger turned to the cinematographer, who looked back through the camera. They were scared. Blood dripped down Slim's forehead. His one eye brow was gone. All but the eye he held to the camera was scorched and covered with soot. Through the camera Slim could see that the water was still inflames in spots. The wreckage had already slipped into the sea. There was no sign of Gwen or Cooper. It was already too dark to tell if they had made it or not.

Roger studied Slim, who seemed reluctant to stop shooting the camera. "He's out there, isn't he?"

"No man or woman could've lived through that. And if either did...the sharks will get them," Slim said.

"You mean...." Roger took over the camera. "You don't know Cooper, like I do. He's one lucky bastard."

"Luck hell, that was one talented son-of-a-bitch we just blew to smithereens. I should hire stunt men so good."

"He's out there, Gwen's with him. I can feel it. And they have something that is very precious to me."

Slim studied Roger. He wasn't sure what this was all about, beyond the script, and the production. And didn't care. But he knew there was a reason De'Ogo kept this messed up actor alive. It had to be something more than finishing this movie. There had to be an alternative ending somewhere. He just hoped he was still alive to shoot it.

11 COP WITH A GRUDGE

"What do you want?" Marty asked with a sleepy voice through the locked door.

"Cooper."

"He's not home, yet."

"Where is he?"

"Your guess is…wait a sec." Marty drew back the curtains and turned on the porch light. The voice sounded too ghostly familiar."Have we had the pleasure?"

Brubaker stood in his street clothes at Cooper's front door. He wanted some answers and he wanted them now.

Marty checked him up and down."You a cop?"

"Good to see you haven't lost any of your reasoning, Marty."

"Jesus. Brubaker?" Marty opened the door and filled it.

"The one and only."

"I'll be goddamned. How you been?"

"They haven't made me leave town yet."

"Heard about your wife."

"She was a bitch anyway."

"Haven't lost any of the old charm."

"I've worked on it by desk phone."

"Right. Look, what can I do for you?"

Brubaker opened the next day's Daily News in front of Marty's face. He pointed to an article circled in red. There was a two-inch shot of Cooper."What do you know about this?"

"Nothin', I swear."

Brubaker snagged the test page from a friend about an hour ago. Research."You wouldn't be dishonest to an old buddy, would you, Marty?" He folded the paper up and stuck it back under his arm. He had traded the exclusive of how Cooper was pulled over in his car the night before. Just the bare facts, of course. He hadn't mentioned anything about the other speeding car because he hadn't figured that one out. But tomorrow Cooper would be a laughing stock and behind bars for murder.

"Honest. Look, Coop had nothing to do with those stiffs."

"He told you that?"

"He didn't have to. I know Coop, that's good enough."

"He was there."

"So?"

"There's a witness claiming Cooper wasted Jerry Goodricke."

"I heard the news. They say someone came and went out an open window."

"According to Cooper. Why was Portland there?"

"I don't know, I swear. Look, he'll probably be home soon. Why don't you call him later. Say, mid-October. I'm sure he'll give you an exclusive." Marty tried to close the door.

Brubaker blocked it. "Don't get wise with me, Marty?"

"You on duty?"

Brubaker pulled back his leather jacket to show how well he was hung."I'm here on a sincere social call."

"Oh, yeah?"

"Yeah."

"Then, sincerely buzz off."Marty slammed the door.

Brubaker cocked a half smile, causing a hundred wrinkles to run across his smoker's face. God it was great being out on the street. The public treated you with utter disrespect. And Portland Cooper was in bad trouble again. Shit, life was great. Pleasant revenge. He turned to face Victory Boulevard. His pale blue eyes took in the sparse night traffic. Heavy thumping boomed through the shell of a new low-riding Nissan 280ZX

2-seater as it cruised east toward Laurel Canyon. Maybe he'd celebrate and pistol whip some dumb pothead.

His last year on the force and they stick him with a god-damn rookie, do-gooder, college-boy. But nothing could bust his chops now. He was free on the streets once again. He took his non-filter Luckys out of his pocket and stuck one in his face. He lit it. Portland Cooper was his. He drew on the cig. It smoldered in his eyes with evil intent. He may not have killed Jerry or the old bag, but he was in on it. Probably caused it by sticking his foolish nose into things that were none of his business again.

That Datsun Roadster chasing him was his proof that Cooper was up to no-good. For years Cooper got away with it. But not this time. Because Brubaker was back on the beat for an encore hard-ass performance. A new man with a new per-spective of how to kickass on the streets of LA. One last year. One last chance. He exhaled. He loved being a cop. The tough guy doing good things as he saw them. Portland Cooper hacked that up for him by putting his fanny behind a desk.

They made him drop the ten pounds he'd gained to get back out. Those arrogant a-holes downtown. Analyzed him, asking all kinds of stupid questions, before they would let him back on the street. To make sure he wasn't harboring anger that would make him a liability. He had to take three physicals and let some pretty boy doctor stick his finger up his ass for Christ's sake. This stinking world. Not even a cop's ass was sacred anymore. But it was Cooper who caused all this. He made a mockery of his career. Altered the natural course of his life. Him and that crummy Corsa...and that bum actor, Roger Kelemen's 911.

It nearly killed him, but he made it back. He couldn't say the same for his wife. The bitch. But he loved being a cop still the same. The man who cleared the streets of little no good lubricant-balls like Portland Cooper. He'd get him. Somehow, somewhere he'd get him for something and make him do some time. He'd put that lousy Corsa off the road for good. All he had to do was find Cooper and feed his ass to the courtyard-sharks.

12 THE END TO PRINCE OF PARADISE

Sam De'Ogo had beaten Brubaker to the feeding. Because at that very moment, on the seaward shore of Catalina, the opposite side from Avalon, lay an uncharted cove at the end of Cottonwood Canyon. If the cove was viewed from the south side, a rock formation called Indian Head Rock unmistakably watched the sun plunge into the sea, marking the burial grounds inhabited by peoples of linguistic affinity--the Takic branch of the Uto-Aztecan language family.

Which was humorlessly coincidental, because at that very moment about a gunshot away was a much better known cove fittingly called Shark's Harbor. There, of all places, about six hundred yards out, were Portland and Gwen, floating on a single Huey seat cushion while wave after wave lifted and dropped them back into the sea.

The wind had blown the fog in over the island so that the half moon hung high in the sky making the dozen or so shark fins circling them all too easy to see. It was a nice place for a honey moon if your idea of a romantic time was ending up in each other's arms as shark bait.

"Keep your hands out of the water, damn it."

A large wave washed over Gwen's head. She came up choking. "Oh, shut up. You mean, after all those Bar mitzvah gifts, Jack's not even Jewish?"

"I can't wait to see Irene's face."

Gwen glanced to her left again. She didn't want to look, but fear kept getting the best of her. She squinted into the night. A cold shudder rippled through her body. If the sharks did attack, at least they wouldn't get a warm meal. "I'm freezing."

"Keep pedaling."

Gwen pedaled. But she also thought of the two kayakers off the Ventura County coastline who became numbers seven and eight last January to die from a shark attack in California waters. At least, none of her new friends seemed to be a great white. Not so for Roy Stoddard and Tamara McAllister...she cursed herself for having such a good memory. She hated sharks. And pedaling was all she could do.

"Can't you shoot one of them, or all of them?"

"Great, we'd be swimming in a pool of blood."

"Maybe one of those over there."

"Gwen. The gun is empty."

"What?! You could've at least saved two for us."

"Sorry, the next time we are about to be eaten by something I'll shoot us both twice. I promise."

She gripped Cooper's forearm. At least she had Portland. Thank heaven for Portland.

"What?"

"I love you."

"I love you, too. Will you marry me?"

"Are you kidding?"

"I'm serious. I just want you know I have always planned to marry you. So, yes or no?"

"Yes, of course I'll marry you."

"Okay, then we're officially engaged. Consider this ring of fear as my token of affection."

"Only Portland Cooper would pick a moment like this."

"Hey, I was waiting for the appropriate one."

"What do you say we go down in history as the first humans to die of shark bites while making love."

"Intriguing, but I'll pass. By the way, you haven't started your holiday yet, have you."

"You are disgusting."

"Hey, Geraldo would want to know."

She laughed as Portland pulled her close to give her a kiss.

"Keep pedaling."

"I've got to go."

"Go."

She tried but couldn't. Her mind wandered back to Florida, when she was a young lady. Though she was born in Hong Kong, her father was, according to legends, a Malaysian Island Prince. And she was her father's little princess. He spoiled her so much. That stay at the Riverside Hotel, just six small cabins across the channel from Jupiter Island, was their last trip north from Miami together. They had stopped there that afternoon because business friends had asked if James wanted to invest in developing Jupiter Island. They had spent the day exploring. It had intrigued her father because of it being an isolated island, yet only across the channel from Route One to West Palm Beach. He was considering buying the island himself to keep it from being completely developed. It would've been their own private jungle, with birds, snakes, black panthers, and as many seashells as they could collect. Gwen fell in love with growing up on her own private island, still so close to everything a spoiled little princess could ever dream of owning.

Gwen's mother, Irene, never came on the book tours. They were doubtful that she would ever approve to living on the island away from it all. She didn't care for the idea of James traveling the world, as it was. While she was stuck at home on Kuali Rhu listening to Tattooed Orang Asli Warriors, the indigenous jungle natives, who slept below the cliffs of their home in long huts. They beat on their drums, hunted wild animals and cooked them on open fires that drifted up into her windows at night. Just knowing they were down there, even though they were the best of security, kept her awake. At first they tried Hong Kong to be around better healthcare until Gwen was three. Then they moved to New York where her father hated the enclosure of high-rises and the clamor of the city just as much as Hong Kong. They had compromised on Irene's home town of Miami, where Irene had friends, could entertain with dinners parties, and James had coconut trees to read his father's books under. Gwen never really knew what her father saw in her mother, until she was old enough to understand her grandmother. James had married a girl just like mom. Refined, beautiful, and pretentious. So, it was the two of them on the open road, in her father's brand new black 64 split window Sting Ray. They were just starting another book signing junket for her grandfather's then latest book.

Gwen hadn't realized how important she was to the marketing of the books, until she saw how much she resembled her aunt's photos on the cover of the books and how people clamored to take pictures with her. Her grandfather who never left the islands he wrote about, used his own daughter's childhood photos on all the covers. He claimed his isolations had something to do with a curse put on him by local natives. But James assured her that the books were nothing but stories made up by his father to support the island jungles to keep them from being developed. So it was up to her father and aunt, who handled the Asian and European markets, to do all the book marketing for the massively popular children's adventure series, 'Little Island Princess,' that were written in twenty-two languages. The sales were imperative to the survival of the island wildlife. Though her grandfather never claimed the stories of her ancestors were true, it was widely believed to be based on a cave civilization that once thrived below the islands of Malaysia.

Portland loved the islands. Went there as often as he could. Her grandfather had even entrusted him with a remote corner of a mangrove swamp, a calm cover, to run his engine boat shop. How that occurred, Gwen wasn't fully knowledgeable on. But Portland had helped her grandfather on a few adventures they wouldn't talk about, so she was sure it was something manly between them. She knew that no money changed hands.

That last day, after their Jupiter Island exploration, her father was standing alone on the end of the dock with his back to the island when a single rifle shot struck him square between the shoulder blades, killing him instantly. One 30 caliber bullet. And a great man who was widely admired and respected by so many around the world, died alone.

It was the fall of '63. Gwen was up in the Riverside Motel's bar eating dinner. She was starved, but her father chose to smoke a cigar. He didn't care to smoke in doors. He said he had some thinking to do before he made his call to his friends. He was found by, Fred, the owner of the motel and restraint when he went down to clean bait off the docks. His random murder was never solved. Whoever pulled the trigger had left from the other side of the island. It was well over an hour before anyone could take a boat back over to search the island, and by then it was getting dark. Whoever altered their lives forever had ample time to be far away out to sea. Gwen knew from that day forward that it was a sick and dangerous world they lived in. On land or at sea. The things Portland had to get done over the years for her never surprised her. All she knew for sure was that she had fallen in love with the right man.

In the spring of '65, Irene, who had lived and grown up in Miami, met Jack Rotenberg. He was making a beach party film starring a young actor named Roger Kelemen and wanted to rent their Miami Beach home exterior for a particular scene. Irene was so impressed that she said yes to the movie over dinner. That led to an intense romance. They married, packed and left Friday night pizzas and their past behind for Bel Air.

The home Gwen had grown up in was still there. Irene didn't own it now. But to honor James, Gwen still drove the black Sting Ray with the same Florida plates. She missed her father so much. And wanted to see her grandfather right then.

"Grandpa," Gwen said, trying to walk on water to him.

"Stay calm. Breathe. The waves are taking us in."

Gwen took in a deep breath as the fins circled closer and closer. She stiffened. "Something just touched me!"

"Keep pedaling."

Any harder and she would fly. "Here they come."

Two fins charged directly at them before dipping below the surface of the waves.

"Portland!"

Gwen wrapped her arms around Portland as another wave washed over them.

"Been a hell of a good time. Thanks." Portland's words came out mostly under water. The reality of them froze the moment.

"I wouldn't have changed a thing. I love you!"

Something nudged them both and they kicked at it. There was more than one, three or four. Something pushed up on Cooper's foot. He suddenly realized he was missing one of his work boots. His left one. But something was going on down below them. Something turbulent. They could feel the swift swishing motions under their feet.

"What's happening?"

"I don't know."

Just then a bottlenose dolphin, a Tursiops truncates, stuck its head out of the water, followed by another squeezing itself between them. Gwen and Portland screamed as another wave hit them sending them tumbling under as their gurgling, relieved laughter faded into the frigid surf.

13 POWDER BURNS

In the ship's captain's quarters, Roger sat on pins and needles across a thick wood table from Sam De'Ogo. He sweated like a lam with its hooves stuck in a sea hammock. De'Ogo waved the chubby Chinese waiter out. Roger flinched. De'Ogo could and possibly would kill him at any given moment. Why not, as a boy, Roger unintentionally shot Tim Waller once. The bullet made mincemeat of his spleen and had lodged against his spine. Removing it could've caused him to be paralyzed from that spot down. It was an accident! At least he thought it was. Wasn't it? He needed a blast, but the old man with the bullet in him didn't approve of Roger doing such things around him. Drinking himself into mush to hide his own pain was okay, but drugs...never! Well, he had pain to hide, too! The sentimentality of it all was killing him.

De'Ogo lifted his dead eyes from his seafood platter. He licked the butter off his fingers that dripped from a tasty Alaskan snow crab. His death-stare rose from the tips of his fingers and settled on Roger's wiped-out ashen face like a crazed giant squid. "What makes you think Portland Cooper is still alive?"

"The man was thrown from an airplane once and lived." Roger pulled his wet shredded sport coat off. The white shirt underneath was stained with as much dirt and blood. "You don't know him like I do."

De'Ogo laughed as he drank directly from the near empty bottle of Jack Daniel's. "You're paranoid, Mr. Kelemen. Too many drugs. I don't like this game of blackmail any longer. And for what, a key and a tape I already paid for? I once made them make you a fortune and you stuck it up your nose. The nose I bought for you. The face I fixed for you. Now you want another fortune. Again I've made them give it to you. I've always liked you, Roger...you were such a smart, friendly young man. Even if you did shoot me. So willing to learn. But now you not only look like shit, you smell like something that grows on the ass of my ship." De'Ogo laughed at his little joke. "I have no more noses to give you. So you best keep yours out of my way."

He picked up a silenced pistol beside his dessert spoon and slammed it down onto the snow crab's head to smash its shell. He set the gun down and picked through the mess with his stubby ring-covered fingers. His horsehide-skin was so tanned it could cover a saddle. His thick curly gray hair was died black with white streaked racing stripes that looked better on a zebra."So don't provoke me into killing you. I'd be deeply saddened. Because of your foolishness I had to dispose of Ruth and Jerry. Perhaps my step niece and the talented Mr. Cooper as well. Such a waste of great talent. So now," he picked up the silenced pistol again and this time pointed the sight at Roger's heart, "our deal has changed. The tape, give it to me or die."

A demented smiled curled on Sam's lips as he studied the horrified look in Roger's eyes. How easy it would be to dispose of this once talented young man out here at sea. The boy who had done so well in school when he was just a talented innocent youth. Having to hide the truth from the snooping rag press of what really happened to him. Because it was Roger who had shot him, one of his own honors students. Sam did not want to expose who his foster parents were. Being in the hospital led to the downfall of everything he and his brother had built.

That goddamn rag-paper snoop, wouldn't leave it alone. Their whole private school scam came crashing down on their heads when the bodies of the Jacksons were found in a pound. Yet, by chance, Sam and Jack were able to escape that disaster and build a bigger and better life with help of this same little boy. Jerry and Ruth, also known as the Duncans had taken the fall for them. Now they are forever out of the way for creating waves. It was fortunate they had let the little nickel-boy live. Watching him go to another foster family, hoping never to see him again. It was Sam who cast the vote to not run him over in the street. It was Sam who had voted thumbs up again when Roger found them.

That all seemed such a long time ago. Yet, here he was, this arrogant little boy, with greedy, dirty hands out again, asking for another nickel. Another nickel. Little Roger, the nickel-boy, always wanted a nickel. Any work for a nickel. Fetch the paper for a nickel. Wash my car for a pocket full of nickels. Do the dishes. Clean his room. Take a bath. Always for nickels. He was never good for nothing. He had thousands in his own bank account when he hit those streets from all those nickels. Sam dug in his pocket and searched for a nickel. Surely he had one. The movement made his back ache. He found one and rotated it between his stubby thumb and index finger.

Roger saw the coin. His eyes narrowed. Sam was mocking him. His past, his childhood, the things they made him do. For those nickels. The bastard! If it weren't for all those nickels he would've starved on the streets of Hollywood. Done who knows what to survive.

"It's imposable to get to the tape without the key, so forget it. It would destroy something very personal to me."

Sam flipped the nickel onto the table. It rolled painfully slow, wobbling but staying upright toward Roger, tinkling off a crystal water glass before dropping into his lap.

Roger's eyes followed the nickel. He didn't move to stop it. He couldn't touch it. A stinking nickel. It fell from his crotch to the Oriental rug below the table. The bastard and his nickels. His eyes rose out of his lap at the sound of the safety clicking back on Sam's gun. He wondered if the old fool knew how close those nickels came to ending his absurd life.

"Then give me the key."

Roger shook his head. "I don't have it."

De'Ogo pulled the trigger.

It put a powder burn on Roger's white shirt. Roger flipped over in the chair.

De'Ogo fought back his laugh but it was no use, his drunken sinister snigger filled his quarters with demented short echoes.

Roger picked himself off the rug, examining himself for any unnatural blowholes.

"Blanks."Sam turned the gun toward a bowl of whole fruit. He pulled the trigger again and this time an apple burst, sending its remains onto Roger.

Roger picked up the largest apple fragment and bit into it. The defying act did not escape Sam's eyes as he scooped oyster Rockefeller into his mouth. A spark of life, some self dignity still existed. There was hope for Roger yet. Perhaps he could convince him to rid his life of drugs again after all. If he truly wanted to direct his script himself and not rely on everyone else to pick up the slack, he would need his wits about him. His wits could save his life.

"Cooper still has the key."

"Well he's dead now, in pieces at the bottom of the sea."

"No, he's not. He's on that island. I swear I can feel it."

"Relax, he's dead. I'll put the word out, just in case."

"Give me two men and I'll bring him back. This time we'll do more than just beat the son-of-a-bitch!"

"You're insane, Roger. I truly think that's why I tolerate you. We have much in common. So be it. If you want to waste your time. Get yourself cleaned up. Take whomever you want, but nobody without a silencer. Mark my words. There's people on that island with a plane. Don't let Mr. Cooper get to them or this will end badly for you."De'Ogo aimed the gun at Roger again, his sick laughter fought its way through a mouthful of oyster and spinach."You better hope this something personal is worth your dying for if you come back empty handed."

Roger disappeared by crawling out of the captain's quarters. With mood swings like Sam De'Ogo's, there was no reason to give him an easy target.

De'Ogo waited until he was alone. He fired again. A juicy Bartlett Pear exploded this time. His laughter subsided as his thoughts turned to the disturbing Mr. Cooper. He picked up a lemon and sucked on it. Jack would be very angry with him for having killed his beautiful stepdaughter. He almost hoped she had survived. But her violent death was unavoidable under such perplexing circumstances. Siding with the talented Mr. Cooper was a deadly byproduct of love. If Jack had allowed him to do away with the Duncans years ago, none of this would've taken place. Roger would have been just the pleasant memory of a dishonest old man who once pretended to be someone else so he could run a private school and make a modest fortune.

Now this situation had grown like a bad case of herpes that kept popping up at the most embarrassing moments. Roger Kelemen, the bastard hadn't even bothered to change his name.

Suddenly the sound of a screaming little girl filled his mind. Sophie's little girl. Such a beauty. His hand shot up to his head with the pistol. He held it to his temple. How many times had he wanted to pull the trigger? How many times had he found himself alone in bed with a gun to his head staring up at himself at the gaudy reflection of his pathetic self.

It could be so easy. Death would be so undemanding. No more pain. No more ungodly yearnings, desires, or needs. Nothing, no after life, no God, no Devil, just gone to the sea. The pain! The doctors had tried to relieve the pain from his back but anything more and he might as well be dead. The pain that shot down his lower back and legs was unbearable. The pills and booze had only dulled it and drove him mad, forgetful, and sad. So he cut out the pills. The damage a bullet could do. Eating at his brain. If there was a God, then this would surely be his punishment. To live a life of pain and misery was indeed living an eternity in hell.

The Chinese waiter reentered with a steaming tea pot at that sad moment to find Sam there, tears streaking his bloated face, the gun to his head. He stopped and tried to back out. But Sam took the gun away from his head and aimed it at the chubby waiter and pulled the trigger. A fine hole appeared directly over the Chinaman's heart. His eyes widened in disbelief. It was unthinkable. He was actually dying, needlessly so. He crumbled to his knees. Blood oozed through his white uniform, and he plopped face first onto the rug, spilling the tea.

Shit, what a squander of a good servant, Sam realized. He pushed a button between his legs under the wood table.

"Yes, Mr. De'Ogo? Is everything satisfactory?"the head chef asked in a thick French accent.

"The dinner is superb. But the dead waiter is bleeding on my carpet. Could you send in your boys to remove him for me, please? Chum for tomorrow's dinner perhaps."

"Fresh shark. Yes. Right away, sir."

What a pity, De'Ogo thought, the little man perhaps saved his life but caused himself to die in return. Life was full of silly tradeoffs. He studied his plate. "Ah, how could I miss scallops?

14 HIGH ON THE MOUNTAIN

Gwen and Cooper were let out at the entrance to the Catalina Airport by a skittish hippy camper in a tie-dyed t-shirt who had a weeklong overnight camper's permit for Little Harbor. He came across the two marooned castaways while meditating on a cliff above Shark's Cove. He had watched them climb up on the rocks and hold each other so tenderly, and with so much real love as they sought warmth, that he couldn't say no when Portland asked about a plane to the mainland. He hemmed and hawed for a moment. But finally, the hippy implied something about immigrant pot smugglers who he heard ran an operation out of the airport. Chances were the hippy was keeping an eye on his own crop with his camping permit. It didn't matter to Gwen or Portland. A ride was a ride. Except for Cooper's one work boot, they were barefoot, wet, singed, beat-up, and dead tired. They sure didn't feel like walking it. So on the ride up to the airport, the dry dirt on the back roads that had curled up behind the VW Thing and clung to them was barely noticed.

Upon arrival, they had tenderly hurried inside past a black heavyset janitor pushing his 60s in a blue cap, light blue shirt, and nerdy dark blue shorts. He mopped the outside ceramic tiles under the terracotta overhang with an air of prolonged loneliness. Once inside, Cooper and Gwen didn't like the sight of the empty lounge. There was no heat in the stone fireplace and the rows of picnic tables were void of life. In fact the only sign of life beyond the air smelling of wet mop and floor cleaner, were the various Indian artifacts hanging on the wall. They went out to the front veranda to speak to the worker and found the man was gone. They went up a set of stairs to the flight offices on the second and third floors, but were extremely disappointed to find it all closed up and locked. Gwen kept Copper from breaking in to get to a phone...for now.

They rested their backs on the white adobe wall. From the top of the stairs they could see out over the runway. There were no lights so there'd be no night takeoffs. Shit. If anyone came looking for them, they'd be sitting ducks up here on this two thousand foot mound to nowhere. There were three ways in by road if they had to walk it out. West on the dusty back road toward Hidden Ranch on Via del Rancho, the opposite direction across Black Jack Mountain heading southeast toward Avalon Bay, or north through the Valley of Ollas toward Two Harbors. Gwen took Portland's hand. Going back the way they came was out, Two Harbors could prove helpful, but Avalon seemed the logical choice. Which was why they wouldn't go there.

"You want to try a pay phone?"

"Yeah, give me a minute to think this out. Marty should be at my place having dinner about now."

"I'm starving."

"Me too. There's a kitchen down stairs. We'll check it before we leave. My guess, they sent someone out for our bodies. Not finding them, they're probably already working their way here, with someone watching the harbor. This De'Ogo will have pull on the Island, so we can't just call a cab to come get us."

Cooper studied the runway. He knew the airport was called Airport in the Sky and it lay near the island's highest point at an elevation of 1,602 ft. If anyone was after them it would take a while to get here on foot because all roads to the airport climb steeply upward. The fastest way up directly from the ocean was the back road they had taken in the VW.

The airport itself was leased by Wrigley to the Navy during World War II because of its short runway and how it dropped off. It was ideal for training pilots to land and take off of aircraft carriers. If he had to, he could take off in a small plane in the dark. Short of hot wiring one and chancing ten years in prison, he was fresh out of honest ideas.

They came back down the stairs as Roger, Bill, and Harry rattled to a stop at the airport's entrance in the same VW Thing that had dropped them off. The hippy wasn't with them. Cooper grabbed Gwen's hand and pulled her under the stairs out of sight. Just then the janitor exited what appeared to be a supply room with a fresh pail and a clean mop. Cooper and Gwen waited for him to enter the building then slipped inside.

The janitor watched them duck inside through the glass doors and began to mop up the trails from their dirty wet feet. That girl sure had dainty feet. Damn he liked that. Such an elegant footprint, like an angle had passed that way. Shit, just thinking about them made him forget that he had already cleaned those tiles. His wife had big ugly feet. They kind of puffed out of her high heels. He never told her, but he hated that. It's one of the main reasons he left. That and the way she eventually puffed out of everything else. Damn. He'd wake up in with her getting bigger, puffing out of her nighty like rising bread dough. So much so it gave him the willies.

He exited the building and continued to mop up the foot prints leading to his work room as fast as he could. He recognized the VW but not the men in it. When he realized that he wouldn't get all the prints, he dumped his bucket and went on mopping as though everything was the way it was. He glanced up to see the look on Roger's wasted face. Whoever these men were, they were up to no good. That was certain, he thought. Where there was no good, there was good, and when you can combined the two you could usually make a quick buck keeping them apart or puttin' them together. Sort of like a broker, so to speak. All you had to do was choose sides. He decided to put his money on the little lady with the wet, perky, slim ass, and the dainty feet. The woman had style. Hot dang. Now the white dude with the battered face and the bozo suit was probably the origins of all her troubles. He didn't seem half as harmful to the sweet thing as these three shits did.

Roger, and the two stunt guys, Bill and Harry, entered, walking over the wet floor. They had cleaned up and changed clothing. Roger's first shower in days. Somehow not noticing the mess they were making, or getting into. They searched the corridor only to find the janitor contemplating his work.

"Hey, you!"

The janitor looked off in the other direction in silent protest of being yelled at. He eventually looked back and pretended to suddenly realize he was not alone. "Yes, sir. Place is closed. Be open first light in the mornin'."

"Did you see anyone come in here?"

"Yes, sir, I sure did. Just a few minutes ago." He was as polite as he could be. "They went right down yonder." He pointed in the opposite direction at an empty locked hanger.

"Stay here, Bill." Roger and Harry went out the door.

The janitor went about his work, finished up, and carried his bucket and mop to the supply room where Cooper and Gwen hid. He stepped in with his things and closed the door.

"Leave the light off."

Gwen was sitting on the sink. Lost in the dark silence the janitor could hear a tinkle of her urine running down the drain. It stopped. Gwen ripped paper towel from the dispenser and wiping herself. Damn.

"You through?"

"Yes. Sorry...I...." She ran the water.

"Never mind, I've pissed in it once or twice myself. But I generally use a light."He flicked it back on. He examined their ragged wet clothing. Their almost shoeless feet. At Cooper's puffy cut face. They'd been through Harlem and back again.

"You two in trouble, boy?"

"We've been in worse."

"Much worse and she'd a carried you in here."

"The thought had crossed my mind."

"The name's Cooper."

"Same here."

"Don't suppose you're a cousin."

"Probably distant."

"Yeah, most likely." The black man smiled. This bozo wasn't so bad. Sure looked like hell though. He turned around and pulled down a medicine box. He handed it to Gwen. "Let me have a look at those wrists."

"No, they're...."

"Let him look."

The janitor took off the remnants of the costume material from Gwen's wrists and hands and cleaned the cuts.

"Your friends, they want to do more than just find your ass."

"Ouch!"

"Hold still. There's a mirror over there if you want to see how ugly you got," he said, motioning to a dirty, paint stained mirror on a shelf. "Better put some of this on."

Cooper took the peroxide and some cotton balls over to the mirror. "Looks normal to me."

"You lookin' for a plane off this burg?"

"You got one?"

"I got a friend. He's got a scrappy little Piper."

"How much?"

"Five hundred cash. Five-fifty plastic."

"Plastic."

"MasterCard or Visa?"

"Visa. Nonsmoking."

The janitor chuckled. "The man's got a sense of humor about him. It's a wonder he ain't dead already."

"I keep telling him that."

The janitor examined their battered faces. He looked at the inventive way Cooper had stopped the bleeding. The Superglue was still holding the cuts closed. Cooper had lost the Scotch Tape to the waves. He knew about the ship. Heard all the shooting and explosions. Film people they claimed. He knew of the one they called De'Ogo who owned the ship, too. If this man had run afoul of the likes of what he had heard of De'Ogo, and helped this angel get away, then this guy was not a man looking for or needing any further trouble. If he was cause of the ruckus this afternoon, then he probably wasn't there willingly. Yes, the janitor had heard stories about Sam De'Ogo. He heard what he was capable of doing to people. He purposely stayed clear of him for good reasons. But this guy in the Bozo suit had gumption, he thought. He made it off that ship. Probably had to shoot his way off. If he needed help getting this young woman to safety. It didn't matter the reason why. He had expected others to come looking for this one. Now it was his choice on whose money to take. Of course, it would be easier to just hand this one over. It would be just as easy to take money from both. To him it was business. But the woman. Man, she sure had nice feet. The janitor scratched himself and nodded his approval.

Cooper bent down and twisted the heel of his remaining boot. Its shoelace was tied to his bleeding ankle where it had dug into his skin. He slid out a Visa card. Also inside the heel were Roger's key and a key to the Corsa. He put the Corsa key in his pocket.

The janitor pulled a credit card machine out of a briefcase, put in a credit card form and ran the card. He read off Cooper's card number to make sure it printed correctly. He turned back to Gwen and Portland. "Nothing personal, you got ID?"

"Would a Cooper cheat a distant cousin?"

The janitor handed the slip and card back to Portland. Cooper signed it. The janitor shut off the light.

"Jose. He's at the snack bar."

"We were just in there. Alone."

"If he wants you to see him, you will. But don't take lip off the little cockroach. Here, out this door." He opened the door and walked out with a broom. He waited a moment to see if anything was moving. So far so good. "Just show him your receipt. Go around this way, follow the walk to the back of the kitchen. It's unlocked. Go in, but look out for your friends. Jose will be there."

Cooper and Gwen left the janitor under the stairs. They headed toward the runways on a narrow walk that led around the blond adobe building. In the back were more offices with their lights out. The walk was lit so Portland pulled Gwen out of the light. If Roger was to pass by, chances were they could get a jump on him. They moved along as silent as cats, peering into the windows as they went by. The place seemed deserted. What Roger and his boys were up to was hard to tell. On the other side of the dark office, Portland found the kitchen. It was small and only set up for easy prepared fast food. He stuck his head in the back door. No one seemed to be there. But outside the front kitchen door a man's back leaned up over the bar. They were listening to the Angel's game on a radio. Angels had a chance for their first postseason appearance and everyone was on the bandwagon. Another man had his bolding head on the bar. He sat on a stool on the customer's side of the counter. The man with his back toward the kitchen had work clothes on. He had a tool belt around his waist. Both men were drunk as brewer's farts, one more so than the other. Portland motioned Gwen inside. He pointed to some bread on the counter. He told her to stay hidden until he was able to check the men out.

Cooper followed the path up around the kitchen to a back veranda. He glanced up to the red tile roof to make sure no one could get the drop on him from up there. He got on all fours and crawled among the row of picnic tables. He made his way to the wall below the kitchen service window and listened. All he could hear was the game on the radio and a clink or two from a bottleneck on shot glasses. Nolan Ryan was pitching for the Angles in the first inning.

He crept to the door and looked in. He hadn't noticed before but there was a large wild boar head above the door. The men at the counter were about six feet away. Cooper eased the door open and moved in, keeping low. The man standing behind the counter looked at Cooper as though crawling on the terracotta flooring was something every man tried once in his life. He motioned to a stool and poured a glass of tequila for Portland. Portland made it to the stool and slid in beside the seemingly passed out amigo. He took the drink and saluted the workman behind the bar. His hard dirty face didn't register Cooper in return. Portland swished the liquor around his sensitive teeth. The workman just watched him. Cooper spit it and blood out onto the floor. The workman winced this time and poured him another. Cooper downed it this time. Voices came toward them from outside the front door. The workman turned off the radio. Cooper failed miserably to leap over the counter. The workman lent a hand and Cooper sprawled onto the disgustingly sticky rubber matting on the floor at the workman's feet.

Roger came in first, followed by Harry.

The drunk draped on the bar moved his hand over slowly and slid Cooper's blood stained glass in front of him.

Bill, the helicopter pilot, came in from the hall leading to the restroom on the other side of the fireplace. Roger looked at him. Bill took off his damp Yankee cap and shook his head no. They stopped when they realized they weren't alone.

"Hey."

"Something I can help you chums with?"

"We're looking for a couple of friends. A guy and a girl."

"Good looking girl, dark hair? The guy looked beat up? Like maybe he'd been in an accident? Wore a funny white jump suit?" The workman poured himself one more shot, in case it was his last, and downed it.

"Yeah, that's them."

"Haven't seen 'em."

"What?"

The workman gave out a robust laugh.

Roger pulled out his silenced handgun and cocked it. "I need to find them."

"What's it worth to you?"

Cooper wasn't sure what to do. The son-of-a-bitch sounded like he was about to sell him out. He started to crawl away. The man standing over him stepped on his leg.

"Maybe your life," Harry answered.

"My life ain't worth maggot shit and my friend's is worth even less. So maybe I've seen them, maybe I haven't."

Roger walked over and put his gun to the man's head at the bar. "Maybe your friend saw them."

"Jose, you seen anyone?"

Jose looked up at his friend. His eyes, painfully bloodshot, were slits at best. He turned toward the gun and tried to focus on the long-silenced barrel. He rocked from a stomach spasm, his cheeks bloated and he forced down puke. Roger stepped back. The next one Jose let it fly onto the floor. He retched over and over. Each one as disgusting as the last, until the last one was a dry heave.

"Oh, Jesus H. Christ. What a stinkin' pig," Harry said.

The man standing on Cooper's leg handed Jose a bar towel. "I guess he ain't seen no one either."

Roger pulled out his wallet. "I have fifty bucks."

"That wouldn't get you a reach around on this hill."

"Shoot the bastard," Bill said.

"Shut up, Bill. My watch is worth fifteen hundred."

"I don't care what time it is."

"Where the hell are they?!"

Bill walked to the bar with his wallet out. "Three hundred."

The man behind the counter took the three fifty in cash and Roger's watch. His dark eyes looked the Rolex over. "Real nice."

"So where are they?" Roger asked.

"Who?"

"Why you…." Roger raised his gun to kill the man.

"I wouldn't if I were you, white trash."

Roger stopped. He turned around to find himself facing an AK 47 assault rifle.

"Good evening."

"What the hell is this?"

"This is your last moment to breathe if you don't get your asses back in that Thing and get out of our airport. If you hurt our friend who owns it, we'll find you."

Roger backed out away from the counter. "You don't know what the hell you're getting into."

"Then maybe I should just kill you now to make sure you don't come back to inform me."

"Screw it, man, I'm out of here."

"Me, too."

Roger looked at Bill and Harry as they put away their guns.

"What's it going to be, little man?" the workman behind the counter asked.

Roger turned back around to find a Franchi SPAS-12 combat shotgun at his back.

"Now get the hell out of here before I stain the floor."

Roger put away his Chinese silenced pistol. Sam felt they would keep things quieter. Little did he know how useless they would be. "All right. Let's go."

Bill and Harry eased by the janitor. Roger followed.

The janitor grabbed Roger by his leather jacket as he went by. "You Roger Kelemen?"

"No. I used to look like him."

"Good thing. Cause he's an asshole."

"Yeah, word's getting around."

Roger followed Bill and Harry to the Thing and got behind the wheel. They drove off and made a left toward Avalon.

The janitor watched them go. "They'll be back."

Cooper slowly got off the floor. He went around and sat next to Jose. He reached over and poured himself another drink from the bottle and downed it. "Thanks."

Before Cooper blinked Jose had a shaky knife to his throat.

"You lookin' for me, Senor?"

Cooper took out the receipt."Jose?"He looked for the old janitor for help, but he was gone.

Jose took the receipt. "Maybe, maybe not."

Gwen came out of the kitchen."What's the score?" She leaned against the door jam. She had found something shiny to straighten her hair in and adjust her clothing.

Jose looked at Gwen. "Did I die?"

The workman turned up the radio. "Sounds like the Angles are up in the first. You want something?"

"Champagne?"

"I got tequila or tequila."

"Agreed. Hold the worm." Gwen downed the shot, flushed a little and left to wash-up in the ladies room, turning back to smile at Cooper and the two awestruck men."There's a phone in the kitchen. I called Marty. They'll be expecting us for dinner."

Cooper had to smile. "Mind?"

Jose lowered the knife, and gave the receipt back to Cooper after looking it over at his friend."Where to?"

Cooper poured another round."Mainland."

Jose picked his drink up and downed it. "No airports."

"Parking lot?"

"I can land only in the water, Señor."

"How about a parachute?"

"Two hundred, cash." He glanced toward the restrooms. "But I only have the one."

"Three hundred credit card?"

Jose looked at the man behind the counter who seemed impressed and nodded yes again.

"I can do... but no guarantees on the chute."

Cooper took out the credit card. "Chanced it before."

The workman ran the credit card.

Jose poured another drink and downed it, stood up, flashed his gold filled mouth and passed out. Cooper caught him and sat him back down on the stool. He looked at the workman.

"I just fix 'em."

15 FLIGHT OF FANCY

Outside, Roger, Bill, and Harry had left the VW Thing parked up around the bend. Thinking they could prevent anyone from flying off the rock, they made their way across a slope toward the back of the locked airplane hangar. They reached the top, out of breath where they were stopped by a barbwire fence that none of them wanted to climb.

Across the parking lot, behind a passenger waiting area, Cooper and Gwen helped Jose into a beat-up Jeep's front seat. Gwen climbed in back. Cooper reached in and pulled it out of gear and gave it a push down the slope.

Roger and Harry made their way across the parking lot toward a patch of cactus gardens when they heard the squeaks and fender rattle from the Jeep. They chased after it on foot. Roger stopped Harry from shooting. They were out of range and he knew after meeting these guys to heed De'Ogo's warnings.

Cooper jumped in and rode the Jeep down the slope. He let it coast as long as he could before he popped it into gear making the engine jump to a rough life. He aimed the Jeep into the dirt to throw up as much dust as possible to give them cover. "Hang on." He cut across a clump of dried brush, through a short gully toward a trampled spot in the fence. Jose's head smacked the dash. Gwen had driven with Portland enough to know better and hung on for dear life. With a jolt from hitting a mound of dirt, a wave of dust lifted into the air behind them. He cut a hard right over to the dirt road heading west and down to the ocean. The sign read Hidden Ranch - Wrigley Family - Via Del Rancho, Escondido.

"Pig!"

Cooper swerved to miss a wild boar. "Was that Roger?"

"Not funny."

By the time Roger and his two pals reached the Thing, Cooper and Gwen were only a bad memory drifting away in a cloud of island dust. So they had lived, the both of them, Roger thought, as he shifted into high gear. Blown out of the damn clear blue sky before his very eyes, yet here they were, shoveling them dust from a feedbag. It didn't surprise Roger. Nothing every surprised Roger when it came to that son-of-bitch Portland Cooper. The bastard was always so goddamn lucky. Only Cooper could fall out of an airplane and into a vat of shit and come up smelling like roses.

He knew Cooper had lived. He had felt it. But Gwen, now that did surprise him, as well as disappointed him. He was looking forward to killing Cooper personally after what he did to him out there. But now he would have to kill Gwen, too.

They couldn't leave this island alive. De'Ogo would have his hide. Gwen couldn't get back under Jack's protection or Jack would have his hide. On the other hand Gwen might not say anything to anyone. It was her family, step family as it may be. There was always Irene to contend with. Shit! He'd have to let De'Ogo handle the details. All he had to do was make sure Cooper didn't get off Catalina Island.

"Pig!"

Roger was way into his head and ran it over. It squealed bloody murder as the Thing bucked up and skidded off the road and ended up in the drainage ditch as the dust trailing them caught up and settled onto them.

"What the hell, man?"

"You killed it."

"Get out, and push us out of here."

Roger looked down the hill as the dust brought tears to his eyes. Cooper would pay for all of this. Every last bit of it. He wiped his face streaking it with mud.

"Are you crying?"

"Shut the hell up and push."

In a small inlet a camouflaged seaplane floated on the waves hidden by scrub brush netting. In the surrounding area, no natural scrub brush grew. But under the chin of the Indian Head at the end of Cottonwood Canyon a thicket of plastic brush clustered together in what seemed to be a natural cropping but wasn't.

Just above that, Cooper cut sharply off the dirt road toward the dry wash bed of Cottonwood Canyon. The Jeep bumped and jumped through the hard underbrush. The one working headlight wasn't much help but Portland wasn't applying for a chauffer's license. About thirty yards from the Indian Head, the Jeep hit a sharp runoff gully, bottomed out, ripping off the exhaust and stalled.

"My Jeep, you pinchi gringo."

"Send her a bill. Move it."

"I give the orders here. Now, help me out."

Portland grabbed Jose by the back of his jacket and dragged his ass out of the Jeep. "Where's the plane from here?"

Jose stood up trying to get his bearings. "You are very rude, Señor." He threw-up on Cooper's feet. Cooper just looked at him with disgust. Jose pointed his finger straight down the canyon.

Cooper dragged Jose along.

Gwen had her feet wrapped in oil rags to protect them from the jagged rocks. She glanced back. Lights were coming down the canyon road. "Here they come."

Cooper stopped above a cliff. Down below, the surf crashed on the jagged rocks. "How do we get down from here?"

"Talk to the Indian."

"What?"

"The Indian." He pointed toward the protruding rocks.

Gwen ran along a path to the rock formation. The moon light glistening off the water wasn't much help.

"In the hole. Reach inside."

"What? I'm not reaching into dark smelly holes."

Cooper dragged Jose over. "Reach, Gwen."

Gwen gulped, closed her eyes and stuck her hand into the hole. A cold shiver ran up and down her spine. There could be a rattle snake, scorpions or worse, spiders in there. She touched something ridged and jerked back with a suppressed scream.

Jose laughed. "You can't die from a rope bite unless it's around your neck, Señorita."

Gwen reached back in and pulled it out. The rope had knots all the way down it. She threw it down and it landed among the rocks below. Gwen looked back at Portland.

"Do it."

She gripped the rope. Her feet were killing her as it was. So much for her pedicure.

"Shall I toss you? Or do you want to climb down.

"Last one down feeds the sharks." Jose followed Gwen.

Cooper looked back up to the road. Roger had stopped where the dust had ended. They had gotten out of the Thing and were arguing. Cooper couldn't make out the angry voices. He wanted very much to lay in wait for them and beat the crap out of all three of them. But he had to get to the mainland and to Finn before Roger did. He climbed down the fifteen feet to the rocky beach below. He wasn't looking forward to giving his wounds another salt bath.

The Piper J-3 Cub seaplane sat behind a natural water break, bobbing on its two dented metal floats. Cooper, Gwen, and Jose waded-swam around the jetty. Only, Gwen was lucky enough to be on Cooper's shoulders. A large wave hit them hard. She fell back, dunking herself. Cooper pulled her back up.

"Cuts out of the water, damn-it."

"Oh, shut up!"

"Here they come," Jose yelled.

Sharks appear in the water.

"Faster, faster."

"Spur me again, I flip you."

Jose started shooting over his shoulder. Cooper made sure Gwen didn't get hit as they fought harder through the waist-high water.

Jose made it to the plane first. The camouflage brush tarp around it fell away with one tug on a rope.

"Help me pull this shit ashore."

They piled the tarp on the rocks and waded back out to the Piper and climbed in. Cooper got behind the lifeless-looking controls that hadn't seen repairs since the mid-forties.

"Can you fly, Señor?"

"Can this?"

"It could this morning."

Roger, Bill, and Harry had by then figured out where Cooper had gone off into the canyon and were yards away from Jose's Jeep. They were too far behind to have seen them get into the seaplane and didn't take notice of it until they heard the roar of the Continental A-65 engine. Roger pulled his gun out and ran down the canyon. He tripped and tumbled as he went. He was beside himself. Cooper had gotten to a plane. Twice Bill helped him up. They stopped at the edge of the cliff beside the Indian Head. Down below in the moonlight they could vaguely make out the plane but they could hear it loud and clear.

Cooper had definitely gotten to a plane! But it wasn't running well. Could his luck have run out and he'd get stuck out in a dead plane? Please. The plane's engine roared louder. That lucky bastard. He was getting away. Roger shot in what he thought was the direction of the roar from the engines. It was hard to tell because of the echoing off the cliffs. Bill and Harry pulled out their guns and joined him. Their silenced guns were giant spit wad shooters in an echo chamber.

Gwen screwed-up her face and held her breath as she climbed in back where it was full of cargo. "What is that smell?"

"Something crawled up the wiring and died."

"Smells like a dead body."

Cooper looked over at Jose. He shrugged innocently.

"Sit down, Gwen."

Cooper sat in the torn pilot's seat. The bullets from above whizzed nearby. Jose leaned over and hit some switches after the plane made it past the white caps and got into the rolling swells. Cooper pushed the throttle forward again and the plane began to move faster. The Grass Hopper heaved up and down in the choppy water.

"Find a groove in the waves and ride into the wind, Señor."

The men up on the cliffs continued to fire after the plane as it got farther and farther from the shore. But the distance was too great for them to do damage shooting into the wind with just handguns. The bullets flew harmlessly overhead or plopped into the ocean before them, but an occasional tink on the plane's armor kept their knuckles white. Cooper attempted to get the plane up but it slammed back down in the sea and disappeared from Roger's view behind another bluff.

"Give it more throttle, slowly this time, or she'll choke-out."

Cooper eased up the throttle. The A-65 sputtered a bit then roared louder. He maneuvered the plane back into the wind and revved it twice. At the top of the second rev he gunned it full throttle. The plane rattled and shook violently, threatening to disintegrate right there in the open sea as it gained speed.

"What are you doing?"

"Getting this piece of shit up in the air."

"You'll kill us."

"Portland."

"Sssssshhhh. I can hear what she wants. Sit back and put your heads between your legs."

Jose looked back at Gwen for support."Lunático?"

"Engine whisperer."

The plane rolled over the swells tipping to either side as it lifted and fell, bouncing Gwen like loose baggage from side to side. Cooper held her hard at full throttle, the engine screamed in protest. Cooper's cut hands ached trying to stay in control.

But finally, as though the plan had enough abuse, the Piper lifted off. Cooper and Gwen where free.

"Shit, how did you do that?"

"You gotta listen to her. Or she'll kill you one day."

Jose looked at Gwen again."Who is this guy?"

"Some lunático I picked up in high school."

The men on the cliff watched as the plane lifted out of the sea and back into view above the bluffs. It still struggled to fly but gained strength as Cooper eased up. Within moments all that was left was the sound of the crashing waves below.

Roger rushed back up the canyon to the VW Thing where he had left his bag of goodies. Bill and Harry followed. It was out of Roger's hands now. It was De'Ogo's movie from here on out. Roger got into the Thing and pounded on the steering wheel. The last thing he wanted to do was tell De'Ogo that Cooper and Gwen were alive and on their way back to the mainland. He should have taken heavier guns with him in the first place but Sam wanted things quiet. Well this was what quiet would get him. Those men at the airport would have to be dealt with later. But not by Roger. He wanted only Portland Cooper. Roger pulled the Thing back on the road and drove to where they had left their inflated launch raft. It had a two stroke outboard strapped to it. They had to move fast if they wanted to catch up with Gwen and Portland. With any luck the backup Huey had arrived. Roger stopped the Thing in front of the hippy tied to a fence post. He tossed him the keys.

"You mother....."

Roger put his gun to the man's head. "I left you a pig. You want to live to eat it?"

The hippy nodded his head yes.

They left him tied. But happy as a luau to be breathing.

16 BACK BEHIND THE WHEEL

Roger, Bill, and Harry arrived back at the ship and reluctantly climbed up to the top deck. Sam De'Ogo met them with a stern look. Pounding of an incoming turbine grew in the sky.

"They're on their way back to the mainland."

"What?!" De'Ogo slapped Roger.

"Those men at the airport. They helped them. You sent us out with peashooters. They had machineguns."

De'Ogo turned to Harry and Bill.

"Three of them. The leader was a black janitor and knew how to use an AK47. We weren't expecting them."He had to yell over the throb of the helicopter.

Sam didn't have to hear anymore of this crap. He knew who they were. Drug smugglers, the lot of them. It probably wasn't anything personal, more likely business. He'd settle with them later. But now he had to get to Cooper. If he was heading anywhere, it was back to the little red car and the marina.

Slim showed up with all the stunt drivers as the helicopter touched down on the helipad up above. The copter pilot kept the engine running. He wasn't staying long.

"Slim, get those two dimwits on the horn and tell them to keep an eye out for Portland Cooper."

"I tried. They weren't answering."

"Goddamn it! All right, all of you, in the helicopter. Now!"

The men headed up to the landing pad. Sam stopped Roger. Roger pulled away.

"Put a case of guns on the helicopter."

"Listen, these things aren't worth shit against automatic weapons."

"I like them, there discreet."

"So is a dead man, and I ain't volunteering."

"Load them!" He smacked Roger again. "Or you won't have to." Sam turned to his cinematographer. "Make sure they get on, and check for adequate ammo. I want Portland Cooper alive, Slim. You make sure everyone knows that he doesn't die until I say so and not until we get it on film."

"You ought to just kill him, Sam. Whatever it is you're looking for, a man like that won't just give it to you," Slim said.

De'Ogo turned out to sea. He had his reasons. He needed Roger back under his thumb, or his and Jack's lives would change again. He couldn't destroy their film careers. Jack's life was exactly where he needed it to be. There was so much at stake here. His plans, he had such deep long range plans that included shooting Gwen's father in the back. He could not let this Mr. Cooper get in the way or let Roger not fulfill their agreement if he wanted to keep things moving as they were. Even if Gwen and Irene were to die with Mr. Cooper. He needed Jack in full control of their financial destiny. His next step, to control a publishing empire. The Little Island Princess, and an island paradise hiding a mysterious ancient secret he knew to be all too true. He wanted that discovery on film. He needed it to fulfill his life. His crowning moment, exposing its truth to the world. His academy award. Even if they didn't give it to him, there wouldn't be a person in the world who wouldn't stand in line to see the truth to what lives beneath Kuali Rhu. The old man keeping it from him could not hide forever. Giving Mr. Cooper the backside cove to the island with the threat it posed to his plans would end here. If he had known it would get to this someday, he would've killed Mr. Cooper in that alley years ago. Though he had meant Gwen for Roger. Gwen and Irene were but meager stepping stones to what he wanted and Jack would just have to understand that someday.

180

Karl J. Niemiec

Slim wasn't about to push it. He went after Roger, yelling for Bill and Harry to give a hand.

Sam De'Ogo watched as Slim made sure enough clips where in the ammo bags. He didn't trust these clowns in a big city with automatic weapons. He saw what Cooper was capable of doing to them in the open sea. He'd be even more dangerous with someplace to hide. There was a good chance things were already beyond repair. He just might selvage what he could by getting what's about to happen next on film. If push got to shove on this one, he was shooting a film. That would be his story and he'd stick to it.

Slim came back with a bottle of Jack Daniel's and two glasses. He poured one half full and handed it to De'Ogo. Sam took the drink and waited for Slim to pour himself one. It didn't look like they would finish this film as written. They toasted. No words were necessary. Slim knew what his boss wanted him to do. Make plans to leave U.S. waters. If worse got beyond worse, he'd have to discreetly scuttle the ship once they got out to international waters. What a waste. They watched the helicopter lift off. By the time they were on their second drink, the sound of the turbine engine had disappeared.

"You want to see the film?"

"How did it look?"

"It's a little rough, but this Cooper character and the girl are unbelievable."

"It's amazing what heights mice will climb when they know the cat wants to eat them."

Cooper was still in the pilot's seat struggling to put on his parachute. He kept the seaplane low enough to make out the shapes of land below. He could trace locations by the lights coming through the spotty, low cloud cover that hung along the shoreline. His main concern was flying so close to the airport with a useless radio. A frantic crackling came over the broken headset. He pulled them off and tossed them aside. He was approaching the mainland from the south west and had to swing way north to avoid any aircrafts taking off.

But still someone was trying to reach them over the air. There was nothing he could do about it. He banked the Piper east over Venice Beach and headed south east toward Marina Del Rey directly at the north side of the airport. The controller assigned to him was predictably pulling his hair out. And jets most likely had already launched to shoot them down. Within minutes they'd be joined and escorted down one way or the other. When Jose woke up and found out what a mess he was in with the local Feds he'd sober up fast.

Dexter and Teatro had Cooper dump the Corsa in the Marina parking lot off Marquesas Way while a trailer had just pulled up with six foreign sports cars. Roger had his Porsche there, and from what Cooper had seen, it was somehow the original car's frame and most of the body. Someone had done a lot of work on it considering the condition Roger left it. Presumably Finn had done some. But Cooper wasn't sure what.

Teatro and Dexter were left in the Marina parking lot to look after the stunt cars and were most likely waiting for him by now. His only chance was if Finn was home on his boat getting drunk as usual.

Gwen searched franticly in the back of the plane for another chute. "Portland?"

Jose had his head resting against the door, snoring.

"Portland?"

Cooper managed get his parachute on. He reached over to wake Jose to no avail. So he opened Jose's door and hung him out into the open damp air while holding onto his belt. The air rushed in pinned Gwen down in back.

"Portland!"

Jose was slowly brought to by the cold air. He opened his eyes to find himself dangling from the plane with his head literally in a cloud. He tried to focus his eyes on the lights of the Marina below. When he realized where he was he scrambled back inside. His heart raced like a Greyhound bus, and tequila oozed through his pores.

"You have a dangerous sense of humor."

"I wasn't joking.You ready to take over? We're bailing out."

Jose looked out. "Shit, are you loco? We're nearly over the LA Airport. They're liable to shoot us down!"

"Just you. We're out of here."

Gwen watched the men traded places."Where's my chute?"

Cooper turned back to Gwen."We're dropping in on Finn. So, hurry up, grab on… let's go."

"Are you listening? I don't have a chute. Wait, here it is." She yanked on it. She looked closer. "Holy crap, it's attached to someone."

Cooper looked at Jose.

"My bad," Jose smiled sheepishly.

Cooper gave her a big bridgeless smile."Take it."

"I'm not putting that thing on."

"I'm leavin'." Jose banked the J-3 Cub out toward the sea.

Gwen knew there was no time to waste. She crawled into the front and wrapped her legs around Portland. Cooper opened the door again and jumped out with Gwen clinging to him for dear life. Cooper's fading voice harmonized with Gwen's scream as they vanished into the night. "Plaaaaaane!"

Jose reached to lock the door."Bombs away, crazy gringo." His mind stopped, his eyes opened with shock. "Plane!"

An airliner materialized out of the cloud cover and filled his whole vision. He put the Grass Hopper into a dive and the airliner just missed him by inches. The down draft nearly knocked him out of the sky.

Cooper and Gwen free fell from the plane for only moments. Cooper pulled the cord in anticipation of a sudden uplifting jolt. Nothing happened. He showed Gwen the cord and let it drop from his hand. Gwen pulled herself up and planted a big kiss on him for luck and bit his ear as he groped for the second cord and pulled it. There was a slight hesitation, then the chute shot out overhead and opened. They jerked up into a north westerly draft and began to slowly glide back down to Mother Earth.

"What are we looking for?" Gwen asked.

"Finn's sailboat."

"There's a hell of a lot of sailboats down there."

"We're looking for his blinking red light."

Cooper and Gwen surveyed the marina down below trying to spot their target while Cooper maneuvered the chute.

"There it is," Gwen said pointing and almost letting go.

"Where?"

"Turn left. See it?"

"There he is. All right, let's float in tastefully. We'll likely be met by a welcome wagon if Roger got back on the ship without that De'Ogo character killing him. Just let go when I say so?"

"Go to hell!"

"You heard me."

"You are the biggest...."

Down below in the marina, Finn hosted a party on his overly lit docked sailboat. A big red light blinked at the top of the mask to let his drunkard friends in the area know he was in and open to getting wasted. It was still early, maybe Cooper would find Finn sober enough to comprehend what kind of danger he was in. The quests cheered the Angels' home ballgame. Overhead, the sounds of passing aircrafts faded. Suddenly, a slew of female curses were followed by a huge splash and red light bulb glass tinkling down onto the deck. Finn and his guests scrambled out of the way as they looked up to find a figure hanging from the mast by his parachute cords like a mummified crucifix. There was a moment of silence before they realized the person was choking to death on the parachute's cords. Loud cheering came from the TV. They all turned to watch Nolen Ryan throw a fastball in for a strike three.

Cooper spoke in a strained voice. "Finn, would you mind helping me down?"

Finn, after catching on that it was Cooper, shimmied up the pole like a roof rat and cut his friend down. Cooper hit the deck like a bolder on a mountain road. He rolled over in agony.

"Aaahhhh...thanks, Finn. I could've done that myself."

"Portland! Marty called but he didn't say you'd be droppin' out of the friggin' sky," Finn said, his voice full of whisky. "Holy poker, what happened to you?"

"I'll explain later. Get sober."

Gwen swam over to the side of the boat and some of the guests plucked her from the septic marina water.

Finn helped Cooper untangle himself. "What did you weld for Roger Kelemen?"

"It's a secret. Why, Gwen, thanks for droppin' in."

"We were in your airspace."

Delma, Marty's boxlike estrange wife handed Finn a dry towel and went back to the TV and her Scotch.

"What's the score?"Gwen asked.

"Tied now. One-one in the third. Nolan's pitchin'."

Finn began to towel dry Gwen with great pleasure, pretending he wasn't just groping her body.

"What was it, Finn?" Cooper began to wad up the chute.

"Why do you need to know now? It was years ago...before he totaled it. A little friggin' body work, front end work...you saw it all before."

"Finn! They are on their way here to make sure you can't tell me."

"You mean...?"

"Yes, kill you."

"Okay, a small box under the backseat. You'll see it. Covers the gearbox. He made me sign a contract to keep my mouth shut. Said it was a personal safety deposit box for his belongings."

Gwen took the towel away."What am I, a sports car?"

Finn gave her a mischievous wink and smile. "Just tryin' to be a gracious host."

"And a letch."

"Of course."He turned to Cooper and saw the no-nonsense look on his battered face. "Okay, the box is rigged to kill anyone trying to open it without the key. All right? He paid me three extra grand to forget I ever saw it. So don't tell Rog I told ya."

Cooper finished wadding up the chute and gave it to Finn. "I'm sure he knows I'm headed here. All of you, hide... you're in danger. Hide, Finn, now! I'll get back in touch."

"Oh, and Delma, come get Marty off my Lazy-Boy, he snores and farts."

"Keep his cheating fat ass. I got Nolan Ryan," Delma said.

The guests all looked at Finn as Cooper pulled Gwen down the plank toward the parking lot.

"Lock it up," Finn told them.

Cooper and Gwen ran through the parking lot heading toward Bora Bora Way. "And stay away from Brubaker."

"Brubaker?"

"He's back on the street."

"Holy mother of Corsa. Give me a minute. We'll give you a lift. There's two guys watching that Corsa."

"No time, catch up with us if you can. Come up on the south side to distract them. Then get the hell out of here. Go straight to Holland's, arm yourself, and stay there until you hear from me."Cooper grabbed Gwen by the hand as they sprinted down Via Marina making a right and continued running until they neared Marquesas Way. Gwen's poor toes were killing her. Thank goodness for all those hours she spent barefoot walking on coral as a kid at the beach. They slowed to catch their breath and give their battered feet a rest. After a moment they walked briskly through the parking lot as an overhead haunting throb sank closer and closer and head right toward them.

So Cooper grabbed up Gwen and sprinted the rest of the way to where Roger left his Corsa. Cooper put her down and took the Corsa key out of his pocket and headed directly past the row of six stunt cars to the Corsa. He stopped when he saw the interior had been taken apart and piled in the back. The top was still down. The dash was parted and searched.

Dexter and Teatro strolled through the parking lot from a nearby restaurant. They had a bag of burgers and a six-pack under each arm. They got into the BMW as they noticed the two figures opening the Corsa doors. They couldn't believe the nerts on the thieves in this town. Trying to rip off the Corsa right under their noses. But a car suddenly turned into the parking lane from the south side and came racing towards them. So they left the Chinese silenced guns that Sam had issued them inside their coats as they got out of the Beamer and advanced on the Corsa.

They eyed Cooper's battered face. Recognition washed over them as they realized who they were looking at. When Teatro saw that the car was joining them he reached for his gun. Gwen poked him in the eye and jumped on his back, clawing at his face. Cooper smacked Dexter in the nose, putting the big gorilla down for another eight count.

Finn and two other Corvair Club members got out of his Spider. He went to his trunk and pulled out a rope while his two friends removed Gwen from Teatro, taking his gun, and dragged the two thugs over to the BMW's opened doors. They pushed Teatro and Dexter down to their knees, adding a couple good kicks, and tied them both to the door handles, one on each side of the car.

Cooper took Teatro's knife and walked over to Roger's 911. He knifed a tire, leaving the knife in it.

Gwen smiled as Cooper jumped in the Corsa. He tried the key. The ignition was still connected. The Corsa fired up. He saluted Finn and his friends and drove away. Finn didn't wait for applause. They sped away in the other direction.

The helicopter landed directly in front of where the Corsa had been parked. It threw up a gust of litter-filled wind. Roger and the six other men jumped out. They knew immediately that Cooper had beaten them to the Corsa. Roger could only jump up and down in frustration almost taking his head off with the copter rotor. He ducked down, yelling at the others to find Dexter and Teatro as the helicopter pulled away.

They found them struggling to untie themselves. After a short explanation from Dexter on why they hadn't checked in, and instructions from Roger, the men spread out and got into their respective foreign sports cars.

Roger stopped at the door of his silver 66 Porsche and saw the knife sticking out of his left front tire. He looked at Bill getting into a gold 68 Volvo P1800 and Harry getting into a 66 Triumph TR4. Beyond them, in basin A, Finn's silent sail boat floated with the red light off. So Cooper had put numbers together and they were beginning to add up for him. Finn was a drunk, though basically honest. But drunks had a habit of letting secrets slip. Knowing him, he probably never told Cooper the facts, maybe just a drunken hint over a case of beer. He wouldn't have told a soul the whole truth on his death bed, except for Cooper who had a way of making things sound imperative when it came to dying. The prick.

Dexter got in his 67 black BMW 2000cs rubbing his wrist. He watched Teatro start his powder blue 67 Datsun Roadster. They looked at each other then over to Roger and waited.

Roger looked away from the sailboat. He reached into the 911 and picked up the CB radio and spoke into it. "Come get your damn knife, Teatro." He got into his Porsche and popped the hood and started it. He looked down at the glowing dashboard. The thing was newly decked out to kill. He could monitor everything from tire pressure to gas pains. The Porsche's bored out cylinders roared with power as Roger flexed his foot to warm up his silver bullet. He couldn't wait to catch up with Cooper and that stinking Corsa. He'd show them what a street machine was all about. "And change my goddamn tire."

Teatro and Dexter pulled out the jack and changed Roger's tire with help of Cherry and Paco. Forty-five seconds flat. Afterword, Cherry hopped into a yellow 66 VW Baja Bug, checking the bandage wrapped around his head in the mirror. Taylor lifted himself over the door of a green 65 Alfa 2600 Spider convertible and slid behind the wheel. Paco, with his arm in a sling, got in the navy blue 66 Mercedes 230s1 because it was an automatic. He tested his CB radio. Zev, the tall young Mexican who released the doves on the ship with Paco for Sam came on the line from inside an orange 68 Karmann Ghia. "Hear, you."

"Follow me," Roger said over their CB radios.

"Roger that," Harry said.

"Eat me. Don't anyone ever say that again," Roger said.

They revved their souped up engines and sped off after Roger's wake of smoking tire tracks. Dexter's and Teatro's cars were in stark contrast to the other cars' beefed up shiny road gear. A newly modified tow truck remained behind. Its chrome function panel and empty camera and movie light mounts glistened in the light from the parking lamps above.

Roger headed north on Via Marina, zooming past Admiralty Way to Washington Street and headed east, followed closely by the roar from the pack of stunt cars.

Parked behind the Jamaica Bay Inn, Portland and Gwen watched as the nine sports cars raced by. Cooper got out, his body beginning to stiffen, and went to a pay phone. He spoke to the operator. "I'd like to make a collect call. Thank you."

17 BODY OF EVIDENCE

Outside of Curt's Corvair Auto Wrecking yard, Portland and Gwen waited in the dark along the dusty yellow wood fence. The Corsa sat at the end of Tujunga Avenue in the heart of the Valley's auto junk yards where Roger had originally bought it and began its complete restoration.

Marty's Corvan pulled left off Penrose Street passing a gravel company and did a u-turn to park behind the Corsa. He got out and stood next to the Corsa as though he always window shopped at night outside of junk yards. He checked inside the Corsa. He didn't really expect Cooper to be waiting out in the open like a hand painted duck decoy. He walked over to the front of Curt's and looked in the window. He checked the door. It was locked as expected.

Cooper waited to make sure Marty wasn't followed. "Come out, come out wherever you are." Marty looked around toward the shadows of the dusty yellow fence then across the road to where large earth movers were lined up behind a locked chain link fence. He started to get lonely. "Do I look that stupid?"

"Define stupid." Cooper came into the open with Gwen. They both moved with the brittleness of a hundred and ten year old couple. Every muscle, bone, cartilage, ligament, and internal organ ached. Cooper needed his stomach pumped, he was still pissing blood and eating anything was out of the question.

Marty stopped in his tracks when he saw the condition they were in. Gwen's bandages and her tattered jeans and blouse were still damp and burned. Cooper wore the singed jumpsuit and only his right boot. A pant leg was missing and the arms were slit from both shoulders to the elastic cuffs. But worse of all was his face. It had started to swell so much that his eyes were tiny slits. The Super Glue caused even deeper crevasses like bad surgical scares. He hurt so bad that he couldn't even tell his nose was broken. His cuts were blood crusty slashes leading from one purple spot to another.

"You said it was like a honeymoon?"

"Of the shotgun variety."

"Got your clothes like you ask. Curt said you could use the shower out back of the office. I've been in there. You sure you want to do that?" Marty unlocked the gait to let them in.

"We'll live."

"Speak for yourself."

Jesus, you two look like you just went fifteen rounds in hell."

"Thank you."Gwen took her jeans and blouse from Marty and stepped back into the shadows to a door. "I'll be right out."

"Scream if you see anything moving."

"Mr. Cooper was right, you're a funny guy."

"I'll be right in."

Gwen went in turning on the light to make sure she was alone and let the door click shut behind her. Cooper and Marty waited to hear the water running.

"Jesus, you're a lucky bastard."

"Yeah, thanks, I'm feeling real fortunate, all over."

"How many of them did it take to do that to your face?"

"Only three, but I had my hands tied over my head."

Marty winced."I reached Doc at Kaiser a few minutes ago. He's got a motorcyclist with a few dangling participles but he's on standby like you asked. What do you want me to tell him?"

"Tell him to meet us at Jorge's when his shift is over." Cooper peeled down to his birthday suit and stepped into a clean pair of blue work overalls.

"You're not gonna shower?"

"Maybe later. I've seen enough water today."

Marty handed over white socks and Cooper's old work boots. "God, your whole side is yellowish, greenish, and purplish."

"Make up your mind."

"You figure anything out that might interest me yet?"

"Later. What did the press say about me and Goodricke?"

The water squeaked to a stop inside the shower room.

"No suspects, however a certain individual is being sought for questioning. By strange coincidence he used to look like, but still sounded and had the same name as you. You know him?"

"Portland was there," Gwen said just inside the door. Gwen stepped out of the shower room to take a look at Cooper fully dressed in clean clothes. "You're not going in."

"Too dirty for me with all these cuts."

"Sissy."

"Well, shit, who murdered them?"

"Stick around, we're about to find out that and a whole lot more than I think any of us wanted to know. Right, Gwen?"

"Kiss my royal ass, Portland."

"The honeymoon's over, good buddy."

"You too, Marty."

"Can I go first, Coop?"

Gwen hobbled over, got in the Corsa and slammed the door.

"What's with her?"

"Jack's not Jewish."

"Okay. We found who took the still on Roger's wall."

"Dead, or alive?"

"Dead of natural causes in 1975. Cancer. He worked for the snoop papers. His widow claims he made twenty grand."

"How'd you find her?"

"She's my step-aunt."

"Great. What about the sixteen millimeter?"

"Your guess is as good as mine."

"I have a hunch it was taken by a man named Sam De'Ogo."

"Who?"

"A friend of the family."

"Brubaker's been weaseling around. He's got an early copy of tomorrow's front page. You're on it."

"I figured he would. So, let him. It won't hurt him none." Cooper turned to Gwen. "I think it's time to invite who's left on Roger's list to dinner tomorrow night. Place an extra setting."

"I'll have to ask Mother. What about Jack? I don't know."

Cooper got back into the Corsa. "Personally I can't wait to see the look on their faces. Make sure Roger gets an invite."

"He's back?"

"Tropical storms in Florida."

"What about Brubaker?"

"I guess we play him by ear."

"All I wanted to know was Roger's whereabouts."

"Well, now you know. His whereabouts is south of Heaven. Here's the parts list, Marty. I need you to find Holland. Check The Palomino. Have her call Cal from wherever she's at. He's expecting her. There's a private Beechcraft waiting at Turners Falls Airport booked into Van Nuys tonight. Finn is waiting at Holland's already. I need the rest of these parts in one hour over at Jorge's, so we can get started. This is where they're at. Have Finn bring his mobile equipment and a couple of guys."

Marty went back to the Corvan and took out a twelve gauge pump in a black gun case and handed it to Cooper. He glanced down at the list. "That's a lot of strings to pull. You sure about all of this? Some of these people we don't want to owe favors."

Gwen looked over at Cooper. She knew he was trying to make things right in his own way. He had a need to kick some ass. So did she. Roger needed to be taught a lesson. And Sam De'Ogo needed to be stopped. Jack had a lot of questions to answer if he's not who he told her mother he was. Her poor mother, what would she do if the police got a hold of all this and it got into the newspapers? They'd have a field day. What would her grandfather say? This really took it in the rear no matter how she looked at it. She sucked in a deep breath. Portland and the Corsa Club rules were her only way out. "Pull them."

18 In Laid The Truth

Cooper waited behind a parked car outside of Roger's Sherman Oaks underground secured parking lot until Roger showed up with his Porsche at fifteen to eleven. It was about time. Cooper was hopeful Roger would need a refill on his habit from Nick, his friendly neighborhood pusher. Cooper followed Roger in on foot before the gate closed and hid in front of a white Cadillac Seville. He waited nearly ten minutes before he heard one long and two short blasts from Gwen's Sting Ray horn. Meaning she had received a phone call from Nick, Roger's one legged neighbor. Roger and his two friends were in Nick's condo getting high. Cooper could hear the music turn up which meant Nick was giving them the go. Roger and his friends were sticking around for snow and tell.

Cooper wore a tool belt that included his trusty slim jim and he had full intentions of popping Roger's door, alarm or no alarm. He made his way over to where Roger parked his 911. With one short tug Cooper unlocked the Porsche by sliding the slim jim down along the glass and hooking into the lock mechanism. He didn't bother with trying to bypass the alarm. Roger was hip to that game.

The alarm went off. Cooper was expecting it and pushed up the driver seat. He flipped up the bottom of the backseat and pulled back the carpet revealing a triangular metal plate. It was held in place by Phillips screws, an access to the shift rod coupler. Cooper unscrewed and lifted the plate. Welded in the hole was a small locked box, not much larger than a cassette tape. A metal tube ran out of the bottom of it.

Cooper unfolded a piece of paper with a electrical scheme drawn on it. According to Finn, Portland had one try to disarm the bomb, grab the tape, and get his butt out of there before Roger came inquiring with his friends. Or he blew himself up.

Cooper inserted the key and slowly turned it counter clockwise as instructed. The tricky part, Finn had told him, was to pull the tape out while the key was inserted and turned, otherwise the explosives would be activated and it would be bombs over Peoria and Cooper would be disarmed instead. Cooper pulled, the tape out quickly. Once the tape was out releasing a spring trigger, the explosives were null and void. Not even a head on collision would set it off now. He reached back inside to the shift rod coupler with a pair of pliers. He pulled out a cotter pin before he let the carpet drop and put the seats back. He could hear oncoming voices even though the alarm was still blaring in his ears.

He'd been in Roger's car for about twelve seconds. He closed the Porsche's door, resisting the urge to carve his name in its new paint and ran toward the street. Gwen's Sting Ray pulled to a stop with the door opened. Cooper got in and they were gone. Eighteen seconds tops.

Cooper showed her the tape. "Want to hear it?"

"I'll wait for the movie."

The garage elevator opened. Roger, Bill, and Harry came out glassy eyed. Roger beeped the alarm off as he ran to his car. It was still locked and looked to be untouched but he knew it wasn't. "Have a look around." It was Cooper, Roger could feel it in his bones. Finn had talked.

Bill and Harry ran to the opposite ends of the underground garage to have a look around. Roger opened his Porsche. The backseat and carpet were back in place, but something looked different. The dust line was off. Roger pulled up the front seat and lifted the back to find the plate under the carpet was upside down, the box open and the tape gone. He hurried to put everything back in order and got out of the car as Harry and Bill came back.

"Nobody's around. They take anything?"

"No, nothing, it must've been a cat or something."

"Yeah, well, I don't like it. I'm gonna look around a little outside. Get some Cools around the corner."

"Good idea... get something to drink for the girls."

Bill went and let himself out into the street. He wiped his runny nose. Dickens was vacant of anyone suspicious, except for himself. So he headed for a liquor store at the end of the block and up on Ventura Boulevard.

Roger and Harry reentered the elevator. As the door closed Roger looked away from Harry so the rage in his eyes wouldn't show. Now Cooper had his key...and his tape.

Hello, if you're enjoying this romantic action adventure about my beloved Blood Red, please leave a review.

Thank you.

Karl J. Niemiec

19 BUILD IT AND IT WILL RUN

Nobody in their right mind lived in Burbank across the road from the newly named Burbank-Glendale-Pasadena Airport. Yet three million people lived within 20 miles including the three homes at the end of Jorge's street, Ledge Avenue, where it intersected in an angle at San Fernando Road.

Because the price was right, Jorge had lived there all his life. So had his father. It was home turf. His mother left him the house so he stayed with his wife and three kids. It was a standard stucco two bedroom, one bath with a garage large enough to paint cars in at the rear of the back yard, built in the early '40s. The back of the garage opened into a parking lot of a boot manufacturing company. No one seemed to mind. Jorge had cut a hidden gate in his fence to the lot years ago so he could unofficially enter his garage from the back. He kept it locked and not looking like an official gate, so no one ever said he couldn't.

That was where Jorge, Marty and Holland sat on crates munching burgers and sucking milk shakes, while serenaded by a nasty pit bull and the roar of private jets.

"Shut up!" Holland yelled at the dog.

"Hey, don't talk to Jorge's kids like that," Marty said as a glob of ketchup dropped down on to his green bowling shirt.

"Bring extra ketchup other than what's on your bozo shirt?"

"Shoot, that's the third bozo shirt today. I got extra everything." Marty dripped on his shirt again. "Shit."

"Put your butt over there, Marty. It's bad enough I got to eat this gringo shit," Jorge said. He flung what was left of his first burger over the fence, but it never hit the ground. The pit bull wasn't so picky. But it shut him up for a moment. He probably fed the dog more than its owners did.

Holland and Jorge turned away from Marty.

"You ain't no pictures of health either, guys."

Roger's Corsa and Gwen's Sting Ray pulled up in the parking lot. Finn pulled in behind them in a yellow and white Rampside. Holland got up and opened the gate for them.

"Hey, Portland, Gwen, just in time for Marty's slob fest."

"You're not eating?"

"If you want to call it that," Jorge answered.

"Stop, there are goodies in the Vette."

Jorge slam-dunked his second burger into a trash dumpster. "My heroine." He followed Holland out to retrieve the food.

Marty remained outside the back gate trying to wipe the Ketchup from his shirt. It only made it worse. "Shit."

Cooper drove the Corsa through the gate and into the garage.

Finn lugged in a welding tank, while Cooper went through the tools to make sure he had everything he needed.

"Oh boy, when Gwen says food, she means real food that's digestible," Holland said, coming back into the garage.

"We ready to get to work here?"

"Everything's ready to go...look at this, home boy food, all right." Jorge pulled out a chicken burrito.

Holland took out two boxes of assorted sushi. "Gwen, this is terrific. If you were a man, I'd do ya. Even at my age. So, Coop, what the hell is going on? And who do we get to kick the shit out of for the look on your face."

Marty helped himself to a taco and three or four different kinds of raw fish. He dropped a California roll to the pavement. He tried to kick it out of sight, but the sticky rice stuck to the broken concrete so he put it back onto his plate. He caught Gwen's disdainful eye.

"You're disgusting, Marty."

"I do my best."

"So?" Holland asked again.

"I want to tell. But I can't. It'll only endanger you guys."

For whatever reason the dog decided to leave them alone. A radio played two doors down and a drunken Mexican tried his best to keep up with the music. Cooper went over and looked out over the neighbor's backyard. Maybe it just got bored. Or they let him inside. Or maybe it hated sushi as much as he did. Cooper searched the dark for anyone including the dog. It was gone. And no one was hanging out listening. He knew he was acting paranoid but who wouldn't in his position?

Holland got up and started to take parts out of her '62 Corvair Rampside truck parked in Jorge's work yard. Jorge grabbed the tools out of Marty's Corvan also parked in the yard. Finn set up his cutting rig and tanks inside.

"By the way, Finn. Thanks for the help earlier."

"No problem. But screw the danger, mate."

"All I can tell you is that Roger has gotten himself mixed up with a rough crowd and we're about to kick hell out of them."

"Drugs?"

"Cars, boats, planes, movies, snuff films, murder with all the Hollywood frills." He grabbed a taco and picked at it. His face and mouth hurt so badly. "I've gone over this with Gwen. She'll explain what I need from each of you to pull this off. Tomorrow Gwen will have little gifts for you?" He put down the taco and picked up a Styrofoam cup of split pea soup.

The men turned to Gwen eating. "Don't get your hopes up. They're Cellular phones."

"You guys ready for a little action?"

"Hell yes... just like old times!" Marty said.

"Good, Marty, then go change your shirt."

Marty's face dropped as the others chuckled at his expense.

Cooper went over and gave him a hug."I mean it, put some overalls on, we're about to get dirty.

"Well, okay. Screw you guys. You ain't half the man I am."

"Shit, I ain't a third of what you used to be."

"Yuck, yuck."

In Jorge's next door neighbor's yard Brubaker pressed his ear to the back of the fence. He had to kill the dog to get it to shut up. It's amazing what a metal softball bat will do to the head of a pit-bull. He felt like taking out the drunk who fancied himself a Spanish Sinatra, but he might have three kids if he worked and five if he didn't. He couldn't hear anything at the moment but he heard enough to know something was up and was going down tomorrow night. He didn't have to hear where. If it was Cooper and cars then Brubaker already knew. And he'd be there. Waiting.

Cooper was mixed up in the Goodricke murders somehow. In what way he didn't know. But it didn't matter. If Cooper was involved or better yet pulled the trigger, he'd find out. From what he had heard so far, this all had something to do with Roger Kelemen but he had checked on the bum actor earlier and no one seemed to know where he was. His neighbors that would answer their doors weren't talking. So he staked out Holland's place and watched as car after car stopped and dropped off parts. Then Finn showed up excited as hell over something but got back into his car and headed out the way he came. A few minutes later, Marty and Jorge showed up and the three of them loaded Marty's van with parts and equipment and came over here with Brubaker as their tail in his Dodge.

It was now three minutes to midnight. He made himself comfortable between the shed and the fence on old plumbing pipe probably stolen from an abandon home. The yard was full of junk bathtubs, sinks and toilets. Who could tell if the guy inside was a plumber or a thief? The weeds were up around his neck as he sat there. And stank to high hell. He was sure spiders were keeping an eye on him. What could he do but sit there, listen, and die for a smoke. At least he didn't have to spend his night off listening to his partner. Here he was alone, just a cop and some fool's dead dog. He looked closer at the leaves in his face. He smelled them again. Shit, this was dope growing wild. He looked around, making sure no one was watching. Better safe than stupid. He cut off a few leaves and put them in his mouth and chewed them. Not a bad chew.

Inside the garage, the Corsa was up on four floor stands. Cooper was prone on a mechanic creeper under the front end. He had the front end apart fitting in fast ration steering arms. Next to him lay heavy duty gas shocks, a hydraulic system and Crown stabilizer bars.

Jorge took the street tires off, preparing to revamp the break system.

"Finn, did you see the drawings on the fabed flair fenders?"

"Yeah, Coop, I saw 'em."

"Let me know if you want Jorge to get started on anything."

"I got guys coming. I brought the cutouts."

"Weld the doors shut, too."

"Plan to. Got some plates to lay in."

"That works for me, just get it done in time to paint." Cooper looked over at Marty who wore Cooper's helmet trying to make room for electronic gadgets. "That make sense to you, Marty?"

"What? Yeah, yeah, sure," Marty said.

"That's a relief."

Marty took off Cooper's helmet. "What?"

"Nothing, Marty. Just messing with you."

"What a surprise."

"Holland, check on that flight again."

"Cal said your dash will be here, so it will be here. You should've had them land right here in Burbank."

"My accounts in Van Nuys."

"We're still talkin' these fifteen-fifties series, right?"

"Right, we'll want the off-roads to fit inside the fender well with enough room for these mud guards to protect the body." Cooper held up a set. "I'm expecting a lot of cement buildup, so leave me enough room to clump and drop as I go."

"We're good then. These two guys on their way can cut and weld whatever we don't get done."

"Thanks, guys."

Aspirins had helped Cooper's aching body, but his face was killing him. He already threw up and got his bridge back. He had stopped passing blood. But if Doc didn't get there soon to give him something for the pain and stitch him up, he wasn't sure if he could pull his plan off. At least not for tomorrow night. He kept his mind on revenge and kept on working.

Finn leaned inside the trunk with a torch, cutting the trunk bottom open. The gas tank lay over by a stack of batteries. "Coming through, Coop."

Cooper reached out for his dark goggles and readjusted his light and tools.

Marty continued trying to figure out how to rig a headset to Cooper's racing helmet without destroying its integrity so it fit him properly."I'll have to drill holes into your helmet, Coop. There's not enough room to run both systems."

"Whatever."

Gwen thumbed through an old September issue of Business Week that had a picture of Dick Tracy holding a cellular phone on the cover. She held it open for Marty to see. "Can you rig a full plug-in module that dials on voice command?" Gwen asked.

"You get it here, I'll set it up," Marty said as he walked over to the back of the Corsa and examined its tail. "I'll have to drill new antenna holes."

"Pull the radio's too," Cooper told him as he reached for the hydraulic wrench and put the final touch to a small grommet on a stabilizer bar bushing. He rolled out from under the Corsa.

Cooper leaned into the trunk. "How's it going in here?"

Finn straightened up, stretching his old back. He flipped his goggles back."It'll fit nice. I ran extra steel down along the sides in case things get rough. You want me to put some in the doors when I weld them shut?"

Cooper moved over toward Gwen as he cleaned his hands, thinking it over. All he needed now was to take a bullet.

"Six inch spots along the support bars. Follow the line where my body will be. Put a plate behind the seat too. But no more. You'll have this thing crouching like a tiger."

Gwen held up a taco to Cooper's crusted lips. "Eat." Cooper nibbled at it. It was no use. Soup was all he could take. She gave him another cup of pea soup.

Later, just past one-thirty in the morning, Cooper continued under the rear end by putting in a rear stabilizer bar and heavy duty gas shocks. Gwen was on the phone trying to get the electoral parts Marty needed. She woke up a lot of people.

Finn's guys had come and gone. Jorge had already prepared the Corsa for racing stripes and numbers by cutting from a roll of brown paper. Strips hung from the rafters as he taped them together. The break system was upgraded, the tires were now covered in sheet plastic and tape. Jorge was itching to paint.

At the workbench Holland had already returned from the airport with the dash and gages from Clark's. She helped Marty gut out a small tape recorder which Marty was turning into a signaling device. Marty had the circuit board in his hand. He pushed the play button and a light flashed on a devise on the workbench.

Holland looked up."You're a genius."

"I can bug a vibrator."

"Marty."

"Don't worry, it wasn't yours," Portland said.

Gwen kicked Cooper in the boot. The rest of them got off easy with a stare as they laughed. Gwen was used to these guys ganging up on her and knew how to handle them.

It was after two o'clock by the time Cooper bolted down a padded roll bar and new racing seat belts.

"Where'd you say you got this cage from?"

"I don't know what you're talking about," Holland said. "I've never seen it before in my life."

Cooper looked at the suspicious hacksaw marks on the base of the cage."I better not find out this came from a stockcar parked in some poor guy's backyard."

Holland looked over at Finn and smiled because it probably did. "You know me better than that, Portland."

"Yeah, I know you all too well."

"He wasn't using it. He's halfway through doing ten. And will probably end up doing life when he gets out."

Cooper knew better than to argue. He backed out of the way, and Finn tacked the cage down with small spot welds.

Doc had arrived about an hour ago. He cleaned Portland's wounds and given Portland something for his pain. He was now asleep in the house on the couch waiting for Cooper to finish so he could put some stitches in him. Cooper accepted the new scars. Gwen felt Portland's face had enough and argued that Cooper should get stitched before Doc went to sleep. Cooper didn't want to stop, and felt he would chance tearing them out. Gwen stopped speaking to him.

Cooper left the backseat out along with all the door and side panels, and the front passenger seat. He stripped the Corsa of all its remaining padded dash, unneeded gages, radio and glove box. He had to make up for the extra weight Finn was putting in the doors and seats.

Finn, having finished in the trunk with the hydraulic mounts, had put back the reinforced gas tank and hooked up the extra batteries. He laid the floor support bars and was rigging the doors with cross bars and steel squares where Cooper's body would be. He slid the bar in a hole he had cut through the side of the door. He ran it back past the rear side panel to the frame above the wheel well and welded it all in place. He did the same to the other door and spot welded them closed forever. He then cut the stitching from the leather driver's seat so he could weld a steel plate inside.

Cooper finished it off by anchoring the front roll bar by drilling holes down through the added floor supports, using the hydraulic wrench to tighten them down. He looked at the cage he'd be sitting in. It was a lot of extra weight. He'd have to spend a whole day in the Corsa just to get the feel of it again.

Jorge was under the front end with a Phillips screwdriver and a razor blade modifying a new front spoiler. He trimmed the excess hard rubber with the blade. Afterwards he drilled two holes into the back deck for the hard plastic rear spoiler. He'd put them on after he painted and it dried.

Marty hopped on the door and sprawled over the remaining front seat, his big hairy belly was rudely exposed as he reached under the stripped dash to splice the bugging transmitter into the wires meant for the radio. The transmitter stuck out of the dash through the slightly enlarged radio hole. Marty clicked from channel to channel manually as Gwen wore the helmet letting him know she had sound from both ear phones. He gave her the okay and Gwen said their names one at a time into the helmet's mike, clicking off in between. At the bench, Holland fielded the phones as they rang, whispering dirty things to her, getting a stiffer finger solute each time.

About an hour later, Cooper was back underneath the rear end bolting in the straight pipes and headers Finn had slightly modified to fit around the hydraulic motors. Marty had finished in the car and was outside with Gwen and Holland as Jorge finished up masking the Corsa for new paint. Jorge put on a mask and tested the paint gun filled with flat black.

The top was up and covered with paper and tape.

"You in a hurry, Jorge?"

"No, I always paint at three a.m. to cut down on sleeping."

"We're out of here, Coop." Holland said. "I'm taking Gwen."

"Behave yourselves."

"See you in the morning."

"Thanks, Marty."

"No problem."

They left, leaving Cooper and Jorge. Cooper pushed himself out from under the Corsa. "She's all yours. I'm waking up Doc."

"This will be the baddest Corsa to hit any street."

"With any luck, I'll live to prove it." Cooper went out looking back over his shoulder as Jorge pulled the garage door down behind him. He knew Jorge loved these moments just before a new paint. So he left him to do his thing. Cooper wiped his hands and headed towards the house. It was time to pull the glue off his face and put in a few stitches. He felt tired, beyond tired, dead came to mind. His boots were heavy, though thanks to Doc's bag of medicine, he didn't hurt so much. But his ass was dragging and he needed sleep.

At sunrise, Cooper was asleep in the Corsa. The paint fumes had subsided with the doors open. He was now snoring painfully because his nose was stuff full of cotton and he was forced to breathe through his mouth. He was alone. Most of the swelling had gone down in his face and his cuts were now covered with clean bandages, including his broken nose.

The Daily News paper covered him like a tramp on a park bench. His picture was on the front page. The caption read: Nude Ex-Corsa Race Driver Sought in Goodricke Murders. Nothing was sacred in Tinsel Town. Brubaker was behind this.

The sun shot through the open windows ricocheting off the freshly painted Corsa like a laser show. The car now sat on its new set of off road paws and rims. Racing nets hung down from the top's frame over the open windows, and stone guards were over the headlights. It looked too hip to flip with its in-your-face flat black stripes on the hoods and the broad black sixty-six on the doors.

Any kid would have killed to own it. Even if Cooper was pushing thirty and just might have to.

On the other side of the fence in the patch of wild weed, Brubaker slept like a stoned cold baby. When he woke, he had multiple spider bites covering his neck and arms.

20 DEADLY DINNER PARTY

Irene ushered her early guest into the dining room. She was noticeably upset. Mostly because no one would tell her what was happening in her precious home. Jack seemed distant. Her daughter asked her not to light the fireplace and to wait and see what happens. The others seemed pensive and frightened. Especially Frank. He kept breaking out in an uncontrollable sweat and pinching his knees together whenever Gwen entered the room. His eyes were so sad.

Something was happening big-time and it only frustrated her not being included in the know. However, Gwen did fill her in on one major detail. Portland Cooper would be attending dinner. Though no one else attending was to know. Somehow this bit of news managed to placate her. If they didn't want to confide in her, well, one could play the game as well as five.

Jack, Elliott, and Frank remained in the living room. They stood next to the high-resolution telescope, watching out the bay window that overlooked UCLA. Maybe they were expecting the end of their world to flash before them. Things had changed so fast. Things that they had no control over. Things that could ruin their lives forever. They looked over their shoulders at Roger Kelemen entering the dining room with Tracey. That son-of-a-bitch had ruined everything they've built.

"This has gone far enough," Frank said, his face flushing red with as much anger as fear. He wanted to cry.

"We don't deserve to be treated like this, Jack," Elliott said.

"Look, I don't mind being grabbed by the short hairs," Frank said. "But the fiendish little bugger nabbed my beach house."

"Screw your beach house, Frank. I'm renting office space from Roger. In my damn building," Elliott said.

"Stop acting like this is my idea. He's got my ranch, too. I haven't had the nerve to tell Iren or Gwen yet."

"Then do something about this," Elliott said.

"You want to end up like Ruth and Jerry? Sam means business. Ask Gwen about that. Those men Jerry hired grabbed up Gwen and Portland outside of your house, Elliot."

"What? Did anyone see them?"

"Ask Sophie."

Elliott looked at Sophie from across the room. "She didn't tell me they came to visit."

"They were taken to Sam's ship. He's trying to take care of us. They beat Portland up pretty bad. Apparently he's got something Sam wants. I heard he put on quite a show getting Gwen back to the mainland alive. Sam filmed everything."

"Filmed it? That's evidence against us."

"And shear madness," Frank added.

"It's part of Roger's script. Portland dies in the end inside that car of his."

"I read that script. No one dies in the end," Elliott said.

"It's Sam's way of protecting us. He was supposed to have Portland's death on film. A stunt gone wrong. It's the deal he cut with Roger to keep him from doing this to us again."

"You've got to put a stop to this, Jack. You're letting a drugged out has-been actor and a complete homicidal lunatic direct the ending to our lives," Frank said.

"I'm not allowing anything. I'm as stuck in this shit as deep as you two are. Don't think Sam wouldn't kill me."

"He stuck our asses into a beehive this time. You don't piss off a roughneck like Portland Copper and not get knocked on your ass for it," Elliott said.

"You think I don't know this? I haven't spoken to Sam about this in person yet. I will. Gwen won't talk about it. But she has cuts and bruises all over her."

Frank and Elliott looked at each other.

"You can't trust a man who tries to kill your own family, Jack," Frank said.

"I know. They've brought this mess back into my own home. Irene nearly cut my head off forcing this damn dinner so she could see Roger for herself. I haven't been able to tell her a thing. And won't until this is over with. Now shut the hell up and let's see what happens next."

"Happens next? We could all see prison time. That's what we'll see happen next," Frank said.

"All we have to do if this goes south is stick together and say Sam made us do everything. Or he'd kill us. Jerry and Ruth are proof of that," Jack told them.

"Our careers are ruined if this hits the press," Elliott said.

"Irene and Gwen will fry me over this regardless. I'm about to lose half of everything I own. And that's only if I get lucky and don't die and lose everything first."

"Does Portland have the tape, or what?" Frank asked.

"Why is Portland Cooper even involved? Wait, he's not coming here tonight, is he?" Elliot asked.

"He wouldn't dare come to my home and pull what he did the other night," Jack said. "I'm sure he's hiding someplace."

"You better hope so, if you want to keep Irene out of this."

"Don't act stupid, Frank. You don't keep a smart woman like Irene in the dark for very long. Not unless you want to live in agony. Trust me. Gwen got Portland involved looking for Roger, and he's soon to be ex-involved, if Sam can find him."

Jack caught a movement from the corner of his eyes. He looked across the living room, past the piano, and through the bar area, to the den. A pair of men's legs in black pants and glossy shoes showed in an overstuffed arm chair. He hoped it was Sam. But Portland Cooper's beat-up face popped into view around the chair. A big smile grew on his broken lips as he tipped his beer toward Jack. Jack's blood pressure rose like an exploding geyser as waves of panic and anger rushed to his heart and brain. Frank and Elliott followed Jack's eyes over to Cooper's friendly tooth-gaping smile. They both fought back the urge to run. Elliott caught a hold of Frank as his legs began to waver.

Cooper chugged the rest of his cold Miller. "Third act is about to begin. Shall we?" He stood up in a rented tux. He didn't even pretend to hide the beating on his stitched up face. He flashed them his best I love shooting turkeys out of season grin. With great care not to show how much pain he was in, he walked toward them. He attempted to leave the empty beer bottle on the bar, but couldn't get his arm up that far. The bartender graciously grabbed it and threw it out.

Portland held out his bruised and cut hand to them. None of them had the nerve to take it. He left the three distraught men with their mouths open in his wake as he walked over to view a new painting on the wall. He pretended not to wait for Gwen to give him the okay to come into the dining room.

Jack started in after Cooper. He wanted to end it now, right here forever. The nerve of this son-of-a-bitch, barging into his home to throw twenty years of crap into his family's face. He wanted to shoot him. He wanted to kick the life out of him. Tear him limb from limb. He stopped in his tracks when Cooper turned to lock eyes with him.

"Does Roger know you tried to kill him, Jack?"

"What? When?"

"You did something to his car to make it lean into me. And filmed it. Maybe Jerry was in on it?"

"Don't be ridicules."

"I've got stitches above my ear that says you did."

"If that's true. You've got no proof that I was involved."

"If you hadn't've threatened to kill Gwen. I would've found something wrong with that 911 eventually."

"I have no idea what you are talking about."

"Let's ask Sam when he gets here, if you were involved," Cooper turned away and entered the dining room.

Elliot and Frank moved closer to hear what was being said. So, Jack held his tongue. The shit was in his home. As long as he was he wouldn't, couldn't do a damn thing. He tried his best to control his anger as he followed Cooper into the dining room. He could only assume that Sam knew Cooper was there by now. What he would do about it was anyone's guess.

Elliott caught a hold of Frank who changed his mind and tried to make it to the front door. The ship may be sinking but nobody gets off until it hits rock bottom. Sam would only waste them. Elliott was sure of it. He proved that much already with Ruth and Jerry. Sending a message to the rest of them that was bloodletting clear. He was capable of killing them, anywhere, at any sign of weakness.

Elliott looked into the dining room at his wife as he crossed the living room. What else hadn't she told him about this mess? True Sophie was always a bit of a tramp. With a body like that, he didn't really mind. She had needs he couldn't fulfill and he found the stories rather tantalizing. But the child. Christ the child. It happened so fast, casting them all forever in a drama careening out of control to this bad ending.

Finally, after all these profitable years writing Roger Kelemen drivel, they had arrived at their own third act. There was no way to rewrite it to fix this plot point. It was sharp and pointed, and would make them all bleed to death one way or the other by its end.

Gwen knew, Mr. Cooper knew, and Elliott was sure all of their club friends knew this whole sordid story. Thanks to the insufferable Roger Kelemen and his goddamn weakness, the hole in his soul, drugs. Mr. Cooper now controlled proof of what happened that night in that very room. How they rewrote it. The deal they cute between them and Sam. How it all dissolved to...this scene. How could he have been so stupid to sign onto this? All his upbringing, all his schooling, his religious beliefs. How could he let himself contribute to this sad story? He looked at the love of his life again. He cherished every moment with her. He knew damn well it was his desire for Sophie that had trapped him. From the moment she first walked into this room with that child needing someone to rescue her. He was trapped. Agreeing to this tail, knowing it would keep her by his side. He had agreed to this ending. He wiped the sweat from his face. He found his customary chair and reached for his water glass and emptied it. He smiled at Sophie, reaching over to pat her hand.

Sophie smiled at her husband. Her radiant teeth flashed across the room. She knew he loved her. That was good enough. She got what she wanted from that night. She had a life beyond what anyone from her family could've imagined her achieving. They had expected nothing from her. Despised her for wanting to make something of herself. If they had known what she did to get to that moment, chances are they wouldn't have been surprised. Both her parents were from generations of working stiffs in the mines of Kentucky and making moonshine. She knew she was right to leave that short lifespan after her father died in the 1970 Hurricane Creek mine disaster and her mother drank herself to death. She heard her brothers went on to grow marijuana and were both murdered in a gun shootout. She saw her relatives suffering early horrible deaths all around her. Visited their graves. When she was ten and got the first look at what her body was to be, she knew that using it was her ticket out of that filthy place. Something she wished her mother had realized. Getting knocked up for the ride out wasn't part of the plan. She tried to do it on her own. Raising a child, doing extra jobs, waiting tables, a commercial here and there. Then finally when her daughter blossomed into a gorgeous young thing herself, Sophie got a shot to put Sahara to work by signing with Jerry and Ruth. Just to help her pay the bills while she pushed her own career. Something was wrong though. Sahara wouldn't pay close attention. She didn't want to be there. She didn't understand how lucky, how important it was to take advantage of natural gifts. Sahara, was so beautiful, so innocent. Just thinking her name after all this time hurt to Sophie's vary soul.

It was an accident, she knew this. She believed it. She had to believe or it would've killed her years ago, eaten her alive from inside. It didn't excuse what they did afterward. What they convinced her to let them do to Sahara. More than anyone else she loathed herself for not exposing the truth. It would've made a spectacle of her life. Ended any chance of her having an acting career of her own. Proving her family right about her. That she was no good. But it wasn't just herself she hated. It was all of them. None more than Sam De'Ogo. That filth, that bastard. Making them go along with Roger's blackmail. Allowing him to recall Sahara's spirit back into this room after all these years, and use it to take her husband's office building when eventually the building and its income would've been hers.

Now this. She looked over at Gwen speaking to one of the waiters. She didn't tell Elliott that Gwen and Cooper had stopped by to caution her. She wasn't participating anymore. She was in this for herself now. This would not end well for any of them. She caught Irene looking at her. She smiled and tipped her class. Boy, did Irene have a high horse to fall from. The vision of Irene's painful tumble back to earth actually made her laugh, knowing exactly what Irene would do to Jack.

But now after all these years, this sordidness of what really happened to her daughter coming to light could actually revive her own career if handled right. She was tricked, forced to go along with the charade of her daughter's death. Never reporting her missing. Gone, vanished as though she never existed. She could almost see the book signing tour, the talk shows, the press junkets with Sahara's picture on the cover. Sahara would get the final say in how this all ended. The last words would be her daughter's sweet revenge on all of them. Sophie's laughter bubbled up to her lips again. Elliott reached over and squeezed her hand, thinking it was nervous laughter. If he only knew what she had planned for him no matter what happened.

Frank pulled Tracey close. "Keep your damn mouth shut. Do you hear me?" Tracey nodded yes. Frank glanced toward Roger. That dirty son-of-a-bitch. Look at the coked-out mess he was. Dragging them all down to mingle in his filth. Again.

He looked over at Irene. How much did she know? Nothing probably. Frank wanted out. He was against it then and he's against it now. Jack was right. They made him be part of all this. Held a career over his head. Held dying as a promise if he changed his mind. That's how he'd play it.

But this, giving up so much valued real state to that little overacting prick. His beloved beach house. He had wasted his whole career directing the pieces of shit Elliot had to write for Roger. He came into this town from college a nobody. Now with all the crap work he'd done over the years. The kind of low budget shit Sam produced, he'd die or sit in prison for life as a nobody. How could Sam let this night happen? To murder their dear friends over this. None of them were safe. None of them would walk out of this unscathed. Sam was a lunatic. He slowly showed signs of madness for many years now. Sailing seas in a pink and blue ship and that band of dangerous, drunken, marauding misfits he called filmmakers that he'd put together. Taking shit from that cinematographer Slim Thompson and his crew all these years. Stuck traveling the world filming bullshit films most people in the US never saw. He had nobody he could trust because of this endless traveling. Nobody to really love, be one with. Now this. He'd kill himself first before he'd face a world that knew what they did in this room. He would have years ago, if he had the nerve.

Gwen had unlocked a glass door leading out to the pool patio when Cooper moved his gaze from a new oil painting in the living room and entered the dining room. She would've loved to hear what Jack had to say for himself.

Cooper headed around the table where he met Gwen in front of a fire place. They stopped and looked into it. Gwen held his hand tight. All this time, all the fires she had enjoyed in it. She could never light one again. Did the others notice that there was no fire this evening? She turned away and Portland helped her with her chair. He sat down next to her where he had asked to be seated. Making sure he could keep an eye on all the exits. He patted Gwen's left hand. She pulled up her elbow length cream colored evening gloves that hid her bandaged wrists. She smiled at Portland, assuring him that she was ready when he was, no matter what happened next.

Roger choked on his bourbon and coke as he turned from Tracey to see Cooper's battered face sitting across from him. He wiped the front of his shirt as the others settled down for what promised to be a very enlightening dinner. He looked at the others. They hated him. So what. They would eventually get over it when he was a bankable star again. It looked like the joke was on him though from the looks on their disgruntled faces. He was the last to know that Portland was here. He shot Gwen a look. She looked right through him. So that's how it was. He smiled at Irene. Irene smiled slightly back. At least she was glad to see Cooper hadn't killed him on the high seas. Nothing was new with these others. He'd been a joke to them for years. Suffering through the crap Sam made him act in. They all made so much money off his films. It was only fitting he took some of it back when he needed it. Well, he had a few more jokes of his own to tell. Cooper wasn't getting out of this room alive. Unless they planned on spilling the beans on everything, they'd have to agree to another cover-up or die. The cover up of Cooper's death. He needed a blast up his nose so bad that his gut wrenched in violent pain. So hard he virtually vibrated, making the ice tinkle in his glass. He noted the lack of flames in the fireplace. This did not go unnoticed by anyone at the table.

Cooper used the tinkling from Roger's glass as a cue to get the evening's festivities started. "Well, Roger, how's Florida this time of year?" Cooper asked.

The waiters started to pour wine. Clearing his throat, "Hot," Roger answered. Roger took a look at Gwen. No wonder she refused to talk about it. The bitch knew Cooper would be here. He glanced quickly over at Jack, Frank, and Elliott again. They squirmed in their chairs. Jack shook his head to calm Roger down. Screw him. Cooper had to die. If they took out Gwen, Irene would have to go. The maid. Shit. This was complicated. Gwen would just have to learn to keep her mouth shut. Become one of them. Live with the past like they had. Jack better see to it. Or Roger would.

Gwen smiled at Frank and Elliott. They smiled back. She wasn't about to hurt these people by bringing all this out in the open beyond this room unless she absolutely had to, to stay alive. The scandal would be a horrible experience for Irene to go through. Once the press got a hold of them and connected them to 'The Little Island Princes Series' this scandal would rock the publishing world. Even though Gwen had nothing to do with it. She had no choice but to trust Cooper and stick to his plans. Let him teach these people a lesson in his own way. They messed with him. Destroyed his beloved Corsa. Tried to kill him and she was sure had other violent plans to get out of this mess that had nothing to do with Portland walking away. If she could, she would put a bullet into Sam De'Ogo's head herself.

Cooper caught her tugging on her white glove again. He held her hand still and she looked at him, smiling because she knew Cooper understood what she was thinking. The lines left her forehead and a calmer twinkle returned to her eyes.

Irene noticed the look in Gwen's eyes. All the eyes at the table for that matter. Something was happening around her and still no one seemed to want to share it. It was so damn mysterious to have everyone dancing around like fools. Her first husband, James, Gwen's father did this to her often when she'd visit the Islands. Nonsensical things were always going on to promote his father's books. But it was non-the-less annoying as this. Her friends were all squirming with hot pokers up their bottoms, pretending everything was rosy at court. Those cream gloves. What does Gwen mean by wearing those god-awful gloves to dinner? She tried not to stare at Portland's face. He hadn't looked this bad in years. Surely Gwen had gotten him into another mess. Now Roger was back. His appearance was horrid as well. He was strung-out on something. She knew it. The look in his eyes when he glanced at Portland and Gwen. She couldn't even begin to think of the Goodrickes.

She took in a deep breath. She'd gone through a horrible unsolved scandal with her first husband's death. Gwen's Grandfather never blamed her for his death. But his funeral on the Kula Rue was the last they had seen of each other. The worse of it was never knowing who had really killed him or why. Living with the speculations in the paper that he was tied up with some very bad people dealing with his father, the books and the Islands. If he was, he never let on to her that any of the rumored past was true. So Irene never believed it was anything more than a random killing. It didn't make it any easier.

She wasn't sure she could bare another marriage scandal so late in her life. But what did she really know about Jack? She knew nothing of his family. None to speak of other than what he told her of distant cousins he had never met. Beyond these friends at the table, Jack didn't have an immediate family. This was his family. A film family. They have become hers over the years. But what did she really know about these people? She knew nothing more than that they produced TV and silly movies that made a lot of money. She never saw them. Not even on TV. She loved Jack. Had almost from the start. He was sweet to her. Gave her everything she needed in life. Came into her life when she needed someone most. He loved her back, with all his heart. She knew this. She looked at Jack. Jack didn't look away. His eyes were so sad. He was so sorry. For what she didn't yet know. She knew he was in trouble. What had he done? Who exactly was she in love with? The mystery of it was painful. She had a feeling that Portland and Gwen had stumbled onto something while looking into Roger Kelemen's whereabouts and now a very large piece of crap was about to hit the Hollywood fan page and become an eternal centerpiece on her dining room table. She picked up her glass. "Please, a moment of silence for Ruth and Jerry," Irene said.

Everyone bowed their head. Tracey even managed an honest sniffle. Life was tough in the unemployment line.

"All right, tomorrow we bury them, for now let's enjoy what their friendships have meant to us." Jack ordered another scotch on the rocks from a waiter.

"So, Elliott, who do you think killed Ruth and Jerry?" No sense wasting time, Cooper thought.

"Not at dinner, Portland," Irene said.

"Sorry, Irene, I have a few interactive questions. How about you first, Tracey?"

"I don't know anything. You had your naked picture in the paper about it. Why ask me?"

"Because maybe you're planning on taking over the agency, and shot them to get them out of your way."

"Don't be...could I do that, Frank?"

"I told you to keep quite. But yes. Maybe. Now, shut up."

"Well, I didn't. And I wouldn't even if I thought of it."

Cooper could see the biz wheels turning in Tracey's head. Another waiter began to serve a mixed green salad with edible purple and yellow flowers as garnish. Much like the pansies sitting at this table he planned to kick the stems out of.

"The police are looking into it," Jack said.

"They don't know you upstanding movie people like I do."

"Why would anyone harm them?" Tracey ignored the look on Frank's face. She didn't work for him.

"Maybe Roger will tell us."

"Look, I've had it up to here with your bullshit. I didn't kill either of them and you know it."

"Back to you, Elliott? Did you kill any of Roger's friends?"

"I spent the day with Frank at the Studio pitching stories."

"We have plenty of witnesses."

"I bet. Jack?"

"He was with me all day," Irene said.

"Moments later I found Sophie naked by her pool.

Elliott looked at Sophie who shrugged.

So, who does that leave? He looked about the table knowing he had covered everyone. "Okay, let's just say it was a silent partner. Now, let's guess at why. Any guesses at why a silent partner would want both Jerry and Ruth dead?"

Even the waiters were silent.

Cooper took out the recorder Marty had worked on. He didn't give a shit about the answers. He was waiting.

"You're not much fun. Hey, let's have a little sing along. You remember the campfire words. If you would, Gwen. We don't want anyone but us to hear this."

Gwen got up and motioned the waiters into the kitchen. She went in behind them to make sure the waiters stayed out.

Roger watched her suspiciously, fingering the forty-five he had stuffed in his sport coat. He wasn't playing around with Sam's peashooters from now on. He turned back to find Portland setting up the recorder when Gwen sat back down.

Sophie covered her face with her hands. "Please, no."

Roger pulled the gun. "The sock hop is over. The tape."

Cooper tossed the cassette across the table. It bounced off Roger's chest and plopped on top of his endive before he got a handle on it. He wiped off the dressing with his napkin and examined it. "What is this...a copy?"

Glances pinballed around the room. Cooper had just racked up a thousand points and got a free ball. Irene and Tracey were completely at a loss. But every time Tracey tried to say anything, Frank dug his nails deeper into her arm.

"My favorite oldies. Your meal ticket is in your Corsa."

Sophie blew her nose. Thank goodness he hadn't planned to play it for them at the table. She wiped the streaking mascara on Irene's linen napkin. The nerve.

If someone didn't explain things to Irene soon she would start slapping people. She looked over at the maniac expression on Roger's face, then down to the gun in his hand. Well, maybe she'd wait a bit.

Cooper just sat there grinning.

"Now he's into our pants," Frank said.

"Don't flatter yourself, twinkle toes."

"Put the gun away, Roger. What do you want, Portland?"

"Sam De'Ogo."

"If you have a beef with Sam, take it up with him."

"I'd rather wait for your short, fat, ugly, sort of looks like you, with a little less hair....older brother, right here."

Jack glanced at Roger. Roger looked away.

"You dumb shit, Roger."

"Sam brought him onboard, not me."

"You never told us Sam was your brother," Elliott said.

"Is that why you've pushed us into doing all his bullshit?"

"You both could've walked away."

"Where's your little girl, Sophie?"

Sophie was horrified by the question. Where was her little Sahara? She was dead. She was dead, that's where she was. It was such a long time ago. But now that it was finally coming out in the open, it hurt so deep inside that the pain just bubbled up like lava suppressed for a billion years. She held back the tears so hard her face bloated. "God help us."

"Sam De'Ogo accidently killed her, didn't he? He was trying to make her his next meal ticket. But she didn't want to be an actress. She had a lack of short time memory that wouldn't allow her to remember simple lines. So she refused to try. Sam got frustrated with her, shook her and she fell back and hit her head on the mantle. Roger got it all on audio tape. Right down to the cremation in the fireplace right here in this room."

Everyone looked over at the fireplace behind Portland.

"Roger blackmailed you all," Portland continued, "because you all were here. He forced you all to make him a star. But he made you a lot of money doing crap films that nobody cares about. So now he wants it all back, because you never really believe in him as an artist. You used him. Became very rich while you let him destroy himself as long as it didn't affect you."

"What?" Irene couldn't believe what she was hearing.

"Yes, yes, yes, yes!" Sophie couldn't hold back the flood of tears any longer. Irene reached out to comfort her from across the table, but she pulled away. "Oh, my little Sahara."

Cooper looked at Sophie. How much of that was acting, he wasn't sure. "Both Ruth and Jerry had enough. I heard them arguing with you the last time I was here, Jack. That's why I went to their place first. They were the weak link. They did time to cover Sam's ass from the life you were hiding and they weren't giving in to Roger's bullshit again. So Sam plugged them...enjoyed it probably."

"What life, Jack?" Elliott asked

"Would someone mind telling me what we're talking about?"

"Me too. I never burned any babies," Tracey said.

Frank dug his nails deeper into her arm again until she slapped him for it.

"Cut it out, Frank. It seems that Mr. Cooper has stumbled onto our little secret past before you came along, Irene."

"A bunch of nasty ones they are, huh, Eddie?"

Jack glanced over at Roger. Roger nodded yes. Cooper knew all about Eddie and Tim Waller. Jack couldn't believe Roger could be so stupid.

"Jack, your name is Eddie?

"Eddie Waller," Portland said. "And he or his brother Tim tried to kill Roger when they made him crash his 911. Blamed it on me. Threatened to harm Gwen if I didn't stop snooping."

"Never mind, Irene, I'll explain later," Jack said.

Sam De'Ogo entered the room from a little breakfast alcove near Cooper's right. He was as close to being behind Cooper as the room allowed. Cooper didn't like that. Leave it to De'Ogo to pick Cooper's weakest point.

Sam carried his favorite weapon, his Chinese silencer by his side. He slowly brought it up and leveled it on Roger. Roger put his gun away. Sam slid its elongated barrel over toward Cooper.

Jack knew his brother was in the house. He could tell by their faces the others hadn't. Not even Roger. But Jack could see Cooper did. Sam never came to any of Irene's dinners, but he was often in the house, entering and leaving doors that Jack would leave open for him. So he could listen to what was being said. Back when they were Eddie and Tim, he'd do the same things. He seldom socialized. The constant voyeur. Two-way mirrors, milking bedrooms, cameras in the johns. Sam was a sick man to be sure. Him and his little games. Jack had gone along with it to keep an eye on his troubled older brother. He had even introduced Ruth and Jerry to Sam who brought them on as teachers. He met them in a strip joint. He discovered that they were the foster parents of a talented, good-looking kid. Said they wanted to put him in a local private school, but couldn't afford it. Sam did one better than give Roger a scholarship. He had arranged for them to take the place of two teachers he had hired that went missing. The two that somehow never made it all the way to the school. The two found in the retaining pond years later.

Yes, Jack had introduced them to his brother, Tim, who had three years before taken the identity of the new principal and owner of the private school. Who knows what he had done to the real principal and owner of the school. Jack didn't want to know. He only knew Tim had been watching him for years. Waiting. Something he had done since they were young kids growing up in Brookline after their parents were killed in an apartment fire. When he left his old public school to start his own private school, Tim had made his move. Tim never let anyone take his picture. So no one was the wiser. It started off with simple things like crashing parties and events to get free food. Then they moved on to jumping people to stay in their homes, sell things if they could. Always on the move, never staying long enough to get caught. Until the school. That was meant to last. But no. A supposedly accidental bullet from Nickel Boy started that down fall. The reason for the accident, and why he had access to a gun at school was between them. The rest was history. Jack, then known as Eddie, had already taken up a business at a local photo shop, processing eight and sixteen millimeter film. He hated the smell. But it was good steady money. He made a little extra by printing copies for his brother of anything fun that could be edited into something it wasn't supposed be and sold overseas. It's how they started their distribution end of their lucrative business of selling films.

So he couldn't blame all this on Sam. Not even Roger, for that matter. When one got right down to the nitty-gritty of all this sordidness, it was Jack, Ruth, and Jerry sitting in that bar, watching the women shake their privates in their faces. He didn't have to spend the whole night with Henry and Bertrand Duncan, the Goodricke's real names. Ruth was a surprising plum when she was young. She hadn't smoked herself into a dried prune until she was halfway through their prison term. That night, they had tied his hands and beat him silly...and he loved it. No, he couldn't blame Sam for that one night. True, Sam was a sick killer, but Jack had no one to blame...except for his own distasteful past.

"Well, speaking of nasty things."

"Please come with me, Mr. Cooper."

"Sorry, I'm rather washed-out from our first honeymoon."

"I want the tape."

Cooper pulled a piece of paper out of his pocket and placed it neatly under his coffee spoon.

"This is where I'll be. One hour. Come get it. Bring helmets."

Sam's eyes narrowed. A challenge. The defying Mr. Cooper wanted to take him on in the streets. Intriguing as it sounded, he knew Cooper couldn't walk out of this room unrestrained. "I don't think so," De'Ogo said. He pointed the gun.

Cooper hit the play button on Marty's rigged recorder. The lights throughout the house and grounds blinked once. Everyone froze for a moment to make sure it wasn't an earthquake or something worse, the ghost of a child.

Roger caught Gwen's look. He reached for his wine glass, a smile on his face. Cooper had finally met his match. If he got lucky, he might even get the opportunity to watch Cooper die, and not have to do it himself.

"I'm no longer amused by your troublesome behavior."

"Sam, not in my home."

Cooper thumbed the button again and this time all the lights went off in the house. He dove for the floor throwing a strike with the recorder at De'Ogo. Sam pulled the trigger, a glass shattered, and a body hit the floor followed by a lot of shattering crystal. The women's screams were joined by Roger's and Frank's. Under this, Cooper scampered on his hands and knees to the unlocked patio glass door leading out to the pool.

He pushed his body through its pain and took off running past the built-in Jacuzzi, down a slope in the grounds, toward a white cement wall.

Roger sat in his seat and plucked glass from one of Irene's irreplaceable wine goblets from his teeth. He had a splendid fruity California blush all over his face and tie. He wasn't so sure Sam hadn't just tried to kill him.

Frank was under the table, white knuckled to a table leg.

De'Ogo lay stunned on the floor of the lunch cove with the recorder lying near him. His back was throbbing from the fall onto a side table full of crystal. Cooper had aimed well and hit Sam in the head. Jack had to help his brother up. He was as much disgusted with him as he was angry at Cooper.

Roger and Sam went to the open patio glass door.

Jack stormed out back through the kitchen. The kitchen staff was sitting along the low back wall overlooking the tennis courts below. They were eating the meal they were supposed to have served. They stopped when they saw Jack. Jack told them to go home. They immediately began to pack up their van.

It was obvious that the lights were tampered with.

Someone had to get into the power shed to cut all the lights at once from the main. Somehow Cooper had rigged the tape recorder to signal that person and he or she had thrown the circuit breaker only to find out that they had automatically switched to auxiliary circuits. But it didn't take the person long to fix it. Jack had an idea who the genius was. The fat one would have to die for knowing too much. Any of the other Corsa members who got involved, as well.

He stopped when the realization of what he was thinking washed over him. This would never end. The list was borderline mass murder. No matter if they killed Portland and got the tape back tonight or not. He looked at his magnificent home. He planned to die here. Of old age. The life he had built. It was coming to an end way too soon. Irene was slipping away from him. He could feel her fingers let go of his hand inside that dining room. How he truly loved her. What an incredible woman. A spectacular wife. How lucky he had been to have found a woman like her to spend his life with. A phony like him. With his past. Living a lie, becoming who he was because of her. He hadn't invented himself this time at all, Iren had made a better man of him. He liked himself. This would rock her world. What would she think of him? Tears beaded up in his eyes. How quickly they had fallen in love. It was over now. This was the end. He could hear it in her voice. See it in her eyes.

His goddamn crazy brother. If Cooper hadn't pulled Roger out of that 911. If Roger had died as Sam had planned in that damn race. This night would never happen. Sam and his death on film. He should've just grabbed Roger up and taken him out to sea and fed him to the sharks and filmed it like he and Jerry wanted. But no, he's still alive and up to the same blackmailing bullshit. Wanting way more than ever before. Millions in real estate, property that took years for them all to acquire.

That and to direct his own script. The directing was the deal cut with Sam. Roger had written the one thing in the script he knew Sam couldn't say no to…real death on film. He had finally fixed his script by writing the death of Cooper in it. It actually worked as written. Did Roger know that they tried to do to him what they now planned for Portland Cooper's death. Had he figured it out? Did Sam tell him? Maddening, all of it.

Jack was stuck in the middle. He had no way out of this. He knew it. He could feel the blood draining from his brain as his wonderful life escaped him. He had to grab for the support of the carport to steady himself. He got a good thorning for it from the damn bougainvilleas. Drawing blood. Irene had insisted on them after moving in. Messy nasty things constantly dropping and blowing around the driveway. How fitting for his last moments here he should shed his blood by her.

Outside, on the other side of the garage at the far end of the pool, Cooper and Marty ran along the wall. They made their way to a hedge and used it to help them climb over the wall. Silenced shots sank into the wall's white paint. Lucky for them,

Sam had difficulty holding up a pistol with his weak upper back and was much more accurate with a supported rifle.

Roger and De'Ogo turned from the glass patio door as all the lights inside the house and the grounds came back on. Shortly afterward, Jack reappeared through the swinging kitchen door. Irene wouldn't even look at him. De'Ogo didn't want Roger firing a none-silenced gun and he knew Jack didn't want any shooting at all. Roger reluctantly put his gun away. Gwen held Irene's hand and Tracey consoled Sophie at the table. Frank crawled out from underneath it as De'Ogo came over and picked up the paper that Cooper left. De'Ogo deliberately stepped on Frank's fingers as he read Cooper's intriguing note. A sinister smile developed across his face as he thought over the note. Live prey once again.

So Mr. Cooper wanted to turn this into a little game of skill, did he. Sam liked that. He liked men who knew how to interest him. This Mr. Cooper was extremely interesting. He knew how to reach out and whip the primitive desires of a sadistic man like Sam. What a young man he must have been. The thought even aroused him more than he had experienced in years. So be it, Mr. Cooper. He'd play your game. What had he to lose? One way or another life as they all knew it was over. He and Jack would have to morph again. He had waited for this move. Wanting it, but Jack's happiness had held him back. They kept amassing an enormous financial wealth making low budget films and ridicules television series. But now, it was time for someplace greater than this. Someplace where he had laid the groundwork of becoming someone great. But this...this game was a fitting way to let it all go. He'd catch Portland Cooper and he'd get what he wanted from him and then he'd kill him if he wasn't already dead by car crash. If everything was done quietly...well, he'd have to wait and see, he'd have it on film at least. And this Mr. Cooper would not be able to attempt to get in his carefully studied plans again. It would almost be like killing two birds with one bullet. Killing Mr. Cooper from this life to keep him out of his next.

"Roger, get the boys together. Meet me at this address." He handed Roger the paper.

"Jack, get Elliott and Frank my telescope."

"I don't want any part of this," Elliott said. "I'm done."

"It's over, Sam," Frank said as he got back up in his chair. He gulped his wine.

De'Ogo pointed his gun at Elliot. "Both of you get in Elliott's car while you still can. Do you hear me? I can and will find you both and take you out to sea and chum my dinner catch with your chopped up carcasses."

Elliott, nodded his head. He helped Frank out of his chair.

De'Ogo and Jack turned to leave the room. Jack stopped to look back at Irene. Irene looked up to find him watching her. Tears filled her eyes. "Goodbye, Irene. I love you. I always will."

"Please, don't come back."

"I know."

Jack looked at Gwen. Gwen pulled her mother close. It was over between all of them.

Elliott and Frank looked at each other, not knowing whether to run, scream or piss their pants. It was quite obvious to them that Sam was out of his mind. They both knew one wrong word could make them end up like Jerry and Ruth...stiff, cold, and uninvited to the Academy Awards.

Irene started to go after Jack but Gwen stopped her from saying anything more. Tears welled up in both of their eyes.

"It's better this way, Mother. You know it. Come on now, we still have guests. I'll have them continue dinner without the others." Gwen went into the kitchen and came out momentarily after discovering that the help were packing up.

"Mother, remember how after Daddy died we ordered pizza on Friday nights, just the two of us?

Irene sniffed back a tear. James was such a good man.

Gwen took her in her arms. "Come, Mother, let's have pizza and make the call to your lawyer. I hear he's single again."

21 DEMOLITION

Across the street from Curt's Wrecking, deep in the heart of Sun Valley, massive earthmovers lay asleep like slumbering dinosaurs, just beyond a chain-link fence. The landfill was dark from the cloud cover that hung near the top of the distant hills to the east and north. Interstate Five growled softly to the west. The lock on the gate had been cut and the gate was pushed wide open. The wood guard gate that usually housed at least one armed man was empty and the lights were off. A single set of fresh off-road tire tracks led into the newly muddied ground.

Jack's white Jag' stopped just outside the gate. Behind him, the nine foreign sports cars that went after Cooper at the Marina, led by Roger's Porsche, roared up in all their shiny fresh paint, looking tough and ready for action. Roger designed most of them himself. The drivers wore helmets and their cars were equipped with CBs. Including Dexter's and Teatro's who drove their own with the slim guarantee that theirs would be replaced if they lived. They all sat wondering the same thing. What did Portland Cooper have in store for them this time?

Dexter's BMW pulled up beside Teatro's Datsun. As dim as he was, he knew this was dangerously nuts. He looked over at his Japanese pal. Teatro shrugged. He wasn't thrilled about it either. Considering what they had done to Portland's Blood Red, going up against him out here in another one didn't seem to be the smart thing for them to do. They had a taste of how Cooper handled the little red American, rear engine, sports car.

Neither was hungry enough for seconds. But Sam insisted they join in the fun or die on some dusty back road.

The souped-up tow truck pulled to a stop behind the others. It was now fully armed with three remote control cameras and five movie lights bolted on hydraulic mounts. Slim, De'Ogo's longtime cinematographer from the ship, stood in the open back, behind his pivoting high-speed 35mm camera. Before him the control panel was lit-up and ready for action. He was to pull focus himself again as he preferred it. Lee, a tall heavyset young man with blond hair and a goatee, sat in the cab behind the wheel. De'Ogo had the camera truck specially rigged for the car race scenes and despite everything wasn't about to lose the opportunity to test it.

Jack spoke into his car phone. De'Ogo sat next to him with a CB radio mic in his hand.

"Can you make us out from up there, Elliott?" Jack asked.

Way up top of Mulholland Drive, near the intersection of Wrightwood, where one could spy over the east valley, Frank looked through the telescope. Elliott stood nearby outside his Mercedes Benz. He spoke into the car phone. On the car's roof was an opened map and a flash light.

"Like fly shit on a skyscraper."

Out in the middle of the Sun Valley landfill, down below a steep slope in the ground, Cooper sat in the Corsa listening to the bugs he put in Jack's and Elliott's cars. He wore his old helmet, fully wired for both the bugs and his cellular phone. It was a big bulky thing bolted to his dash so he could keep his hands free. An earplug and mic cords ran from it and plugged into his helmet from the headrest. Somehow Marty had made it voice activated and a closed circuit between the Corvair Club.

His black racing gloves were a little stiff after all this time. The red and black jumpsuit a little dry and tight. It felt good just to have them on again. He had deliberately designed the jumpsuit with red sleeves and a black body so that it matched his own Corsa's seats. It almost made him disappear into the upholstery of the remaining bucket seat. What you can't see, will beat you, he thought. And just might kill you.

He double checked his shoulder harness and tugged on the strap to his helmet. It was times waiting like this when he wished Gwen hadn't made him stop smoking. He looked to his left through the racing nets hanging over the side windows at the moving car lights splashing on the ground as De'Ogo's men jockeyed for position amongst themselves.

"Do you see him?" Jack's voice came over the speaker in his helmet. Cooper adjusted the volume. He left it up high because once the cars began clashing he'd need the extra volume.

"All we see are your lights," Elliott answered.

Cooper reached over and flashed his lights on and off.

"Lights just flashed!" Frank yelled back at Elliott.

"Did you catch that?" Elliott asked.

"Yes we did, over a ridge, about seventy yards back. Keep us posted, Elliott," Jack said.

"Roll cameras," De'Ogo said to Slim over the CB. He sat back in his brother's comfy Jag cushion to watch the live show unfold before him. No matter how it ended, he knew his kid brother's life was again changed forever. He looked over at Jack. He took note of the blood dripping from his index finger and that Jack did nothing to stop its flow. It dripped onto the floor mat below as though it dropped straight from his heart. A symbol of his living pain. Sam knew they would build another life together. His plans would work. Something he thought Jack would both be surprised and eventually approve. He knew his heart was shattered inside over losing Irene, his home his business. There was nothing either of them could do about that. Portland Cooper would die. Roger, too. If all played as planned. Even with the information kept from the press, Iren and Gwen knew. Jack would never let him harm them to make them understand. So they would move on. He'd have it all on film. He looked forward to watching people die. And with paid-up life insurance on Roger the shoot would pay for itself as the race was supposed to have paid for Jerry and Ruth. If it weren't for that kid in the funny blood red car. All he needed was popcorn. He pulled a flask from his coat. "Let's get it done."

Everything that was said over the CB was picked up by Jack's bugged car phone. Cooper couldn't believe his ears. It sounded like Sam was shooting his car movie after all.

"Rolling," Slim answered.

"Roger, did you see the lights flash?"

Roger picked up the CB, dropped it to the floor and retrieved it between his legs. He dropped his nose spray. Shit. The helmet was driving him crazy, stifling him. These damn stinking seat belts. He struggled to reach the spray. He stuck it up each nostril and gave it three quick blasts. Ahhhh, he felt better. His nose bled.

"Roger!"

"What?"

"Stay with me, Roger. Or I'll feed your ass to the wind. Did you see the lights?"

"Yeah, it's him, he's out there...waiting."

Cooper listened. "Gwen." The cellular phone auto dialed.

Gwen picked up. "Yes?"

"Stay online for a minute, I want you to hear all of this. I'm picking up everyone who has a CB through Jack's telephone."

"From that one bug?"

"And Elliott's. Cockroaches with ears."

"Take the boys in and flush him out," Sam said.

"It's dark out there."

"That's telling him, Roger."

"Now! I want footage," Sam clicked off the CB. He pounded on the dash. "The little shit, I'm gonna...."

"Relax, we still need him," Jack said.

"I'm not sure," Cooper said. "But it sounds like Elliott and Frank are up somewhere on Mulholland."

"Sam made them take the telescope out of the house. I'm on my way up there."

Roger put his Porsche in gear as he continued to talk into the CB. "Cover your asses, you guys...or he'll hand them back to you gift wrapped in dirt." He wiped his nose again.

"Shit, I ain't afraid of him. Let's show that horn dog sucker what driving's all about, boys," Harry said.

Roger hung up and gripped the steering wheel tight. He knew better. These assholes probably won't know what hit them. Where'd Sam find these clowns anyway? A camera truck. Sam was actually shooting this. Directing it himself. This was crazy. This is not how he envisioned it. He was not directing. Cooper had taken over the picture. Didn't anyone learn anything out in that water. They weren't playing with some dumb grease pit carhop here. Some piss ant short order mechanic. This was lucky son-of-a-bitch Portland Cooper. And Coop had them right where he wanted them. Bunched up in the mud in the dark. He'd pick them off out here. One kill after another. He'd leave Roger's movie cars rattling and decaying like bloody dead animal carcasses on a desolate road at night.

Roger had to laugh, Coop was eating this up. He just knew it. Sam agreeing to this madness. Gwen and the other Corsa guys would all be in on this somehow. Cooper never did anything without a big picture plan that included them all. But it would be all these cars against the Corsa out here in the open ground. The odd car out. With the lone duck driver. The sheriff on the highway to nowhere but death. Roger just needed one opening to end it all. Destroy Cooper's grand plan. Friggin' Cooper.

Sam probably thought it was some kind of fun game, too. Footage. When Cooper and Sam were done destroying these cars he'd be left with nothing for his film crew to shoot. It's just like Hollywood to let some hack driver rewrite his script. All those drafts, all those late night strung-out hours to make the story work. Nobody believing he could. Shit. Let's get it over with. He let out his clutch and eased forward leading the other eight foreign stunt cars two-by-two past Jack's Jag. They rumbled out into the wet earth. Come on, Sam, this is a set up. Mud? It hadn't rained in months. Cooper's up to something. God damn it, can't you see it? He's up to something!

The camera truck followed. It turned on its movie lights. The lights glared up over the slope but the Corsa was still out of sight. Cooper reached down and turned the key. The Corsa roared to life. What a sound. The feel! Cooper couldn't help but smile. Shit it felt good. Where had the time gone. He should've stayed on the track. Gone with a different car when he came back from Corpus Christi. But what? He was out of the pits, retired, left with his funny little red car, dead before its prime. Well, tonight it lived...alive and in blood red color, about to kick some ass and loving it. Here we come boys. Grab your privates. Cooper waited on the advancing rumble just over the slope in front of him and to his left. He eased the Corsa into gear. Timing.

"Speak up if you see anything," Roger said.

"Remember the prize money, boys," Sam reminded them.

"Save him for me. I'm gonna kick his ass until his brain bleeds," Roger said, feeling good.

"I love actors," Cooper said. "Roger?"

Roger's phone rang. He looked down at it. Who the hell would be calling him now? It certainly wasn't his agent. He let it ring. Damn, he didn't want to answer it. He took another blast up his nose. He picked up the phone. "What?"

"I'm waiting," Cooper said.

"I'm gonna...!"

Cooper clicked off. He put the pedal to the metal, the 190 sitting behind him revved up sending its comfortably loud RPMs vibrating through the rest of the car. Cooper's fingers tingled in his gloves. He let his left foot slide. The clutch slapped back in place. The back two off-roads dug in the dry dirt sending it fifteen to twenty feet behind him. The Corsa picked up speed and hit the ridge at forty-five. Still in second gear the Corsa flew ten feet before coming back to earth broadside left of the nine sitting mallards. Cooper cut the Corsa into the center of the foreign cars as they bunched up in panic. He hit his breaks, cutting the wheel to his left, sliding the Corsa. Cooper deliberately flung the mud forward, until the Corsa stopped sideways with a painful crunch into Bill's gold 68 P1800 Volvo.

The other cars spun around in the mud trying to get traction like heifers on ice. The cinematographer and the camera rose up on a hydraulic lift as Lee drove and followed the action. Different lights turned on and off at Slim's will as the car action moved from place to place. Harry managed to pull up alongside Cooper in the TR4 and took aim with his Chinese silenced gun at where he thought the engine was. The shot skipped off the front hood and blew out a side window on the Volvo. Cooper slammed it into reverse and dropped back. Bill sat behind the shattered window picking glass out of his neck.

"Sorry, old buddy." Harry's voice came over the CB.

"The engines in the back, you butthead," Roger screamed.

Portland Cooper raced backwards to the front of the pack. He slammed into Roger's Porsche, taking off the driver's side mirror. The blow also smashed out his own left tail light.

Cooper waved. "Hi, Rog. Can I have your autograph?"

Roger stared back, not amused. He aimed his gun, but Cooper was gone again. He drove down a dusty road leading past the row of earthmovers. As planned, he was screened from the others by his trailing dust. He turned right in behind the dinosaurs and looped around others and killed his engine.

The pack of foreign cars headed into Cooper's drifting dust and stopped before reaching the earthmovers.

Roger watched as the silt drifted down on his window. First the mud and now this. Cooper was unbelievable. He must've had Marty and Jorge out here spreading whatever this filth was all over the place. What the hell was it? He rolled down his window and wiped some off his door. He turned on his interior light. Cement. The son-of-a-bitch was covering all the cars with cement dust. Roger reached for his nose spray.

"What's going on, Roger?" Sam asked.

"Everything's under control."

"Like hell, that son-of-a-dead-dog is playin' bumper cars out here!" Bill said.

"So what? You're driving a stunt car."

"Can it, you two! Stop that car!"

"What the hell is this shit in the air? It's clinging to my car like cement?" Teatro yelled out his car window.

"It is...he's turning us into modern art," Dexter answered.

Cooper waited between the two earthmovers. He listened in.

"What can you make out, Elliott?"

"I can't say for sure. He went behind some large dark objects about halfway in."

"Earthmovers."

The rumble of the pack of foreign sports cars crept forward. Cooper waited.

"Portland?"

"Yes?."

"I just reached Mulholland."

"How does it sound?"

"Elliott's a little faint, but I'm getting it all."

Roger snuck forward as the dust began to settle. He turned his windshield wipers on and sprayed the silt from his window before it could dry. It was still a strain to see.

Jack looked at Sam. "Portland confronted me about Roger's crash. He knows we tried to kill Roger."

Sam looked at his brother. He smiled. "So?"

"He also knows it was us who beat him and threatened to kill Gwen for snooping around the yard?"

"We'll be okay. I've got us covered."

"Let Roger live if he destroys the evidence of that night."

"Why?"

Jack watched the blood drip from his finger."Taking both Roger and Portland from Gwen. She's good. Let him live."

"We'll see how this goes."

Sam looked away from his brother. Jack was always the gentler one between them. Falling in love again. Sam smiled.

"Careful, Roger, he's in amongst those dinosaurs."

"No shit," he said to himself taking another blast up the nose again. His nose ran. He wiped it on his sleeve.

Cooper, listened to Jack and Sam as he waited for Roger to pass. He knew it all along. It wasn't just a race accident. They tried to kill Roger. Roger had falsely blamed Cooper all these years. And they planned to kill Roger again. Jack was having second thoughts about it. It was almost touching. But Sam was calling the shots. Always had. In the end, Jack would do what had to be done. They would cover their tracks and take Roger out if he didn't get the tape back and destroy it this time. Knowing he had Roger's life duct taped to the seat under his ass made Cooper smile. Roger would get his audio tape back. But not until Cooper kicked the tar out of him first. He started the Corsa again and went flying among the cars striking Roger's 911 on the taillight and knocking the Baja Bug sideways smashing its fiberglass right front fender, putting out its head light.

Shots came from Teatro ripping two holes through the Corsa's top. Dust refilled the air.

Cooper cut a zigzag through the oncoming cars, making them slam into each other. Cooper rammed Teatro's Roadster head-on. Teatro's teeth bit through his lower lip. Blood gushed.

"Prick!"

Cooper pushed the Datsun away and headed down another dusty road. The stunt cars regrouped and went after him.

The road wasn't close to a smooth ride. Cooper reached with his thumb and pushed a red button on the steering wheel that used to be the horn. The Corsa body lifted up three inches.

Sweet Cherry in the Baja Bug handled the jittery road best so he kept close, eating Cooper's dust like a gas powered pooper scooper. He shot at Cooper again. It shattered the Corsa's glass rear window and ricocheted off Cooper's helmet sending oceans of deafening static through Cooper's head.

"What was that!?"Gwen screamed.

"Either a bullet or I just swallowed a satellite."

Cooper slammed on his brakes. Cherry cut to his right to avoid the Ghia and hit a rock with his left front tire. Impact with the rock sent the Baja into a complete barrow roll. It ended upright as the other cars zoomed past. Cherry shook his head clear and reentered the fray at the back of the pack.

"I found Elliott and Frank. They're on the straightaway just west of Wrightwood peak."

"Don't let them see you." He hung up. "Marty?"

"Yeah, Coop?"

"Any long arms?"

"Not yet. But you're making a hell of a racket."

"Ten minutes. Be there." He hung up. "Gwen."

"Here."

"Cover the five."

"On my way."

Teatro, in his 67 Datsun Roadster, missed a turn that the others had made easily while trying to avoid Cherry's Baja and rolled his car bad. It came to a stop halfway inside a bulldozer's scoop. Teatro scrambled out. He pounded down his helmet in disgust, yelling a few foreign obscenities in Cherry's direction. He looked back at his Roadster. It was bad, dented all to shit, and covered with who knew what. His roll bar was the only thing that saved him. He put his head down, wiped the blood off his chin from his gashed lip, and headed back across the open field toward the mud and the gate.

Cooper was now on the far side of the work roads weaving in and out of the slopes in the ground on his way back toward the mud. He made sure they were all close behind him when he got to the mud pit. He downshifted and slid sideways until his tires grabbed again and he headed up into the middle of the field. Roger's Porsche was the first one to reach the mud. He started to hit his breaks to go after Cooper but stopped in time to save himself when he realized what Cooper was causing. He put his foot back on the gas and cleared the mud toward the dinosaurs.

But Dexter in the '67 BMW 2000cs didn't know Cooper like Roger did. He hit his breaks trying to make the turn and ended up sideways sliding into the mud. Before the BMW could regain its traction, Cherry in the yellow Baja Bug, passed the others and slammed into it, caving in the passenger door. The Baja ricochet clear before the other cars, attempting to make the same move, careened sideways into Dexter. The cars spun, bounced and crashed out of the mud, leaving behind the dead BMW completely washed with sludge and cement.

Dexter climbed out of his smoking car tripping over his own exhaust system and fell to the ground on his hands and knees. His head spun. He wasn't sure where he was at first. Once he got a load of his once shiny black BMW it all came back. Smoke was billowing out from under the hood. It seemed to crawl along the underbelly toward the gas tank. He stopped in his tracks and leaped away from the car as it burst into flames.

Teatro strolled up behind Dexter sitting in the mud watching his car burn into the stench of plastic and oil. Teatro's lip still bled. The roar of the cars came from the back of the landfill arching its way south and headed back toward them. Dexter took a good look at his pal, back at his burning vehicle, and out toward the roaring engines getting louder. "I don't care what De'Ogo said. I'm killin' that arrogant bastard."

Just then the Corsa came airborne over the same ridge it had hid behind earlier. This time followed by the others. Paco nearly lost it in the 230s1. He barely kept himself from rolling. Cooper headed straight toward the burning BMW. He didn't see Dexter or Teatro until it was too late. Their guns flashed off to his left as he went by. Both shells struck the driver's door ripping holes. They shattered the window inside and broke into small fragments on the steel slabs. One of which managed to strike Cooper just above the left knee, ripping his jump-suit.

"Ahhhh!"

"Portland!"

"I'm okay."

Blood seeped through Cooper's racing jump-suit. He downshifted to test his knee on the clutch and headed in the dinosaurs' direction. It hurt, but so did the rest of his body.

Cooper hit the brakes, spinning the wheel to the right and spun the Corsa completely around in the dry road. He headed back into his own cement dust toward the onrushing cars with his windshield wipers on and his headlights off. He caught them all off guard trying to clear their windows and scared the hell out of them. They smacked into each other again in the mud. The camera truck cut to the left. He avoided smashing Roger from behind but ran its left front tire over top of the Mercedes. It crushed the trunk hood while Slim held on to the mounted camera for dear life.

Cooper headed back toward Dexter and Teatro who slopped with their backs to him through the mud. They turned to see Cooper and started running like rabbits in season. Out in the middle of the mud Cooper caught up with them. He swung the rear end of the Corsa out as he passed by knocking them both down with the onslaught of mud. He cut a donut around them, drenched them thoroughly from head to toe, then headed for the gate as the other cars caught up with him. Bullets zipped harmlessly overhead.

Bill, in the Volvo, made a deadly mistake. He got up beside Cooper as they approached the chain link gate. Cooper took that opportunity to nudge the Volvo toward the sturdy iron post. At that speed there wasn't a thing Bill could do but cover his face and scream.

Jack couldn't stand to watch but Sam yelled for Slim to get it as the Volvo hit the post head on and bounced back into the oncoming cars. The others hit their brakes while still in the mud and slid into the back of Bill. They demolished the Volvo into a huge gold accordion. Cooper slipped past the nice clean white Jag, showering it with brown globs from the Corsa's off-road tires. Cooper headed down Penrose towards San Fernando Road. The cars untangled and Bill's Volvo was a pile of junk. Harry helped Bill out and over to his TR4. Jack looked through his spotted window at the filthy, banged-up stunt cars. Jesus. Slim crept up behind them to a stop, filming everything. Dexter and Teatro neared the Jag's, walking past the truck.

"Cut!"

Jack's window rolled down. "And you call yourselves killers."

"I ain't ever seen drivin' like that," Dexter said, clearing mud out of his ear.

"What's he got in that thing?"Teatro asked.

"Brains. Hurry up, and ride with us."

"But...." Dexter protested indicating their muddy clothing.

"Never mind, just get in back," Jack said.

Roger pulled up alongside of Jack."Damn, did you see that?"

"He made you guys look like schoolgirls."

"Wait until we get on open road with those tires. I'll show him what this 911 is all about."

Jack started to roll up his window. The mud streaked.

He stopped halfway."This isn't one of your teen drags, Roger. Don't make it one." He got back on the phone.

"Where is he, Elliott?" The window shut in Roger's face.

Roger tried to see the two men in the backseat. The mud made it hard to see into the car. He studied Jack and Sam in the front seat. He could just make out the two idiots in the back. A thought of déjà vu crossed his mind. He smiled to himself and let it pass.

Bullet Hole Drive

22 OPEN THROTTLE NIGHT

Elliott hung on the phone while keeping a lookout for the cops. "He stopped at the Roscoe onramp to the Hollywood Freeway."

Cooper listened in while putting a tourniquet around his leg. The pain wasn't so bad considering all he'd gone through.

"What's the son-of-a-bitch doing there?" Sam asked.

"Waiting for you clowns," Cooper answered him.

"I can't tell. But he's alone at this point."

"How do I get there?" Sam asked.

"As far as I can figure, you turn around and head west on Tuxford until it turns into Roscoe as it passes under the Hollywood. Two minutes away."

"Put your seat belts on, boys, this car show isn't over yet," Sam said.

Jack looked back through his rearview mirror, taking in the two men in the back. He looked over at his shorter brother.

Sam glanced back at Dexter and Teatro. He nodded to Jack as he spoke into the CB. "Listen up. Follow us. And remember, silencer or no silencer, gunfire will bring the cops if we get up on the freeways. So force Mr. Cooper off the road and make him crash. If you can catch him. Just make sure Slim catches it on film. Anyone needing gas, do so, and rejoin us. If you're stopped, keep your mouth shut until you hear from Slim."

Cooper sat under the Hollywood listening in. The Corsa was dented and dirty. The back right tire was quickly deflating. He put his head against the headrest, watching in the mirror as headlights danced in the distance. He listened to the engine breath. He deciphered sounds and vibrations that worked their way up and through his pain filled body. The two primary carbs needed minor adjustments. The left header was surprisingly loose. He smiled. Gwen called him The Engine Whisperer. Hey, just like a good woman, Corvairs talk. You gotta listen, if you want them to stay hot for you and love you back.

"Marty." The phone dialed.

"It's us, Coop." Marty's van pulled up beside Cooper. Jorge and Marty hopped out. Marty moved to the front of the driver's door and refilled the Corsa with two five gallon gas cans as Jorge jacked up the front end with a speed jack and an air compressor gun that ran back into the van. He lug-nutted back on the fresh set of street tires he had taken off the night before.

Copper hobbled out, leaving the Corsa running, and opened the engine hood.

"Someone just pulled up beside him. Looks like a white van. I see two people. One big, one small."

"We're almost there. Roger."

"Yeah."

Cooper used a screw driver from a tool kit stored inside the engine compartment to take off the two primary chrome air cleaners.

"Mr. Cooper has company. A white van."

"That would be his Corvair buddies."

"They're gassing him up and changing tires."

"Goddamn it."

Cooper used a Uni-Syn carb balancer to eliminate the rough idling. "Roger."Cooper's helmet autodialed Roger again.

"What do you want?"

Cooper listened to the engine.

"Cooper?"

He adjusted one carb. "I'm coming for you." Then the other.

Roger knew damn well what Cooper was doing to the Corsa. The grease ball engine whisperer. "You'll need more than a carb adjustment to catch me, you prick," Roger said and hung up.

"How's it going so far?"Marty called out.

"Three down, six to go. Move fast, they're on to us."

"You're bleeding."

Cooper crawled underneath as Jorge brought the backend up and tightened the header making noise. He rolled out and Jorge finished, threw the off roads and jack into the van and jumped in behind them. He popped off the air-wrench and slipped on a turbo water spray nozzle. He handed it to Marty.

"Stand back," Marty said.

Cooper stepped back. Marty cut loose with the pressurized water hose. The cement residue dissolved from the Corsa. Marty got on his back and made sure the Clark's valve covers, oil pan, dual exhaust, clutch linkage, oil cooler, lower shrouds, steering package and the axles were all clear of cement and free of dirt. He rolled back over and handed the spray nozzle back to Jorge. He got up and jumped back into the van.

"What, no tip?" Marty asked.

Cooper checked his watch. "Forty-three seconds, not bad. See you at half past."

Marty gave him a worried look.

"I'm okay. Disappear."

The roar of the foreign sports cars approached. Marty got behind the wheel and drove off.

Cooper eased himself back into the nice clean, dented Corsa and waited for the muddy, cement-caked foreign stunt cars to come into view. He pressed the red button on his steering wheel again and the hydraulic shocks lowered over the new set of high-performance street radials. The front spoiler was barely an inch off the road. Just the way he liked it. He made sure the others saw him before he pulled the Corsa onto the onramp and took off headed north on the Golden State.

The remaining foreign cars zoomed past the Jag and, led by Roger, went after Cooper. The tow truck followed them. Cooper sped north on the Five. He politely passed cars as he went. He looked back in his mirror to find Roger had positioned himself right on the Corsa's tail. Right where Cooper wanted him.

Roger checked his speedometer. It showed 95 M.P.H. and holding. He swung the 911 out to the next lane on Cooper's left as they passed a Toyota truck. He pulled effortlessly alongside of Cooper. Roger smiled his baddest smile as Cooper looked over at him, letting Cooper know who was who. Cooper kept his eyes locked with Roger's and stepped on the gas. He sped up to 110 M.P.H., leaving Roger in his wake. The sports cars merged into traffic with the Hollywood Freeway.

Cooper's headset rang."Yeah?"

"Brubaker is sitting on the Five."Gwen sounded worried.

"Shit. Thanks. Marty."

"Yeah, Coop."

"We got company."

"Cops?"

"Worse. Brubaker."

"Okay. Bring him in. We'll be there."

George and spider bait Brubaker watched from the parked Mustang as the remaining sports cars zoomed past them. They clocked the cars as they went. The Corsa, 911, Karmann Ghia, Alfa, Baja, TR4, and the 230s1 - all of them banged up, dirty, fast and loud.

"110, damn that Corsa looks hot! Who the hell's driving it?"

Brubaker rubbed the spider bites on his neck."Who the hell do you think is driving it?!"

"I couldn't see anyone. Could you?"

"He's in there. Let me drive, George."

"I'm not lettin' you put me in the hospital. I can handle this."

"All right, get us in position. "Brubaker picked up the cell phone and dialed. He had no intentions of getting on the cop channel on this one. That was no way to catch Cooper at his game. "Here he comes. Get ready. A red Corsa or a silver Porsche is all I want. Both 66s. Portland and Roger. You can have the rest. Do what you want with them."

George got off at Osborne as Slim filmed him in the passing tow truck. He went back under the freeway to the south bound onramp and pulled to a stop at the top of it.

Cooper slowed when he saw Roger's Porsche followed by Paco in the 68 230SL get off at Van Nuys Boulevard for gas and a wash. Roger knew what he was doing. Cooper had to hand it to him. Despite the drugs, Rog was still hip to Portland's old road kill game and would be waiting for Portland to swing back. Just as Cooper hoped he would.

By the time Cooper started up the ramp onto the 118 the remaining foreign sports cars were bunched up right behind him. They were pulling a lot more weight around with them thanks to the drying cement. A quick slam on the breaks could have taken out two or three of them right there, but that would have felt like a premature ejaculation. Cooper preferred to wait and take them out one at a time.

As they came down onto the 118, Cooper hung in the merging lane letting Zev pull up along the left side of the Corsa in his dull Orange 66 Karmann Ghia. Cooper looked through the racing nets at the young Mexican and gave him a big grin and flipped him the love bird. Tacky, but it worked.

Zev's eyes narrowed to slits at the insult. He eased over into Cooper's lane trying to force Cooper into the merging traffic. Instead, Cooper cut his wheels into the Ghia throwing sparks flying as Zev's right front fender crumbled under the blow. The Ghia bounced away from the Corsa. Cooper kept his lane. Zev came at Cooper again. He dug his fender into the Corsa's door. The Ghia's headlight exploded as the fender bent inward. Cooper saw it as Zev pulled back for another strike. Zev cut the tires back toward Cooper. Cooper sped up to take the blow on the reinforced door. The Ghia's fender dug deeper into its own tire tread. Cooper glanced in his rearview to check on the other stunt cars. Taylor in the green 65 Alfa 2600 Spider was less than a car length away. Cooper slammed on his brakes, nearly giving Taylor a heart attack trying to avoid him. Cooper downshifted as Zev's tire blew. The Ghia faded into Cooper's lane. Cooper cut to his left into Zev's lane and pulled up along the left side of the floundering Ghia. Zev fought to keep control as they went under the Sepulveda pass at eighty-five miles an hour.

Cars honked and skidded to avoid them as Cooper leaned the Corsa into the Ghia taking them both across the merging traffic lanes on the west bound 118. Cooper stepped hard on the gas and gave the Ghia one last shove toward the overhead bridge. The Ghia went up the cement ramp and slammed into the underbelly of the 405. It sent sparks jetting against the wall as it lodged itself firmly at the top of the ramp. The other cars zoomed past as Zev angrily rolled out the window of the crumpled Ghia. Slim in the tow truck followed, filming it all.

Jack's Jag sat parked at Moorpark and Laurel facing south into the hills. "We lost another one... Roger, come in. Roger!"

"What is it?" He sniffed his runny nose. "I'm getting gassed."

Cooper continued west on the 118. He checked his gauges. The car was running strong. A bullet rung off the top of his door. He glanced back in the mirror to find Taylor back on the Corsa's tail again. Perfect.

"Kill him."

"Now?"

"You heard me, make him crash."

"Coop?" Holland said.

"Yeah?"

"A long arm is sitting on Balboa at the top of the ramp."

"Looks like Brubaker has them onto us. It's okay, stick to our plans. We'll take it as far as we can."

"He's facing south."

"Thanks, Holland."

"Where is he?" Roger asked.

"He just went up the Balboa exit," Slim informed them.

Cooper went up the ramp and made a screeching left at the light, catching the green. The two cops Brubaker spoke to over the phone sat at the intersection just like Holland said they were. They put on their light and went after Cooper.

Taylor, in the green 65 Alfa 2600 Spider, whizzed through the intersection. The Alfa backfired as Taylor let up on the gas. The two cops never saw it. Taylor bull's eyed the cop car right on the driver's door.

The TR4 and the Baja Bug made the turn narrowly avoiding the wreckage. The tow truck clipped the Spider on the way by. Slim shot it all. He zoomed in on the two cops' angry faces as they got out. The driver had to climb over the hood of the Spider. Slim zoomed out as the tow truck left the Spider behind. He caught the foot action full frame as they dragged Taylor's stunned body out of his seat. The cops threw him belly down over the hood of the cop car and shoved his bloody face down into the broken windshield glass to handcuff him.

Meanwhile, Cooper made it back down the Balboa onramp and was headed east on the118. He had to get Roger back in the game. He didn't have time to deal with the two cars following him. He'd just have to leave them behind. He brought the Corsa back up to 110 as he went past the 405.

The TR4, Baja Bug, and the tow truck were losing ground on Cooper as two more cops entered the race from the 405. Smoke shot out from the Baja's engine, then flames. Sweet Cherry put on the brakes, and slid to a stop. Harry and Bill yelled for Cherry to run for it as they passed by in the TR4. Slim captured Cherry on camera jumping out with a fire extinguisher as the second pair of cops screeched to a stop and got out with their guns drawn. Cherry raised his hands.

Cooper reached the Five in seconds. He slowed to safely merge with traffic and headed south. At Van Nuys Boulevard Roger's nice clean, but dented Porsche and Paco's clean and dented Mercedes joined the TR4 in pursuit.

George and Brubaker pulled into the race ignoring the TR4 at the Hollywood Freeway as it began to groan and drop cement coated rear end parts and came to a rattling stop. Harry and Bill got out as the tow truck went by, cameras still rolling. The second two cops pulled up behind them. Cherry was handcuffed in the backseat. He had his greasy face pressed against the window. Lights flashed overhead. They reflected in his scared eyes. Harry and Bill started across the freeway then changed their minds and ran down the embankment towards some fenced in, dried-up mud flats. The two cops fired into the air then pursued them on foot over the fence. They caught them halfway across the flats in a flurry of contaminated silt.

At Riverside Drive, Brubaker told George to pull the Mustang off the freeway and head west.

Cooper, Roger and Paco cut through traffic at normal speed and left the Hollywood Freeway at Cahuenga Boulevard West. They single filed south to Mulholland Drive.

"Shit, man." George took a left on Laurel. The Mustang's cop lights flashed. "This is crazy. We could've caught him with this."

"Relax. He let us catch him last time. We're gonna beat Cooper at his own game. We'll let him dig himself a grave. Trust me." He laughed thinking of Cooper sitting behind bars waiting for bail the other night. This time there'd be no bail. He must have shit when he read about being busted in his car while nude in the paper this morning. This time it'd be reckless driving. Maybe even vehicular manslaughter if someone bit the big one. That'd be beautiful. No more tickets. No more warnings or suspended licenses. This time he'd have Cooper by the throat and his ass behind bars for an extended stay in the big house. Where he belonged. All Brubaker had to do was catch him red-handed, or was it red Corsaed. He laughed at his stupid joke. He looked at George. He had to get him out from behind that wheel to make this all work.

"What?"

"Nothing. Just drive." Brubaker scratch at his spider bites.

"You wanna tell me where you got all those bites?"

"I was working on a case."

"Looks like you was sleepin' with a vampire."

"Drop it, will ya."

"Then stop scratching like some bitch in heat."

"Warnin' ya."

Cooper listened as Elliott spoke into the phone.

"We've lost him."

"He's heading up toward you on Mulholland."

"We're in plain sight up here. That's it, Jack, we're out."

"Stay put, damn you, Elliott. We're nearly at Laurel and Mulholland right now."

Sam looked at Jack as they traveled east on Mulholland.

"There's no way he could've figured...." Sam reached under the dash and pulled out the bug's transmitter.

Jack's and Sam's eyes met again. They were had by Cooper. Jack looked in the rearview mirror at Dexter and Teatro. Sam pulled off his watch and rings. Jack did the same and pulled off the road. "Here, for your cars, in case we get separated."

"You said cash for the cars."

"Take it or leave it."

Dexter looked at the rings and watch. "Shit, this is worth four times what our cars are worth."

"You serious?" Teatro said. He put on a watch. "Thanks."

"You ever drive a jag?" Jack asked.

Cooper listened as he drove. "Gwen."

"Yes."

"Something's going on in the Jag. I couldn't make out what they were saying. Something about a watch and payback."

"Who's with them."

"The too who torched my car."

"What do you think?"

"Not sure yet."

Roger handled Mulholland as well as he ever did but Cooper was still keeping a comfortable lead. Paco was hanging even further behind. But this time the tow truck had left the chase and continued south into Hollywood. Roger saw that the truck had dropped out. "What are you up to, Sam?"

"Where are you, Roger?"

"We should be coming up on Elliott."

"They're scared. Don't let Cooper get to them first."

Elliott and Frank turned to listen to Cooper coming up the road. Elliott put the telescope into his Mercedes while Frank climbed in the other side of the car.

The blood red Corsa came barreling west on Mulholland. The white Jag came flying east. They both reached opposite sides of the straightaway at the same time. The Jag moved to the center of the road. So did the Corsa. The two cars picked up speed, seventy yards apart, sixty, fifty, forty, thirty, twenty. The Jag cut to its left all the way to the shoulder of the road. Cooper slammed on his breaks, fishtailing into a 180. The Porsche and Mercedes screeched by to either side of the Corsa, just missing it. The Porsche had to squeeze in between the Jag and spinning Corsa. Fear was the only thing that saved Roger. He had his eyes closed. Cooper felt them more than saw them as they went by. Paco ran the Mercedes into the side the hill, sending sparks out into the night. The crash caved in the whole left side of the car. Gravel flew up from under the Jag as it tried to regain its balance. But its tires hit a rut, causing the Jag to tip sideways, its momentum pushing it over the lip of the hill. It hit the dried brush on its top and continued through it as it tumbled down the steep hill. It flipped violently end to end, over and over, until it exploded far down below into a huge ball of orange flames and death.

Cooper watched the ball of flames rise up over the cliff and nearly engulf Elliott's Mercedes. Elliott shut his slack jaw and drove his Mercedes away from the blast with Frank hyperventilating next to him. They headed west and never looked back.

Cooper didn't waste a second. He put the Corsa back in gear and headed east on Mulholland. He left Roger and Paco to clean their own pants. Roger pulled to the side of the road and turned around letting Paco get back on the road behind him. Roger looked over the hill at the glow and smoke coming up from below. He wasn't sure what he felt. Jack and Sam... dead. And all because of Cooper. There wasn't time to think about what he saw with his own eyes. He had to stop Cooper and get the tape back. He'd gotten what he wanted from Jack and Sam, there were still the other properties to consider. None of this could come to light. Without the tape, they might fight it in court. Cooper and that Corsa had to die. He looked back in his mirror to see Paco fleeing east. He got on the CB radio.

"Where the hell are you going, Paco?"

"Sorry, Roger, I'm out."Paco tried to act normal as two cop cars zoomed past him.

"You dirt bag. Get your carcass back here! I own that car."

"Listen, De'Ogo was picking up my tab. He's out, so am I. I'll leave the car in the Marina parking lot with the keys in it."

Roger pounded on his steering wheel and went after Cooper alone. He had to stop him. This wasn't over. Not for them.

Paco smiled to himself as Brubaker and George passed him by. He had gotten away unscathed. He looked up the road to find two figures in his headlights. A surprised, scared look covered his face as he realized who it was. Paco pulled over. "I thought you two were...."

A silencer fired, the door squeaked opened and Paco rolled out onto the road with, a dark hole in his forehead. The two figures got into the Mercedes and drove east on Mulholland as fire truck sirens filled the night air.

Brubaker turned away from the burning Jag. George hung up the car radio and got out to take a look for himself. Brubaker walked past him.

"Anyone need help down there?"

"Not likely."

George looked over the edge. "Jesus Christ." He turned back to see Brubaker pulling away in the Mustang. "Hey!"

"Stay here, George."

"God damn you. They'll have your ass back behind a desk for this." He ran after the Mustang. "Brubaker."

Cooper had waited to let Roger catch up. He got back on the Hollywood Freeway mindful to stay within acceptable speed and headed north into the Valley. Roger was right behind him again weaving in and out of traffic. Brubaker made up time on the Hollywood with his lights flashing. It was just them now. Someone was dead, and Cooper and Roger would pay.

Cooper slowed down and exited at the Burbank Boulevard ramp. Roger caught him at the bottom. Cooper looked back to see Brubaker's flashing lights cutting around the Pinto behind

Roger. Cooper cut his wheels to the right and went around a Dodge Barracuda, over the curb, along a fence, cut in front of the Dodge at the light and leaped into the east bound traffic to the sound of screeching tires. Roger didn't hesitate to stay with him, throwing sparks up as his oil pan struck the curb. Brubaker took out a chunk of the fence and a post. His headlight exploded on impact. He just made the corner without getting broadsided. Cooper sped past a plowed open field that was up until recently a fenced in ball field where Cooper hung out to be cool and smoked cigarettes. He lost ground on Roger and Brubaker out front of a row of houses by slowing to avoid a Studebaker pulling an illegal u-turn from the curb. The audacity! Roger had the nose of his 911 kissing the bumper of the Corsa as Cooper went into a wide right from the left lane at Beck into the neighborhood between Burbank and Chandler.

Roger hadn't anticipated the move and jumped the curb nearly ending it all on a dying Oak. He zipped across the sidewalk taking out a small spruce while squeezing between the old oak and two smaller trees. He wasted the corner hedge that wrapped around a yellow bricked house. A young man was backing out his dented brown VW from the garage. He had to slam on his breaks as Roger came flashing over the sloping curb onto Beck just short of Killion. The move forced Cooper to the outside lane again. An oncoming station wagon ducked into the alley to avoid Cooper.

Brubaker's lights flashed four car lengths behind.

They blew past Albers Street head to head. Cooper hit his brakes at Cumpston, cutting his wheels into Roger. Roger was late in reacting and got his bumper clipped just enough to send him into a tailspin through the intersection. The Corsa crushed its front bumper but Cooper managed to straighten the Corsa out just in time to miss a parked RV. Cooper pointed the Corsa west on Cumpston and hit the gas. Roger didn't lose a beat. He headed back north on Beck toward Killion knowing that Compton and Killion dead ended together at the defunct ball field.

Brubaker made his decision to stay with Cooper. At that very moment a partially stripped blue '65 Pontiac GTO inched forward. It just nicked the front corner panel of the Mustang sending Brubaker out of control. He hit his head on the side window and momentarily blacked out. That's all it took. The unmanned speeding Mustang headed directly toward the south curb in front of the parked RV. It made the curb and took out a yellow hydrant. Now careening out of control, it left tracks across the sidewalk and a torrent of gushing water as it burst through a knee high, flower/butterfly design block wall. The Mustang continued across the dead grass. It skipped up the three red painted cement steps and jetted across the short wood porch, into the cheap imitation cut stone and stucco cracker house. It totally demolished a picture window and ended up imbedded halfway into the living room, on top of the family's twenty-year-old console Zenith TV.

Across the living room, two longhaired teenage boys in tie-dyed Grateful Dead t-shirts smoked pot, munched chips and watched a 'French Connection' video. They stopped dead, too blown away to move, as the glass and sheetrock rained down around them. Brubaker's head ended up out cold on the blaring horn. The flashing blues and reds filled the room with concert light. After a moment of realizing they were not dead, the dirty blond-haired kid took another hit from the water pipe and passed it over to his stunned friend.

"Wow, like killer 3-D, dude."

"Yeah, too bad we didn't rent a porno."

Back on the other side of the street, Finn and Holland snuck away from the parted-out blue GTO.

Unless Cooper turned around, he only had one way out of Cumpston and Roger knew it. Roger made a left off Beck onto Killion and raced down past the row of low class autos where Cooper sat at the corner of Cumpston. Roger slowed. What the hell was Cooper doing? The shit was waiting. Roger shifted into first giving Cooper a chance to make his move.

"Gwen." The phone dialed.

"I'm at the top of the ramp. Don't hurt him, Portland."

Cooper hung up. "Marty." The phone dialed.

"Here. You got three minutes. It worked, Finn and Holland took Brubaker out. We called 911. The fuss in the parking lot has drawn the copter."

"See you at Holland's."

"Good luck."

"Roger."

"Eat it, Cooper."

"Ready to die, Rog?" The phone went dead.

Cooper glanced out at the sky searching for the source of the pounding above. As planned, police helicopter hovered over by the May Company on the other side of Oxnard where some of the Corvair Corsa Club members were turning doughnuts and pretending to be drunk. Lights flashed up on the Hollywood.

Cooper let up on the clutch and inched the Corsa forward keeping an eye on Roger and out of the street light above. Roger hung his silencer out of the window. Cooper revved his engine. Roger did likewise.

Cooper cut the wheels to the right and hit the hydraulic shock button. The Corsa lifted. Roger's bullet hit the top of the door and glanced up harmlessly through Cooper's headrest.

Cooper had the jump on Roger. He barreled down toward the dead end of Killion. Instead of stopping his front wheels hit a wood ramp placed earlier by Finn and Holland at fifty, pulverizing the white wood railing blocking off the back entrance to the plowed field. Roger hit the ramp as the unseen splinters from the railing came back down to earth. Cooper followed a path out to the middle of the field and cut his wheels to spin his backend around, coming face to face with Roger.

Roger put his foot to the floor. His tires throwing up trails of dirt as his engine bucked through the plowed field toward the oncoming Corsa. They passed at sixty-five as the two cars gave out a cry of crunching metal. The Porsche twisted to the right, sliding sideways until Roger could bring it back under control. The Corsa cut up into what once was the baseball diamond and stopped at the ghost of home plate. The Porsche cut back around to the corner of the field where the Hollywood off ramp met Burbank Boulevard.

Cooper waited for Roger to turn the Porsche around then headed back across the field at an angle toward a ten foot drainage drop behind a ridge at the south end of the field.

Roger did the same with every intention of ramming Cooper. The two cars cut a sharp V-shape across the dirt field. First, second, third. Their engines screamed. Porsche, Corsa, Porsche, Corsa, Porsche, Corsa...and met at the top of the ridge with a thundering crunch as both cars sailed out into the darkness. Roger downshifted in midair, his transmission gave out a low metallic grind as his rear tires hit the ground. His door jarred open. He slid to a stop, blood gushing from his nose. He revved the engine to test it as he looked for Cooper.

Cooper didn't fare as well. The Corsa hit the slope on its weighted front end, murdering the hood. This caused the Corsa to flip over onto its ragtop's frame and continue down the slope tumbling sideways over and over again. The ragtop's frame had ripped from the car and the windshield crushed as its frame gave way. The passenger door rolled over a protruding sewer top and caved in around the roll bar. The Corsa rolled once more before it stopped all together. It ended back in an upright position facing Roger. The engine was quiet. Cooper lay with his head against the headrest, his eyes closed, the helmet was ripped from his head and thrown in the back. Blood ran down from his forehead across his broken nose and stitched up face.

Roger pushed on the Porsche's door, forcing it open to get out. He had finally won. He was almost surprised. He had beaten that son-of-a-bitch Cooper at his own game. He snickered to himself as he got out of the Porsche. He held his gun to his side in case anyone should be watching, and walked toward Cooper in the crumpled blood red Corsa. He could see its skin was ripped back to the supports Finn had welded in it. He looked up at the sound of the helicopter now hovering over where Brubaker had crashed. Squad cars sped down the

Burbank exit ramp, their lights flashed and sirens blared from over the ridge. Dogs howled in nearby backyards sensing a death.

Cooper's eyes opened to see Roger victoriously grinning at him from under the gap left in the crumpled hood and the crushed air intake vent at the base of the smashed windshield.

Roger kept trying to see but the distorted glass hid Cooper from Roger. Roger didn't have the information he wanted yet. It was time to finish Cooper off and take it back. Or make sure Cooper wasn't breathing whether he had to pull the trigger or not. How fitting it seemed to Roger for Cooper to die by his own hand behind the wheel of a funny little red car. *Bullet Hole Drive*. Sam missed the shot he had wanted. Cooper dying on film. But not Roger. Cooper was dead and or dying in living color before his very eyes. Roger needed a blast to heighten the moment. He felt, his pocket, he'd left it in his car. It didn't matter. The Porsche was victorious at last. It was finally over. Roger did it. Everything would be his. All that property. All that money. With no Cooper in his way of enjoying being rich. Maybe Gwen, no not Gwen, that was surely over. But he drove the last car running. His precious 911, lived at the end of this demolition derby to the death. He was finally the winner. The way it should've been so many years and operations ago.

Roger wiped his bloody nose on his sleeve bringing his gun up to where Cooper could see it. Cooper used this moment to reach down with the slightest of movement and turn the ignition key. The Corsa jumped to life as Cooper revved it up to nearly redline RPMs. The running lights came to life like two yellow demon eyes opening in the dark to see its prey.

Roger stopped in his tracks. His breath choked on his own blood. How could it be? How could it be? The Corsa was still alive! Roger stumbled back at the sound of the revving engine. It cracked and it popped, but it lived. Cooper put the Corsa in gear. Roger was beside himself. He was helplessly out in the open. He had to get back. He had to get back into his womb. His Porsche...his...he turned and ran. He shot back reaching across his body as he turned, punching holes in the already shattered windshield and the crumpled hood until his gun clicked empty.

Cooper sat back up in his seat, and eased the clutch out. The left front spring groaned from being pushed against the steel supports in the trunk. Roger fell and crawled the last ten feet back to his Porsche. He got in and fumbled to reload his gun, but his hands shook. He reached to close the door. It creaked and stuck. He got out and tried to push it. It was no use. The door wouldn't close. He turned to see the Corsa creeping toward him. He gave up on the door and got back in. The hell with it. He revved the Porsche's engine. Its Weber carbs sounded healthy. He tried to put it in gear but it wouldn't slide in. He pounded on his steering wheel. He tried second. Nothing. It felt funny. Panic raced through his coked out brain as he fought to calculate what the solution might be.

Cooper crept forward in the Corsa.

Roger tried reverse. Shit! It went into third. He looked up at the slope in front of him. He'd never make it up in third. His only chance was to take it at an angle. The Porsche moved three feet and stalled. Roger looked over at the Corsa. He could barely see Cooper's eyes from under the gap in the hood. The look in them as blood ran down his face was deadly. Are you ready to die, Roger? Is any man ready to die? Roger could hear the answer as if he had asked the questions out loud. No! He was not ready to die.

The Corsa ruined, the Porsche ruined. Fear, honest to goodness fear, rocked Roger's body from head to toe. What had he done? His friends - Gwen, Portland, Irene, Jerry, Ruth, Jack, Sam. What had he done? For what? A key, a tape? Coke? To resurrect his acting career from the dead? For millions in their property? To direct his own film? To get even with Cooper. What? Was he as sick as Sam? Did Sam see himself in him? Is that why he kept him alive? Was he that low. He reached for his bag and held it to his chest. His life spent on drugs. "Please, God, help me!"

Cooper floored it across the short distance. Roger covered his face with the bag. Resolving himself to die, crushed between the two beloveds. Impaled by the Corsa, embedded into his 911. Cooper put it into a skid and stopped right in front of Roger's Porsche, taking off the door. He backed up about twenty feet and got out dragging his leg and carrying his automatic twelve gauge pump. Roger uncovered to find himself staring at the end of the cold steel.

"Get out!"

"Go ahead, waste me. Please."

Cooper slid the barrel over just far enough to blow out the 911's backside window. Roger nearly flew out of the Porsche on his hands and knees. Cooper stepped back and fired all but two shells into the silver bullet tearing it up. He reached into the Porsche and pulled out Roger's handbag and gun. Cooper took out Roger's checkbook, emptied the coke into the dirt, grinding it in with his boot, and threw the empty bag back into the 911. He put the empty silencer in his pocket.

The sirens got closer and closer. The dogs continued to howl. A group of neighbors began to grow at the dead-end street. Roger went for the coke.

Sam De'Ogo's voice came over the CB, "Roger? Rog..."

Roger leaped back. "Jesus Christ!"

Cooper unloaded a shell at the Porsche's gas tank. It burst into flames. Roger hit the dirt. Cooper just stood there, his blood glistening in the flames. The Corsa was behind him, still running loud and breathing free. They looked at each other knowing Tim and Eddie had done it again. Teatro and Dexter were the only ones in the car. It must have been Dexter driving, but everything happened so fast who could tell with the windows streaked with so much mud.

"For the record. Sam had something done to your 911 to make you lean into me and make it look like I pushed you into that wall. Jack and Jerry just wanted to take you out to sea and feed you to the sharks."

"Don't give...."

"Shut up. I bugged their cars. I heard them say it. Gwen heard it, too. I was right all along. They threaten to kill Gwen if I kept looking into it. So I stopped nosing around. I thought it was over the insurance on the movie, but they had taken out life insurance on you and planned to collect. It was to be Jerry's and Ruth's payback for doing time because of you."

"So what?"

"If you get rid of that tape for good, they might let you live. I heard Jack ask Sam. Rog, you and I are the only ones who know they are not dead. They might not come back if you do the right thing with that tape."

"Okay. When I found that footage on my wall of our race , I felt something was up. Sam shooting the whole thing. He would only if he knew or thought one of us would die. So, say you are right. What now?"

"It runs great. Sign a check for the engine I built for you or we both wait here for them." Cooper indicated the cops.

"I'm not signing dirt over to you."

Cooper ejected the shell and pumped a new one back in. He pointed the shotgun at Roger. "I didn't say alive." Roger got up to face Cooper. They looked eye to eye. Both had blood down their face, both looked like road kill, and now neither of them had their dream cars. Roger smiled.

"You won't kill me."

Cooper swung the butt of the shotgun up and clipped Roger on the jaw sending him up against the Corsa.

"Maybe not, but I'll hurt you real bad."

"Okay, okay, how much?"

"Three grand. As agreed."

Cooper gave Roger his pen and checkbook. Roger wrote the check on the shattered Corsa windshield. Cooper got back into the Corsa, taking the check and putting it in his breast pocket.

"Get in."

Roger looked at Cooper, then climbed over the caved-in door and sat on the carpet. Roger knew Cooper was telling him the truth about Sam and the others. He had no reason to lie.

Knowing Sam and the film he bought up, Sam wanted to see him die on film. Just like he wanted to see Cooper die on film. Roger looked over at Cooper.

"You're a true American asshole, Cooper."

"You're an international one, Roger. You're just too messed up to see it."

Cooper backed the Corsa up and took the slope in first and headed across the field to the Burbank off ramp. He dug in his breast pocket and pulled out the cotter pin he had taken out of Roger's shift coupler. "Here, you lost this."

Roger took the cotter pin and rolled it between his fingers, immediately knowing damn well what it meant. He couldn't help but smile. "You cheated."

"Yep."

"Then I want a rematch."

"Anytime, anyplace."

"I'll be there, grease ball."

"I don't race scumbag, preppy drug addicts anymore, Mr. Super Star. So clean up your act if you want another shot at me on the open road. Or I spill my grease ball guts about everything. And I mean every last slimy detail."

Gwen waited there at the red light in her Corvette. Cooper got out of the Corsa and grabbed his helmet from the back. He slipped the car phone base out of the dash, leaving Roger and the keys. He stepped through the fence, thankful he didn't have to crawl over it. Brubaker had conveniently taken it out. He handed the shotgun to Gwen who put it in its case.

Roger could see he wasn't invited. "Wait. The tape."

"It's taped to the bottom of the Corsa's driver's seat." Cooper got in Gwen's Sting Ray and shut the door. The window was down.

"How the hell do I get out of here?"

"In your blood red, Rog."

Gwen looked past Portland at Roger. Years of knowing and loving him washed away. It was up to him. Roger looked at them both. He'd messed up good. He hung his head, blood dripped from his nose. A man only had so much. Gwen put the Sting Ray in drive, turning right on Burbank and left at Lemp.

Roger looked up as the helicopter's light edging into the open field and the sirens raced closer. He put the Corsa in gear and was halfway to the gap in the fence when the abandoned ball field flooded with cop cars. They were loaded with all the stunt drivers in handcuffs. Another patrol car blocked his escape through the fence. The police helicopter's light locked in on the Corsa as Roger pulled to a stop. He was surrounded by the black and whites.

Brubaker got out of one. His head was bandaged. Roger raised his hands and placed them on his helmet.

"Where's Cooper?"

"Who?"

"Cooper. Portland Cooper!"

"I don't know what you're talking about, Brubaker. I haven't seen him in months. This was a stunt car. Someone tried to steal it and we just got it back."

"Bullshit, Kelemen!"

"Check the registration and ask them. We have permits in place to shoot a car stunt movie starting next week. They'll tell you everything you need to know."

Brubaker turned to the stuntmen in the cars. They all nodded. Brubaker turned back to the cruddy, lying, son-of-a-bitch actor. His face bloated with anger. He'd been had. He'd end up with his ass retired for sure now. Someone was going to pay. And someday it'd be Cooper. Portland-goddamn-Cooper!

Roger couldn't help but smile.

Holland opened her garage to let Gwen's Vette in. She shut the door behind them and went into her house. Gwen and Portland sat a moment. Cooper was in too much pain to move.

"Doc's in the house."

"I want to sit here for a bit."

"There will be other cars, Portland."

"I know."

"Let's go inside."

"You'd better go be with Irene. She'll hear Jack is dead."

"How?"

"His Jag went off Mulholland."

Gwen looked away, not sure how to take it.

"Jack and De'Ogo weren't in it."

She turned back to Cooper. "You think...?"

"I do. Whoever they find in it, won't be them. Pick me up here tomorrow for brunch and we'll go over to the police station and try to clear this mess up."

"What about Roger?"

"What about him?"

Gwen didn't need to say anything. She just made a face.

"All right, I said I'd help him. So, if our pal agrees to enter a drug rehab that Irene oversees, I'll do what I can. Otherwise I don't know him and I don't want to know him ever again."

Gwen gave Cooper a gentle kiss. "Thanks...you're a swell guy, you know that, Mr. Cooper?"

"Yeah, yeah...you'd better use the alley."

Cooper got out slowly and opened the back garage door leading into the alley by pushing a button. He hobbled to Holland's house as Gwen drove away. Inside a card game took place. The excitement from the night drained out of his body like stinky sewage down a drainage pipe. He felt like shit. His body hurt in places only a kid with straight As in school ever heard of. The muscle tissue around the frag in his left leg throbbed to the beat of his tired heart. His face was killing him, and his insides ached with every sore breath. He had bruises on his bruises, bumps on his bumps. And a few bald spots.

"You gonna deal those cards or hatch 'em?" Finn asked inside at the kitchen card table. Portland knocked on the door.

"Who is it!?"

"Cooper."

"It's open."

The game went on. It felt good to know that some things never changed.

23 IT'S ALIVE

Gwen was still parked outside the station when Cooper came down the steps on crutches. She got out to help as Cooper approached.

"How did it go?"

"He agreed."

"He did? I mean, good, he did."

Cooper just smiled knowingly.

"That was pretty easy."

They got into the Sting Ray. Gwen drove off.

"After I threatened to beat him to a pulp."

"But he's agreed to join?"

"Under the agreement that we'd stay out of all this and let Roger straighten things out his way."

"What about Elliott, Frank, and Sophie?"

"I don't think Roger plans to open that bag. He does have all that property and money legally in his name. It includes Jack's ranch. You get to visit and ride your horse anytime."

"I'll rip his heart out. By the way, Jack's will was intact. Mother gets everything they could find. Nearly a hundred mil in assets. And they're not done looking."

"How is Irene taking all this?"

"She went and had her hair done. I heard back from your Coast Guard friend. He was very nice. No ship like the one we were on was reported in American waters."

"At least we know the ship's fast...and the two bodies?"

"Beyond recognition...they'll be cremated tomorrow. We will attend the services as planned."

"Good. Last night they found a third body up on Mulholland. With a shell in his head from the same gun that shot the Goodrickes. It's probably how Jack and Sam drove away."

They drove on for a moment. Cooper watched out the side window trying not to think of what he knew to be all too true.

"What are you thinking about?"

"Somewhere in the world, Tim and Eddy Waller are getting away with murder...again."

"It's a big world."

"Not anymore. They'll be back."

They drove on in silence again. Gwen stopped at the light at Victory and Whitsett Ave.

"Poor Roger," she sighed.

Cooper gave her a nasty look.

"Well, how will he explain all this?"

"Don't worry about Rog. He's a pretty good actor, but he's a great liar."

She drove on again.

"You shouldn't close the shop over this."

"Who said I...Marty, that big mouth. I was just thinking maybe of staying in Kula Rue for a few months and catch up on and some boat engines for a while."

"Let's go...I can take a couple months. Grandfather would we thrilled to see us."

"Fly. No ships."

Gwen made a left into the alley and pulled up just outside of the work yard gate with Cooper's Corvair Shop sign on it. Cooper got out with great care. He studied the sign. It could use some paint. And the walls could use a coat. Maybe he'll have the place painted while he was away. Have Marty take care of things for him while he's staying there.

"Coming in?"

"I've got a real job, remember?"

"I'll call Irene and see if she'd like to have dinner. My treat."

"That'd be nice."

"Am I being nice again?"

Cooper leaned in to give her a gentle kiss.

"I told Mother you didn't put those foot prints on her carpet after all."

"Did she believe you?"

"Of course...well, she's skeptical."

"She'll get over it."

"I love you, Mr. Cooper...you brute."

"You'd better. You agreed to marry me."

"I'm gonna set the date while we're on the island. So you better not run."

"You'll know where to find me."

"I will, mister."Gwen stuck her tongue out, backed out of the alley and drove off. She was so incredibly beautiful.

Cooper made sure he was alone and let himself in the gate to find a car with a cover over it parked next to the pile of metal that was once his beloved blood red Corsa.

He went over to it, hesitating only for a moment before he pulled off the cover. Underneath was a beat-down but restorable red Corsa. The tires were flat and the top and interior were shot but there was very little rust. It must've come out of a barn or a garage somewhere below the salt belt.

Cooper couldn't believe his eyes. On the hood was his set of Kelsey-Hayes chrome wire wheels and the heads Marty hocked in the card game at Holland's.

There was a note on the antenna. Cooper took the note and opened the Corsa's door. It groaned in protest of being touched after so many years of neglect. He eased himself in to sit on the rotted seat, and put his head back, letting the pain subside. In the dash, all set up and ready to operate was his cellular phone. His helmet sat on what was left of the passenger's seat. He opened the note. It was from Marty. Cooper smiled as he began to read it.

"She's all yours, Coop. What a beauty, huh? Kind of gives you watery eyes and the urge to blow snot, doesn't it. Roger called me. He found her after he started rebuilding the other one. He wanted you to have it. Said he got your design from the old car mags. He also said you can partout the one you beat up last night. He actually apologized. Can you believe it? Told me to tell the guys. Actors, huh? Holland says you owe her one for the heads, but I'll cover it for you. Oh, Gwen gave us the money to buy your wheels back from a couple of milk-bones who hadn't a clue as to what they were worth. Marry her, stupid. Speaking of witches. I've moved back in with Delma. What did you say to her? God help me. Love, your pal, Marty."

Cooper closed his eyes and sat back and smiled. He opened his tired eyes again and looked at the phone. He picked up his helmet, saw that it was hooked up and ready to go.

"Dad."

The phone auto dialed. A Miami number rang on the other end. A smile slowly developed on Portland Cooper's face again. The smile just kept on growing and growing. Maybe he'd get lucky and someone would come along and dump six feet of dirt over him and the beast. The thought made him laugh. The laugh made him hurt. This was absolutely the last time he'd ever help one of Gwen's crazy friends.

"Hello?"

He spoke into the helmet's mic. "Dad?"

"That you, Portland?"

"You bet."

"How are you, boy?"

"Still scraping it off the boot. How's mom?"

"Playing golf with the gals. How's the Corsa business?"

"It's alive."

THE END

About The Author

After years of living and working in LA, Karl J. Niemiec is now raising his young family and fulfilling childhood dreams in Carmel, Indiana as the Publishing and Enrichment Program Director at LapTopPublishing, KJN Original Studios and Noir Pictures.

You can find more of Karl's books at: http://amzn.to/karlniemiec

Don't miss Karl's Blood Red Corvair in:

Jozeph Picasso's Alien Trilogy – Filmmaking Adventures. Alien Made, Alien Biz and Alien Mobster.

Hello, if you enjoyed this romantic action adventure about my beloved Blood Red, please leave a review.

Thank you.

Karl J. Niemiec

CORSA CHAPTERS

Corvair Society of America
Corvair.org

Air 'Vair Group
Galion, OH United States
airvair@richnet.net

Alamo City Corvair Association
Seguin, TX United States
tjgirgus@gmail.com

Arkansas Corvair Club
Little Rock, AR United States
eking@aristotle.net

Association of Corvair Nuts
Rochester, NY United States
chuckflo2@cs.com

Bay State Corvairs
North Providence, RI US
dmac632000@yahoo.com

Bayshore Corvair Association
Howell NJ, United States
bjdoe1@verizon.net

Beaver State Corvair Club
Eugene, OR United States
gregorymiller69@comcast.net

Blue Mountain Corvair Club
Stroudsburg, PA United States
jfwells@ptd.net

Boise Basin Corvairs
Meridian, ID United States
taysndogs@msn.com

Bonneville Corvair Club
Clinton, UT United States
benfwofford@att.net

Cactus Corvair Club
Phoenix, AZ United States
inafix@live.com

Capital City Corvair Club
Madison, WI United States
dadblanco@aol.com

Capital District Corvair Club
Delmar, NY United States
newell6055@roadrunner.com

Caveman Corvairs, The 1960 Group
Morenci, MI U S
rjennings@cass.net

Central Carolina CORSA
Manning, SC United States
air_cooled63@yahoo.com

Central Coast CORSA
Atascadero, CA United States
corvair@charter.net

Central Florida Corvair
Ormond Beach, FL US
central_florida@corvair.org

Central Kentucky Corvair
Lexington, KY United States
scarboro@trgpsc.com

Central New Hampshire Corvair
Contoocook, NH United States
ginnyb@empire.net

Central New York Corvair Club
Jamesville, NY United States
ddunlap3@twcny.rr.com

Central Pennsylvania Corvair
Dauphin, PA United States
w061772@comcast.net

Central Valley Corvairs
Modesto, CA United States
papamodesto@cs.com

Central Virginia Corvair Club
Hartwood VA United States
scout1977@hotmail.com

Chevrolet Corvair Club of Paris
91410, Dourdan France
paul.dupuis-philipponnet@
industrie.gouv.fr

Chicagoland Corvair Enthusiasts
Matteson, IL United States
clbiddle@comcast.net

Circle City Corvairs
Indianapolis, IN United States
valveclatter@aol.com

Classic Corvairs of River City West
Sacramento, CA United States
hbspence@pacbell.net

Colonial Corvair Club
Arlington, MA United States
a65corvair@comcast.net

Columbia Basin Corvairs Rich-
land, WA United States

Connecticut CORSA
Plantsville, CT United States
ctcorsa1@yahoo.com

CORSA of Baltimore
Towson, MD United States
klinzey@acm.org

CORSA Ontario
Burlington, ON Canada
njdl@sympatico.ca

CORSA Oregon
Portland, OR United States
wjabs@cascadeaccess.com

CORSA South Carolina
Greenville, SC United States
bwschug@att.net

CORSA West of Los Angeles
Mission Hills, CA United States
sixtysixturbo@sbcglobal.net

CORSA/N.C.
Raleigh, NC United States
gmcvair@juno.com

Corvair Atlanta
Smyrna, GA United States
corvairatlanta@corvair.org

Corvair Club Nederland
1071 VS Amsterdam, Netherlands

Corvair Club of Cincinnati
Hamilton, OH United States
mdemeter@fuse.net

Corvair Houston
Magnolia, TX United States
corvairhouston@yahoo.com

Corvair Midwest
Lincoln, NE United States
jb30343@navix.net

Corvair Minnesota
St. Louis Park MN US
jherkenramp@juno.com

Corvairs Northwest
Tukwila, WA United States
info@corvairsnorthwest.org

Corvairs of New Mexico
Albuquerque, NM United States
jimp@unm.edu

Corvanatics Pine Mountain
Valley, GA United States
corvanatics@gmail.com

Coyote Corvair Club
Vista, CA United States
kennedyautorepair@sbcglobal.net

Dayton Corvair Club
Dayton, OH United States
greg.hanlin@earthlink.net

Delaware Valley Corvair Club
Cinnaminson, NJ United States
bvair@hotmail.com

Derby City Corvair
New Albany, IN United States
actken@insightbb.com

Desert Corvair Club
El Paso, TX United States

Detroit Area Corvair Club Swartz
Creek, MI United States
corvairkid1963@aol.com

Dirigo Corvairs
Gorham, ME United States
4carbcorvair@gmail.com

East Tennessee Corvair Club
PO Box 928Kingsport, TN37660
United States

First State Corvair Club
Newark, DE United States
mslotwinski1973@netscape.net

Friends of Corvair
North Canton, OH United States
tcarpenter@neo.rr.com

Greater Orlando Corvair Assn.
Saint Cloud, FL United States
govairs@aol.com

Green Country Corvair Group
Broken Arrow, OK United States
okieguy@hotmail.com

Group Corvair
Bowie, MD United States
simpsonj@verizon.net

Gulfcoast Corvairs
Sarasota, FL United States
tonycorsa@juno.com

Head of the Lakes Corvair Assn.
Superior, WI United States
upnorth1@gmail.com

Heart of America Corvair Owners
Belton, MO United States
mdawson1961@sbcglobal.net

Heart of Georgia Corvairs
Leesburg, GA United States
lawjandl@aol.com

Indian Nations Corvair Assn.
Oklahoma City, OK US
teermin8r@mac.com

Inland Empire Corvair Club
San Bernardino, CA US
yenbat@aol.com

Inland Northwest Corvair Club
Spokane, WA United States
daveeva@icehouse.net

Iowa Corvair Enthusiasts
Davenport, IA United States
monza67@aol.com

Keystone Corvair Club
Martinsburg, PA United States
fcvairs@atlanticbb.net

Knoxville Area Corvair Club
Maryville, TN United States

Lehigh Valley Corvair Club
Northampton, PA United States
rcwvair@rcn.com

Lone Star Corvair Club
McDade, TX United States
amescua@academicplanet.com

Long Island Corvair Association
West Babylon, NY United States
longisland@corvair.org

Low Country Corvair Assn.
Ladson, SC United States
2donn@att.net

Mad Anthony Corvair Club
Fort Wayne, IN United States
keithcherimiller@verizon.net

Mid-Continent Corvair Assn.
Derby, KS United States
mcca@corvair.org

Mid-Maryland Corvair Club
Rohrersville, MD United States
corvair@xecu.net

Mid-Ohio Vair Force
Ostrander, OH United States
martzo@live.com

Milwaukee Corvair Club
Milwaukee, WI United States
wbaranowskijr@yahoo.com

Music City Corvair Club
Nashville, TN United States
wayne.stutts@comcast.net

Nature Coast Corvairs
Inverness, FL United States
nccorvairclub@yahoo.com

New Jersey Assn. of Corvair Enth.
Ridgewood, NJ United States
vairtec@optonline.net

New Orleans Corvair Enth.
Denham Springs, LA US
msyvairs@aol.com

Niagara Frontier Corvair Club
Tonawanda, NY United States
gswiatowy@rochester.rr.com

North Cascades Corvairs
La Conner, WAUnited States
fredngale@wavecable.com

North East Wisconsin Corvair
Neenah,WI United States
arndt2205@sbcglobal.net

North Texas Corvair Assn.
Irving, TX United States
contactsmu@yahoo.com

Northern Virginia Corvair Club
Fairfax Station, VA US
bryan@skiblack.com

Performance Corvair Group
Derby, KS United States perfor-
mance@corvair.org

Philadelphia Corvair Assn.
Leighton, PA United States
kcorvair@ptd.net

Pikes Peak Corvair Club
Colorado Springs, CO US
halpinem@comcast.net

Prairie Capital Corvair Assn.
Springfield, IL United States
prairiecapital@corvair.org

Queen City Corvair Club
Monroe,NC United States

Resurrection Corvairs of Yonkers
Yonkers, NY United States
npasquale@smtplink.mssm.edu

River City Corvair Club
Evansville, IN United States
nepstudio@sbcglobal.net

Roanoke Valley Corvair Club
Roanoke, VA United States
yenko66@cox.net

Rocky Mountain CORSA
Denver, CO United States
rocky_mountain@corvair.org

Sacramento Corvair Tour Group
Sacramento, CA United States

San Diego Corvair Club
San Diego, CA United States
redbadgett@aol.com

San Francisco Bay Area CORSA
Orinda,CA United States
corsanews@bigfoot.com

San Joaquin Corvair Club
Fresno, CA United States
jim_a_b3@hotmail.com

Show-Me Corvair Club Saint
Charles, MO United States
cavajopphr@sbcglobal.net

Silicon Valley CORSA
Santa Clara, CA United States
silicon_valley@corvair.org

South Coast CORSA
Santa Monica, CA United States
vargascorvairmonza@hotmail.com

South Florida Corvairs Lake
Worth, FL United States
gailvair@att.net

South East Corvair Council
Ormond Beach, FL US
sarahvair@juno.com

Southern Oregon Corvair Owners
Medford, OR US
stanleyfamily1@attbi.com

Stock Corvair Group
Virginia Beach, VA US
whubbell@umich.edu

Suncoast Corvairs
Tampa, FL United States
suncoast@corvair.org

Swiss Corvair Club
CH-2540 Grenchen, Switzerland
utgrenchen@bluewin.ch

The 1969 Corvair Group
Wallingford, PA United States
1969@sashimi.org

Tidewater Corvair Club
Virginia Beach, VA US
annie-bo@cox.net

Tucson Corvair Assn.
Tucson, AZ United States
tucsoncorvairs@yahoo.com

Ultra Van Motor Coach Club
Manteca, CA United States
lew111@verizon.net

V-8 Registry
Harrison, OH United States
v8registry@hotmail.com

Vacationland Corvairs
Painesville, OH United States
rampside@ncweb.com

Vegas Vairs
Las Vegas, NV United States
vwh5574@frontier.com

Ventura County Corvairs Fill-
more, CA United States
venturacountycorvairs@yahoo.com

Vermont Independent Corvair Enth.
East Arlington, VT United States

Vintage CORSA
Brea, CA United States
webmail@vintagecorsa.com

Vulcan Corvair Enthusiasts
Chelsea, AL United States
rtnoble@southernco.com

West Florida Corvair Club
Milton. FL United States
wfcc@juno.com

West Michigan Corvair Club
Ravenna, MI United States
wmcc@corvair.org

Western Canada CORSA Port
Coquitlam. BC Canadain-
fo@westerncanadacorsa.com

Western Pennsylvania Corvair Club
Plum, PA United States
pggreen233@netzero.net

Yenko Stinger Group
Oshawa, ON Canada

CORVAIR PARTS AND REPAIRS

	Full Time	New Part	Used Parts	Repair Shop
Arizona Corvair Corral Apache Junction AZ United State 480/242-121	Yes	No	Yes	Yes
Avery Corvairs Campobello, SC United States 828/342-0953	Yes	No	Yes	Yes
C J Corvair Services Lakehurst, NJ United States 732/370-3844	No	Yes	Yes	Yes
Charlie of Phoenix Phoenix, AZ United States 623/247-3272	Yes	No	Yes	No
Clark's Corvair Parts, Inc. Shelburne Falls, MA United States 413/625-9776	Yes	No	Yes	No
Corvair Ranch, Inc. Gettysburg, PA United States 717/624-2805	Yes	No	Yes	Yes
Corvair Repair LLC Isanti, MN United States 763/444-9334	Yes	Yes	Yes	Yes
Cotrofeld Automotive East Arlington VT United States 802/375-6782	Yes	No	No	Yes

	Full Time	New Part	Used Parts	Repair Shop
Dahlquist Automotive Inc. Lockport, NY United States 716/434-5286	Yes	No	Yes	Yes
Demo's Automotive Houston, TX United States 713/526-3781	Yes	No	Yes	Yes
Don's Corvair 12057 N. Saginaw Rd., Clio, MI. (810) 515-0800	Yes	No	Yes	Yes
Fred's Classic Radios & Clocks Lenexa, KS United States 913/599-2303	Yes	No	Yes	Yes
House of Corvairs Rorbas-Zurich, Switzerland 01-8760537	No	No	Yes	Yes
John's Corvair Parts Stoneboro, PA United States 814/336-9033	Yes	No	Yes	Yes
LeVair Performance & Restoration Michael LeVeque 4627 North State Road 9 Anderson, IN 46012 (765) 617-9307 mlevair@sbcglobal.net	Yes	Yes	Yes	Yes
Maplewood Motors Cape Neddick, ME United States 207/361-1340	Yes	No	Yes	Yes
Meadows Automotive Oviedo, FL United States 407/366-0974	Yes	No	No	Yes
Mel's Vairmart Mel Raven 1443 Laurelwood Road Santa Clara California Phone: (408) 267-8164 Fax: (408) 267-8164	Yes	Yes	Yes	Yes

	Full Time	New Part	Used Parts	Repair Shop
Paul's Corvair Indianapolis, IN United States 317/636-0154	No	No	Yes	Yes
Rafee Corvair Wister, OK United States 918/753-2486 Corvair1.Com	Yes	Yes	Yes	Yes
Rear-Engine Specialists Golden, CO United States 303/278-4889	Yes	No	Yes	Yes
Red Line Auto Restoration Dexteria, BC Canada 250/472-2605	Yes	No	No	Yes
Shade's Classic Corner Hastings, NE United States 402/463-5577	Yes	No	Yes	Yes
Shepard Corvair Repair Matthews, NC United States 704/554-6769	Yes	No	No	Yes
Silicone Wire Systems San Jose, CA United States 408/247-2237	No	Yes	No	No
Stinger Motorsports Roanoke, VA United States 540/204-0917	No	No	Yes	Yes
Vaca Valley Corvair Vacaville, CA United States 707/446-3769	Yes	No	No	Yes
Vair Shop Frankfort, IL United States 815/469-2936 vairshop.com - larry@vairshop.com	Yes	No	Yes	Yes
Wolf Enterprises San Antonio, FL United States 352/588-0645	Yes	No	Yes	Yes

CORVAIR MUSEUM

Located inside the **Chevrolet Hall of Fame** at 3635 U.S. 36
Decatur, Illinois 62521

Please call 1-888-9-bowtie or 217-791-5793 for more information. http://www.chevrolethalloffamemuseum.com/

CORVAIR FORUMS

CorvairForum.com
Corvair Society of America - Corvair.org

FACEBOOK CORVAIR GROUPS

Corvair-Owners-Group-COG
https://www.facebook.com/pages/Corvair-Owners-Group-
COG/124200804308827

Pikes Peak Corvair Club
https://www.facebook.com/groups/patl80820/

Mid-Continent Corvair Association
https://www.facebook.com/groups/105523176146520/

Corvair Preservation Foundation
https://www.facebook.com/search/top/?q=corvair%20preservat
ion%20foundation

Meet the Makers of Chevrolet Corvair
https://www.facebook.com/search/str/Meet+the+Makers+of+C
hevrolet+Corvair/keywords_search

www.ingramcontent.com/pod-product-compliance
Lightning Source LLC
Chambersburg PA
CBHW061131200626
46817CB00016B/714